"It is a calling. You're being summoned, Watcher."

Haern tried to think it over, but he felt so tired, so unprepared. The dead boy's face kept flashing before his eyes.

"How do I know this isn't a trap?" he finally asked.

Alyssa looked away, as if embarrassed by what she had to say. "Because of you, my son lives," she said. "And because of you, I was able to bring vengeance to the one who tried to kill him. I will never betray you. Someone murdered powerful citizens of Angelport, my friends and colleagues, and is using their blood to send you a message. Help me find him. Help me stop him."

Haern sighed.

"So be it," he said. "When do we leave?"

By David Dalglish

—

Shadowdance

A Dance of Cloaks

A Dance of Blades

A Dance of Mirrors

A Dance of Shadows

A Dance of Ghosts

A Dance of Chaos

A DANCE OF MIRRORS

SHADOWDANCE: BOOK 3

DAVID DALGLISH

www.orbitbooks.net

Orbit
Hachette Book Group
237 Park Avenue, New York, NY 10017
HachetteBookGroup.com

First Edition: December 2013

Orbit is an imprint of Hachette Book Group, Inc. The Orbit name and logo are trademarks of Little, Brown Book Group Limited.

The Hachette Speakers Bureau provides a wide range of authors for speaking events. To find out more, go to www.hachettespeakersbureau.com or call (866) 376-6591.

The publisher is not responsible for websites (or their content) that are not owned by the publisher.

Library of Congress Cataloging-in-Publication Data
Dalglish, David.
A dance of mirrors / David Dalglish. — First edition.
pages cm. — (Shadowdance ; Book 3)
Summary: "Man or God; what happens when the lines are blurred? Haern is the King's Watcher, protector against thieves and nobles who might fill the night with blood. Yet hundreds of miles away, an assassin known as the Wraith has begun slaughtering those in power, and leaving the symbol of the Watcher in mockery. When Haern travels south to confront his copycat killer, he finds a city ruled by the corrupt, the greedy, and the dangerous. Rioters fill the streets, and the threat of war with the mysterious elves hangs over all. To stop it, Haern must confront the deadly Wraith, and the man he might become. A Dance of Mirrors was previously published as A Dance of Death."—Provided by publisher.
ISBN 978-0-316-24245-5 (pbk.) — ISBN 978-1-4789-7910-4 (audio download) — ISBN 978-0-316-24247-9 (ebook) 1. Assassins—Fiction. 2. Corruption—Fiction. 3. Imaginary wars and battles—Fiction. I. Title.
PS3604.A376D365 2013
813'.6—dc23
2013018995

10 9 8 7 6 5 4 3 2 1

RRD-C

Printed in the United States of America

For Mom, who kept every story I ever wrote,
and every award I ever won

Rigon River
Bone Ditch
Northern Plains
Helforn Forest
Queln River
Crestwall Mountains
Felwood Castle
Sully Lake
King's Forest
Green Castle
Riverrun
Hillock
Citadel
Weldaren
Woodhaven
Kinel River
Beaver Lake
Kingstrip
Kiln
Nellassar
Queln River
Erze Forest
Council Towers
Kinamn
Henn
Ramere
Quellen Forest
Omn
Rigon River
Jex
Clubfoot Mnts
Ghostwood
Quellassar
Angelport
Ashhur's Bridge
Karak's Bridge
Riverend
Haven
N
W
E
S
Neldar

PROLOGUE

Torgar staggered out of the tavern with the blood of a stranger on his knuckles.

"I want my sword," he said to the four burly men who had persuaded him to leave.

"Come get it when you're sober," one said as he shut the door.

"Well, at least give me my damn drink!"

No such luck. The sellsword cursed and howled until his lungs hurt. Feeling better afterward, he made his way through the streets of Angelport back home. Home, of course, was his little room in the Keenan family's magnificent estate, as captain of their mercenaries and guards. Not that he needed to do much anymore. With the thieves' war ending nearly two years ago, his life had grown significantly quieter. And quieter meant boring. He wasn't quite as young as he once was, either. When he first agreed to work for Laurie, he would have crushed at least a dozen skulls before they flung him out the door of a tavern. But now?

"Getting old," Torgar grumbled, bracing a hand against the

nearby walls to steady his walk. "How in Karak's name did that happen?"

Surely it wasn't that long ago he'd been a feared mercenary. The Bloody Kensgold was…gods help him…seven years ago? He turned and spit. On that night, he'd hunted thieves, drunk himself stupid, rescued Madelyn Keenan from Thren's little hideout, and overall had himself a glorious time. A shame those days were behind him. Well, all but the drinking part.

Without his sword, he felt naked traversing Angelport's streets. Big as he was, he doubted any ruffians would be dumb enough to try hustling him. That, and he certainly didn't look like a man loaded with coin. But he liked having his weapon with him anyway. All it'd take was one bad turn, one lucky snot with a dagger and a hungry belly, and he'd go from Laurie Keenan's trusted mercenary to just another rotting hunk of meat to be cleaned up by the city guard. Thankfully he encountered no one on his way home. The streets were strangely quiet. Laurie had mentioned something about the elves; perhaps that was the reason. The whole city stank of nervousness.

At the gates to the Keenan estate, he saluted the single guard keeping watch.

"Morning," Torgar said.

"Not for four more hours."

Torgar grinned. "Aren't we picky?"

The guard looked him over. "You're early. And where's your sword?"

"On loan. Care to let me through?"

Drunk or not, Torgar was still the boss, and the guard begrudgingly turned and unlocked the gate.

"Take the servants' entrance at least," the guard said. "Lady Madelyn's getting tired of you waking her up."

"That so, eh?" Torgar asked, heading straight for the front doors. "Too fucking bad."

Halfway across the expansive lawn, he began singing a tune, butchering half the lyrics but not caring. When he put his hand on the door handle, he stopped and sighed. Laurie's son, Taras, slept not far from the main entrance, and he'd been having a devil of a time catching winks because of his newborn. Madelyn could rot in an open grave for all he cared, but he held a soft spot for Taras.

"Fine," he said, thudding his head against the thick wood of the door. "You owe me, bud."

He left the main path and walked the worn dirt track around the mansion. Compared to their first home in Veldaren, it wasn't nearly as large, but it housed over fifty members of the family, plus guards and servants. Torgar spotted a couple hiding behind a tree, no doubt a guard and a maidservant having themselves a good time. He resumed singing to startle them, and grinned while imagining their surprise. Their lack of reaction left him disappointed. Worse, something about it felt wrong, and he looked back just before turning a corner.

Neither was moving.

"Gods damn it," he muttered, trying to think through his pounding head. "Asleep, right? Just asleep."

He went to check them anyway. Slumped against the tree, with their bodies positioned in a mocking embrace, were two guards, their throats slit, their armor soaked with blood. Torgar stared at them for a full three seconds as the alcohol in his brain gave way to his many years of training. He grabbed one of their swords and then checked his immediate surroundings, in case the killer lurked nearby. When he saw no one, he hurried toward the back door. So far no alarm had been raised; otherwise the guard at the gate would have known. The bodies were warm, blood still dripping from their wounds. Whoever this killer was, he wasn't far.

The grounds seemed vacant enough, so he looked to the rooftops, desperately wishing he hadn't drunk so much. He saw several shadows that might have been men hiding, but with his headache it was impossible to know whether his mind was playing tricks. No time, he decided. Raise the alarm. Get every guard armed and scouring the place. He was in no position to play hero.

The servant door was locked, and he pulled out the key from a chain around his neck. As he inserted it and turned, he felt the hairs on his neck stand up. One of the shadows...

"Shit!" he cried, flinging himself back. A dark shape descended, blade in hand. Torgar blocked with his sword just in time. Before he could react further, his opponent landed on top of him, elbows and knees ramming his face and chest. Collapsing onto his back, Torgar rolled, narrowly avoiding a stab to his throat. He continued rolling and did the only thing that seemed logical. He hollered his brains out.

"Killer!" he screamed. "There's a killer out here! Wake the fuck up!"

He pulled out of his roll and onto one knee as his opponent's sword came slashing in. He tried to parry it and was only partly successful. Blood splashed across his vision as the edge tore through his face. He spun from the force, landing on his stomach. Teeth clenched, he waited for the killing blow to land. It never did. Looking back, he saw the door was open, his key still in the lock.

"You left me alive?" Torgar asked, struggling to his feet, his free hand clutching his face. "Big mistake, you bastard. I'll make you pay."

He felt warm blood spilling across his fingers and mouth. A

huge gash across the bridge of his nose was bleeding heavily, and he wondered if he'd pass out before the night was done. Cursing, he cut off a large portion of his shirt and pressed it to the wound. It hurt like blazes, but it was the best he could do for now. Sword held high, he rushed into the mansion.

The hallway was mostly dark, with only small oil lanterns burning at the various intersections. He had no clue who this assassin was targeting, but Torgar knew who paid his wages and that man belonged at the top of the list to protect. Hooking a right, he headed for Laurie and Madelyn's room. He tried shouting for help, but it hurt his nose too much. His eyes watered, hampering his already blurred vision. Several times he rammed into a wall, adding more bruises to his aching body. All throughout, he heard cries from the guards. Most were tracking positions, calling out all clears. But every few moments, they let out frightened shouts, if not death screams.

Reaching Laurie's room, he felt hope at seeing the door closed. He kicked it open and barged in, only to have something hard and blunt strike the back of his head. Torgar dropped to his stomach, and he vomited uncontrollably.

"Damn it," Torgar said, glaring at Laurie standing to the side of the door, dagger in hand. His wife sat on the bed, also holding a blade.

"I thought you were the intruder," Laurie said, offering his hand. Torgar ignored it, instead using the wall to brace himself as he stood.

"You're an idiot, Laurie. Why the hilt?"

"I wanted you alive for questioning."

Torgar looked back to the hallway, listening for sounds of battle.

"Next time, use the pointy end," he said. "Stay in here and bar the door."

A trio of guards approached, and Torgar saluted with the hand holding the bloody bandage.

"Any clue where the fucker is?" he asked.

"Toward the front," one said.

Torgar's ears were still ringing from the blow, his vision so blurred he couldn't make out the man's face. He took a wild guess at his name, not caring if he got it right.

"Stay here, and guard them with your lives," Torgar said, nodding toward Laurie's door. "Gary, you're in charge."

"Where are you going?" asked the one on the left.

"To make him pay for this," Torgar said, gesturing to his nose. He rushed toward the front half of the mansion, and sure enough he heard sounds of battle. His gut sank at the noise. This was no normal assassin sent to smother a sleeping man or pour poison into a bottle of wine. This guy could *fight*. Torgar listened for steel hitting steel, or people dying. All around him, he heard doors locking, the servants barring their rooms and staying inside like he'd trained them. Good. Last thing he needed was a bunch of frantic idiots crowding the halls.

As he neared the front entrance, he stumbled upon five corpses of his guard, their blood staining the blue carpet. Torgar could hardly believe the sight. Surely it wasn't just one man doing all this?

And then he heard a scream.

"Taras," he whispered, his blood running cold.

It took him a moment to remember the way. Gods, what he'd give to be sober! He passed by three more dead guards, confirming his dread suspicion of the assassin's target. Despite the pain it caused, he screamed as loud as he could.

"Everyone to Taras! To Taras, now move your asses!"

At his friend's bedroom, he found the door already open. A dead guard was propped against it, the wood's white paint stained red with gore. Heart in his throat, Torgar stepped inside. Despite his years of training, warfare, and executions, he was still not prepared.

The assassin knelt amid the carnage, his sword deftly slashing at a bare spot on the floor. Torgar must have made a noise, for the assassin looked up. His face was hidden by a heavy black hood, his body wrapped in cloaks.

Torgar lifted his sword. "Come on," he said, wishing he felt as tough as he sounded. "Come die, you sick fuck."

The assassin stood, and his head shifted so Torgar could see a faint glimpse of his face in the dim moonlight streaming through the broken windows. He was smiling.

"Not tonight," the man said. Smoke burst at his feet, flooding the room. Torgar coughed as it stung his eyes and throat. He slashed wildly a few times, but no attack came. When the smoke cleared, the man was gone. Torgar walked to the center of the room, creating footsteps in the drying layers of blood. His sword shook in his hand.

Taras and his wife, Julie, lay dead and in pieces. Their maidservant's body was slumped against the closet door, her throat opened by a gash that went from ear to ear. As Torgar's heart caught in his throat, he heard a horrific sound break the silence—their newborn girl, Tori, wailing. Guards flooded the room as he picked up the child from the stained bedsheets. Her wrappings were bloodied, but she was unharmed.

"Where'd he go?" a guard asked as the others gasped and cursed at the sight.

Torgar shrugged, having no answer.

"Like a damned wraith," said another. "We'd see him, and then he'd be gone."

Hearing a cry, Torgar looked back to see Laurie fall to his knees before the doorway. Madelyn stood behind him, her face like glass but for the tears that ran down her cheeks. They dared not enter, for there was no reason, no way to clutch the bodies to their chests. The massacre was too horrific. Too complete.

"Who?" Laurie asked. "Why?"

Torgar looked to the symbol at his feet, drawn in Keenan blood.

"I don't know," he said.

"Give her to me!" Madelyn cried, her sudden outburst startling.

Torgar carefully stepped across the gore-coated floor, gladly handing Tori over. All he felt was rage. Having a child in his hands didn't seem right.

"I'll find out who did this," he said. "I promise I'll make him pay a thousand times over."

Little comfort for any of them, but it didn't matter. The assassin had left his calling card, and because of that, it would be his death. Few crossed a member of the Trifect and lived. As Laurie and Madelyn were led away from the scene, Torgar stabbed his sword into the center of the symbol, which seemed vaguely familiar. He'd seen it before, years ago, or at least heard it discussed. And then it hit him.

A single open eye, drawn in the victim's blood.

"The Watcher," whispered Torgar.

CHAPTER

1

Haern pulled his hood low over his head and tied his sabers to his belt as the leader of the Eschaton mercenaries, the wizard Tarlak, sat at his desk and watched.

"Do you want our help?" Tarlak asked, picking a bit of dirt off his yellow robe.

"No," Haern said, shaking his head. "This one needs to be a message for the underworld of the city. Brann crossed a line that I need to make sure no one else ever crosses. I'll do this on my own."

Tarlak nodded, as if not surprised.

"What about Alyssa?"

Haern tightened the clasp of his cloak. They'd heard word that Alyssa planned some sort of retaliation against the thief guilds, though the reason was unclear. Their source was fairly respected in the Gemcroft household, so much so they had no choice but to take it seriously. At some unknown point in the night, there was to be a meeting at her mansion to discuss the circumstances.

"After," Haern said. "I'm sure you understand."

"I do," said Tarlak. "Good luck. And remember, I can't pay you if you die on me."

"I won't be the one dying tonight," Haern said, feeling the cold persona of the King's Watcher coming over him.

He left the room, descended the staircase to the tower's exit, and then ran the short distance toward the city. A dozen secret passageways, ropes, and handholds were available to him as a way to cross the wall, and he drifted to the southern end before climbing over. Alyssa's potential conflict with the thief guilds was a greater threat in the long run, but Haern could not bring himself to focus on it just yet. His target was a piece of scum named Brann Goodfinger. He operated in the far south of the city, and it was there Haern went.

Normally he felt pride as he traversed the rooftops, carefully observing the doings of the various guilds. Ever since the thief war ended two years ago, the factions had settled into an uncomfortable truce. The first few months had been the worst, but Haern's sabers had spilled torrents of blood. Through sheer brutality, he had brought both sides to their knees. He was the silent threat watching all, and tolerating nothing. But tonight his accomplishment felt bitter. For the first time, his plan had been turned against him in a most cruel, personal way.

Thieves who stole from the Trifect died. They all knew this, knew that every night Haern patrolled the city as the King's Watcher to ensure the agreed-upon peace. And so Brann had recruited children, a bold dare against the Watcher's threat.

"Where is it you hide?" Haern whispered as he lay flat atop a roof. For two days Brann had eluded him, and his children had gone unchecked. No longer. He spotted one of their youngest, a boy surely no older than seven. He was exiting the broken window of a shop, a handful of copper coins clutched to his chest. He ran, and Haern followed.

The boy tried to vary his pattern, as he'd no doubt been trained to do, but against someone like Haern the tactic was a minor inconvenience, nothing more. Haern kept far out of sight, not wanting to alert him to his presence. Twice he'd tracked Brann's child-thieves, but one had spotted him, abandoned his ill-gotten coin, and fled. The other had been killed by a different thief guild before he could question him. Children bled out on the streets of Veldaren. The Watcher's wrath would be terrible.

Haern turned a corner and watched the child hurry inside a warehouse. Approaching the door, Haern slipped into the shadows and looked through the crack near the hinges. A faint lantern burned inside, and from what he could make out, two other children were within. Hoping it was Brann's hideout, and not a simple gang of orphans, he drew his sabers. There would be no stealthy entrance. This wasn't a time for quiet deaths in the night.

He slammed the door open with his shoulder at full charge. Without slowing, he took in the surroundings, his finely honed instincts guiding him. The storehouse was full of crates and bags of grains, limiting his maneuverability. At least twenty children were gathered in a circle, and before them, his dirty face covered with a beard, was Brann. The man looked up. His jaw dropped, and then he turned to run.

"Stop him!" Brann shouted to the children.

Haern swore as they drew small knives and daggers. He leaped between them, twirling his cloak as a distraction. A sweeping kick took out three, and then he pushed through the opening. The storehouse was divided in two by a high wall, and Brann vanished through the doorway in the center. Haern raced after him, again slamming aside the door with his shoulder. To his surprise, Brann was not the coward he'd believed. His sword lashed out from behind the door. Haern's speed was too great, though, and he fled beyond Brann's reach, pivoted on his heels, and jumped again.

Brann was only a gutter snake, a clever bully who relied on size or surprise to defeat a foe. Haern had fought his kind, knew their tactics. With three strikes, Brann's sword fell from a bleeding wrist. Two kicks shattered a kneecap, and then he fell. Haern clutched his hair and yanked his head back, his saber pressing against Brann's throat.

"How dare you," Haern whispered. His hood hung low over his face, and he shook his head to knock it back. He wanted Brann to see the fury in his eyes.

"You hold this city prisoner yet ask me that?" said Brann.

Haern struck him in the mouth with the hilt of a saber. As Brann spat out a tooth, the children rushed through the door, surrounding them both.

"Stay back," Brann said to them, and he grinned at Haern, his yellow teeth stained red with blood. There was a wild look in his eyes that made Haern uncomfortable. This wasn't a man who cared about life—not his own, nor that of others.

"What game is this?" Haern asked, his voice a cold whisper. "Did you think I wouldn't find out? Using children, here, in my city?"

"Your city?" Brann said, laughing. "Damn fool. All the rest are scared, but I know what you are. They think you're as bad as us, but you're not…not yet. Once the thief guilds find out, they'll have your head on a spike."

He gestured to the children, all prepared to attack. Haern didn't want to imagine what Brann had put them through to achieve such a level of control.

"Kill me," Brann said. "Do it, and they'll swarm you. You won't die—you're too good for them—but you won't escape without killing at least one. So what'll it be, Watcher? Can you take my life if it means taking the life of a child?"

Haern looked at the twenty children. Some were as young as seven, but others were maybe eleven or twelve. All it'd take was one lucky stab by any of them and he might go down.

His saber pressed harder against Brann's skin. He leaned closer to whisper into his ear.

"Nothing, Brann. You know nothing about me. You die, they go free."

"I die, then innocents will as well. You don't have the stomach for it. You aren't the beast the others think you are. Now let me go!"

Haern glanced at the children, all poised to act. He tried to decide what to do, but he knew what life someone like Brann would lead them to. No matter what, no matter the risk, he couldn't allow it.

"This was never a choice," Haern whispered.

He slashed, spilling blood across his clothes. Hoping to move before the children reacted, he turned and leaped, vaulting over their circle. They gave chase, not at all bothered by the death of their master. Haern rolled to his feet, his sabers crossed to block their weak stabs. A quick glance showed no exits except the door he'd come through. Doing everything he could to fight down his combat instincts, he shoved through the group's center. His cloak whirled and twisted, pushing aside feeble attacks.

Pulling out of the spin, he lunged for the door. One of the older boys was there, and Haern felt panic rise in his chest as he saw the deadly angle of the boy's thrust. He reacted on instinct, blocking hard enough to knock the dagger free, then following it up with a kick to send the boy flying. Breaking back into a run, he kicked off a pile of crates to vault into the air, catching a rafter with one hand. Swinging himself up onto a perch, he stared down at the children, several of whom gathered around the body of the one he'd kicked.

"Listen to me," Haern said to them, trying to forgive the children's attack. They didn't know any better. The rage he felt was misguided, born of frustration. "Your master is dead. You have no hope of winning this fight."

"Fuck you," said one of the kids.

Haern swallowed down his anger at such disrespect. They were frightened and living in a world Haern knew all too well. If reason would not work, he knew what would.

"Say that again, and I'll cut out your tongue."

The boy stepped back, as if stunned by the coldness in his voice. The rest looked up at him, some ready to cry, some angry, but most were heartbreakingly indifferent. Haern pointed to Brann Goodfinger's corpse.

"Take his coin," he said. "Go, and make better lives than this. Remain thieves, and you'll fall to the guilds, or to me. I don't want to kill you, but I will. There is no future for you, not in this."

"None for you, either," said another, but Haern could not tell who. With practiced efficiency the children took everything of value from Brann's corpse and vanished into the streets. Haern didn't know where they went, nor did he care. He only felt fury. Brann had died quickly, hardly the example Haern desired to set. As for the boy he'd kicked...

He dropped from the rafter, landing lightly on his feet. Gently he rolled him over, put a hand on his neck. No pulse.

"Damn you, Brann," Haern whispered. "I hope you burn forever."

Leaving the body there was not an option. Haern considered himself better than that. Lifting him onto his shoulder, he rushed out to the streets, praying no gutsy member of a thief guild spotted him and tried something incredibly heroic and stupid. There were several gravekeepers in Veldaren, plus another who burned bodies instead of burying them. Haern went to the burner, picked the lock of his door, and went inside. The owner was asleep on a cot in a small room, and Haern woke him with a firm prod of his saber.

"What? Who are... Oh, you."

The elderly man, Willard, rubbed his eyes, then opened them when Haern dropped a handful of coins onto his lap.

"Spare no expense, and bury his ashes."

"Who was he?" asked Willard, looking over the boy's body as Haern set him down on the floor.

"An accident."

"Then what shall I engrave on his urn?"

"Pick something," Haern said as he left.

In a foul mood, he raced off for the Gemcroft estate, wishing he could put the prior events out of his mind and knowing there'd be no such luck. Brann's death would still be a warning to the others against using children to break the arrangement between the guilds and the Trifect. He'd accomplished that, though not how he'd hoped. But it was that nameless boy who haunted him, made his insides sick. Brann had been convinced Haern would not have the stomach for what might happen. Turned out he might have been right.

Scaling the fence around the Gemcroft estate was easy enough, though avoiding the guards was another matter. There was a secondary building in the back, where he'd been told the meeting would take place. Most of the patrols kept close to the mansion, which helped tremendously. Haern lurked beside the gate, running along it when outside the patrols' vision and lying flat amid the shadows when they passed. At last he reached the small building. Timing the patrols, he knew he had about thirty seconds to slip in and out without being seen. Faint light burned within. He pressed his ear against the door and heard no discussion.

Too late, or too early? The door was unlocked, so he opened it and slipped inside. The room was surprisingly bare, containing only a single bed atop a padded floor. Hardly the servants' quarters he'd expected. The lone lantern kept the place dimly lit, with plenty of shadows in the far corners. So far, it appeared empty.

"Damn," he whispered.

He headed for the far corner, figuring to wait a few hours just in case the meeting was yet to transpire. In the center of the room, though, he stopped. Something in the corner wasn't right, the shadows not smooth...

Haern lunged for the door, his instincts screaming *trap*. Before he could get there, something latched on to his cloak and tugged, hard. He spun to the ground, torn between attacking and tearing his cloak free to flee. Already furious because of Brann, he kicked to his feet and attacked. To his surprise, his sabers clashed against long blades, his thrusts perfectly blocked. He was already preparing a second strike when he saw his opponent's outfit. Long dark wrappings covering her body—all but her shadowed face.

"Enough, Watcher," said Zusa, her slender body contorted into a bizarre defensive formation. "I am not here to kill you."

Haern pulled away, and he put his back to a wall, the door at his side.

"Then why are you here?" he asked.

"Because I desired it," said a voice at the door.

Haern turned, then dipped his head in a mock bow. "Lady Gemcroft," he said. "It is good to see you, Alyssa."

The ruler of the Gemcroft fortune smiled at him, not at all bothered by his tone. Zusa sheathed her daggers, though her hands remained on their hilts. She joined Alyssa's side, her dark eyes never leaving him. Alyssa seemed relaxed, far more so than when Haern had last seen her. Of course, he'd been trying to kill her at the time, back when Alyssa was flooding the streets with mercenaries. She wore a slender dress underneath her robe, her red hair let down loose about her shoulders. Haern almost felt flattered she'd dressed up for him, as if he were some noble or diplomat.

"I was told of a meeting concerning the thieves," Haern said. "Was there any truth to this?"

"I assure you, Terrance is loyal to me, and me alone," she said.

The side of Haern's face twitched. Terrance had been his informant, of course. He felt at a disadvantage, with no clue as to the reason for their meeting. He didn't like that. The two also blocked the only exit. He really didn't like that.

"Then I was told a lie, just to bring me here," he said. "Why is that, Alyssa?"

"Because I want to hire you."

Haern paused, then laughed at the absurd notion. "I am no pawn for you to force your will upon. And if what you say is true, why this secrecy and deception?"

"Because I don't want anyone—not the guilds nor the Trifect—to know. I leave for Angelport, and I wish for you to accompany me and Zusa."

Haern's hands fidgeted as they held his sabers. Answering

such a request with someone as dangerous as Zusa blocking his way out was not his idea of a fair bargaining position.

"What reason could you possibly have?" he asked. "I assure you, Zusa is quite capable of keeping you alive."

A bit of impatience finally pierced Alyssa's calm demeanor. "Someone broke into Laurie Keenan's home, slaughtered his son and daughter-in-law, along with a dozen guards. I'm going for their funeral services, as is appropriate. I want you and Zusa to hunt down this killer and bring him to justice while I'm there."

Haern shook his head. "I can't leave Veldaren," he said. "The peace I've managed to create—"

"Is no peace at all," Alyssa said. "The thief guilds prey on each other, killing themselves in an endless squabble over the gold we pay them. The few that steal are more often caught by their own kind, not you. No one will know you've left, not for weeks. It's been two years, and you've spilled enough blood to wash the city red. Those who remain have settled into their comfortable lives of bribes and easy money, and you know it. You've become a figurehead, a watcher against only the most reckless of the underworld. The city's changed. It won't miss you while you're gone."

Haern did know that, but that didn't mean he liked it.

"This is your problem," he said. "I've had enough dealings with the Trifect to last a lifetime. Find your killer on your own. Now let me through."

Alyssa glanced at Zusa, then nodded. They stepped aside. As Haern walked out into the night, Alyssa called after him.

"They found a marking," she said. "Drawn in their blood."

Haern stopped. "What of?" he asked.

"A single eye."

Haern turned, and he felt his anger rise. "You would accuse me of this crime?"

"No accusation," Alyssa said, stepping out. "I have already looked into the matter and know you were in Veldaren both the night it happened, plus the nights before and after. Laurie's kept word of it a secret and told only those closest to him of its presence at the murder. He knows you didn't perform the deed, though he still fears your involvement somehow..."

Grinding his teeth, Haern tried to think through what any of it meant, but it left him baffled.

"This makes no sense, Alyssa," he said. "Why would someone frame me so far away? I've never been to Angelport, nor used that symbol for years. Not since the war between the Trifect and the thief guilds ended."

"It's not a frame," Zusa said, as if it were so simple. "It is a calling. You're being summoned, Watcher."

Haern tried to think it over, but he felt so tired, so unprepared. The dead boy's face kept flashing before his eyes.

"How do I know this isn't a trap?" he finally asked.

Alyssa looked away, as if embarrassed by what she had to say. "Because of you, my son lives," she said. "And because of you, I was able to bring vengeance to the one who tried to kill him. I will never betray you. Someone murdered powerful citizens of Angelport, my friends and colleagues, and is using their blood to send you a message. Help me find him. Help me stop him."

Haern sighed. "So be it," he said. "When do we leave?"

"Today?" Tarlak said, leaning back in his chair with a bewildered look on his face. "You're leaving *today*? But we still have that contract with the Heshans, and I haven't tracked down that damn prostitute killer Antonil paid us to find. How am I supposed to find the bastard without your help?"

"Start spending time with prostitutes. Well, more time."

Tarlak raised an eyebrow, then laughed. Still in his bed robes, he stood and gestured about his office, which was a haphazard mess. "Clearly this place will fall apart without you," he said. "But go and do what you must. Can't have someone giving you a bad name, after all."

They embraced, Tarlak smacking him on the shoulder.

"Don't get killed on me," he said.

"I'll try not to."

Haern exited the room onto the circular staircase of the tower. Heading up a floor, he entered his barren room. After stripping down to his underclothes, he slipped into bed and slept. When he awoke, it was to something poking him in the shoulder. He looked, then groaned and rolled over.

"You're risking death, Brug," he muttered.

"You're the one heading off after someone brave enough, or dumb enough, to taunt you," said the short, burly smith. "Besides, the day's almost over. Get your ass up. Oh, and I have something for ya."

Haern rubbed his eyes, then looked again. Brug stood beside his bed, a pair of shoes in hand.

"Shoes?" he asked.

"Not just shoes!" Brug said, flinging them at Haern. They smacked against his chest. "I've spent two months making them things for you, so you can show some damn appreciation."

Haern sat up and examined them. They were gray, made of soft cloth thickened on the bottom. They would muffle any footsteps, though he wondered how long they'd endure his chaotic sprints across rooftops.

"You made these?" he asked. "I didn't know you could sew."

Brug blustered, and his neck went red. "That's not the point," he said. "With Tarlak's help, there's a bit of magic in them. They won't wear out, but the real fancy part is they'll make your footsteps quieter than a mouse's... Forget it, no reason I should tell you. Find out on your own."

He stormed for the door, stopping only when Haern called out for him.

"Miss you, too, Brug."

"Whatever," Brug grumbled, but he hesitated before leaving.

Once he was gone, Haern dressed, put on his soft leather armor, and prepared to leave. Down the stairs of the tower he went, into the warmly lit and furnished bottom floor. It was empty, the fire in the fireplace burning low, the padded couch bare. Frowning, Haern swallowed his disappointment and exited the door.

Delysia was waiting for him outside, leaning against the tower with a smile on her face. Her soft white robes were immaculate, her red hair pulled back into a ponytail.

"Planning to leave without saying good-bye?" she asked him.

He shrugged. "Thought you'd be waiting for me inside."

"You still left when I wasn't."

He had no answer to that, so he smiled at her and stepped close so she might embrace him. When he tried to pull back, she held him tighter still, and he was surprised by her sudden boldness.

"You be careful," she told him. "Tarlak told me everything. Anyone who can do what that... Wraith person did, and then taunt you for it, is someone to worry about."

"Fearing for my safety, are we?" Haern asked, trying to make light of her worry—and trying to ignore how much having her hands wrapped around his neck made his heart jump.

"I fear every night you go out on watch. But this time I won't be waiting for you should you get yourself hurt. Please, be careful."

No making light this time. He put his arms around her waist and pressed his forehead to hers, the tips of their noses touching.

"I promise," he said, smiling. "It's going to take more than some cowardly pretender to take me down."

"Good."

She pressed her lips to his, and after a stunned moment, he kissed her back. When it ended, she stepped away, dipping her head so her hair fell forward to hide her blush. When she spoke next, it was as if everything were fine and normal.

"Is that all you're bringing?" she asked, gesturing to his single outfit, his sabers, and the cloaks he carried in his hands.

"Yes," he said. "Why, something wrong with this?"

"Ever the poor boy," she said, laughing. "Good luck, and make sure you come back."

He bowed low. "I wouldn't dream of doing otherwise," he said. "Keep Tarlak in line for me while I'm gone."

"I'll do my best."

He headed down the pathway toward the main road south, a bounce to his step. The daylight made him feel uncomfortably exposed, but he did his best to quell the feeling. Once he reached the main road, he found Alyssa's caravan waiting. It was only three wagons, far smaller than he expected. Alyssa had told him she wished to leave with little fanfare in hopes the thief guilds would not find out. Turned out she wasn't kidding. He found her sitting in the first wagon, with Zusa beside her. They both tilted their heads as he approached, and he realized without his hood, and under the bright sun, they could clearly see his face.

"Watcher?" Alyssa asked, as if to confirm just in case.

"Haern," he said, standing before them. "That'll do for now."

Zusa offered her hand, and he took it.

"To Angelport?" he asked as he sat across from them.

"Indeed," Alyssa said before calling out the order for their driver to begin.

CHAPTER

2

Eravon used the cover of night to hide his exit as he put the walls of Angelport far behind him. Spring had officially come, but the air still had a bite to it, and he kept a thin cloak wrapped tightly about him as he followed the path north. Though he'd lived for centuries, for the first time he experienced the sensation humans called "feeling old." His joints throbbed in the cold, and the days seemed to pass ever faster. Though his elven skin was smooth, he knew that in another hundred years or so he'd start to get a few wrinkles on his face, and his time among the humans would be at an end.

Not that he'd miss them.

The signal was subtle, just a few leaves placed in a specific way, with pebbles atop them to ensure they did not scatter in the wind. Eravon left the path, climbing up a nearby hill. On the other side was a tent, without a single torch or fire to give away its location. He tightened his cloak, then approached. The tent was large, the front flap open. When he stepped inside, he bowed to the two elves waiting for him.

"It is good to see you again," said the first, a young elf barely a hundred years old. His hair was short and golden, his eyes a vibrant green. Eravon accepted his embrace.

"You as well, Maradun," he said before turning to the other, who remained seated. "Does your leg trouble you so much that you cannot stand, Sildur?"

The silver-haired elf waved a cane, the only sign that he walked with a limp and that he was even older than Eravon.

"We have much to discuss, and little time to do it," Sildur said, motioning to an empty seat before them. "Sit, and tell us what the spoiled children of the brother gods have to say."

Eravon sat, and he accepted the cup and pitcher Maradun offered. He drank, purposefully delaying his report. Sildur might have outranked him back in Quellassar, but they were in human lands now, and Eravon was their ambassador. His importance could not be denied. That, and Sildur was always a dour one, as if Celestia had made him with mud in his veins instead of blood.

"Talks are yet to officially begin," Eravon said, setting down his cup. "What I know is only bluster and promises, which humans possess an infinite capacity for. But in this, I do not feel they will back down. Either we grant several of the human lords access to our forests for hunting and chopping, or prepare for bloodshed."

"Blood has already been shed," said Sildur.

"More blood, then."

"Can we not come to some sort of compromise?" asked Maradun. He glanced at the two of them. "Surely they do not desire war."

"Humans always desire war," Sildur said, fire in his voice.

"You know what they did to our Dezren brothers. Chased them halfway across the continent and burned Dezerea to ash. Their desire for war runs deep in their veins. All our talks are nothing but a waste of time."

Eravon sighed. Sildur spoke the truth, no matter how harshly. He only echoed what they all knew.

"I see little choice," Eravon said. "We must cede parts of the forest to them. It should be enough to sate their appetites, as well as calm their lord."

"Ingram is a fool who pales at the very sight of us," said Sildur. "He will not be calmed until we are dead and gone from all of Dezrel."

"But what else can we do?" Maradun asked. "I have slain several who came to our forests with axes, yet every week their numbers increase. What do I tell my masters in Quellassar? We continue to overlook many excursions, hoping to prevent escalation, but we must come to an understanding soon. Humans cannot trespass upon our lands forever, not without consequences."

"There is another way." Sildur's eyes sparkled. "Instead of running from war like frightened children, we embrace it. Turn our bows and blades toward their cities. The humans are like animals and will learn only when struck."

The three fell silent. Eravon put his hands upon the table and forced himself to keep calm. Sildur said nothing he had not heard a thousand times before over the last decade. Against that, he had the same tired argument, but no matter how tired, it remained truth.

"We might slay ten to our one," he said. "But our numbers dwindle, while the humans spread like insects. We must not forget the lesson of the Bloodbrick, where our greatest died. Despite the thousands our casters killed, the humans have recovered, while we will never see those ten replaced in our lifetimes. No matter our skill, there is little we can do when they come with fire and pitch, outnumbering us over a hundred to one. You cannot stop a swarm of ants with an arrow or a blade. If we come as the aggressor, their king will send troops from every corner of Neldar. Our people, our loved ones, will die for nothing."

Sildur's eyes flared wide, and he opened his mouth to argue, but then stopped. Eravon felt a chill pass over him, and he turned, following his companion's gaze. A man was hunched at the door, his body covered with dark clothing and a long cape. A sword hung from his belt. Despite Eravon's excellent night vision, his eyes could not penetrate the deep shadow across the intruder's face. Only his mouth and chin remained visible. He was smiling.

"Who are you?" Sildur asked, his hand drifting to the long dagger at his hip. "Speak your name!"

The intruder let out a chuckle. "I've heard many amusing names given to me, but if you insist, I will choose one of them for you. I am the Wraith."

"Wraith?" said Sildur, hardly impressed. "What brings you here with your face masked and your identity hidden?"

The Wraith jumped from where he stood, landing atop the table with a clatter of cups and silverware. A hand on the hilt of his sword, he grinned at them all.

"Why do you discuss in secret?" he asked. His voice was strangely soft, and would have been charming if not for how coldly amused he sounded. "Do you fear the ears of man? Do you plot his downfall, or wonder for a way you might go crawling to lick their boots while somehow maintaining your dignity?"

Eravon prepared to draw his own sword. He would endure no insults from such a disrespectful whelp.

"I don't know how you found—"

He stopped as the Wraith whirled on him, staring with unseen eyes. The intruder grabbed his face with his fingers, in a movement so fast Eravon did not have time to react.

"I found you by following the stench of cowardice. You leaked piss all the way here from Angelport, like a frightened dog."

Maradun stood, a sword flashing in his hand. "Let him go," he said.

The Wraith laughed. "As you wish."

He shoved Eravon aside, then spun atop the table. His foot lashed out, the heel smashing Maradun's face before he could lift his sword to block. Eravon drew his sword and slashed, but the Wraith pulled his own blade. As the sound of steel rang out, the elves fled from the table, standing at the far reaches of the tent. Only the Wraith remained in the center, turning so his back faced none of them for long.

"Do you fear me?" he asked. "Good. Then perhaps you will remember the message I bring."

"What is that?" Eravon asked, stealing a glance at Maradun, who clutched his face with his free hand, blood dripping between his fingers from what Eravon guessed was a broken nose.

"Do not ask as if you don't intend to listen, Eravon."

The Wraith leaped, his body changing from relaxed to taut in an imperceptible moment of time. Eravon blocked his brutal chop during the descent, but his skills were with words and schemes, not blades. He parried the next few swings, then overextended to block what turned out to be a feint. Before the other two could come to his aid, the Wraith's sword pierced his side. Gasping in pain, Eravon fell to one knee. When the Wraith pulled the blade free, blood poured across the grass.

"Don't do anything foolish," the Wraith said, turning on the other two. "I will kill you all if I must."

"Speak," said Sildur. "Give your message."

Eravon tried to stand, but his head felt light, and his muscles refused to cooperate. He collapsed onto his side. Beneath him the grass warmed from his own blood. With fading vision, he watched the Wraith approach, his footfalls frighteningly silent.

"You are not wanted," the Wraith said, grabbing Eravon by the hair and lifting his head back so they might see eye-to-eye. "Leave, tonight. The people here do not need your meddling. Stick to your forests. One day, axes and fire will come for your borders. Remember that the next time you think of returning to Angelport."

Eravon's vision was nearly dark, but he still saw Maradun launch himself into an attack. The Wraith let him go, then twirled, his sword a blur. Eravon felt something wet splash across him, and then Maradun fell clutching a bloody stump, his arm gone from the elbow down. Trying to stand, Eravon succeeded only in rolling onto his back. The Wraith stood above him, looking down. Still smiling.

His sword sliced into Eravon's flesh, never deep. The sharp stings were nothing compared to the deep ache in his side, but still his anger grew.

"We'll kill you for this," he said, coughing.

"Many will try," the Wraith said, his sword twirling in his hand, flicking blood all across the tent. "But not you."

The blade descended straight for his eye.

"There it is," said Alyssa, hopping down from the wagon. "Angelport."

Haern followed, and as the rest of the travelers set up camp, he looked out over the city. It was smaller than Veldaren, but not by much. Three walls formed concentric circles enveloping the city, all of them stretching out into the water. A sprawling port lined the far side, and in the light of the setting sun, at least a hundred boats shifted about like ants. Haern was stunned by the sight. He'd never seen a single ship before, so to find so many coming into port or sailing out for the far reaches of Dezrel impressed him greatly.

"Why do we camp here?" Haern asked. "The city is not far."

"Because I want to make sure you know your part in this charade," Alyssa said, looking him over, then sighing. "Gods help me, you couldn't appear more uncomfortable if you tried."

Haern rolled his eyes and then went to help the others unpack. They'd kept a small supply of kindling and firewood, replenishing it as needed during their journey. Once their bonfire was roaring, and tents set up for those who would not sleep in the wagons, the servants began cooking their meal. One continued on the path, sent to receive word on the state of the city.

All the while, Alyssa drilled Haern on customs.

"Deepen your bow depending on their station relative to you," Alyssa said, smoothing out his silk shirt. "Since you'll be a distant relative of mine, that means nearly every member of nobility and the Trifect is significantly higher than you. If in doubt, bow low and avert your eyes for only a brief moment. Just make sure you don't ever tip your head to a commoner. Kind words in greeting are fine, but don't overdo it."

"I'd rather stick to killing people," Haern said. "Can I do that instead?"

She gave him a look he'd seen many times on their journey. The first had been when she realized he had packed a single set of clothes to wear for months at a time, his dark gray shirt and pants coupled with his cloaks. Wishing he'd heeded Delysia's advice, he found himself inheriting a wide assortment of outfits from Alyssa. They were poofy, silken, and more expensive than anything he'd ever owned in his life. And they itched.

Alyssa continued grilling him, seemingly determined not to risk the slightest error.

"Who rules the city?"

"Lord Ingram Murband. Pompous. Overconfident. Legally responsible for all the lands south of the Kingstrip known as the Ramere."

"Who *actually* rules the city?"

"The six men known as the Merchant Lords. Over the past ten years they've slowly taken over Laurie Keenan's shipping empire, and if not for Laurie's control over the growth and sale of crimleaf, he might lose the rest of his vast wealth. Of course, I'm to be annoyed by such ridiculous rumors about Laurie going broke, since I'm a silly dumb relative of yours who cannot think for himself and would never accept the idea of someone else being wealthier or better off than us."

Alyssa rolled her eyes at his gross oversimplification of her original identity she wanted for him.

"Tell me your name," she said.

"Haern Gemcroft, third cousin by marriage."

"And Zusa is?"

Haern rubbed his temples. "My wife. Zusa Gemcroft, originally of the Gandrem family line, having fallen for me at a ball celebrating Nathaniel's safe return. Apparently I was a skillful dancer."

"And why are you here?"

Haern muttered through his answer, wondering for the hundredth time why he'd agreed to go. As nice as it felt to get away from the dark streets of Veldaren, he was completely out of his element amid the wealth and traditions of the Trifect.

"It's our... honeymoon," he said. "You agreed to take us so we might see the port and buy presents from afar."

Alyssa sat down beside the fire, accepting a bowl of soup, and frowned at him as she sipped. "I hope you can put on a better act when we're inside the city."

Haern accepted his own food and ate. Alyssa finished, and while Haern took seconds, she went off to their wagon to see how Zusa fared. She, too, had been unhappy with Alyssa's scheme to get them into the city unnoticed. But Haern could not deny the usefulness of the ploy. Wherever Alyssa went, they could follow, yet at the same time they had a ready-made excuse for when they needed to search the city unnoticed. Of course, come nightfall, the real work would begin, and he could don his cloaks while Zusa covered herself with her wrappings...

Alyssa stepped back into the light of the fire, Zusa trailing behind her. Haern nearly choked on a piece of potato. The slender woman wore a loose dress with a wide V-cut between her breasts that ran all the way to the belt at her navel. Her skirt was long and violet, swaying about her legs. Apparently lacking Haern's discomfort, Zusa twirled once, then curtsied as if she'd been raised in court her whole life.

"It's a bit...revealing," Haern said, immediately realizing that was far from the compliment he meant to offer.

Alyssa looked ready to murder him.

"It's the style there, brought over from Ker by their sailors. Be glad I dressed you in Veldaren fashion. You'd have half your body exposed otherwise."

Haern scratched at his neck. "Would it be less poofy?"

"More and more I doubt the wisdom of your assistance," Zusa said. She ran her hands through her short hair. "At least you are handsome. No one would believe me marrying you otherwise."

"No one's going to believe it anyway," Haern said. "I've still got scars from when you tried to kill me."

"You tried to kill Alyssa first, remember?"

"Such doe-eyed lovers," Alyssa said, sounding like a tired mother. "I swear, sometimes I wonder why I brought *either* of you."

Haern laughed. He'd feared awkwardness given her station, and his history, but she seemed sincere about her gratitude for what he'd done for her son Nathaniel. Currently he was up in the north, under Lord Gandrem's protection. Haern almost wished the boy had come. It would have been nice to have a familiar face around, even if Nathaniel had not been conscious when he carried him to safety after an attack by an ambitious lover of Alyssa's.

Zusa left to change into clothes more suitable for sleeping. While she was gone, the servant returned from the city. At his sour expression, Alyssa urged him to speak.

The servant glanced once at Haern, then said, "Lord Keenan has cremated both Taras and Julie and delayed the burial for your arrival. He is thankful for your appearance and looks forward to your company. As for the city... the business with the elves has grown significantly worse. Not long ago, a cloaked man killed the previous elven ambassador and wounded those with him."

Haern straightened, and he exchanged a look with Alyssa.

"This man," she said. "Do they know who he is? Did he leave a symbol or name of some kind?"

"While the two survivors watched, he cut an eye into the ambassador's chest. He calls himself the Wraith. That is all anyone would tell me, though I would not be surprised if Lord Keenan knows more."

Haern swallowed, his mouth dry. Alyssa dismissed the servant, and when Zusa returned in a simple robe, they informed her of what they'd heard.

"First the Trifect, now the elves," Haern said, his voice low as he stared into the fire. "What does he want with me?"

"Have you ever heard that name before, this Wraith?"

Haern glanced at Zusa, then shook his head. "No. I'll need to speak with the elves who survived, learn anything I can of him."

Another servant arrived, carrying a small cask of wine and a trio of cups. They all accepted, and then Alyssa led their toast.

"To a long life," she said. "Something I feel none of us shall have."

Haern clinked his glass against hers. "A wonderful toast," he said, trying to imitate Alyssa's noble attitude while bowing low.

"Laurie will never, ever believe you are a member of my family," Alyssa said, sipping from her glass. "Let's pray he's more understanding when he realizes you're there to keep me alive."

"And find his son's killer."

Alyssa downed the rest. "That too. Good night, Haern. Tomorrow morning, we ride into the city. Try to sleep well. It will be a long day."

She left Haern alone with Zusa. He shifted uncomfortably beside the fire. Zusa always made him feel awkward; he was never sure of what she thought or might say. She often stared at him and was never self-conscious enough to hide it.

"Do you know where we might start looking?" he asked, breaking the silence.

"We start with the Keenan mansion," she said. "From there, the elves. After that, we listen for rumors and search for others he might have killed. I found you, Watcher. We can find this pale imitator."

"That servant said something about the business with the elves having grown worse. What did he mean by that?"

Zusa glanced to the city. "I don't know much, but what little I do know is grim. Disputes over territory, particularly the Quellan Forest, have put the elves and the people of Angelport at the very precipice of war. Tomorrow, we ride into a pile of kindling and oil. The slightest spark will set it off."

Haern chuckled, earning himself a raised eyebrow.

"Nothing," he said. "I just have a feeling, given how my life has gone, that we're about to be that spark."

Zusa lifted her glass, and finally she smiled. "To starting fires," she said.

Haern smiled in return. "To starting fires."

CHAPTER

3

Ulrich Blackwater stepped onto the deck of the *Fireheart* and scowled.

"Where's Pyle?" he asked two nearby crewmen, bare-chested lads soaked with sweat as they labored crate after crate toward the plank leading to the dock.

"The captain's in his cabin, milord," said one, bowing low. "Busy."

Ulrich weaved through the various ropes, cargo, and men until he reached the captain's quarters. Without knocking, he yanked the door open and stepped inside. Despite the overall size of the *Fireheart*, the quarters were cramped, just a bed, a desk, and a few maps tacked to a wall. On that bed, with a naked whore riding atop him, lay Captain Darrel Pyle. Seeing his entrance, Darrel laid his head back and sighed.

"Didn't they tell you I was busy?" he asked.

"Perhaps." Ulrich glared at the woman, who slipped to the side and grabbed her clothes. "Leave us."

"Don't go far, girl," Darrel said as the whore hurried half-naked past Ulrich and out the door. With only a blanket keeping him decent, Darrel leaned against the bedpost and scratched his neck. He was a burly man, with skin darkened from months spent in the sun. A long scar ran from his lip to his chin, leaving a gap in his brown beard.

"Shouldn't you be helping them unload?" Ulrich asked.

"My men know what they're doing."

"It's not your men I'm worried about. It's my cargo."

Darrel stepped off the bed and pulled on his trousers. "Your damn wine is safe and dry," he said, buttoning them. "Not that I give two shits. I could piss in every bottle and still the scum here in Angelport would consider it fine vintage."

"I would still prefer it if you oversaw things, in case such a respectable crew as yours decides to help themselves."

"You telling me how to run my ship?"

"*My* ship," Ulrich said, glaring. "You may captain it, but this is my boat, my cargo, and my reputation on the line. Besides, I don't give a damn about the wine. You'll be carrying something worth a thousand times more soon, and I need to be certain it is kept safe and untouched."

The captain pulled a white shirt over his head; it was hopelessly stained with sweat.

"What could you possibly have that's worth more?" he asked.

In answer, Ulrich took out a small pouch from his pocket and opened the drawstrings. From within he drew a single leaf, tore off a small piece, and handed it over. It was green with strange purple veins, and Darrel grunted as he examined it.

"What is this?" he asked.

"Bite, but don't chew. Keep it crushed between your teeth and focus on breathing steady. Oh, and I suggest you sit down first."

Darrel shrugged. No stranger to various drugs and drinks, he seemed unimpressed with the simple leaf. Ignoring Ulrich's advice, he popped the leaf into his mouth and chewed. Within seconds his expression changed, and his chewing slowed. Ulrich watched as Darrel's pupils dilated and his hands started to twitch. Taking a seat at the captain's desk, he patiently waited for the drug's effects to pass so he could continue their conversation. After about five minutes, Darrel's legs wobbled, and he fell hard onto his elbow. Even though the jolt caused him to bite his tongue, he barely reacted. Blood dribbled down his chin and into his beard.

"Unbelievable," Darrel said, his voice strangely dreamlike.

Ulrich found the captain's private stash of alcohol and poured himself a drink. Behind him, the captain remained oddly quiet, other than for the occasional grunt of pleasure. After Ulrich had finished his third drink, Darrel finally came around.

"How long?" he asked, spitting blood to the floor.

"About fifteen minutes," Ulrich said.

"Damn. That was better than fucking." His eyes were bloodshot, and he stared at the pocket where the rest of the leaf remained in its pouch.

"That was just a piece," Ulrich said, holding in his grin. "Imagine a whole leaf. You'd be out for hours."

"If I could just have..."

"No," Ulrich said, standing. "No more, not while you are captain of my ship. In a day or two, it'll be gone from your blood, and you'll be able to control your desire for it. But while you sail for me, I can't risk it. I'm sure you understand."

For a moment, Darrel looked ready to strike him, then regained his composure.

"Gods damn it," he said, rubbing his eyes. "Give me that bottle."

"It has several names, but the one most use is *Violet*," said Ulrich as the captain downed half the bottle in a series of gulps.

"Never felt so good in my life," he said, wiping his chin. He looked down at his pants, realizing they were stained with semen. Instead of being embarrassed, he laughed.

"We have only a little, but I anticipate more soon." Ulrich tossed the captain a rag. "We've known of its properties for a few years now, but it was passed among the lords, always expensive, always rare. But things are changing, Darrel. Soon we'll have a nice, steady supply of Violet to spread throughout the world. Clean yourself up and get the rest of the crates unloaded. Whatever untrustworthy crewmen you have, get rid of them. When the first shipment of Violet sails north, nothing, and I mean nothing, must go wrong. For now, I'll be loading a single crate into your hold, for safekeeping only. You are not to open it, let alone take a leaf, understand?"

Darrel stared off for a moment, as if still longing for the leaf, then shook his head to clear it. "You'll make a fortune with that," he said. "Give me even a few samples, and I could get everyone west of the rivers hooked." He sniffed his fingers. "This stuff even legal?"

"For now, and I've taken steps to keep it that way. Good day, Captain. I have matters I must attend. Stay in port and wait for my orders. It may be a few weeks, but I'm sure you will find a way to pass the time. Make sure the crate is kept carefully guarded."

He turned for the door, then stopped. It was ajar, but only slightly. He was certain he'd closed it.

"Such interesting pleasures," said a man perched atop Darrel's bed, his legs crossed beneath him. Both whirled, and Ulrich drew his dagger. Wrapped in cloaks and black leather sat someone Ulrich had thought only existed in rumors and stories. His face was hidden by heavy shadows cast by his hood, but his grin remained perfectly visible.

"The Wraith," Ulrich said. "That's who you are, isn't it?"

"Such brilliant wisdom," said the intruder. "Though perhaps I give you too much praise. You would have noticed me ten minutes ago if you were truly clever."

"What in blazes are you doing on my ship?" Darrel asked. He took a step back, to where his sword hung on the wall. The Wraith tsk'ed at him, and he put a hand on the hilt of his blade.

"Stay still, sea vermin. I have no reason to kill you, but I will if you do something so irrevocably stupid. I come bearing gifts for our dear Merchant Lord."

Ulrich stood straighter, and he tried to put on an air of superiority. "So be it, stranger. I will accept your gift, if it is worthwhile, but then I must demand you leave the *Fireheart* at once."

"Demand," said the Wraith, his grin growing. "You amuse me."

He tossed Ulrich a heavy bag that had been hidden behind his back. It thudded to the floor. Slowly Ulrich bent down, opening the top to look inside. His throat tightened, and he stepped away.

"What is the meaning of this?" he asked.

"I told you, a gift."

Ulrich kicked it to Darrel, who opened it without hesitation. Pulling it out by the hair, the captain held a severed head, all the blood drained so that it did not drip across the cabin. The face was familiar, despite its pale color and obvious mutilation.

"Who...?" Ulrich asked, trying to swallow down the lump in his throat.

"Must I do everything?" The Wraith stepped off the bed, the movement startling both of them.

Ulrich felt certain the man would draw his sword, but he kept it sheathed...for now. Once again Ulrich looked at the severed head, trying to make out the face. The bulbous nose, the slender chin. Familiar...

When it hit, he put his back to the wall and held out his dagger.

"An attack on one of us is an attack on us all," he said, wishing he sounded braver than the panicked whine that came from his lips.

"Please," the Wraith said, offering him an elegant bow. "I look forward to your retaliation."

He kicked open the door and sprinted across the deck, leaving their line of sight before either could react. The moment he was gone, Darrel tossed the head back into the bag.

"What the *fuck* was that?" asked the captain.

"I don't know," Ulrich said, feeling his legs go weak. "But you're holding the head of William Amour."

The two exchanged a look. William Amour, one of the six Merchant Lords of Angelport, of which Ulrich was also a member...

"Shove a rock in its mouth and toss it overboard," Ulrich said. "I will accept no blame for this."

"Will do."

Still trying to regain his composure, Ulrich exited the cabin. Much of the cargo was unloaded, and his own people scurried about the dock, directing the crates to various stores, merchants, and warehouses. If any had noticed the Wraith and his strange garb, none showed it. He spoke with a few to calm himself down more than anything else, then hurried north. With the sea vanishing behind him, along with its salty smell and vulgar cries of sailors, Ulrich felt much better. As he walked, he checked to make sure nothing untoward stained his fine clothing. He would be arriving late to the funeral, but so long as he looked dashing, he wouldn't mind.

Normally Ulrich traveled without guards, but the incident with the Wraith had him rethinking that policy. Still, the streets were generally regarded as safe, so long as you were of high enough station that the city guards left you alone. At various gateways between walls, soldiers made sure the riffraff stayed in their appropriate place. In the outer ring, Ulrich curled south to meet his brother in the Keenan mansion. At their gate, he was searched well, which would have insulted him if he hadn't known of the attack weeks prior. Doing everything he could to push the Wraith and that severed head from his mind, he joined the service held within.

About fifty people mingled throughout the first few rooms of the mansion, drinking wine and conversing in soft tones. Many candles hung from the ceiling, but only a third were lit, keeping the mood of the place somber. The walls were elegantly painted into a representation of stone, the carpet a deep blue, which seemed to grotesquely resemble blood in the dim orange light. Before anyone noticed his arrival, Ulrich spotted his brother Stern alone in a corner and joined him.

"I assume I haven't missed the burial," he said, motioning over a servant so he might have a drink. He knew he was pushing it given how much he'd downed in Darrel's cabin, but he needed all the help he could get to remain calm.

"Lady Gemcroft just arrived," said Stern. "It'll be a while before the pointless introductions are finished and we can begin. At least the Conningtons are still bickering about who will be ruling what. There's a few minor members from their household here, but no one powerful enough we have to kiss their ass. And no one as fat and disgusting as that fat bastard Leon was."

Stern looked him up and down, then frowned. "Are you all right?"

The two were not twins, but they looked enough alike that most people thought they were. They had the same blond hair, pale skin, and brown eyes. Stern was older, though, and taller by an inch. That was often the only difference. They'd gotten along well enough that when their father died, the two had amicably split the inherited wealth, vaulting the both of them into powerful positions among the Merchant Lords. With how similar they were, and how alike their minds worked, Ulrich was not surprised that Stern could sense his unease.

"Do not worry about me," he said. "I'm here for you, after all. To lose Julie like that..."

Stern finished his glass, then set it down hard on a nearby shelf. "It's the damn Trifect," he said. "They're no better than the thieves they warred with for years, and my daughter had to get into the middle of it. Madelyn won't even let me hold my own granddaughter—you know that? As if *I* am the dangerous one. Knew Julie shouldn't have married Taras, married into that privileged, murderous circle of—"

"Enough," Ulrich said, glancing about to make sure no one heard. "You know why we let her, what we all stood to gain. Their marriage was to help create peace. Don't ruin that now by ranting like a drunken idiot at their funeral!"

Stern took a deep breath and nodded. "Forgive me," he said, tears breaking through his steely façade. "I have not slept well in weeks. She was everything to me, Ulrich. Now she's gone, and why? The whim of a madman? What could he want?"

Ulrich thought of the meeting with the Wraith on the *Fire-heart* and decided now was not the time to discuss it.

"Go wash your face," he said, squeezing his brother's shoulder. "I'll mingle fine on my own while you compose yourself."

Stern thanked him and left. After refilling his drink, Ulrich wandered through the mansion, paying more attention to the art than the people. The three families of the Trifect might be arrogant, overconfident, and wasteful, but they had good taste in paintings. While admiring a portrait of a paladin, the right half of the canvas purposely charred and burned, he heard someone clear their throat behind him.

"Glad for you to be here, albeit late," said the soft-spoken Laurie, offering his hand as Ulrich turned around.

Ulrich shook it while looking over the grieving father. His dark skin looked pale, and he'd cut his long ponytail as a sign of mourning. Ulrich tried to hide his annoyance that the ever-perceptive Laurie had realized he'd arrived late. Some might consider that an insult, and he did his best to apologize.

"Pressing matters delayed me," he said. "I fear someone lost their head over them."

Laurie winced, and Ulrich had to bite his tongue to keep from chuckling. He'd forgotten the most prevalent rumor was that Taras had been found decapitated, with his wife's head lying in his lap. Ulrich had doubted the truth of it, but Laurie's reaction made him wonder. Well, that and his little present in the bag earlier on the *Fireheart*.

"I hope business continues well for you," Laurie said, pushing the conversation to safer topics.

"Better than ever. There's an opportunity we've discovered that should bring our wealth right up with yours, Laurie. I wonder, do you think there's any more room in the Trifect for a promising merchant like myself?"

Laurie's smile was so patronizing Ulrich once more bit his tongue.

"In hundreds of years, we've never had more than our three families," said Laurie. "If you truly desire it, though, we can arrange a marriage, perhaps with one of Jack Connington's nieces—"

Ulrich snorted. Some niece? He wanted his family brought into the Trifect, not pushed aside to be married to some far-distant relative's brat.

"Sorry," he said, interrupting Laurie. "I don't much care for arranged marriages. They rarely turn out well."

The barb hit like he'd hoped, and Laurie's anger shook through his carefully controlled performance.

"Pardon me," he said. "I should speak with the priest before he begins the services."

With him gone, Ulrich wandered further, seeing few familiar faces. It was only because of his brother that he was there at all. The Trifect kept to itself, except when it came time to collect its debts.

A lovely lady caught his eye, distracting him from the paintings. She wore a revealing violet dress, and unlike most women of Angelport, she kept her hair cut short at the neck. Running a hand through his hair to make sure it was smooth, he joined her side.

"Would you like a drink?" he asked, seeing her hands empty.

"Are you a servant?"

Her voice was husky, deep. Her exoticness elevated her beauty in his eyes.

"Of course not," he said, laughing as if amused by the error. "I am Ulrich Blackwater, merchant and proprietor of many wondrous items from all across Dezrel. I merely ask because you seemed alone, and I would hate for your shyness to keep you from enjoying yourself."

"Not alone," she said. "I am merely watching."

She nodded toward an elegantly dressed woman across the hall. Ulrich tried to see if he recognized her, but did not. One of the lesser ladies of Angelport, perhaps, or from nearby Omn?

"I have given you my name but have not had the pleasure of yours," he said, bringing his attention back to her.

"Zusa Gemcroft," she said, still cool toward him.

Ulrich took another drink, not yet frustrated. Something was clearly off with this woman, which made her all the more interesting.

"Gemcroft?" he said, feigning surprise. "Are you with Alyssa, then?"

"I am."

That explained the other woman across the hall surrounded by guests. No doubt they were all busy kissing Alyssa's ass.

"I know a little of the Gemcroft family but must confess I have never heard your name mentioned before."

She blushed a little, then pointed to one of the men near Alyssa, though who exactly Ulrich could not tell.

"I am newly married into the family."

Ulrich's smile widened. He loved seducing newlywed women. So nervous, so excited, and always a challenge. That, and it forever gave him power of blackmail if successful.

"I am truly envious of whoever the lucky—"

"Excuse me," interrupted one of the servants, immediately bowing in apology. "The service is about to begin. If you would, please follow me to the gardens."

Zusa shot Ulrich a smile he could not decipher.

"I will see you another time," she said, curtsying once before returning to Alyssa's side. Ulrich watched the sway of her hips as she went, then glared at the servant.

"I know where the gardens are," he said. "I'll be there shortly."

"Of course," the servant said, bowing again.

Ulrich had no intention of going, having little interest in the prattle of priests and crying of women. He wandered deeper into the mansion, hoping for some solitude. Once everyone was dismissed, he'd slip back among them, say his good-byes, and hurry off to more pressing matters. The Amour family, for example, needed a new head appointed, after the loss of the last one.

He chuckled at the grim pun. Perhaps he shouldn't have tossed it overboard. It might have been amusing to present it to William's wife. He'd always hated that hag. Turning a corner, he was surprised to find he was not alone. A blond man stood in the doorway of a nearby room, staring. Ulrich vaguely recognized him, then remembered he'd been at Alyssa's side. He looked too nicely dressed to be a servant. Distant cousin, maybe?

"Lost?" he asked, deciding it best to make the other man explain his reasons for being there so he might not ask the same of him.

"Only looking." He gestured to the room. "Was this where it all happened?"

Ulrich looked inside, realizing they were at Taras's bedroom. "I believe so. What brings you here? Morbid curiosity?"

"Something like that."

Ulrich offered his hand. No doubt the stranger wished to avoid the service as much as he did. Already he liked him.

"Ulrich Blackwater," he said.

"Haern . . . Gemcroft."

Ulrich lifted his eyebrows. Were the Gemcrofts suddenly mating like rabbits? Here was yet another he'd never heard of.

"Well, Haern, what brings you to Angelport?"

He hesitated a moment, then looked back to the room. "It is my honeymoon."

"Is it, now? Well, a funeral is hardly the place to be. Or were you scouting for available bedrooms? I doubt this one will be used for a while." He laughed, then had a thought. "Say, you aren't married to a lady named Zusa, are you?"

Haern's pause was enough. Ulrich smacked him on the shoulder and was surprised by how firm his footing was. Almost felt like hitting a rock.

"You lucky bastard. Wouldn't blame you for fucking on a dead man's bed when the woman is that fine."

Haern looked too embarrassed to respond, which amused Ulrich all the more. He was a handsome man, and with startling blue eyes. Seducing Zusa away from him for a tryst would be that much more of a challenge. As much as he liked the man, he might have to use a bit of poison to ensure Zusa was his at least once before they left for Veldaren.

"Do you know what happened here?" Haern asked, stepping into the bedroom.

Ulrich followed, also curious to see. "Only rumors. You'd think a hundred men hacked them all to death, if you believed the rabble. I think it was just one man, though, a fool the commoners have begun calling the Wraith. He slaughtered guards left and right, butchered Taras and Julie, and then vanished in a puff of smoke."

"Smoke?" Haern whispered. "I see."

The room had a clean yet barren feel to it. The sheets had been stripped from the bed and not replaced. The carpet was so immaculate it had to be new. The windows appeared new as well. Even the walls glistened with fresh paint, the room still stinking from the application. Haern looked about, then pointed upward.

"Damn," Ulrich said, finally spotting it.

They'd changed the sheets, the floors, and the walls but had missed a faint spray of blood across the ceiling.

"This was no assassination," Haern said, his voice soft. "I

doubt he cared one way or the other about the couple. This was a message, and he made sure it carried far."

Something about the way he spoke, the way he carried himself, gave Ulrich a sense of unease. For the first time, he realized the man had a pair of sabers sheathed at his belt.

"Consider me curious. What makes you think someone would cut off a person's head, rip his entrails from his stomach, and fling his blood about like an insane painter, yet *not* care one way or the other about him?"

Haern walked over to the window, testing its lock. "He let the baby live. I saw Madelyn holding her."

Ulrich's eyes narrowed at such perception. "What is your relation to Alyssa again?"

Haern looked back. "Second cousin."

"Who is your father?"

"Is this a test?"

Ulrich slowly reached for his dagger. "That's a poor answer."

Haern turned where he stood, and something odd came over him. His face darkened, and a hard edge entered those blue eyes. His stance shifted slightly, the muscles in his body relaxed yet at the ready. While still at his sides, his hands brushed the hilts of his sabers, clearly ready to draw.

"I am a guest in the Keenan family's mansion," Haern said. "I was not aware I had to explain myself to you."

Ulrich suddenly felt nervous, his every action scrutinized with deadly intensity. With a startling clarity, he realized he felt the same as he did when in the presence of the Wraith.

"Forgive me for any insult," Ulrich said, letting go of his dagger. "After what happened, we're all a little nervous of assassins."

Haern's eyes seemed to sparkle at that. "I'm not one to live in fear of assassins."

"I can imagine."

Haern left the room, passing a mere foot in front of Ulrich. For the briefest moment he thought to draw his dagger and stab him in the back, but he let the impulse pass. Such a confident display was not made carelessly. This Haern had looked him over, then dismissed him as being no threat. The thought burned like fire in his gut. Smoothing out his shirt, he returned to the main parlor of the mansion to await his brother, enduring the many insulting glares he received from the serving staff.

After what felt like forever, the first of many guests returned. Ulrich remained seated, standing only when Stern finally showed. The wait had left him irritated, eager to deal with the business at hand instead of more false sympathy and tears.

"Something wrong?" Stern asked, seeing his brother's obvious displeasure.

"We need to go," Ulrich said. "Been delaying long enough as is."

"Delaying what?"

"The inevitable. Not too long ago, William Amour's head was cut from his shoulders and tossed into the ocean."

Stern looked like he'd been slapped, and a bit of anger cut through his grief. "Who would dare do such a..." He stopped, and then shook his head, having read Ulrich all too well. "Him, isn't it? That Wraith? What have we done to earn his wrath?"

"Lower your voice," Ulrich said, grabbing his brother by the arm and leading him to the exit. "And I don't know. Call a meeting of the Merchant Lords, and set it for tomorrow. We'll let the Amours have a day to prepare their funeral and appoint one of William's sons in charge."

"And what is it you hurry off to do?"

"None of your concern."

The Keenans were waiting by the door, with Madelyn holding the newborn child just as Haern had said. The two brothers said their good-byes, then left. They split, each heading for their homes. Trusting Stern to spread the word (assuming the other Merchant Lords didn't know already), Ulrich traveled through his spacious, but empty, home to his private room. No kids, no wife, no family. Just as Ulrich preferred. After he'd stripped himself of his uncomfortable clothes and locked the door, he pulled out the pouch from his discarded shirt. But first he covered up the large glass window. Sunlight always hurt his eyes afterward.

Tossing an entire leaf into his mouth, he bit down and then breathed deep. As his head grew light and his blood pounded through his veins, he thought of what Zusa might look like naked. Amid the euphoria, he felt a certainty overcome him, one that lasted throughout the next two hours. No matter the cost, he would have her, and he'd make damn sure that arrogant prick Haern knew it. But mostly he thought of Zusa, of taking her against her will, until at last the Violet faded and he fell asleep with his seed spilled across his hand.

CHAPTER

4

Alyssa played the kind supporter as the proceedings ended, and the guests trickled out one by one. She endured a hundred greetings, treating them all as if they were with a long-lost friend.

"Will you be all right?" Zusa asked her when she closed her eyes and rubbed her forehead.

"I'm fine," she said. "It's just...all this makes me miss Nathaniel for some reason."

"We wallow in the sorrow of others. Of course you'd fear for your own loved ones."

"Doesn't mean I like it, nor wish to think of it."

"Then drink," Zusa said, handing her a glass. "Wine is excellent for forgetting."

Alyssa chuckled. "At least there is that," she said, hoping the burn of it going down her throat would banish her tiredness. As she did, one of Laurie's servants came to inform her that her room was prepared.

"What of Zusa and Haern?" she asked.

"They have a room of their own, though it is near the back with the servants. I hope there is no offense."

"That will be fine," Zusa said. "I only hope we do not keep the servants awake at night."

The servant, a young, clean-shaven man, blushed and hurried away without a word.

"This is amusing," Zusa said, glancing at her own cleavage. "I should show my body more often. It makes the men so much more pliable and stupid."

"Body like yours, surprised you weren't showing skin the moment your breasts budded," Alyssa said. She winced. "I'm sorry, Zusa. I forgot."

When Alyssa had first met Zusa, she had been a member of the faceless women, a sect created in punishment for priestesses of Karak who broke their rules of sexuality. They'd kept her body covered in tight wraps, her face hidden behind a thin cloth. Zusa still wore the wrappings, though for what reason Alyssa could only begin to guess. At least she no longer hid her face, except when absolutely necessary.

"I will blame the wine, and not you," Zusa said.

Alyssa felt her head swimming and set aside the glass. Enough with that. She rarely succumbed to weaknesses, and she would not drown herself in alcohol just because she was a lovesick mother. Glancing about to make sure no one might overhear, she leaned closer to Zusa and began to whisper.

"What will you and Haern do first?"

"We'll go to the streets," she said. "Every city is alive with its own crude personality. We must learn of Angelport, and from there, learn of every hole someone might hide in."

"Good luck. Just make sure you two are back before morning. No one will be surprised if you sleep in."

Zusa bowed, then left to find Haern. Alyssa felt unsteady on her feet, so she found herself a place to sit in front of a fireplace. The chair was overstuffed and a dreary red, but she sank into it quite comfortably. Alyssa let out a sigh. She couldn't remember when she'd last eaten. Stupid of her to drink on an empty stomach.

"Are you feeling ill?"

She looked up to see Madelyn taking a seat across from her. She shifted baby Tori from her left arm to her right, stroking her face with her fingers. Tori was awake, but only barely, her eyes slowly opening and closing as she snuggled.

"The journey here was long," Alyssa said. "I think it's worn me out more than I expected."

"It is a trip I've taken for every Kensgold. I'm well aware of its toll."

"You could move back to Veldaren."

Madelyn shook her head. She had always been incredibly beautiful, increasingly so over the years, and seeing her holding a newborn made her all the more stunning. But when she looked up and spoke the name 'Veldaren,' she looked shockingly ugly.

"Veldaren? No, girl, I will not move back to that terrible place. You may choose to bed with thieves, but I will not. There is no safety there."

"Nor here," Alyssa said, knowing she was crossing a line but not caring. Madelyn clutched the babe tightly to her chest, hard enough to make little Tori cry.

"The mongrel you dealt with, that killer...the King's Watcher? By his blade you pour wealth into the streets, and for what? It was his sigil left written in my son's blood. Veldaren was your mess, and you helped create him. Far as I'm concerned, your hands are just as guilty."

"Enough, woman," Laurie said, stepping between them. Neither had heard his approach, so focused were they on each other. He glared at his wife, then bowed low to Alyssa. "Forgive her, she speaks out of grief."

"As do I," Alyssa lied.

"Tori should feed before she sleeps," Madelyn said, standing. "Excuse me while I fetch the nursemaid."

Laurie grabbed his wife's arm. Her eyes flared, and Alyssa felt she looked upon a wild animal, not a noblewoman. Madelyn stood there, staring, until at last he let her go without saying a word. He didn't seem offended, only sighed and took her seat across from Alyssa by the fire.

"She has not taken this well," Laurie said, sounding tired beyond his years. "Sometimes I think that baby is the only reason she continues on at all."

"Forgive me, Laurie. I did not mean to provoke her. I only suggested she return to Veldaren. It might do her good to be out of this house and its... memories."

"I have expressed the same," Laurie said, leaning back. He snapped his fingers, and a servant rushed over with a drink in hand. Downing its contents in rapid gulps, he had it refilled, then waved the man away. "But she will not heed my words. To her, Veldaren will always be the place she was taken hostage by Thren during the Bloody Kensgold, and as long as that spider's alive, she'll never return."

"Laurie, I meant to mention this earlier. My guests—"

"This about your, what were they, cousins?" Laurie laughed. "I've spent every waking moment of my life surrounded by men and women who dine with golden spoons. It doesn't take much to know neither has had the Gemcroft name for long, if ever. Who are they really? Bodyguards?"

Alyssa bit her lip, trying to think of the proper answer. "In a way," she said.

Laurie shifted in his chair, his hand drifting to his neck

before returning to the armrest. No doubt he missed the long braid that used to fall over his shoulder. Touching it with his fingers had been a nervous tic of his, and now it was gone.

"I understand you wishing for extra safety, given what happened. I trust they will be with you at all times."

"Not exactly..."

Wishing for her own drink, Alyssa swallowed and pressed on. Laurie was much older than her, and with Leon's death two years ago, he had become the eldest ruler of the Trifect. She'd always felt intimidated in his presence, however soft-spoken he might be. Something about him always seemed vulnerable and made her want to trust him, but she could never forget the ruthless stories she'd heard growing up, of what he'd done to make the thief guilds truly fear him. Still, she did not want to lie to her host, especially when he was her ally and friend.

"I have brought Haern and Zusa with me so they might hunt down the one who killed Julie and Taras, this man you call the Wraith."

Laurie set down his glass hard enough to chip a side. For a long moment he sat there, leaning forward in his chair, thinking. Alyssa did her best not to appear nervous or uncertain. At last he looked up at her, tired eyes bloodshot and a frown on his lips.

"The past few weeks have passed in agony," he said. "Each moment crawls like a day. I could tell you down to the hour how long it has been since my son left this world. And I assure you, for every one of those torturous seconds, I have had my men scouring Angelport in search of him. We have found nothing, heard nothing, other than more names claimed as his victims. It doesn't matter who you brought. It doesn't matter how much you paid them, or how good you think they are. They won't find him. If this is the gift you've come to offer me, then you waste your time."

He stood to leave, but Alyssa stopped him with a sentence. "I brought the Watcher with me."

He turned, something dangerous stirring in his eyes. "Who, Alyssa?"

"The King's Watcher," she said, refusing to back down. "The man I brought... that's who he really is."

"You brought *him*?" asked Laurie, his voice strained, hands clenched into fists. "Into my home? Beyond my walls? It was his mark left to me in mockery, and you bring him here?"

"It was not him," she insisted. "I am certain of it. The travel between our cities is too great, Laurie, and the Watcher was spotted dozens of times in the weeks prior to your son's death. Whoever this Wraith is, he chose that symbol for a reason. It's a challenge, Laurie, a challenge to the Watcher, and I could think of no one better to hunt him down and lay his body at your feet."

"You bring a murderer to find another murderer." He shook his head. "You've always been willing to lower yourself into dealing with scum to solve your problems. One of these days, Alyssa, you'll learn that if you lie with enough dogs, you'll catch their fleas."

"I do what I must," she said, straightening in her seat. "I will bear no shame in that."

Laurie chuckled, and it seemed all his fearful intensity bled away, and he relaxed back into his seat. Once more, he became the charming man he so often was.

"If you insist, then let us see how your Watcher fellow fares here in our city. I'll tell Torgar to let him come and go as he pleases—within reason, of course. And I suggest not telling Madelyn that the Watcher sleeps under her roof. The results would not be... pleasant."

He smiled, and Alyssa could not help but smile back. Despite the redness of his eyes, he finally seemed to show a trace of his old self. The man he'd been before his son was brutally murdered in his room.

"Pleasant night, Lady Gemcroft," he said, bowing.

"And pleasant dreams."

Left alone, Alyssa finally relaxed, glad to have that confrontation over with. His certainty about the Wraith's elusiveness worried her a little, but she brushed that aside. There were plenty that the Trifect had tried to track down, yet failed. Thren Felhorn was a prime example of that, eluding capture for more than a decade. Yet she had the Watcher at her disposal, the one who had found those she could not, frightened those who felt no fear, and forced an entire war to end with just his bloody sabers.

If there was anyone who could find this Wraith, it was him.

"We're never going to find this guy," Haern said as he tightened his hood. "A skilled assassin in his hometown, one daring enough to strike at a member of the Trifect? He'll know every nook and cranny to hide in, nooks and crannies we know nothing about."

"You whine like a child," Zusa said, looping her dark purple wrappings about her neck. She'd been half naked when he entered their room, so he dressed with his back to her as she slowly covered her body.

"That must take forever to put on," he said after stealing a glance to make sure she was decent.

"It was part of our punishment," Zusa said, grabbing another roll of cloth and pressing it against her chin. "The idea was that with how much time it would take, we would be more able to resist our womanly urges."

"It work?"

The wrappings covered her face, cheekbones, and forehead, with only a long gap across her eyes.

"There are many ways to find pleasure, even fully clothed. Trust me. We faceless women discovered them all."

Haern felt himself blushing and quickly changed the topic. "Where is it we should go first?" he asked.

"The docks."

"Any particular reason?"

Zusa smiled at him; her lips might have been covered, but he could tell by the way her eyes sparkled.

"I will explain when we arrive. Now let us hurry. Alyssa said we will be allowed to come and go as we please, but I still think it best we not let many know of our presence here."

Haern inched open the door and looked out. The hallway was dark and empty. The entire mansion had been laid down for rest, the sun long set. Nodding to Zusa, he pulled his cloaks tight about him and led the way. They kept to the servants' side, since they were closer to their exit. When they were to leave, a burly man stood on the opposite side of the door, his arms crossed. A wicked scar ran across the bridge of his nose. He was past his prime years but still looked like he could tear Haern in half with his bare hands.

"You're blocking the way," Haern said, keeping his tone flat as he came to a stop before him. "Move?"

"You're that Watcher guy, aren't you? Laurie said you'd be coming and to let you do as you want."

"How kind of him. Care to do as he says?"

Instead, the man drew an enormous sword off his back. It had to weigh a ton, but he handled it with ease.

"They tell me you weren't the one who killed Taras," he said. "But I saw the symbol. You might not have done it yourself, but that don't mean you're innocent. I fought that Wraith bastard. If the rumors about you are even half true, this guy's still better."

"We don't have time for this," Zusa whispered behind him.

The man let out a roar, as if he were trying to intimidate them. Haern winced, but only from the heavy stench of alcohol that assaulted his nostrils.

"Who are you?" Haern asked.

"Torgar. I'm in charge of Laurie's mercenaries, as well as keeping the family safe. If it were up to me, I'd have you hanging outside the—"

He suddenly tensed, and his jaw dropped a little. Zusa stood before him, her knee rammed into his crotch, her left hand holding his neck to keep him steady. Her dagger pressed against his abdomen, just below his leather armor.

"Move," she breathed into his ear, just before kicking the side of his head. Torgar dropped to his rear, and he howled out his anger.

"You bitch!"

Zusa blew him a kiss as she ran on. Haern followed, offering the mercenary a sympathetic shrug.

"A little harsh," he said as they vaulted the walls of the Keenan estate.

"The oaf thinks with pride and alcohol. I have no patience with either."

"I'll keep that in mind."

They kept to the shadows as they hurried down the street toward a main intersection leading to the docks. Their first obstacle was one of the three walls that divided the city, its gateways well lit and carefully guarded. They slunk to the side of a home and peered around.

"Doubt they'll let us through," Haern said. "Not armed and dressed like this."

"We could take them out. Not fatally. Don't give me that look."

Haern glanced at the wall. It wasn't that tall, and with so many homes built up against it, just maybe...

"Follow me," Zusa said, interrupting his thoughts. She ran until out of sight of the gate, then turned and vaulted high into the air. Haern could hardly believe what he saw. She landed atop the roof, without needing to grab hold or climb up. Without slowing, she took two more steps and jumped again, catching the top of the wall with her fingers. Climbing up, she then leaned back down and offered her hand.

"Jump or climb," she said.

He took his own running leap, caught the roof with a hand, and used it to pull himself up. As for the wall, he jumped toward it, kicked off with a foot to lift higher, and then caught her hand. With minimal effort she pulled him up, and together they overlooked the docks.

"You need to teach me how to do that," he said, shaking his head.

"Run fast, then jump. I didn't think it was difficult." She pointed. "There."

"What am I looking for?"

"You'll know."

Haern followed her finger, then saw a trio of men lurking in an alley. They certainly looked up to no good. Nearby torches burned, lighting up taverns that bustled with activity.

"What is your plan?" he asked. "Assault random thugs and hope one of them knows the Wraith?"

Zusa let out a sigh. "Sometimes I wonder how you achieved as much as you have."

"A lot of luck was involved."

She drew her daggers, twirling them in her hands. "This

Wraith sent you a message for a reason. I say we send one in return. Let him know you're here in Angelport. Let him find you, instead of us finding him."

A grin spread across Haern's face. At least in this, he felt right at home.

"Those scoundrels," he said, gesturing to the men in the alley. "They're about to have a very bad night, aren't they?"

Zusa shot him a wink. "Lead on, Watcher."

Haern dropped from the wall onto a roof, rolled to the street, and shook off the jarring landing. With Zusa following, he weaved toward the taverns. He stayed close to the walls and peered around corners to ensure they never saw his approach. The three men were all heavily tattooed, but most striking was the sword blade tattoo across their right eyes, stretching from chin to forehead.

"Do you know what it means?" Haern whispered.

"I don't," said Zusa, shaking her head.

Haern shrugged, then resolved to watch. The men kept their attention focused on the nearby taverns. They were waiting, and Haern was patient enough to find out just what for. He would not attack men just for standing in a dark alley, despite the short swords they carried. He needed intent. He needed proof.

"They wait for a victim," Zusa said. "Perhaps we should give them one?"

Haern shrugged. "Wait here."

He looped around back so that the three would not see his approach. Pulling down his hood, he turned a corner, making it seem as if he'd just come from one of the taverns. Walking with an uneven gait, he purposefully stumbled closer to their alley while making sure his sabers remained hidden by his cloaks. The outfit would label him an outsider, and he hoped that would help convince the men to make their move.

Crossing the alley, the three men stepped out, their short swords drawn.

"Don't seem from around here," said the biggest of the three.

Haern turned his head aside, not wanting them to get a good look at his face. As they neared, he tugged his hood lower, as if he were scared.

"Visiting a friend, that's all," he said, doing his best to sound afraid.

"Then come over here and hand over what you got," said another, stepping quickly to cut off Haern's retreat. "You need to pay to stay safe in this town, stranger."

"I don't got much to live on," said Haern.

"I'm sure your friend'll help you out."

Haern laughed. "That she will."

Zusa fell upon the one blocking his way, her daggers slicing across his neck before he even knew she was there. Haern spun, drawing his sabers. The other two men swore, unprepared for his vicious assault. Only one managed to defend himself, and Haern batted aside his weak parry with ease. He gutted the nearest, then kicked his head to knock him on his back to die. The other turned to run, but Haern was faster. His saber slashed heel, and down he went. The man rolled, then stopped when he hit a wall.

"You can't do this," he said, spinning over to face them. "You'll hang, the both of you!"

Haern pressed a bloody saber edge underneath the man's chin, lifting his gaze so they might stare eye-to-eye.

"If you have any sense, you'll shut up now, before I slice out your tongue," he said, covering his face with shadows cast from the distant flickering torchlight.

The man swallowed, then carefully nodded.

"That's a smart man. Tell everyone you know, whether they'll believe you or not, that the King's Watcher has come to Angelport. Your time draws to an end. Every one of you thieves risks death when you enter the shadows. The shadows are where *I* live. Tell them."

The tattooed man laughed, stopping only when Haern pressed the tip hard enough to draw blood.

"Thieves? Are you fucking stupid?"

"You can deliver my message, or I can write it with your blood across the wall behind you. Your choice."

The man swallowed. "I'll do it," he said. "Just let me go."

Haern pulled back the blade and gestured for him to leave. He did, limping away from the docks. Zusa joined his side, wiping her daggers clean on the dead man's shirt.

"He is not to be trusted," she said.

"Then what do you suggest?"

She knelt before one of the bodies and dipped her fingers into the gaping wound across his stomach. Once coated with blood and gore, she walked to the wall and began to write.

I am here, it said, signed with the name *Watcher*.

"Let there be no doubt," she said, smearing the rest into a vague circle about the message.

Haern looked at the two dead men, feeling vague unease. Something about it all wasn't quite right. Perhaps he should have waited for them to attack first, to at least confirm their intentions had been fatal, and not just for a bit of coin. That tattoo... surely it signified their guild affiliations. Veldaren was not Angelport, but he had a hard time believing the cities would be so different.

Still, something about the way the man had laughed in mocking when he called him a thief...

"We're done for now," he said, sheathing his sabers. He glanced about, but no guards or drunken workers were near to see what they'd done.

"We have only begun."

"Search if you must. After the trip here, I could use a good night's rest. We've delivered the message you asked. What else could you hope for?"

Zusa gave him a disappointed look, and he tried not to let it get to him.

"To deliver it, again and again."

Haern thought of killing more, and it put a bad taste in his mouth. "This isn't my city," he said. "I've done enough."

He left, and Zusa did not follow. Back at the Keenan mansion, he slipped into his room, stripped off his clothes, and climbed into bed. Several hours later, he heard the door open. Zusa slipped inside. He shifted over, to let her share the bed, but she did not join him. Without a pillow or blanket, she slept on the floor, still in her wrappings stained with blood.

CHAPTER

5

Ingram Murband, lord of Angelport and ruler of the Ramere, listened to the guard's report with a growing rage.

"You're sure it isn't this Wraith character I've been hearing rumors of?" he asked.

The captain of the guard shook his head. "Different weapon used to kill them, plus a different name. Only one person's lived to see him, but he also listed clothes that don't match what the mercenaries at Laurie Keenan's mansion saw."

Ingram leaned back in his chair. They were in his modest throne room, for unlike most lords, he had no castle. The walls and water of the city were enough to keep him safe. His mansion was an impressive structure, however, with a surrounding wall built of stone imported all the way from Ker. In its center was his throne room, with no other purpose than meetings with various minor lords and commoners pleading for their simple definitions of justice. The walls were dark stone, and barren of any decoration. Ingram thought it made him seem all the more confident by not covering the walls with beheaded animals and war trophies to exaggerate his prowess.

"I won't put up with this," he said. "I want it dealt with, and harshly. Whatever the reason he is here, we need the entire city turned against him before he sways any hearts."

"What do you suggest?" asked the captain.

"Take it out on the prisoners, ten for every one. Make it public. I'll bear their hatred just fine. Will he?"

"Very well," the captain said, bowing low. "Shall I send in the first of your guests?"

"If you must."

As the soldier left, Ingram rubbed his eyes. Things had grown so tiresome of late. First the Wraith was making his life a living torment, and now the mysterious Watcher of Veldaren had to come to his city. As if the elves didn't give him enough trouble. Thinking of the elves, he wondered when their new ambassador would arrive. He'd been told to expect him today. He'd greatly appreciate restarting their talks.

The double doors opened, and in walked the two most prosperous and powerful lords of the Ramere: Yorr Warren, tall and thin, his oval face covered with a beard, and the other, Lord Edgar Moss, muscular and dark-skinned, with two elegant rapiers hanging from his belt. Between them, more than half of all lands that stretched from the southern coast up to the Kingstrip were within their power. There were other lords, minor nobles and owners of land, but Ingram knew they were all in either Yorr's or Edgar's pockets. Both men bowed to Ingram, who gestured for them to continue.

"We've come as you've requested," said Yorr. "Did the elves finally gain some sense and accept our proposals?"

"Not quite," Ingram said, leaving his throne. The three took a seat at one of the two tables in the room, with servants rapidly appearing to pour them drinks and bring them small meats and breads to eat.

"Then what are we to do?" asked Edgar. His fingers twirled the hilt of a rapier, as if by habit. "Every week I must replace men riddled with arrows, all because they don't want us to chop down a few trees or set foot in their sacred lands. Sacred? What a joke."

"You're better off than I am," said Yorr. "If my peasants even step within bowshot of the Erze Forest, they get an arrow through their throat."

"I understand the difficulty," Ingram said, sighing. "But King Edwin refuses to declare war. In this, our hands are tied. We must reach a favorable agreement with the elves, for if we provoke battle, the king will not come to our aid. Only if the elves seem the aggressor will he bother. Edwin knows of their aggressive defense, yet does nothing."

"Probably thinks it's our own damn fault," Yorr muttered.

Edgar sipped his wine.

"Given what those pointy-eared bastards went through over in Mordan, it doesn't surprise me. Still, such aggression needs to be punished. They came into our lands, built a home in our forests, and now deem them sacred without need to share. How else are we to build our homes, our ships?"

"Their ambassador should come today," Ingram said. "We must show strength and back down on nothing. The prosperity of our city depends on the resources they covet. King Edwin is a young, easily frightened brat. He'll insist we handle this ourselves, and leave us to our fates, But if the elves leave their forests and begin burning fields and villages, he will have no choice but to interfere."

"We play a dangerous game," Yorr said. "How do we know Edwin won't leave us to our fates instead of embroiling Neldar in war?"

Ingram chuckled and shook his head, thoroughly amused. "Because our king is human, Edgar. No human would dare side with a lying, deceitful, worthless race of elves over his own kind. Not when they have a choice. That's as it should be, and how we must proceed in all matters with these heathen creatures. Let them worship the stars and trees like fools. We serve the true gods. Our progress is inevitable. King Baedan figured this out. He burned Dezerea to the ground and sent the Dezren elves fleeing east, toward our homes, our lands. If we are strong, we will one day achieve a victory far greater than that."

A soft clang marked the opening of a side door, and in stepped the captain of the guard.

"The elven ambassador has arrived at the gates of the city," he said, saluting. "Shall I let him in?"

"Send him this way," Ingram said, pushing away his plate and standing. "Be firm, you two, and do not hide your anger when we make our demands. Such prideful creatures, the elves cannot stand being treated as they should. Use it to our advantage."

They waited, fixing their clothes and making sure they stood just right. When the double doors opened, Ingram went to greet the ambassador.

"Welcome to our city," he said, all smiles.

The elf was slender, and tall for his race. Flowing emerald robes brushed against the stone floor as he stepped inside, and his sleeves fell low when he gracefully bowed. His hair was long and golden, his eyes a vibrant green.

"Greetings, lord and ruler of Angelport," said the ambassador.

"My name is Graeven Tryll, and I have come from Quellassar to seek peace with men."

"As do we also seek peace," Ingram said, not bowing and hoping the ambassador would notice the slight. "Please, let me introduce my companions. This is Lord Yorr Warren, who rules the northern reaches of my land. To my left is Lord Edgar Moss, in charge of the west. They have the most experience when dealing with your . . . kind."

Graeven bowed a second time. "Your names are familiar to me," he said. "I greet you, and wish Celestia's grace upon you both."

"Flattered," Yorr said dryly.

"I'm sure your trip was long," Ingram said, letting a hard edge creep into his voice, "but given the many deaths our loyal citizens suffered by the tips of your arrows, I would like to begin negotiations as soon as possible."

"I agree," said Graeven. "But I do not speak for all elvenkind. I only come to prepare the way for the lady who shall. Our Neyvar has sent Laryssa Sinistel to meet with you and has given her authority to speak in his name."

Ingram felt his heart jump. "Laryssa?" he asked, trying to show no emotion. "Your king has sent his daughter here?"

"Neyvar, not king," corrected Graeven. "And yes. She should arrive in a few hours, and I come to ask permission for her and her escort to enter within your walls—"

"Wait one moment," Yorr interrupted. "How large an escort?"

"Large," said Graeven. "Along with Sildur Kinstel, Maradun Fae, and their own escorts. Surely you understand, given our concerns for safety."

Ingram felt ready to explode. That damned Wraith had killed the last elven ambassador, and while Ingram had been amused at first, now he wished to throttle the strange assassin. To have someone as important as Laryssa within his grasp could mean everything, but to invite that many bodyguards, all on high alert, sickened him. Elves walking freely within his walls, doing untold damage with their blades, bows, and poisons. Gods, what if they spent their seed among the loose women and whores about the docks? What bastard children might one day inhabit his city?

"Can you swear to the safety of my people?" he asked, but the words felt hollow. As if the promises of an elf meant anything.

"I can promise nothing," Graeven said. "Only that they are here for protection, and nothing more. I do not want to imagine the consequences if something should happen to one of our wise leaders."

It didn't take much to imagine what those consequences were, of course.

"Where is it you will stay?" Ingram asked.

"We have been graciously offered a place by one of your city's fine men. I assume this will not be a problem?"

"Of course not." Despite the bad taste it left in his mouth, he smiled and bowed once more. "Let us resume talks tomorrow. Make sure you send someone to let us know where you will be staying, so I might send servants to tell you when we will convene. We'll meet here, your representatives, mine, and the Merchant Lords."

Graeven spun on his heels and headed for the door. When it closed, Ingram stalked back to his throne, sat upon it, and shouted for a drink.

"Hardly the angry display I was told to expect," Edgar said, unable to conceal his sarcasm.

"Shut up, you fool," Ingram said, gulping down his wine.

"This changes everything. Laryssa did not come here without reason. Ceredon is playing games, and we must discover his aims. I'll save my anger for the morrow, when they are together. Besides, if something should happen to her, something no fault of our own... but enough of that. Send word to your camps, both of you. I want their forests crawling with men. I don't care how many die, so long as they learn that we will never, ever stop. Oh, and find out who that damn traitor is that's willing to house the elves."

The two lords bowed, and Ingram dismissed them with a wave. It wasn't until they were gone that Ingram realized Graeven had not bowed before his exit. Such disrespect left him calling for more wine and wishing he had loosed his temper on the ambassador after all.

That same morning, Haern joined Alyssa and Zusa as they walked amid the hundreds of shops lining the roads just north of the docks.

"I'd prefer the few extra hours of sleep," Haern said as they looked at a strange assortment of dresses whose cost he couldn't even begin to guess. Forget cost, thought Haern. He couldn't even decide which was the front and which was the back. Never before had he been so keenly aware of how secluded a life he led. Here in Angelport he saw styles from all four nations, tattoos drawn in bright colors, and animals in cages he had only heard of in passing. All his life he'd danced in the underworld of Veldaren, oblivious to the greater world beyond its walls.

Still, that didn't change the fact he'd rather be sleeping than keeping up his façade of being newlyweds with Zusa.

"Come, husband," she said, flashing him a smile, looking

beautiful in a red dress that left her shoulders naked. "You treat me so distantly. Has our passion already faded?"

Haern hurried past a merchant selling a brightly colored bird with a silver beak. "I can't imagine so. Ours was a marriage made for the ages."

She snickered, then grabbed his hand. "For show," she said, winking.

Haern shook his head and laughed. "You're lucky you're beautiful," he said.

Zusa's smile lost its joy, and he saw her exchange a look with Alyssa.

"Yes," said Zusa. "Lucky."

Haern didn't understand, but Zusa offered nothing more, so Haern let his mind wander. Watching for thieves kept most of his attention. They were everywhere, lurking in corners, doorways, and the sides of stalls. They had a look to them, a wariness they could not hide from someone so familiar with their ways as Haern. Twice he'd caught a man sliding through the crowd, spotted the mark, and then put himself in the way. The first one he'd asked for directions, letting the noble lady move on to a much more occupied booth. The second time, Haern only grabbed the man's arm and smiled.

"Lay off," the thief said, yanking free.

"Pardon me," Haern said, grinning while still blocking his way. "I thought you were someone else."

By the time he let the thief free, the mark was gone. Zusa chided him for being childish.

"You cannot stop every crime," she said, squeezing his hand. "The world is bigger than you."

"I can at least stop the ones I see."

"Even that will one day kill you. We are not in Veldaren, and right now, you are not the Watcher. Relax. We're supposed to be in love, remember?"

He chuckled, and he felt his neck flush despite himself.

"Right," he said. "How could I forget?"

They rejoined Alyssa's side and continued browsing the selection. At one stall Haern finally found something that caught his interest: a wide variety of swords, all exquisitely made. He was holding one, examining its hilt, when he heard a loud cry from the guards.

"What was that?" Haern asked the shopkeeper.

"Sounds like a hanging," the burly smith said. "You look new here, so go take a gander. Shame I'll miss the fun, selling wares and all."

Haern replaced the sword, tilted his head in a manner of respect Alyssa had showed him, then returned to Zusa's side. They were already making their way north, toward a large open square.

"You hear it too?" she asked him.

"Partly."

Zusa shot him a glance. "They're calling for the Watcher."

Alyssa crossed her arms and leaned closer to the two so she might not be overheard among the din. "Do not interfere," she said. "Watch, and watch only. If either of you are revealed, the blame will fall upon me for bringing you here. I have no intention of spending my stay here in a dungeon."

"Watcher!" the city guard cried again, a single man bellowing above the crowd. He stood atop a wooden platform, with five nooses hanging behind him. Haern felt his mouth go dry as a row of dirty, malnourished men ascended the stairs, their arms tied behind their backs. "Watcher of Veldaren, come forth!"

"What's going on here?" Haern asked.

"Isn't it obvious?" Zusa whispered.

Perhaps it was, but Haern didn't want to believe it. The crowd quieted as the guard began crying out anew. Worse was the tattoo he saw on the city guard's face, the same tattoo many of the city guard wore: a sword across the right eye.

"Murderer, coward, and butcher known as Veldaren's Watcher, know that Angelport is no place for you. We will not accept your presence. Last night, you slew two of our city guard and harmed a third. For every innocent man you attack, ten from our dungeons shall hang. So declares Lord Ingram Murband."

The crowd let up a cheer at the hooded executioner's arrival. As he slipped noose after noose over the heads of prisoners, Haern felt his hands shake.

"How dare they?" he whispered.

Zusa squeezed his hand tight. "Criminals," she said. "Outlaws. Their lives are nothing."

Once bags were over their heads, the executioner stepped down and circled around to the back of the platform. Hanging underneath were ropes attached to thick planks of wood. With a pull on a rope, it'd drop open, allowing the man or woman above to fall. Meanwhile, the city guard walked from person to person, shouting out their crimes. Murderer. Thief. Rapist. The crowd cheered as the executioner took the first rope and wrapped it around his beefy arm.

He pulled, and the man dropped.

"Not in my name," Haern whispered. "Damn it, not in my name."

One after another, the executioner pulled the ropes, until all five were dead.

"We killed guards," he said, feeling his insides roil. "Not thieves. Guards."

"We didn't know," Zusa insisted.

It didn't matter. Two dead guards and the third left alive to deliver his message. Thirty men and women to die in return. Haern's rage grew, and he tried to let go of her hand. She refused, instead pulling him closer. Alyssa glanced over, her face coldly passive, but she said nothing.

"No," Zusa whispered. "Accept no blame, Haern. Stand and watch. This is the path we chose, and we will bear the consequence of our mistake together."

Five more, their crimes read. The crowd cheered, the executioner did his work, and then they hung. As the bodies were carted off and the next set brought on, Haern listened to their crimes.

Avoiding taxes. Striking a guard. Stealing food. Speaking ill of Lord Murband.

They were hanged like the rest. Still the crowd cheered.

"I can stop it," Haern said. His sabers were clipped to his belt, and every part of him screamed to draw them from their sheaths. "I can kill them all."

"You will die," Zusa said.

"It doesn't matter. I could still...no. Ashhur help us, they cannot..."

Two of the next five were children, no older than ten. The executioner had them stand on stools above the trapdoors. They were called thieves as their heads were covered with bloody cloths. When the first rope pulled, Haern took a step forward. It didn't matter he had no disguise. It didn't matter there were hundreds of guards crawling about. Another child still stood with a noose about his neck.

"No!" Zusa cried, blocking Haern's way and grabbing his head with her hands. He clutched her wrists, but she was strong. They stared face-to-face, Haern nearly delirious with anger. Her gaze held him, the force of her will incredible.

"We are the ones who own the night," she said, pressing her forehead against his. "We are the ones with blood on our hands. Look at me, just me. Ignore all else. We are the reapers, the demons, the dark shadows wielding steel. We will not be denied our vengeance, but it is *not now*."

The crowd cheered, and he felt oblivious to them, lost in a sea of dirty faces and black hearts. Her eyes were beautiful, though, and he wished he could lose himself within. But even there, he saw the child drop, the noose snap taut, followed by the image of that other lone child in Veldaren. Not his fault, he'd told himself then. Not his fault, he tried to say now. But it was. The dead belonged to him.

"When?" he asked, trying to control his fury. "And how can we do what must be done when every guilty man I kill leads ten more innocents to their deaths?"

Zusa offered no answer.

Alyssa stepped between them, and she motioned for them to go.

"I know what you're thinking," she said as they left the gallows. "But you cannot let Ingram's madness deter you. The Wraith must be found and killed."

"And what of Ingram?" Haern asked. "Do you think I'll let such an act slide?"

"He killed thieves and criminals to send a message, same as you. You're hardly any more innocent than him, Haern. Don't get yourself killed trying to prove otherwise."

Her words stung far deeper than she could have possibly known. Haern pulled away from Zusa and stormed off. Zusa called his name, but he ignored her.

"Are you watching, Watcher?" the city guard cried behind him. "Do you see the fruits of your labors?"

He did, enough of it anyway. Wanting to be as far away as possible, he wandered the streets north, toward Angelport's entrance. On his way, a thief, probably not even out of his teens, slipped beside him and reached for the coin purse in his pocket. Haern's first instinct was to reach for his sabers, his first desire one of bloodshed, but the realization chilled him to the bone. So instead he slapped the thief's hand away, whirled, and grabbed his throat.

"You should be dead," Haern said. "Now go."

"Fuck you, mister," the thief said, knocking over two other kids as he fell back. His demeanor weakened at the fury in Haern's eyes, and he fled down the street without another word. Haern glanced at his clothes, fine silk and soft cotton, and realized he looked like a noble. More than ever he wished to return, put on his old clothes, and vanish amid Veldaren's crowds. Not wanting to be anywhere near the Keenan mansion, he passed through a second gate. The guards let him go with only a salute, but the same could not be said for those whose clothes were stained with dirt and whose hands bore the calluses of the docks.

"That's a good lady," one of the guards said to a mother, dumping half of her collection of coins into his palm before tossing the worn bag at her feet. "Even whores need to pay their taxes, aye?"

The woman nodded, her heart clearly not in arguing. Haern swallowed hard, and his hands itched to draw steel. The thought of ten more swinging from the gallows moved him on. His walk took him to the city gates, and he heard a growing commotion near them. Mildly curious, he wandered closer. As he did, the crowd parted to either side of the road. Not wishing to stand out, Haern did the same. A trumpet sounded, and then he saw the first of the elves.

They walked with their heads held high, their fine clothing glittering in the sunlight. They wore earthen tones, greens and browns, but the fabric was highlighted with gold trim, their belts shining with silver buckles, their ears glimmering with emerald rings. Among them were the warriors, their leather armor well oiled and intricately decorated. Large swords hung from their backs, except for those wielding bows slung over their shoulders. Among them were elf men and women riding horseback, their lords and leaders, all heavily flanked by warriors.

Haern stood in awe of the spectacle. He could only begin to guess why they had come. He counted at least a hundred, closer to two. At first the human crowds watched, also in awe of the wealth and majesty before them. Then came the many shouts, first hesitant and from the back, but the anger and hatred spread like wildfire.

"Murderers!" they shouted. "Heathens! Butchers!"

Haern could hardly believe what he heard. They cried against the foreign elves, deeming them murderers, even as their own lord hung thirty people for crimes not their own? Was this the true face of the city?

"Why such protest?" he asked a man next to him. He'd kept his calm, unlike most others.

"They're killing our friends and families," said the man. "But they can't hide in their forests forever, not when we want what they have."

"Do you not share the crowd's anger?"

"No point. Their time's over. They can ride in all high and mighty, but it won't change nothing. Besides, they don't hurt my business any."

"And what is that?" Haern asked.

The man chuckled, and he turned to leave. "I build the coffins," he said. "There's always enough wood for that."

A few brave souls began throwing stones. The elves ignored them, reacting only when one came too close. The warriors would reach for their swords and move with such precision the crowd scattered. Hearing the shouts, and seeing the bruises build across the warriors' faces as the rocks came down like hail, Haern's gut filled with venom. In all of Angelport, he saw little kindness, little worth saving.

Worse, he knew Veldaren was no different. He'd grown up there, and familiarity had blinded him. But here he saw vileness, cruelty, and such a callous attitude toward life it stabbed straight to his heart. These were the people he'd struggled to protect? These were the ones for whom he spent years of his life freeing from his father's war against the Trifect? What was it he'd truly accomplished? Anything at all? Come his death, it'd all come crashing down. Everywhere, men were the same, and he knew their nature well.

But worse were Alyssa's words, painting him in a light he'd hidden from, revealing a self he never wished to see.

He killed thieves and criminals to send a message, same as you.

Was he the same? Was that the carnage he unleashed, all to the cheers of the populace as he left corpses in their gutters so they might pretend to safety and justice? Once he'd thought himself a monster, the monster his city needed. But as a ruthless peace had settled over Veldaren, he'd allowed himself to believe he'd become something more. The King's Watcher. Such a joke. The hood he wore... the man upon the gallows had worn the same. The King's Executioner. That should be his name.

"No," he whispered as the elves vanished around the corner,

out of sight because of the mob. "I am not the same. I cannot be. I escaped that fate."

Hollow words that did nothing to ease his troubled mind. But what did give him relief was the thought that, come nightfall, he'd pay Lord Ingram a visit and show him how dangerous a monster the Watcher could truly be.

CHAPTER

6

Ulrich drank a glass of whiskey to chase away the lingering effects of the Violet. He'd taken half a leaf in the morning, more than the quarter he usually allocated. Supplies were incredibly limited, but if everything went well over the next few weeks, he'd be buried in the rare leaf. When he left his mansion, he found his brother waiting for him outside the gate.

"About time you're ready," Stern said.

"Who are you now, our mother?"

"Mother rests in a deep grave. I have no intention of being her for a very long time."

Ulrich laughed, then caught his brother staring at his eyes.

"What?" he asked.

"I'm no fool," Stern said. "I can see the yellow in your veins. You're addicted to the Violet."

"Nonsense," Ulrich said, brushing his brother aside. "Keep your damn opinions to yourself. What I do on my time is my own business, not yours, and you're a fool for thinking I'd be weak enough to become slave to a plant."

"As you wish," Stern said, but Ulrich could hear the condescension in his voice, and it irritated him to no end.

They walked down the street, passing unquestioned through one of the interior city gates. When they came to the docks, they entered an unremarkable building titled PORT AND LOAN. Inside led to a small entryway, guarded by two men in chain mail.

"The rest are waiting for you, my lords," said one.

Stern nodded, then glanced over at Ulrich. "If the room's dark, they shouldn't notice," he said, once again referring to his eyes.

"I know you're still upset about Julie," Ulrich said, biting down his initial retort. "But keep your head up high. We Blackwaters never show weakness. They might press hard to change your mind if they think you're still grieving."

"As you so eloquently put it, keep your damn opinions to yourself."

Ulrich grabbed his arm, stopping him from pushing in the door. "This is serious," he said, meeting his brother's eye. "With Tori set to one day inherit the Keenan wealth from Madelyn, the others will wonder where your allegiances now lie. Is it with us, or her?"

"The Trifect is a disease," Stern said, pulling free his arm. "Freeing Tori from their influence is the best thing I could ever do for her. Anyone doubting my intentions does so at their own peril. Right now, running someone through with a sword would do wonders for my mood. Now come on."

Stern entered the gathering room, and Ulrich followed.

The space inside was grand, shaped into an oval with an abundance of empty space. A map of the known world was painted across the walls, the seas finely detailed and interlaced with many monsters and fish, both real and fantastical. In the center of the room was a circular table, and despite its size, it had only six chairs, all equidistant from each other. The Blackwater brothers took their seats and greeted the other four Merchant Lords. Unlike true lords, they owned no lands and had been granted no official power by the king. But the vast majority of ships that sailed the seas belonged to them, and for several decades their family had banded together, uniting against a common enemy: the Trifect.

Their eldest, and official leader of gatherings, was Warrick Sun, a salty old man who had spent half his life on the ocean. The latter half he'd spent indoors, reaping the bounty of his impressive fleets carrying the Sun banner. His white beard was braided tight and decorated with beads of gold and silver. Warrick stood in greeting, and the others followed suit. Beside him, looking young and out of place, was Flint Amour, the firstborn son of the deceased William. Recently entering his twenties, he had a box beard that was thin and unimpressive, but he sported a healthy tan from his many hours upon the boats. Ulrich was glad to see him as William's successor. Flint was rumored to be the toughest of the lot, and that was exactly what they wanted among their ranks.

"Glad for you to finally join us," Arren Goldsail said to Ulrich as they entered, flashing them an earnest smile. Years of experience had taught Ulrich just how fake that smile was. "I was beginning to think you'd chosen to stay among more feminine company instead of attending your own meeting."

Arren was thin and pale, having never once sailed across open waters. He was an excellent barterer, though, and had a way of making a man agree to twice what he intended, yet simultaneously feel he had the better deal. While the others controlled ships, Arren had contacts and trade routes stretching across all four nations of Dezrel.

"It takes time to please that many ladies," Ulrich said, accepting a drink from one of the many servants lingering near the walls. "Isn't that right, Durgo?"

The last of them, Durgo Flynn, rolled his eyes. He was a giant of a man and dark-skinned, yet he spoke with a soft voice. For several years, Ulrich had carefully spread rumors the man preferred the company of little boys to grown women. He had no clue if it was true or not, but it amused him, and pissed off Durgo immensely.

Together, the six were the Merchant Lords of Angelport. With power derived from their wealth and ships, not position or birth, Ulrich knew every single one sported a chip on their shoulder and a desire to prove their influence. He himself was no exception. Every meeting of the Merchant Lords was a great clash of egos. For someone like Ulrich, it was also an incredibly amusing game.

"Things have changed since our last meeting," Warrick said, always one to keep things on task. "First and foremost, we welcome a new man to our table. Listen well, Flint, and ask questions if you must. We do not know how much your father told you of our dealings and would prefer you to make wise decisions instead of rash, unfounded ones just to hide your ignorance."

"Thank you," Flint said, bowing his head respectfully. "I will do my best to be a boon to this council."

"Keep the cum cleaned out of your ears, and you'll be a better man than your father," Durgo said.

Ulrich hid his laugh with his palm. Flint flushed red and said nothing. William had been considered one of the more slow-minded merchants and was poorly received by the other five. His death was no great loss.

"Let us not disrespect the dead," Stern said, his harsh tone startling the rest. "Besides, his death is why we're here. Twice now this man known as the Wraith has struck at us—first my daughter, and now William. What are we to do about it?"

"What can we do about it?" asked Arren, picking at one of his smooth fingernails. "The Keenans have already put out a tremendous bounty, and his mercenaries have scoured every corner of every street. If that Wraith's not been found yet, there's little we can do to help matters."

"We are masters of places in Angelport the Trifect doesn't even know exist," Durgo said. "I say we put up our own bounty, as well as some of our men. I won't be losing my head next."

"We're ignoring the larger question," Warrick said, and he squinted in the candlelight. "Why has he targeted us at all? I thought perhaps the Trifect had hired him, but then why kill Laurie's son?"

"What about Ingram?" Flint asked. The others sighed or rolled their eyes, with only Warrick remaining patient.

"Lord Murband's rule on Angelport is tenuous at best," the old man explained. "He would not dare make enemies of both us and the Trifect. With just temporary cooperation, we could cast him out with nary a bead of sweat on our brows. The king may grant Ingram lands, but it is we who control the money and trade."

"Then what of the elves?" Ulrich asked. "Perhaps they wish to weaken our resolve?"

"Perhaps," Arren said. "But then why kill their own ambassador and maim another elf outside the city?"

Ulrich shrugged. "Elves are liars. We have little proof that events transpired as they claim."

Warrick shook his head and lifted his hand so the others would pause for him to speak. "No," he said. "I fear we have a murderer who owes allegiance to none. He kills elves, Trifect, and merchants alike. In this, he is a greater threat than any other we have faced before. He has made no demands, offered no ransoms, and left us guessing his motives. Hunt him down and execute him. I call for the hiring of skilled men to end this threat. Do any object?"

None did, for despite their bickering, Ulrich knew that a threat against one was a threat against all. It couldn't be allowed. Warrick called over a servant with a ream of parchment, a quill, and an inkwell. He carefully recorded Warrick's orders, then faded back into the shadows among the walls. As the discussion stalled, Ulrich called for more wine. For some reason, he found himself incredibly thirsty, and the strawberry flavor tasted divine on his tongue.

"Putting aside this Wraith," Warrick said, "we have another test of our influence. Our men scour the Quellan Forest for Violet, but our casualties increase daily, and the amount brought back is too little for real exportation. From what I see, we have three options. Either we receive significant concessions from the elves, reach an acceptable trade agreement, or abandon the project altogether. Tomorrow we meet with Ingram, the Trifect, and the new elven representative. Come then, we must decide our most profitable fate."

"Ingram is easily manipulated," Arren said. "I have no fears there."

"What of the Trifect?" Durgo asked, looking to the two Blackwater brothers.

"Laurie's shaken up by the loss of his son," Ulrich said, stealing a glance at Stern. "I think he'll side with whatever ends this nonsense the quickest. As for Alyssa…that girl is lightning with tits. There's no predicting her."

"And the elves?" asked Warrick.

"It doesn't matter," Stern said, looking as if he were forcing himself out of a daze. "If we keep the right lords bribed, Ingram won't be able to stop war from approaching. Long as loggers and hunters press the forest boundaries, the conflict will escalate. The elves will eventually appease us, or risk extermination in a long, bloody conflict."

"And what if they choose war?" Flint asked.

"A good question," said Arren. "Surely a middle ground would be easier for the elves to accept. We need not grow the Violet ourselves if the elves give it willingly."

Ulrich shook his head. "The elves cannot realize the Violet is the true reason for this conflict. Demand for food to live on and lumber to build ships and homes is something they cannot deny without looking petty, but a simple weed? We lose our pedestal. If it must come to war, then let it come to war. We'd profit from it, like we profit from everything. Now if you'll forgive my audacity, I request the right to represent us tomorrow at the meeting."

"You?" Warrick asked, lifting his bushy eyebrows. "Why is that?"

Ulrich thought of Zusa, and how she would most likely be with Alyssa, or at least nearby. "Because we need someone who won't put up with shit from anyone," he said. "You all know I'm the one for that."

"Perhaps I would be better for so delicate a matter," Arren said.

"Only you would think so, Goldsail," said Ulrich. "This isn't a barter, not anymore. It's time we make demands, and make them realize *we* control this city. I want my Violet. Once we have it, everything else crumbles at our feet. Ingram, the Trifect, the elves... I won't risk losing a single scrap of that victory. Put it to a vote, now."

Warrick shrugged his bony shoulders. "All who favor Ulrich Blackwater speaking for the Merchant Lords, lift your hand."

Flint was first, immediately endearing the kid to Ulrich, who of course voted for himself. *Two more*, he thought, glancing about the table. Arren refused to meet his eyes, which was answer enough. Warrick stayed back, to vote last as he always did. Durgo crossed his arms, not looking pleased at all. Stern finally lifted his hand, and Ulrich tried to hold back his anger at such a delay. How could his own brother not trust him so?

"Will there be any others?" Warrick asked. "Then so be it. I cast my vote for you as well, Ulrich, though I do so with a heavy heart. It is one thing to chase gold, another to be blinded by it. The Violet may bring us wealth unimaginable, but it also may lead us to our doom. Acknowledge that threat."

"Of course," Ulrich said, all smiles.

The major issues decided, they closed a few more minor points of contention, then ended the meeting. As Ulrich was heading out—last to arrive and first to leave as always—Flint hurried to catch up with him.

"I'm not scared of war," Flint said, earning him a raised eyebrow.

"Is that so?" Ulrich asked, a little puzzled.

"I just…I asked back there only because I'm still trying to learn. But I'm not my father. I am not afraid of the elves. No matter what they say, I know they killed my…I have no intention of making deals with those backstabbing monsters. Whatever you need, know the Amours are behind you."

Ulrich smiled, and he clapped the young man on the back. "How solid is your rule over your family's estate?" he asked.

Flint's cheeks flushed. "I have many brothers," he said.

"If anyone gives you too much trouble, you come to me. Consider that a favor for your help."

Flint nodded, looking relieved. "I will," he said, and smiled.

Such an eager kid, thought Ulrich. Good thing he got to him before Arren did. "Come on," he said, glancing back to see Stern discussing matters with Warrick in a far corner of the room. He frowned, but then hurried to hide it. "We should go find ourselves a place to drink the night away in celebration of your new position as head of the household."

"Will you not be going with me?" Haern asked as he pulled his hood low. Zusa shook her head, sliding her wrappings across her face.

"Your vengeance upon Ingram is your own. We sent our message, and I will see if the Wraith answers."

"And if you find him?"

Zusa shot him a wink. "I am capable of killing, same as you. Worry about your own life, Haern."

He left her there while she continued dressing, feeling a small sense of relief at heading out alone. It was what he knew, what he did best. At the servants' exit, Torgar gave him no nonsense, stepping aside when he saw Haern coming.

"Try not to die too painfully," the big man muttered.

Haern smirked. "Zusa will soon follow. Try to behave."

He climbed over the wall and ran.

The city of Angelport was mostly flat, but overlooking the docks was a man-made hill rising from the water. Atop it was a large and fairly modern-looking mansion, with many statues built into various nooks and corners. Its walls were made of a white stone he did not recognize. He was surprised by how poorly guarded the outside was. Easily finding a gap in the patrols, he used the arm of one statue to vault to a second, that of a great bird spreading its wings as if to fly off the roof. Once up there, he searched the windows.

He didn't know what this Ingram fellow looked like, but he knew well the mannerisms of the privileged. There would be no other room as large, no place as well decorated, as his own. Through the third window he saw an extravagant four-poster bed, red silk curtains along the sides. The window was unlocked, another unimpressive bit of security. Sliding it open, Haern slipped inside, drew his sabers, and hopped onto the bed. The impact startled the man awake.

"Wait!" the man said as the tip of a saber pressed against his throat.

"Are you Ingram?" Haern asked, keeping his voice a cold whisper.

The man was tall but hefty, and when he nodded, his cheeks shook and blood trickled down his neck. His dark hair was long, and it fell across his sweaty face.

"Do you know who I am?" Haern asked.

"I do," said Ingram, doing a remarkable job at keeping calm. "You're him, aren't you, the Wraith?"

Haern felt his professional pride take a jab. Being mistaken for another? An unwelcome first.

"No," he said, pressing the tip harder to make sure the man didn't dare cry out for help. "The Watcher. You left me a message. I've come to give you one of my own."

"Is that so?" Ingram said. He swallowed, and the motion rubbed the tip up and down his throat. The sensation made him shudder. "I'd think twice about that. Do you really believe I'd provoke you without expecting retaliation?"

Haern felt the hairs on the back of his neck prickle. Ingram was trying to take control of the situation, initiating conversation while acting as if he were the one with greater knowledge. Not the way he wanted the situation to progress at all.

"Everyone knows they'll die," Haern whispered. "But that makes them no less prepared. You slaughtered innocent people in my name."

"And you killed my guards," Ingram countered.

"Ruffians prepared to rob and beat others. A poor excuse for guards."

"And those I killed were no better. My dungeons are overcrowded as is. You gave me a fine excuse to thin them out, Watcher."

Haern felt his anger flare, and he pulled the saber back to thrust.

"Do it, and hundreds more die," Ingram said. He clenched his jaw and stared Haern in the eye while bracing for the killing blow. Haern almost did it. Almost.

"How?" he asked. "How will so many die?"

Ingram let out a slow sigh of relief. "I've heard many rumors of you, Watcher, but the strangest was that you cared for the commoners. I've given orders to every guard in the city, and my nobles all agreed to do the same, lest they forfeit any chance of inheriting my power. Should I die by your hand, or that of the Wraith, every prisoner in my custody is to be immediately executed, regardless of their crime." Ingram gave him a smile. "As of last count, I have over four hundred people locked away in my cells, minus the thirty we removed today."

Haern struck him across the face with the hilt of a saber. Instead of showing anger or fear, Ingram laughed.

"You really are a weakling, aren't you? Letting a faceless rabble decide your course of action . . . shameful."

"Why did you do it?" Haern asked. "Why such a display?"

"You ask me?" Ingram rolled his eyes. "You appear in my city and kill two of my guards, yet ask *me* why I did it? How about you tell me what you're doing in Angelport? Oh, and keep your damn saber away from my throat if you have no intention of using it."

Haern leaned close enough to whisper into Ingram's ear. "You said your orders were only if you were killed."

He thrust a saber through Ingram's shoulder, pinning him to his bed. Ingram let out a cry, but Haern smothered it with his hand.

"I'm here because another dared challenge me," Haern said as Ingram's struggles ceased. "This fool who calls himself the Wraith will die, and I will be the one to kill him. Last night I thought I killed thieves, not guards, but I do not regret the act. They preyed on the weak, and they deserved to die for it. Until the Wraith is dead, I will prowl the night. Do not try to stop me, nor get in my way. And if you dare consider hanging more innocents..."

He yanked out the sword and let the blood drip across Ingram's forehead.

"I'm not scared of you," Ingram said, despite his pale face and shaking arms. "You're a coward. I'll fill the gallows with necks no matter who you kill. Empty my dungeon, and I'll grab people off the streets to swing."

"Not another body," Haern said, shaking his head. "Not if you want to live."

Ingram laughed. "Come now, this is a gentleman's deal. You now know the cost of doing whatever it is you do. Question is, are you willing to pay it?"

His left foot kicked out, ringing a bell Haern could not see underneath the sheets.

"Oh, and I'd suggest running," Ingram said. "I did prepare, remember?"

Guards burst through the door, all wielding crossbows. Haern turned and dove through the window, furious at his carelessness. He rolled along the roof as bolts whizzed by. Shouts followed him, and he circled about in search of a clear space to leap. The grounds were suddenly crawling with guards. A risky trap, given how vulnerable Ingram had left himself, but it had gone as the lord had hoped. Crossbow bolts thudded all about him, and torches continually pointed in his direction as he fled.

His pulse pounded in his ears as he looked toward the back of the mansion, hoping for an escape. The longer he took, the more guards seemed to appear. He kept his head low and his cloaks spread wide, covering as much of his body as he could. The sky was clouded, the night particularly deep. All he needed was a few seconds lost amid the darkness and he might escape.

"This way!" he heard a voice cry out, but it came from the roof, not those chasing along the ground. He looked over to see a shadowy version of himself, clothed in similar garb only darker, more blacks than grays. In his hand he held a sword, the blade slightly curved. The man's face was hidden by his hood, its recesses so dark only his lips and chin remained visible. He smiled as if incredibly amused by Haern's predicament.

"Follow me!"

This shadow, this mirror, turned and ran along the top of the mansion to its highest point. Once there he looked back, beckoning. Despite the insanity of it all, despite who he feared this stranger was, Haern followed. The man offered his hand, and Haern took it.

"Reach for the heavens," he said before turning and running at blinding speed.

Haern kept up, but just barely. Bolts clacked and buried into the roof on either side. They ran down the slanted front of the mansion, toward a two-headed monster built above the door. Letting go, the stranger took a step ahead and then leaped off. Haern followed, lifting his hands high as he'd been told. The fence about the mansion was near, and as they sailed over, Haern had a half-second to see the man hook his arms about a rope before he had to mimic the action. It struck his elbows, and he looped an arm about it and hung.

"Hurry," the stranger said, swinging once over the rope before dropping beyond the wall.

Haern paused a moment, trying to catch his breath. Large trees grew on opposite sides of the mansion gate's entrance, the rope tied to two branches. Instead of following, he climbed to one of the trees and took cover within as another volley of crossbow bolts flew his way.

"I said jump," the stranger shouted.

"Tell me your name," Haern shouted back.

"You should know it, or my opinion of you is greatly overestimated."

Haern tried to decide what to do, but in the end, he couldn't stay there, not with armed guards rushing from all sides of the mansion toward him. With a kick of his legs he leaped over the wall, rolled to absorb the force of the landing, and then pulled up mere feet away from the man he'd been brought to Angelport to kill.

"Lead on, Wraith," he said.

Wraith's grin grew. "As you wish . . . Watcher."

They ran, two deadly shadows, and left the guards far behind.

CHAPTER

7

Despite what she'd told Haern, Zusa had no intention of searching for the Wraith. She didn't like lying to Haern, but they couldn't trust him yet, despite him remaining true to his word so far. Besides, she had her own business to investigate. Let the King's Watcher deal with an unpredictable animal like the Wraith. Instead, under Alyssa's orders, Zusa went to the docks.

"Where have you hidden it?" she wondered aloud, overlooking the many docked boats, both grand and small. Creeping closer, she noted the ones she had already checked the previous night, when Haern had thought her out and about slaughtering thieves to alert the Wraith to their presence. Despite her unhappiness with the deception, at least it meant not having accidentally killed more of the city guard. She didn't like the idea of more bodies hanging from the gallows because of her actions any more than Haern did.

One by one she went down the docks, lurking in the deep shadows of the starlight. Any boat not owned by the Merchant Lords she skipped, but they were not many. The ones that were guarded she slipped past. Zusa wanted no commotion alerting any to her search. Crates and cargoes flashed before her eyes, yet as the night wore on, she could not find what she was looking for.

By the time she'd checked twenty ships and found nothing of note, she decided she needed a way to narrow down her search. If the Merchant Lords had any of the Violet in Angelport, surely it would be kept well guarded. Focusing solely on the larger boats with visible guards, she continued on.

Her first pick was the *Fireheart*, which she recognized as one of the Blackwaters' boats. Alyssa had considered him the Merchant Lord to watch most closely. Three men stood near the top of the plank leading to the boat. Two were asleep at their posts, the third leaning against the mast with his arms crossed, watching the water lap against the dock. Two torches burned from posts halfway up the ramp. Zusa smiled at the setup. No doubt they thought the presence of so many would deter thieves. She almost wished they'd spent some time in Veldaren, among the presence of true thieves. Then they'd realize how little their guard meant. But between Laurie Keenan, the Merchant Lords, and Lord Murband, all the truly good thieves had abandoned the city for more opportune ground.

Zusa loved vulnerable targets.

She dove into the water a hundred yards away, and with careful patience, drifted toward the boat. The water was cold, but not enough to cause her any harm unless she stayed in it too long. Unseen, she brushed against the side of the boat and used her hands to steady herself from going underneath. Above, she heard someone snoring. Grabbing her daggers, she closed her eyes and waited. Through her lifelong training, she had gained the ability to traverse between shadows as if they were connected doorways. It took much of her strength and had become harder after she turned her back on her god, Karak. But it could still be done, and upon the boat, there were many dark corners.

"I deny you," she whispered, amusing herself with the thought of Karak actually hearing her. "But I take your power still."

She dove underwater, swam directly beneath the boat, and then kicked toward the surface. Instead of striking the smooth undersurface wood of the vessel, she plunged wet and disorientated onto the deck. Taking in her surroundings, she leaped from behind a crate toward the lone alert guard. He'd turned, having heard the thump of her landing but not yet realizing someone had come aboard. Without slowing, she lunged toward him, her daggers leading. One pierced his throat, preventing a death scream. The other slipped through his ribs and into his heart. The man convulsed for a few seconds, then fell limply at her feet.

The two sleeping sailors died where they slept, their throats slit. Afterward she paused, listening for any sort of alarm. She heard none, so into the hold below she went.

It couldn't have been any more obvious. The hold was empty but for a single, solitary crate. Zusa tested its lid, but it was nailed shut, and she had nothing to open it with. Glancing about, she found a heavy sledgehammer and decided it would do. Surely no one would notice a minor commotion in the hold of a boat, not through its thick wooden walls. Lifting it, she smashed a hole through a side of the crate, then reached within. The crate was half full of small, smooth objects. She pulled one out and examined it. It was a simple leather bag. Curious, she opened its drawstrings.

"So you're the Violet?" she asked, hardly impressed. This was the mysterious leaf threatening the Keenan crimleaf trade? "Just a damn weed."

She sealed it, then tied its drawstrings about her wrist. Alyssa's request fulfilled, she wondered what to do about the rest...

Zusa found some lamp oil stowed in the corner, and she poured it inside, soaking the rest of the Violet. Going back up top, she removed a torch from the ramp leading to the ship. With childish glee, she tossed the torch into the crate, which burst into flame. That glee turned to confusion as the smoke billowed into her face, and she breathed in its bitter scent. It hit her like the hammer she'd used to open the crate. Gasping even through the wrappings over her mouth, she crawled for the ladder back up top. Her stomach heaved, and her head felt painfully light. Climbing was a chore, for whenever she released a rung, her hand shook violently. More and more she breathed in the smoke, which had rapidly thickened.

Get away, she thought, trying to push through the fog overcoming her mind. *Keep moving. Move!*

When she made it to the deck, she tore away the wrappings from her face, gasped in the clean air, and then vomited over the railing.

What have you done to me? she wondered, stealing a glance at the bag tied to her wrist. Smoke had begun billowing from the belly of the ship, and she knew she had little time before streams of sailors and guards came to fight the fire. It was a brotherhood thing; no one let another's ship burn if they could help it. She had to flee, but where? She nearly leaped into the water, figuring she'd swim to a discreet location before coming ashore, but stopped herself at the last moment. Her whole upper body was twitching sporadically, and she feared what might happen if she tried to swim.

Like a drunk, she staggered down the plank. Already a guard had come at a steady jog to investigate.

"Is there a fire?" he asked, as if he thought Zusa were a victim of it instead of the cause. When he came closer and saw her strange clothing, he tensed and drew his sword. Zusa knew at any other time she could have cut him down, but not now. Panic swirled through her as her muscles twitched with a feeling that almost approached pleasure. Her brain in a fog, with shimmering lines moving into her vision as if sprouting from her neck, she almost lay down right there and succumbed to the sensation. Instead she swallowed hard, tried to gather her senses, and stumbled on by, ducking underneath the guard's halfhearted swing.

"Stop!" he called out. "Fire!"

Faster and faster she ran. Her heart hammered in her chest so hard she worried it might burst. Every time she thought to hide in shadows, she saw things there, vague and shapeless. Her outfit, normally excellent at hiding her form in the darkness, now only made her stand out as different from the rest. Gasping in air, she cut down alleys and streets whenever she saw someone approach. Her legs felt numb, yet strangely her feet throbbed. She frequently heard the shouts of men chasing, and at one point even a pack of dogs tracking her scent.

No, she thought. *Not real. Think, Zusa. Think!*

But she couldn't. The last remnants of pleasure had faded into stark terror that became overwhelming the moment she stopped moving. Her skin itched, as if spiders crawled underneath her wrappings. She had no idea where she was, how far she'd gone. At one point she wanted to tear off all her clothes and let whoever found her do whatever they wished, so long as she didn't have to be afraid of them. Another time she nearly killed the first shape she saw. She'd even drawn her daggers, but there was blood on them, and for some strange reason that frightened her all the more. It was as if her senses had been heightened a hundredfold, and everything carried hidden danger.

At last she passed a shop that had built a deck across the front. It was low and cramped, but she rolled underneath nonetheless. Finally enveloped in a closed, safe place, she tried to catch her breath. Her heart hammered, and she shivered in wet clothing. She curled her knees to her chest, wrapped her arms tight about them, and waited. Time became meaningless. With each passing moment, her terror subsided, replaced once more by an overwhelming sense of euphoria. Despite her dismal surroundings, she had to fight an impulse to touch herself all over. Teeth clenched, hands gripping her elbows, she rode it out, praying for morning.

Come the rise of the sun, she had not slept a wink. Her whole body felt numb, her mouth dry. Her mind was empty, like someone had scooped out her insides with a spoon. All she could think about was shutting her eyes and hoping the blackness that followed would take those feelings away, but she couldn't. Guards might still be searching for whoever set fire to the boat, and she'd appear quite guilty hiding underneath a deck in strange clothing. Crawling out, her clothes covered with crusted dirt, she looked about to decipher her surroundings. Despite what felt like her eternity of running, she was less than a quarter of a mile from the docks.

The city was yet to wake, though there was a moderate bustle of activity near the docks. Zusa ran for the Keenan mansion, frustrated with the stiffness of her joints. The bag of Violet bounced against her wrist, and she looked at it with far more respect. If any saw her run back, none said anything, and that didn't surprise her. Paranoia seemed to linger in the back of her mind, but she could control it now, keep it at bay. At the front gates of the mansion she tore off the rest of her facial wrappings and demanded entrance. The two guards had been made aware of her stay, and they hurried to open the gate so none might see her.

She used the servants' entrance, went directly to her room, and collapsed on her bed. Hoping to fall asleep any moment, she was annoyed to hear the door open, and then Alyssa stepped inside.

"Are you well?" Alyssa asked.

"No," Zusa said, and she laughed, for she could think of nothing else to say.

"You're soaked," Alyssa said, frowning. Her hand pressed against Zusa's forehead. "Feverish too. Get off the bed. I'll help you undress."

Feeling like a sick child, Zusa sat on the edge of the bed as Alyssa removed her wrappings one layer at a time. Once Zusa was naked, Alyssa pulled a plain white dress over her head. It felt deliciously warm. Only then did she let her roll back onto the bed and underneath the covers.

"I found it," Zusa said, nodding toward the bag that now lay on the floor. "I found the Violet."

Alyssa picked up the bag and placed it in a pocket of her dress without looking inside. "Rest now," she said. "I'll hear of what happened when you're well."

Her body still occasionally twitching, Zusa sighed deeply, laid her head on the pillow, and tried to rest.

"Wait," she said as Alyssa was about to leave. "Where's Haern?"

Alyssa frowned and looked away. "When you're awake," she said, then shut the door, leaving Zusa in blessed darkness.

As they left Ingram's mansion behind them, Haern felt his unease growing. Ahead ran the Wraith, his dark twin, the very man he'd been brought to kill. He'd told Ingram the same. Yet why did he keep his sabers sheathed? Why did he follow, instead of attack?

"You fall behind," the Wraith shouted, glancing back. Despite their exertion, he wasn't even winded, and that faint smile remained. Haern felt challenged, and he increased his pace. He knew he should attack, but two things bothered him: Why had the Wraith helped save his life, and why had he sent him a challenge half a country away? He wanted answers. He'd expected to get them at the tip of a saber, but if he could get him talking first...

They approached the docks. With the buildings built closer together, the Wraith vaulted to the roof of one, pulling himself up by grabbing the edge with hardly a slow in his momentum. Haern replicated the feat, wishing he were as nimble as Zusa. For her, it was as if she could turn off the inevitable fall back to the ground. They raced along the rooftops, the homes crammed together, the roofs flat but for a slight tilt facing the ocean. When they reached a heavy crossroad separating the rest of the city from the taverns and docks, the Wraith stopped.

"You came," he said, smiling nearly ear to ear.

Haern nodded, fighting to catch his breath. He kept his voice steady and slow to mask the attempt. "What choice did I have?"

The Wraith laughed. "Always a choice. Isn't that the way

of men, after all? You could have ignored me. You could have stayed in Veldaren. Instead you traveled here. Why?"

"You're killing innocents, all to send me a message. I couldn't allow it any longer."

"Innocent?" Again, he laughed. "What do you know of this city, Watcher? Nothing. You know nothing, and that is what I've come to show you. Veldaren is a temple of children compared to here."

He gestured to the street below. Wary of a trap, Haern leaned closer to the edge and looked down. Four men gathered in the alley, all with sword tattoos on their faces. At their feet was a corpse, whose clothes they rifled through, taking any valuables. Haern drew his sabers, furious at the sight.

"These men protect the city?" he asked, incredulous.

"Ingram's hired any thug with a blade to work for him. Once they were pirates, mercenaries, thieves. Now they are the protectors of the innocent. Reminds you of someone, yes?"

Haern felt his chest tighten. "You know nothing of me, Wraith. I do not shed innocent blood."

"Is that what you believe? Well, then, neither do I. How much do you truly know of the Trifect, and what it's done? Or how about the Merchant Lords? You've walked into a fire, Watcher, blind and dumb. I must say, I had higher hopes than this." He gestured to the guards below. "Go. Men rob and take from a murdered man. Give them their due."

The Wraith tilted his head at him, staring from beneath that strangely dark hood. Haern thought of the four guards and of the forty that would hang if he took their lives. In Veldaren, he'd have never hesitated. But now...

"If I deliver justice for the innocent, more innocents will die," Haern said. "Is that what you've brought me here to learn?"

The Wraith shook his head, and there was a hint of disappointment in his sigh. "I thought you were better than that. Deliver justice for the innocent without fear, and without remorse. Innocents will always die. The question is, do you let those with power hide behind them forever?"

He leaped off the building, his black cloak trailing behind him. Haern leaned over the edge, and he knew he had only a fraction of a second to decide. The four guards were below, preparing to dispose of the body in a way that would prevent them any trouble. Upon their deaths, Ingram would hang dozens. Dead innocents. Dead children.

Only a fraction of a second, only the slightest hesitation, and then Haern followed after him, his sabers drawn.

The Wraith's descent ended in a bloody eruption of gore as his sword pierced the nearest guard's back, punching through his chest. Upon landing, he spun, yanking the blade free and slashing for a second. It tore through his throat. The guard collapsed to his knees, clutching his neck as it gushed. The Wraith continued spinning, his blade turning on the third. It would have opened his chest, but Haern was there, his sabers blocking the strike.

"Get away!" he screamed to the other two, who needed little encouragement. They fled, all the while crying out for more of the city guard.

The smile was gone from the Wraith's face.

"You protect guilty men, all because you fear the actions of other guilty men," he said, slowly falling into a stance. "A shame."

Haern watched the man's movements carefully. Already he'd seen enough to know he was brutally efficient with his attacks, which came with lightning intensity. The Wraith tilted his sword, shifted a foot, and then lunged. Haern gasped, still surprised by the speed. He blocked the slash for his neck with his left saber while thrusting with his right. The Wraith stepped aside, looped his sword about, and thrust again. When he tried to parry it, Haern found the longer blade shifting aim, a subtle dip that threw his entire defense off. Falling back, he smashed the attack aside with both his sabers. In the distance, they heard guards rallying.

"Tell me why," Haern said, slowly shifting side to side to get his cloaks into motion. "Why did you summon me? Why am I here?"

"I thought you could help me," the Wraith said. "But it seems you are not the man I thought you were."

Haern spun, flinging his cloaks about. It was a technique he'd perfected over years, a dance as familiar to him as breathing. He let the gray fabric hide his movements, disguise the motion of his hands and the location of his sabers. His cloakdance had only one risk, and that was the brief time he lost sight of the Wraith as he turned. On the third rotation, he saw a great puff of smoke where the Wraith had been. Haern hesitated, then realized his error. A heel slammed into his back, and he let out a cry of pain. Rolling across the ground, he desperately blocked as the Wraith came slashing in, repeatedly battering his sabers so they could never settle into position.

The Wraith's movements grew faster, and Haern fought solely on instinct, nervous to use the cloakdance again. A high feint fooled him, and in came the Wraith's foot, blasting the air from his chest.

"You made an entire city fear your name," the Wraith said as his sword stabbed and cut. Nothing about him gave away his intentions, and everything about his stance and reactions was unfamiliar. Haern could not fall into a rhythm. The few times he tried to riposte or counter, he found himself stabbing air, or canceling the hit to prevent having his throat slashed open. The sound of steel rang out a chorus, and Haern knew its song was not under his control.

"I thought you were the best!"

The sword tip cut a gash across his arm, just enough to bleed. Haern retreated on instinct, only to realize he'd put his back against a wall. The Wraith positioned himself directly across, his legs tensed to lunge. There'd be no escaping. The sword was a blur, and Haern blocked the first four hits. The fifth plunged through his shoulder, and he screamed.

"I was wrong," the Wraith said, twisting the blade, eliciting another scream. "A shame you won't be at my side when I set this city ablaze."

A trio of arrows whizzed by, one punching a hole through the Wraith's hood. The man freed his sword and fell back as dozens of city guards came rushing in. Haern tried to give chase, but the Wraith suddenly darted back at him, his heel smashing into Haern's forehead. His vision a blur, he dropped to the ground, his sabers falling from his lifeless hands. As he lay there, he watched feet march by. Rough hands rolled him onto his back and then yanked off his hood. Haern screamed. It felt like pain was everywhere in his body, yet nowhere in particular. Through the tears in his eyes, he saw men peering down at him, familiar tattoos across their faces.

"Sure it's him?" asked one.

"Damn sure. I'd be dead if not for him."

"Thought he went after Ingram, though?"

The rest fell silent. Haern tried to ask for water, but his voice came out a mumble.

"Take him to the dungeon," said the biggest of the men. "We got time to figure it out."

They grabbed Haern by his arms and legs. When they lifted him, his shoulder exploded with waves of agony. He knew ten different litanies against pain, techniques for hanging on to consciousness no matter how horrible the trauma. Haern used none of them and slipped away.

CHAPTER

8

When Ingram awoke, he was in an irritable mood. His shoulder hurt despite the tonic his healer had given him, preventing any real rest after the Watcher's departure. Once out of bed, he bathed in a tub of hot water prepared by servants while he'd struggled for sleep. After bathing, the healer came and changed the wrappings.

"Clean wound," the old man said as he looked it over. "You'll be fine."

"Just keep away the infection," Ingram muttered.

After he was gone, his captain of the guard stepped inside his bedroom and saluted.

"What is it you want?" Ingram asked.

"We have him," the captain said. "The Watcher."

Ingram went through the rest of his morning rituals with a smile on his face. Despite the first major meeting with the elves, all he could think about was making his way to the dungeon.

Leaving his house, he exited the outer fences, accompanied by a small squad of guards. With murderous elves running about his city, he would not travel anywhere unprotected. Dug into the lower side of the hill on which he'd built his mansion was Angelport's dungeon. It had one entrance, sealed and watched day and night.

"He hasn't said a word," said the guard captain as they opened the gate. "Not that we've questioned him much."

"Good," Ingram said. "I want him all to myself. How'd we capture him?"

The captain shifted on his feet, looking slightly uncomfortable. "He was protecting two of our guards from the Wraith. He saved their lives."

Ingram frowned. "Interesting," he said. "I'll keep that in mind. Such actions should at least warrant him an honorable death."

"If you say so, milord."

Lamps lit the dim hallway. The cells had a small hole dug into the hill to give them a speck of light. Most had eight or ten people within, despite how large the dungeon was. In the far back was the Watcher's cell, small and solitary. He was manacled to the wall with an absurd amount of chains. The jailor had clearly been terrified of the man's potential escape. One was wrapped around his neck, then connected with a thick chain about his waist before being bolted to the wall. Another chain kept his arms above his head, his wrists together, and then looped through a second ring attached to the ceiling. He was on his knees, unable to lie down or stand. His hood had been removed, and Ingram saw a handsome man with blond hair and blue eyes. A large welt swelled purple in the middle of his forehead.

"So we meet again," Ingram said, grinning. "I must admit,

I didn't think it'd be so soon. Did you kill any more of my guards, Watcher? Or would you care to give me your real name, since I now see your face?"

The Watcher looked up at him, and Ingram took an involuntary step back. There was something sinister in his gaze, a certainty of retribution that all the chains in the world could not make him feel safe. No wonder the jailor had tied him up so ridiculously. Trying to regain his composure, Ingram smoothed out his shirt, then softly slapped the Watcher across the face.

"Nothing to say? Well, if not a name, how about a reason? My guard captain says you were protecting two of my own from the Wraith. Why's that?"

"You know why," said the Watcher, his voice dry and tired. He nodded to the other cells, where men and women sat dirty in their own filth. "Which of them would have hung from your ropes?"

Ingram scratched at his chin. "Twenty still will," he said. "Two of my guards died, after all. I like to be a man of my word."

"And I'll be a man of mine," the Watcher said. "Another body, and I will make you suffer."

Ingram laughed. "A fine feat that'll be. You're here, Watcher, stuck and chained. You couldn't defeat the Wraith from what I was told. That means you're useless to me."

The comment seemed to burn more than Ingram expected, so he prodded further.

"It is such a shame. To think all your reputation in Veldaren would mean so little in my fair city."

The Watcher flung himself against the chains, moving hardly an inch but causing a loud ruckus. This time, Ingram did not back away, nor show fear. Finally, he was in control.

"It only seems appropriate. You stab my shoulder, another

stabs yours. You won't be given a chance to heal, though. You'll swing from the gallows, in full view of the city. I want that Wraith to know what's waiting for him when we capture him, just as we captured you."

"You won't capture him," the Watcher said, his voice barely above a whisper. "He's beyond you and your men."

Ingram put his heel on the bound man's shoulder and pressed. Despite the pain, the Watcher showed not the slightest reaction.

"I'm sure many people in Veldaren said the same about you," Ingram said, turning to leave. "But don't worry. I'll proudly bear the scar you left me. In time, memories will fade, and it'll be me who took you down, not some nameless guard. Thank you, Watcher. Whatever legacy you had just added to my own."

Ingram left, stopping only to have a word with the jailor.

"Block his window," he said. "I want him in darkness. And have the city guard prepare the gallows. He hangs at sundown."

That matter concluded, he exited the dungeon, only to be surprised by a large contingent of people waiting for him. There didn't seem to be any trouble with them and his guards, but tensions were clearly high. Amid the mercenaries, a lady stepped forth, and she curtsied. Ingram had never met her before, but there was no one else she could be.

"Greetings, Lady Gemcroft," Ingram said. "For what reason have you come to such a dreary place as my dungeon?"

"Rumors, Lord Murband," Alyssa said, her good cheer sounding forced. "Fortunate rumors, if they are true. I hear you have caught the man we know in Veldaren as the Watcher."

Ingram frowned. "I see one of my guards has a loose tongue."

"You hanged thirty people as a challenge to him, then caught him in open streets," Alyssa said. "Surely you cannot be surprised that people talked."

"Perhaps. Would you like to come up to my study and—"

"No. We can discuss it here. The Watcher is a criminal of Veldaren, where he has slain hundreds of men. I want him in my custody so we may send him back for punishment."

"I assure you, a man hanging in Angelport is just as dead as one hanged in Veldaren, miss."

Alyssa's eyes flared at that. "Who said we wanted him hanged? He's spilled a lot of blood, Ingram. We'd like a lot spilled in return. I demand him turned over to me at once. I am no 'miss' ashamed to dirty her skirt, nor afraid of the example his death must set."

"Demand?" Ingram could hardly believe what he was hearing. "You come into my city, my lands, and give *me* demands? And why should I listen?"

Alyssa stepped closer, and she lowered her voice. "Only a fool would willingly make an enemy of the Trifect."

Ingram shook his head, the grin spreading across his face not matching the rage he felt in his chest. "I might have feared you once," he said, gesturing to the many guards about him. "But things have changed, haven't they? The Trifect's power has dwindled, yet the Merchant Lords has only grown over the past decade. You've wasted coin battling scum in the streets, and while Laurie spent all his attention northward, the merchants have stolen away sailors and trade routes and undercut nearly everything he's built. You don't control me, don't frighten me, and unless you want to find yourself banished, you'd better start showing me the respect an appointed Lord of the Realm deserves. That son of a bitch hangs at sundown. Do you understand?"

Alyssa took a step back. All about, her mercenaries bristled at the outburst. But instead of anger, she only curtsied again. "Forgive me," she said. "If you will not hand him over, I ask that you let me question him first. He may know something of the Wraith who killed Laurie's son, and I would prefer to hear everything I can before he goes to his grave."

After a deep breath to calm himself, Ingram nodded. "You may question him as you like, but you go in alone, no mercenaries. If you need to question him harshly, well"—he leered at her—"I'm sure you won't mind dirtying your skirt."

She flushed at the comment but refused to take the bait. Instead she curtsied again, then asked for one of the dungeon guards to lead her within.

"Don't be gone too long," Ingram said as she vanished into the dark. "I'd hate for you to miss our little meeting with the elves."

"Don't worry," she said, glancing back. "I'll be there. After all, it'd be a shame for a war to destroy Angelport."

Ingram frowned as she left, then shrugged it off. He wouldn't let her ruin his good mood. The Watcher had been caught, and surely the Wraith would follow. Her comment about war was just petty, and ill-informed. Sure, his woodsmen pressed elven borders, but the elves were cowards. Should things turn rough, Ingram felt confident he'd have the upper hand in creating peace.

But what if the elves *wanted* war? Ingram pulled at the collar of his shirt as he walked back to his mansion, suddenly filled with unease. In everything so far, mankind had been the aggressor, but what if something made them change their minds? Close to two hundred elves were already within his city walls, and how many more might sneak in at the dead of night in disguise? What if Laryssa's arrival wasn't the desperate attempt for peace he first assumed it'd been, but instead the moving of troops into enemy territory?

Suddenly Alyssa's comment didn't seem quite so easy to

shrug off. War with the elves would be disastrous. He'd not lied about that to the other Lords of the Ramere. Ingram could only bluster, posture, and pretend. It'd take an army to fight off the combined power of the elvenkind, an army that would take far too long to arrive from the north.

"Where are Yorr and Edgar?" he asked his captain of the guard, who walked alongside him.

"At their homes, I believe."

"Fetch them."

Ingram looked over a few maps of the Ramere while he waited in his study. Everywhere he looked, he saw unguarded farmland the elves might burn. There were a few castles near the reaches of the Dezren and Quellan Forests, but they would protect the people, not the crops. Their storehouses could last only a little while under such a vicious siege. King Edwin would come down from Veldaren, but would he arrive in time?

Or would the elves starve and burn his beloved Angelport to the ground, with Edwin rescuing only ruins?

As he was pondering, the door opened and Lord Edgar stepped inside.

"Is there no one else?" he asked, glancing about the study with a hint of nervousness.

"Yorr should be coming soon," Ingram said. "Tell me, have you discovered who reserved rooms for the elves?"

The man crossed his muscular arms, and he leaned against a bookshelf. "Whoever it was, they're incredibly careful. Each one had a mercenary come with a bag of gold, either buying or renting the homes so they'd be available for the month. Once the places were cleared and empty, they hired a single person, one per building, to keep it clean."

"Do they know anything? A name, at least?"

Edgar shook his head. "The mercenary guild's refusing

to cooperate. They don't like anyone looking into who hires them."

Ingram rolled his eyes. "Grab their guildmaster and throw him in the dungeon. We'll hear a name from him by tomorrow."

"You sure that's wise?"

Ingram glared, and he felt his temper flare. "If I didn't think it wise, I wouldn't order it done."

Edgar bowed to show he meant no offense. Ingram walked over to his desk, sat down, and poured himself a drink. As he did, Edgar wandered closer, eyeing the open maps.

"What do you expect from the Merchant Lords?" he asked. "The elves' desires are quite clear, as are ours and the Trifect's. We want food and wood, the Trifect wants to keep the Merchant Lords from succeeding in anything, and the elves want to shoot us with arrows. But what of them, what does someone like Warrick Sun have to do with any of this?"

Ingram leaned back in his chair, enjoying the feel of the alcohol burning his throat. "The merchants?" he asked, letting out a sigh. "They've been insistent that the elves make concessions of land as repayment for so many of their workers dying, and the costs suffered because of it. I'm not sure I believe any of it. Sure, they claim the land will further Angelport's growth, and any disruption to the lumber trade will hurt their ever-precious coin flow when it comes to building new boats. Still, there's easier ways to get lumber that don't involve climbing over dozens of bodies. I understand why you and Yorr struggle with their aggressiveness, but the merchants have so little to do with—"

Edgar put his hands behind his back, and he glanced away. Ingram caught the motion and frowned.

"Do you have something to say?" he asked.

Edgar finally looked him in the eye, and nodded. "It's the Violet," he said.

"The what?"

"The Violet," Edgar repeated. "It's a plant that grows within the elven forests. If you put it in your mouth and bite down, it intoxicates you, far faster than the strongest whiskey, far more powerful than even the finest of crimleaf."

It didn't take long for Ingram to put things together.

"They want the land so they can start farming and selling the Violet," he said.

"I'm certain of it," Edgar said. "And that's why our position is such a difficult one. I tried some of it last night, and I can assure you, they would sell enough to buy a whole kingdom should it reach the masses. But if we accuse the merchants of this being their only reason for involving themselves in matters with the elves, they'll claim we're acting petty and dismissing concerns over the loss of life at elven arrows."

Ingram looked at his empty glass, wishing he could simply think more alcohol into it. "Why didn't you tell me this sooner?"

Edgar shrugged. "I hadn't tried the Violet yet. It was just a hunch, but experiencing that leaf's power…there's a fortune for whoever can sell it in large quantities. I have no doubt now that's what the Merchant Lords are after, and so far it seems the elves are unaware of this, which is for the best."

"So at least we know their reasons now," Ingram said, setting down the glass. "The question is, how can we use this to our advantage?"

"The elves must make concessions of some kind," Edgar said. "I've lost far too many hunters and woodcutters for this to be swept aside. But at least we know now. At least we can watch, perhaps even predict the Merchant Lords' next action. Until then, I say we keep a unified front."

"Indeed," said Ingram, rubbing his hands together. "If it comes to war, they will back down, especially if they feel we will not be the ones to blink as the conflict approaches. Let those merchant bastards rant and rave and pretend to be high and mighty. At least I know *why* they're being such a pain in my ass..."

"Indeed," Edgar said, grinning.

After two knocks, the door opened and in stepped Lord Yorr.

"Forgive me for my lateness," he said, bowing.

"Forgiven," Edgar said, taking a step back from the door and bowing. "Glad for you to join us."

"Yes," Ingram said, forcing a smile. "So glad. We were just discussing our meeting with the elves, and the Merchant Lords in particular..."

The air stank of piss, shit, and stagnant water. Despite holding a handkerchief to her nose, the smell made it through with ease. On either side of Alyssa, men reached through the bars, jeering and crying out lewd comments and accusations.

"Just ignore them," the head jailor said.

Hard to do, given how vile the cries became. One called her a cunt who had sucked him off as a child. In return, the jailor spat in his direction.

"Take him out and beat him," he told one of his guards.

At the far end of the dungeon, in a dimly lit cell wrapped in chains like a cocoon, waited Haern.

"I wish to talk to him alone," Alyssa said.

"Not sure I should leave you," said the jailor. He nodded toward Haern. "That guy's killed a lot of people. You know that. He can hurt you with more than just his hands."

"I've made my desires clear, jailor. Would you interfere with my business?"

The burly man shook his head. "It's your life, milady. Just don't expect me to take any blame if he breaks something."

He unlocked the cell and gestured for her to enter. After she stepped inside, the door shut behind her, the lock clicking loud enough to send her heart jumping to her throat.

"For safety," the jailor said with an ugly smile. Alyssa didn't give him the satisfaction of a reaction. "When you want out, just holler. I'll be near."

"Thank you," she said, her voice cold. She put her back to him and took a step closer to Haern. The man looked exhausted, with heavy circles beneath his eyes. A purple bruise swelled across his forehead, and blood seeped from a dirty bandage on his shoulder.

"What are you doing here?" he asked. His eyes were unfocused, and they didn't look at her.

"I came for you. What happened last night? How did you end up here? All I heard were rumors you'd been captured, and since you hadn't returned in the morning..."

"I fought him," Haern said, finally looking at her. Death hovered in his eyes, and it terrified her. "I fought the Wraith, and I know him now. He wants something, and he'll slaughter every man, woman, and child to get it. Get me out of here, Alyssa. For the sake of everyone, the Wraith must die."

"I don't know if I can," she said.

His gaze hardened, and she took a step back.

"Get me out of here," he said again. "I don't care how. No one else can take him, but I can. I'm the only one, and even I might not be strong enough."

She looked around the dark cell, then stepped closer. Light from a thin window shone upon her face.

"You saved Nathaniel," she told him. "I promise I'll do everything I can. I owe you that, at least."

Despite all the chains, it looked like a weight lifted off him.

"Thank you," he said.

Though his face was battered, he still looked handsome, and she gently leaned forward and kissed his cheek.

"Don't lose hope," she whispered in his ear. "Even if they slip the noose around your neck, do not lose hope. This isn't how you die."

She returned to the cell door, then called out for the jailor. While she waited, she glanced at Haern and fought back a smile.

"I told you to stay away from Ingram," she said.

Even amid his chains and exhaustion, Haern laughed.

Alyssa returned to her mercenaries, led by Torgar on reluctant loan.

"Take me home," she told him.

"As you wish," Torgar grumbled. "So what's going to happen with him?"

"He won't die," she said as they walked down the hill toward the street.

"Everyone's got to die sometime."

She shook her head. "He deserves better than that."

Torgar chuckled, grabbing his huge sword on his back as if out of reflex. "Maybe he don't," he said, glaring at a few beggars who eyed Alyssa hungrily. "Or maybe he deserves far worse, having killed hundreds of people. Not all of 'em could have been thieves or murderers. No one's that perfect, certainly not him."

"It doesn't matter," Alyssa said, thinking of her son. "I'll find a way to help him. Keep this to yourself, Torgar. This business is my own, not Laurie's and not Madelyn's."

The mercenary shot her a grin. "I keep my word, lady, but I only give it out when money's involved."

She reached into her pocket and tossed him some coins. He caught them in his beefy hands, his grin spreading. "Now that's a good girl," he said.

"There's more I need than just you holding your tongue," she said.

When they returned to the mansion, Alyssa went into her room and quickly undressed. Two of Keenan's maidservants came to help her, but she shooed them away. Not that she resented the help, but she didn't want them to see her after she was done changing into her new outfit. The fewer eyes on her, the better. Gone was her expensive dress, diamonds, and jewelry. Instead she put on a plain pair of slacks, a white shirt, and a small triangular hat currently in style. She'd purchased every item the day before, under the guise of simple gifts for her servants.

Finished, she stashed a small sum of silver in her pocket, belted a dagger to her waist, and went to Zusa's room. It was still dark, and she heard heavy breathing from the bed. Alyssa slipped to her side and put a hand on her forehead. She still burned with fever. Alyssa shook her head. Whatever the faceless woman had endured the night before had taken a hefty toll. There was no way she could rely on her to be ready come nightfall, and even if she was…

Haern was a friend and had saved her son. But Zusa was something more. Something Alyssa would not risk. Still, she had to keep her promise to the Watcher somehow, and that left her with one other option. She closed the door, pulled her hat lower over her face, and headed to the servants' back entrance.

Torgar was waiting there as she'd requested.

"Got somewhere secret to be?" he asked.

"Just take me to the gate," she said coldly. "And remember how much I paid you."

He patted his pocket, rattling the gold within. "It'll be hard to forget, not for many glorious nights of drinking and whoring. My tongue's yours, milady."

She hated his lecherous grin, but she bowed her head and gestured for him to lead the way. Following behind as if she were a simple servant on errand, she kept her head low and did not make eye contact with any of the other guards patrolling the area.

"Stay safe," he said when she was at the street, and he shut the gates. "It's a scary place out there for lonely ladies... especially ones who ain't looking like they should."

Alyssa ignored him, and with as much speed as she could muster without looking suspicious, she hurried toward the outer sections of the city. The streets grew less crowded as she moved farther away from the docks and into the slums of Angelport. Most ignored her, only a few tossing her strange looks. Glancing down at her clothes, all spotless and clean, made her realize how naïve she'd been. Simply wearing their clothes would not make her look like one of them. Desperately wishing she'd woken Zusa, she continued on, her jaw clenched to hide her growing fear.

Her destination was a plain enough building, wood walls withered by the salty winds of the ocean and a heavily slanted roof. She let out a sigh upon seeing it, glad no one appeared to have recognized her. She knocked twice, waited, then knocked twice more. From the opposite side, she heard a click and then the door swung open. Stepping inside the small building, Alyssa removed her hat and bowed.

"My, my," said Graeven, bowing in return. All around him, the gathered elves glanced their way. "Are you sure it is wise for you to visit us, Lady Gemcroft? Lord Ingram has been struggling mightily to discover who prepared us these rooms directly beneath his nose."

Alyssa looked about, counting the number of elves in the two-bedroom home. At least thirty, if not more.

"Forget him," Alyssa said, smoothing out her shirt, which had wrinkled from her walk, the cotton inferior in quality than what she was used to. "Are the accommodations sufficient?"

"Cramped, but we cannot complain," Graeven said. "I doubt Lord Ingram would have given us anything as welcoming. Lice-ridden beds and rat-infested walls do not suit me, nor would staying outside the city like unwelcome invaders."

"Though we are unwelcome," said a lady elf who came and gracefully curtsied to Alyssa. Her face was slender and smooth, her hair woven into an intricate braid that fell down to her waist. "You are Alyssa, yes?"

"Indeed," Alyssa said, returning the curtsy despite her lack of a dress. "May I have the pleasure of your name?"

"Laryssa Sinistel," she said, her voice oddly beautiful, like the soft sound of glass chimes. She wore a green dress shining with sapphires shaped like a hundred raindrops. Alyssa had to hide her shock upon hearing the name of the elven princess.

"Your Highness," she said, bowing low. "I am honored to be in your presence."

"You are one of the few in this city to be so honored," Laryssa said. "Words of welcome are not what your people gave to us as we entered the walls." She glanced to Graeven, who sported a swollen cut above his right eye. "No, they hurled stones and curses. I once thought my people were rash to condemn humans, to be so eager for a cleansing war. Now I wonder."

"They are merely scared," Graeven said. "They know little beyond what they are told. It is the human leaders we must convince, and they'll make the rest of the populace follow."

"Perhaps," Laryssa said, and she smiled again at Alyssa. "But we will discuss this all too soon with Lord Ingram and his various puppets. Let us not worry on this now. Why have you come, Lady Gemcroft?"

Alyssa swallowed and tried to remember every lesson she'd ever been taught. She'd have one chance at this. Originally, she'd thought to pitch it to the elven ambassador, but with Laryssa there, it was clear who would be in charge.

"A friend of mine has been wrongfully imprisoned by Ingram—" she began.

"Who?" asked Graeven, interrupting her.

"A friend," she said, struggling not to glare. "I have tried to convince Ingram to turn him over to me, but he refuses. He'll execute him tonight, and I fear I can do nothing to stop him. I know the skill of your warriors—it is almost legendary to us humans. I ask that you free my friend and bring him to me for safety."

Laryssa's oval face remained perfectly still as she listened, her blue eyes staring. Alyssa felt like the young child she was before the ancient elf. When she finished making her request, she crossed her hands behind her back and lowered her head, the best show of humility she could think of. Laryssa brushed aside the bangs of her hair, which was so blond it was almost white.

"What you ask could spark a war," she said. "This friend must mean a lot to you."

"He once saved my son's life. I must do what I can in return."

"So honorable," Graeven said, and he sounded amused.

"And foolish," Laryssa said. She gestured to the many other elves who lingered about in chairs or sat cross-legged on the floor. "We came to prevent a war, yet you would have us openly invite it? Do not deny it—you know the risk in this. Should anyone realize we are responsible for his escape, we risk open battle. Friends and family, people I have known for hundreds of years, might die before my eyes. Is your friend worth that?

To you, perhaps, with your life so short it is but a candle. But he is not worth that to me. We are thankful for your hospitality, Lady Gemcroft, but we will not perform such madness in payment."

"Surely the risk is not so great as that," Graeven said, turning to his princess. "We could easily dispatch a handful of guards, and if done right, no one will know of any elven involvement."

"And what will we say if caught?" Laryssa asked. "That we did so at the request of a friend? We do not know this man, and have no interest in him. Any lie we offer will ring hollow, and I refuse to be put into such a position. I am sorry, Alyssa, but we can offer no aid."

Alyssa nodded, first hesitantly, then more firmly. "I understand," she said. "Forgive me for wasting your time."

"Time with you is never wasted," Graeven said, bowing low.

"Hurry to your home," Laryssa said. "Our first meeting with Ingram is soon, and I would wish you there to help us as promised."

"Of course." Alyssa curtsied, put her hat back on, then exited the home. Barely three steps out, the door reopened and Graeven appeared.

"Do not give up hope just yet," he said, walking beside her. "You are a powerful woman with many resources. I lament Laryssa's hesitance, but we may still help if only in secret. Should you rescue your friend and need a place for him to hide—"

"I'll keep it in mind," she said, trying to disguise her impatience. "Now, please, I don't want to draw any—"

"Say no more," the ambassador said, offering her a wink. "Pleasant nights, milady."

With him gone, Alyssa hurried down the streets, this time willing to run. She'd been gone too long as is and needed to prepare in haste for the meeting. Upon reaching Laurie's mansion, she saw Torgar waiting at the gate. He shot her a pleased grin.

"Did anyone notice my absence?" she asked.

"All lips are sealed," said the mercenary, opening the gate so she could enter. "Now hurry. Laurie's almost left for the meeting, and I think he'll be quite unhappy if you're not there with him."

CHAPTER

9

The dark void of Zusa's sleep slowly filled with dreams, at first calm, then terrifying. She ran through the streets of Veldaren, lions giving chase. Fire consumed their enormous bodies, their roars thundering in her ears. High above shone a bloodred moon. Twice she turned to fight them, but she was naked and held no weapons. At last she stumbled and knew with absolute certainty they would fall upon her. She cried out, desperate for someone to save her, and then the dark-red world turned bright.

Zusa opened her eyes to see her door cracked open, allowing a sliver of light to lance across her face. She sat up, suddenly aware of her full bladder.

"Who's there?" she asked.

The door opened farther, and Alyssa stepped inside.

"Let me light a lamp," she said, closing the door for a few moments. Zusa took the time to relieve herself, then replaced the chamber pot underneath her bed. Alyssa returned with a thin punk, the tip burning. She lit two separate lamps, giving a soft gold glow to the room. With the door closed once more, she sat down on the bed beside her.

"How long did I sleep?" Zusa asked, rubbing her face with her hands. Normally she could awaken fully alert, but this time it felt like sleep clung stubbornly to her mind.

"About ten hours," Alyssa said. "It is late afternoon."

Something gnawed at her, and then Zusa figured out what. "Where is Haern?"

"Captured," Alyssa said.

Zusa felt a lump build in her throat, and then she saw her mistress's hands were shaking. "Ingram has him in his dungeon. He plans on hanging him tonight, come sundown."

Zusa tried to think, and she bit down on her tongue to use pain to focus her mind. It had to be remnants of Violet, she decided. Seeing Alyssa's troubled mind, she thought of what else must have happened. Ten hours gone... that meant...

"What of the meeting?" she asked. "Did that go well?"

Alyssa sighed. "There are so many there. Laryssa and the elves, Ingram, his petty lords, and of course the Merchant Lords made sure their presence was felt. Nothing but an hour of shouting and accusations. Twice I swore it would turn to bloodshed. My head still hurts after that nonsense."

"Anything resolved?"

The question evidently amused Alyssa immensely, and she laughed like one reaching the end of her sanity.

"Lord Yorr demanded a halt to the killings while talks took place; Ulrich and the rest of the Merchant Lords insisted concessions of land be given, along with total access to the forest; Ingram implied he agreed with both without ever saying so;

and the elves threatened war should they lose a single acre of land. Laurie and I were the only ones who even knew the word *compromise.* Perhaps tomorrow will go better. I hope so..."

"Forget about tomorrow," Zusa said, wrapping her arms around Alyssa and pulling her close. Resting her head atop Alyssa's, she stared into the flickering shadows of her room. "Haern hangs tonight, and I know that troubles you. Give me the word, and I will go."

"I can't. I won't let you get yourself killed trying to break into Ingram's dungeon."

Zusa let her go, then removed her dress. She still felt weak, and it wouldn't have surprised her if she still had a fever. None of that mattered. Sitting naked on the bed, she began to put on her dark wrappings. Alyssa watched for a while, as if debating, then stood.

"Let me get you something to eat," she said.

"Thank you."

By the time Alyssa returned with a tray of bread and meat, Zusa had covered all but her face. She tore into the bread, relishing the taste of butter on her tongue. When she had first woken, her stomach felt cramped and angry, and she hadn't thought she could eat much. Smelling the meat and tasting the bread had awakened a hunger that shocked her. She devoured the entire meal, wiped her lips on her wrist, and then began to cover her face with the last of her cloth wrappings.

"Don't get yourself killed," Alyssa finally said, stepping behind Zusa and taking the cloth from her hands. "I'll hate myself forever if you do."

"You'll hate yourself even more if you do nothing," Zusa said, smiling underneath her mask. When Alyssa finished tying the last strand, she gave her a kiss on the forehead.

"Guards are nothing to me," Zusa said. "Rest, and learn

what you can about the Violet. I feel certain that whatever goals the Merchant Lords have, that simple weed is the true cause behind it all. As for Haern, I'll return with him, alive. I promise."

"I'll show it to Laurie," Alyssa said. "And I'll hold you to that promise."

Zusa shot her a wink as she put on her cloak. "I've defeated dark paladins, mercenaries, and even fought the Watcher to a standstill. I fear no dungeons, Alyssa, no jailors. When I return, it will be with Haern, my promise unbroken."

Without another word, she grabbed her daggers and dashed down the hall.

In pure darkness Haern sat and listened to the distant moans. He could see their vague shapes through the bars of his cell, lit by light of slender windows that he now lacked. Not long after Alyssa's departure, the jailor had come with a few bricks to jam into the window.

"Consider yourself lucky," the jailor had said. "They just want it dark. No clubs or pins for you. Damn shame. I'd have loved making you sing."

Haern had given him no reply, for he had no fear of torture. He was the King's Watcher of Veldaren, son of Thren Felhorn. To think a single lowly jailor could break him in a day was insulting.

Hour by unknown hour, time passed. Haern tried praying to Ashhur, but each time he thought of those who'd swung from gallows, his name on the lips of their executioner, his prayers stumbled and ended. Worse was Senke's amulet of the Golden Mountain. They'd taken it from him before chaining him to the wall. He would have given anything to have that meager comfort hanging from his neck. Thinking of Senke only opened old wounds, and he tried to push the memory away, no easy task in the suffocating darkness. All the while, the wound in his shoulder ached with a steady throb.

If he slept, he didn't know it, but he must have. Something pressed against his shoulder, and he startled awake. He saw nothing close, but then a voice whispered in his ear. The sound chilled Haern's blood and for the first time forced him to admit how vulnerable and helpless he was.

"Greetings, Watcher," whispered the Wraith. Haern could almost imagine his grin floating beside him. "I must admit, finding you chained like this disappoints me greatly."

"Why are you here?" Haern asked, keeping his own voice a whisper. He had no doubt the Wraith would execute him immediately should he try to summon the guards.

"To talk to you, of course. Why else? I've given some thought to our last discussion, and I feel I judged you too quickly. I cannot have misread you so thoroughly after your domination of Veldaren. You see, Watcher, you've been dragged into a game with many pieces, yet you are ignorant of their positions on the board. There are few rules, but already you've broken one."

"And what rule is that?"

"Never, ever let compassion blind you to the truth."

The Wraith chuckled. Something slender and sharp ran along Haern's neck. When it pricked open a tiny cut, Haern didn't even flinch.

"Tell me, Watcher, do you know why the elves are here? How about the Trifect? Do you think Alyssa came here solely because of me? And what of the Merchant Lords? Have you wondered what part they play in this, or do you even know who they are? You would condemn me for killing members from all parties, yet you know so little. You killed leaders of the

Trifect and the thief guilds. The men and women I kill are no less guilty."

The side of the blade smacked Haern's face, and he felt blood trickle down his cheek from another cut.

"Tell me, how am I different from you?"

"I never reveled in my killings."

"You are wrong," the Wraith whispered, his tone chilling. "These killings give me no pleasure, no joy. Perhaps with some of them I am amused by their deaths, but only the truly despicable ones. Surely you cannot deny feeling the same as you slaughtered Veldaren's worthless scum."

Haern turned toward the Wraith, and in the darkness, he thought he could see the faintest outline of the man's hood. "Then why the grin?" he said.

"In the face of such madness, what can one do but smile?"

"And kill."

The Wraith laughed. "Yes, and kill. Kill, as you have killed. Inspire fear, as you have inspired fear. Last night, I went to administer the same justice you have dealt out a hundred times. Why did you defend them, Watcher? I have tried to discover the answer, but nothing I've come up with seems satisfactory. Was it truly what you said?"

"Innocents would die. I had no choice."

"Innocents always die. Do you think your little games in Veldaren harmed only the guilty?"

"Not children!"

A hand pressed over his mouth. "Quiet, fool," the Wraith whispered. "Such outbursts...and why do we speak of children? Or do you mean the hangings in the city square, all done in your name? Yes, that was despicable, but I don't expect much better from the scum of this land. Does your conscience suffer? Is that what prevents you from thinking clearly? Children suffer through the actions of their fathers and rulers. Nothing will ever change that. Would you let the faults of this world prevent you from fixing that which can be made better? You coated your swords with blood to end the struggle between the guilds and the Trifect. Why do you hesitate to do so again?"

Haern closed his eyes and tried to think. Too much of what the Wraith said made sense. Did he really think he'd been above it all when he slaughtered members of the thief guilds? But he'd done it in the name of peace and safety. What of the Wraith? What guided his actions? The man was right; he knew far too little of the games nobles and merchants played in Angelport. Swallowing his pride and anger, he spoke words that tasted bitter on his tongue.

"What is it you hope for? If I'm to help you, I must know the end you seek."

"The end is precisely what I seek. You've walked into a house of cards, Watcher. I will bring it all crumbling down. Every piece, every player, seeks to flood Neldar with drugs and war. Ask questions. Open your eyes. If I told you, you would not believe me, so hear it from their own lips. Then come to me and try to tell me I am in the wrong."

Haern felt more than heard the Wraith turn to face the door to his cell, which by the glint of distant torchlight, he could tell was slightly ajar.

"Your friend comes for you," whispered the Wraith. "Many of the guards are... sleeping deeply, shall we say. I can go and let your rescuer find you with ease, or I can sound the alarm and bring the rest of Ingram's guards flooding into the dungeon. Which is it to be, Watcher? Is there hope for you, or should I let the gallows remove your thorn from my side?"

Haern took a deep breath and tried to think over all he'd heard and seen. In the end, he remembered what he'd told

Ulrich back at Laurie's mansion. The Wraith had left Tori, Tara's child, alive. Somewhere in him was a sense of control and decency, despite the chill his presence gave him that seemed contrary to that in every way. No matter how hard Haern wanted to pretend otherwise, he could not sit there in the dungeon and claim to be any more innocent. He'd filled the gutters of Veldaren with blood to achieve his aims, however lofty. Condemning the Wraith for doing the same, without looking into matters further, was hypocritical beyond measure.

"I make no promises," Haern whispered. "But I will discover the truth of this city, one way or another. If I've been played the fool, by anyone—"

"So be it. Perhaps there is hope for you yet."

The cell fell silent but for the soft clink of the door shutting. Haern closed his eyes, hung his head, and wondered if he'd lost his mind. He thought of the rage he'd felt when Alyssa had come, and how he'd promised to make the man pay. A large part of him still felt that way, but he didn't know if it was the better part of him or just his battered ego.

A hand clamped over his mouth, and he startled.

"Quiet," a woman's voice whispered. "Someone has been here before me."

"The Wraith," Haern whispered when she removed her hand.

"Will he stop us?"

He shook his head. "No. I don't think so."

"Then let us hurry."

He heard a clinking sound from above as Zusa began picking the locks of his chains. Haern kept his breathing steady as his pulse began to rise. No matter how many guards Zusa and the Wraith took down on the way in, escaping would be no easy task. The sheer fact that it was still daylight would prove problematic. With a loud rattle, one of the chains slipped loose and hit the floor. Farther down the corridor, several prisoners called out in mocking tones.

"How bad is your wound?" Zusa asked.

Another chain slipped free, this one carefully brought to the ground. Haern tested his shoulder, and he had to bite his tongue to hold in a pained cry.

"Not good," he said through clenched teeth.

"Can you run?"

"Do I have a choice?"

"Not if you want out."

"Then I can run."

The last of the chains loosened from around his body. Despite Zusa's care, their rattle seemed thunderous in the stone cells.

"Who you got with you?" someone shouted from nearby. "You got yourself a whore?"

Zusa grabbed Haern's hand and pulled him to his feet. His wounded shoulder throbbed, and he gingerly touched it. His fingers came away sticky and smelling foul. Most likely infection, thought Haern. Fantastic.

"Where are my things?" he asked.

"At the front, I believe, still guarded. We'll get them on our way out. Ready?"

"Ready."

She took off at a blistering pace, her hand firmly clutching Haern's wrist. From the darkest reaches of the dungeon they emerged into torchlight, and their passing raised a ruckus from the prisoners, who hooted and hollered. At a doorway he saw a guard slumped against the wall. Blood coated his neck and chestplate. Zusa paused to listen for any approaching guards.

"He your doing?" Haern asked.

"Was unconscious when I found him," Zusa said, glancing at the dead guard. "I only cut his throat."

If any guards heard the ruckus behind them, none came to investigate. Haern dared breathe a sigh of relief.

"Come," Zusa said, pulling him along. They passed two more bodies, and Haern had no need to ask what happened to them. One lay on his side, the other on his back, both with huge gashes across their throats. At the major cross-section of the dungeon, they stopped again. To their left and right stretched rows of cells, while ahead was bright light, and escape. Behind them, more prisoners shouted in either encouragement, anger, or jealousy.

"The guards remain there," Zusa whispered.

"How did you get by?"

She pointed toward one of the side tunnels. "Shadows are my doorways, but I cannot take you with me."

Haern didn't like the thought of killing more guards, nor any more prisoners hanging, but the Wraith's words haunted him in mockery. Would he really become a coward, frightened of taking a life, all because of a threat made by someone like Ingram?

"Get me my swords and cloak," he said. "We'll cut through."

He saw her glance at the wound to his shoulder, and he shook his head.

"I can fight through the pain. Now go!"

She strode ahead, releasing his hand to draw both her daggers. At the doorway, a guard stepped out, no doubt to finally check why the others had not silenced the prisoners. Zusa caught him flat-footed, one dagger ripping open the belly beneath his breastplate, the other piercing his windpipe to choke down his death rattle. She kicked him aside and then ran on. Haern followed.

Three more guards sat around a small table, a rack of weapons and crossbows behind them in the small room, along with a heavy chest. Zusa was a blur among them, slashing and cutting before they could even ready their weapons. As the corpses fell with no alarm sounded, she leaned against one of the walls and pointed to the chest.

"In there," she said.

He knelt before it, flicked it open, and found his things. As the cloak wrapped about him, the hood pulled low over his face, he felt his confidence rise. Buckling his sabers to his waist, the feeling was complete. Blood still soaked his shirt, and he knew that once his battle lust calmed he'd be in a world of pain, but for now he could fight. He turned to Zusa and was surprised to see her still leaning against the wall. When he stepped closer, he saw beads of sweat upon the exposed skin about her eyes.

"Were you stabbed?" he asked, though he saw no wounds.

"Fine," she said, pushing off the wall. "I'm fine."

She walked to the iron gate, the last obstacle to freedom. Instead of a lock or key on the inside, a bar blocked the outside. Zusa swore.

"Can we break through?" Haern asked as he inspected the situation. Outside he saw two guards, both positioned adjacent to the door as if they were asleep. All it'd take was a single patrol to notice, and they'd be swarmed.

"Can't," Zusa said. "It's metal. I need to get out there."

"How?"

She pressed her face to the bars of the door, looking.

"Remember?" she said. "Shadows are my doorways."

Zusa retreated into the dungeon, vanishing from view. Trusting her to know what she was doing, Haern waited at the entrance, feeling strangely helpless. Here he was, the deadly Watcher, and he was stopped by a simple barred door?

"How the mighty have fallen," he murmured, pacing to keep his blood flowing.

On the other side, Zusa fell from above the entrance, landing hard on one side.

"Zusa?" he asked as she lay there, very still. "Zusa!"

"Was spotted," she said, her back still to him. "Careless..."

He heard shouts from far away, and his pulse doubled.

"Hurry," he said. "We need to get out of here, now!"

Zusa looked too weak to stand, though, let alone lift the heavy bar blocking the door. She closed her eyes, and then he saw the first guard come running up the hill toward the inlet of the dungeon's entrance.

"Zusa! Get up, Zusa. Focus on the pain, use it, and stand!"

She forced herself onto her knees, and for the first time Haern saw the thick crossbow bolt embedded in her side. The first edges of panic bloomed in the back of his mind. Turning away from the door, he grabbed one of the crossbows and a handful of bolts. Before the first guard could reach her, Haern shot him down through the gaps in the bars. Another guard appeared, and though his first shot missed, the second plunged into his throat.

Zusa grabbed the bar across the door and dragged herself to her feet. Haern reloaded the crossbow, then reached through the bars to cup her face in his hand.

"You can do it," he said. "Don't worry about them. Don't worry about anything. Lift it. Set me free, and I swear I'll protect you."

She tore the wraps free from across her mouth, then leaned her forehead against the bars.

"Too hot," she said, breathing heavily, her eyes still closed.

Haern saw the group of guards approaching, coming up a side path from the mansion.

"Now, damn you," he said to her. "Now, or we're both corpses."

He shot a bolt over her head, then dropped it to draw his sabers. Shrieking at the top of her lungs, Zusa grabbed one end of the bar and forced it upward. As it cleared the latch, she dropped it, and Haern burst through. The pain in his shoulder a distant memory, he launched himself at the six guards, all the while howling like a madman. His sabers danced, and the guards could not hope to match his fury. The first two dropped, their initial attacks clumsy compared to his. Twirling between them, he slashed the back leg of one guard, then lunged at another. Their bodies collided, and the guard went down, Haern's knees slamming his chest. The collision with the dirt jarred them both, but Haern's sabers were there, punching through flesh to keep him still. The final two turned to flee, but he would have none of it. He stabbed one in the back. The other he tripped, cutting out his throat on the way down.

Walking back, blood dripping from his sabers, he passed the guard he'd hamstrung, who pleaded for his life.

"Don't, please!" the man cried as Haern pressed a saber against his throat. Haern felt the cloud of his rage passing, and with it the ache in his shoulder returned with full force. Lowering his weapon, Haern slapped the guard across the face with the flat of his blade.

"Do something useful with your life," he said, sheathing his sabers. He ran back to Zusa, who leaned against the door, clutching the bolt in her side with both hands. As Haern neared, she rammed it through her flesh, punching the barb out her back. In near disbelief, Haern caught her as she fell into his arms.

"Pull it out," she said to him as he held her. Haern grabbed the bloodied shaft, gritted his teeth, and pulled. Only a slight gasp of pain marked its exit. He staunched the blood flow using her cloak, tying it tight about her.

"Leave me," she said. "You won't escape otherwise. Tell Alyssa I'm sorry..."

"You'll tell her yourself."

Bracing her weight on his shoulder, he took a pained step forward, then another. She leaned her head against him, and he was shocked by its warmth. As they gained momentum, Zusa began to recover her balance, and she supported herself more and more. Limping and bleeding, they walked down the hill. The entire complex was walled in, their path leading to a gated side entrance. A squad of soldiers stood before it, manning their post. When they saw Haern and Zusa coming, they readied their weapons.

"Too many," Zusa said, seeing them. "Just drop me and go."

Haern shook his head. "We die together."

Hardly ten paces away they stopped, and Haern released her from his grasp. They stood, weapons drawn. Haern laughed, knowing they must look like the most pathetic pair of killers. Meanwhile, nearly twenty men moved to surround them.

"Let us through," Haern said, pointing a bloody saber toward the man who appeared to be their leader. "Otherwise, you die first."

"Drop your weapons now," the man said, ignoring his demand.

"Only when we're dead, soldier."

The soldiers tensed, and Haern knew they prepared to attack. Zusa slid into a low stance, her arms poised almost as if she were a spider, but he saw the delirium in her eyes. Even in the best of conditions the two would have trouble with so many armored men, but in their current state...Haern pulled his hood lower and grinned. He'd die fighting, regardless of the lack of hope. The Wraith was right. Amid such madness, what else could he do?

Before the soldiers' leader could give the order, a voice cried out from above the gate. Haern looked up to see the Wraith poised upon the wall, his sword drawn.

"Let them go," he said.

"These are prisoners of Lord Ingram," said the squad leader. "Go on your way, unless you want to join them in the dungeon."

"Let them go. I command you."

Whispers grew as several of the soldiers realized who stood above them, garbed in black clothes and a long cloak.

"Who are you to give us commands?"

The Wraith grinned. "This is my city now. Let them go, or all of you will die."

Haern could see the fear spreading through the squad. The Wraith spoke with authority, and even before their greater numbers, he showed no fear. It didn't matter whether they could defeat him, for they knew the massive losses they would suffer. Again Haern witnessed a mirror of himself, of the fear he'd painstakingly created in Veldaren. Seeing it on the outside, it felt so deceptively false.

"Step aside," Haern said, keeping his voice calm. "No one else needs to suffer."

The squad leader took a step back, as if he were going to give way, then suddenly slashed for Haern's throat while crying out for his men to attack. Haern parried it aside as all around him erupted into chaos. Zusa avoided the first two strikes her way, and then Haern was there, guarding her flank. Neither went on the offensive, instead blocking and retaliating against those who struck against them. After killing a single soldier who had pressed too close, Zusa collapsed to her knees, pushing Haern to his very limits to protect her. But after those initial moments, the number of his attackers shrank, for the Wraith had fallen among them, his sword a whirling steel blade of death. The soldiers fell at his feet, no match for his speed or skill. Cutting a bloody swathe through their numbers, the Wraith appeared before Haern, a smile still on his face.

"Sometimes I wonder how much use you might actually be to me," he said before directing his attention to the remaining handful who had fallen back. "Come! Face me! Or are you cowards and fools who can strike only the poor and destitute?"

Haern didn't care either way. Zusa lay at his feet, and he pulled her into his arms. He used his foot to lift the heavy key ring from the squad leader's belt, flicking it up so he could catch it. Sounds of combat came from behind him as he unlocked the gate and shoved it open a little.

"Stay with me," he whispered to Zusa. "We need to get out of sight for a while. I need you to run. Can you run?"

"Don't...have much choice..." she said, and she gave him a weak grin.

Overcome by impulse, he kissed her lips, then shifted more of her weight onto him. "Some honeymoon," he said. "Stay strong. Stay with me."

They ran, leaving the occasional trickle of blood behind them. Given their outfits and wounds, they garnered many stares, but none interfered with their passage. Guards shouted in the distance, but they faded in time. Whether through their speed, the crowd, or the Wraith's interference, they put Ingram's dungeon far behind them. With each minute, Zusa grew weaker, until Haern at last lifted her into his arms and carried her. No more running then, just step after painful step. He felt his own delirium starting to grow, the city strange and unfamiliar about him. Forcing the streets to make sense, forcing his mind to push through the pain, he continued along. The farther they got from the prison, the more people lingered, and several even asked if he needed help. He ignored them, having no spare thought beyond putting one foot in front of the other.

At last Haern collapsed to his knees, Zusa lying unconscious in his arms. Before him was a large gate. Never would Haern have guessed the incredible relief he'd feel seeing Torgar yank it open to greet him.

"Are you out of your fucking mind?" the giant man asked.

Haern wanted to say that indeed he was. Instead he laughed even as the tears ran down his face, and at least fifteen passing men and women saw them brought into Laurie Keenan's mansion.

CHAPTER 10

Madelyn kissed Tori's smooth forehead and then wrapped her swaddling blanket tighter as the commotion grew. Her husband had been in his study when the first shouts came from outside the front door, and while he no doubt rushed to investigate, she retreated farther within her walls, clutching the baby to her chest. Her home was her sanctuary, her place of locked doors and safe walls. Already the Wraith had violated that sanctity. Would someone else be vile enough to do the same?

"Go see what is causing that ruckus," she told her nursemaid, Lily.

"Of course," said Lily, hurrying away. Two other servants were with her, and they stood patiently in the corners of the parlor, one tending the fireplace, the other waiting for orders. She tried to put them out of her mind, instead softly singing a lullaby to the already sleeping baby. After three lines, she stopped, for the commotion had grown louder. Lily returned looking confused, yet trying to hide it.

"Well?" Madelyn asked.

"It's Alyssa's guests," Lily said, the name immediately putting a rock in her stomach. "The newly married couple. They're both bleeding."

Madelyn stood, angry she had not been summoned. To have guests in her house injured, yet not brought to her attention? Still, something was off with how Lily was acting. It reminded her of when Lily had been sleeping with one of the guards, that slight hesitance, her unwillingness to look her in the eye for long.

"What happened to them?" she asked. "Did they tell you?"

"No, but... they are wearing strange clothes. I cannot explain."

Strange clothes? What nonsense was this?

"Lily," she said, adopting a pleasant tone that she knew chilled all of her servants. "What are you not telling me?"

The nursemaid bit the top of her lip and held her arms against her waist. She was still a fairly young girl, though the last of her girlishness would be gone within another year or two. But she was young enough to have lingering instincts to obey a motherly figure, and Madelyn shifted her tone.

"Lily. You aren't in trouble. Now tell me what you're hiding."

"We were instructed not to speak of it to you."

"By who?"

"Your husband, milady."

Madelyn breathed in deep to hold back a retort. If Laurie was hiding something from her...

"His anger will fall on me, not you, now speak."

Lily glanced to one of the other servant girls, and Madelyn's ire grew. Their single look showed they both knew. How many kept this secret from her?

"The two have been sneaking out at night," the third and eldest servant said, standing by the fire. Her face was lined with wrinkles, for she was their midwife, staying in the mansion to ensure all went well with baby Tori. "We've seen them using our door. They dress strange, and they got weapons with them when they do."

"Strange?" Madelyn asked. "What do you mean? Dressed like what?"

Lily looked to the others for support, and she lowered her voice, as if whispering a curse. "Like thieves."

Madelyn was out of her seat fast enough to stir Tori, who softly groaned upon waking. Her servants trailed after her as she hurried through the mansion, heading toward the room they'd given Haern and Zusa for their stay. The room was crowded upon her arrival, Torgar standing before the door, several armed men milling about.

"Is my husband inside?" Madelyn asked, nodding toward the shut door.

"He is."

"Open it."

"It's locked, miss."

"I said open it."

Torgar shrugged. Drawing his enormous sword, he used it as a wedge to break the flimsy lock, jarring the door open a crack. Through it, she saw her husband glance at her in the dim lamplight, Alyssa standing beside him. He had a hard look to his face, and she knew he'd been preparing for her discovery. That fact only infuriated her more.

"Will they live?" she asked as he stepped out to join her.

"I believe so," he said.

"A shame."

Laurie glared. "They are guests in our house, Madelyn. Such callous attitude is unwarranted."

"Is it? Where'd they come from, Laurie? What is it that nearly killed them?"

Her husband looked to the gathered house guards, then shook his head. "Somewhere quiet," he said.

She followed him back into his study. Only Lily remained when he shut the door, accepting Tori into her arms. Sitting down in one of the several padded chairs, she exposed a breast and began feeding. Even in feeding, Madelyn refused to ever let the baby out of her sight. Laurie glared at her but was wise enough not to fight that battle given the larger problem with Haern and Zusa...assuming those were even their real names. Already she doubted their relationship to the Gemcrofts.

"What is it you know?" she asked. "Tell me all of it, and no lies. The gods help you if you've put Tori in danger."

"We're in no danger!" Laurie shouted, the uncharacteristic display startling Madelyn back a step. Feeling naked without Tori in her arms, she crossed them and glared right back at her husband. Laurie looked away, and she could see the anger fuming behind his eyes. Good. Only seemed right he be as angry as she was.

"At least, I don't think so," he said when he'd calmed. "But things are changing fast, and never did I think the Watcher would be so stupid."

Madelyn's jaw nearly hit the floor. "You brought *him* here?" she asked. It felt as if her husband were playing a sick joke on her. "But he...I heard Ingram's announcement. The Watcher was supposed to hang tonight."

And suddenly his wounds made perfect sense. Overwhelmed with rage, she dug her nails into the flesh of her arm hard enough to draw blood. Her precious mansion, her only place of safety, housed one of the most notorious killers alive?

"He broke out," she said, and her husband never contradicted her. "And after he broke out he came here. Damn it, Laurie, did anyone see us taking in a wanted fugitive?"

Laurie sighed. "Torgar says they were most likely seen."

The words hit her like a blow to the chest.

"He'll find out," she said, meaning Ingram. "Half the city guard will surround our home before nightfall. We can't be caught housing them, Laurie. We have to turn them over!"

"Alyssa won't allow that and you know it."

"Then turn over Alyssa!"

He slapped her, hard. She leaned back in her chair, holding trembling fingers against her bleeding lip.

"Alyssa Gemcroft is a leader of the Trifect," Laurie said. "And the Trifect does not hand over its own, not even to kings. I don't care how many soldiers Ingram sends—they won't cross our walls."

Panic crept up Madelyn's spine, and she was helpless to stop it.

"We don't have enough men," she said.

"Torgar's already sent runners to hire every available sellsword in the city, regardless of the cost."

"But the mercenaries are all in league with the merchants. We can't invite them into our home! They'll outnumber our house guards!"

"Damn it, woman, enough! Do you think I'm a fool? I have enough problems trying to keep the damn Merchant Lords from ruining us. I need no grief from you. If Violet gains popularity, and it will, what do you think will happen then? If they ever have the coin to challenge us, to spread out beyond Angelport, nothing stays certain. Nothing stays *safe*."

He said the last word with a cruel edge, for he knew her paranoia and phobias. The open sky was a torment. Unlocked doors were a danger. His shouting upset Tori, who released Lily's nipple and began to wail. Lily shushed her, rocking her back and forth while shifting her to the other breast. Madelyn watched her rub the nipple across Tori's upper lip, and she thought of all that might happen because Alyssa had brought the Watcher and his whore with her from Veldaren. She thought of what the city guards might do to such a helpless thing if they came crashing through the doors. It sent her to tears.

"Why?" she asked. "Why are they even here?"

"Who? The two? Alyssa brought them to hunt down the Wraith. It was her gift, to bring Taras's killer to vengeance."

"She gives us poison and calls it a gift, and yet she stands equal to you in the Trifect? This is madness, Laurie. Utter madness."

He went to her and wrapped his arms about her waist. When he kissed her lips, she kissed back out of reflex, and nothing else. They both tasted blood.

"I promise nothing will happen," he said. "Ingram can only do so much. He needs us, no matter how much he wants to admit it. Without us, our guards, our trade, and our influence, Angelport will suffer greatly. Without us, he cannot stop Ulrich and his madness from starting a war he can't hope to win. He'll bluff and bluster, but the man is a superstitious coward. Do not fear him. When he knows we will not relent, Ingram will turn away."

"I pray you are right," she said, pulling away from him so she could join Lily's side. After Tori was burped, and her bit of spit-up cleaned, Madelyn accepted her back into her arms. Lily covered herself and excused herself from the room. Now fully alone, the two looked at each other, as if neither had anything to say.

"I should go check with the healer," Laurie said.

"Go, then."

With him gone, she rocked Tori back and forth until the baby slowly settled into a shallow sleep.

"I'll keep you safe," she whispered. "Always and forever."

She returned to her own room, summoning her servants. Her arms tired, she passed Tori over to Lily, then waited for the inevitable. After an intolerable length of time, one of her servants came to her, as ordered.

"They're here," she said.

Madelyn went to the front parlor, her servants in tow. From the window, she could see the entire front yard, including the gate. At least fifty mercenaries lined the surrounding wall, many of them unfamiliar to her. On the other side stood a contingent of the city guard, and they seemed not at all surprised when Torgar refused to unbar the gate. Madelyn had a servant open the window so she might hear the exchange.

"Not happening," Torgar said, his deep voice carrying easily. It helped he was shouting, as if he wanted all of Angelport to know he couldn't give two shits about the city guard. "A few money-grubbing peons come saying one thing, and I got Lord Keenan of the Trifect saying another. Who you think you should be believing?"

The leader of the guard looked flustered, and he tried to match Torgar in both volume and depth. He succeeded at neither.

"We come only to search the premises for murderers wanted by Lord Ingram. Even if your master is uninvolved, those we seek might be hiding within."

"You brought a whole lot to be just searching."

The guard sneered at him. "It's a big mansion."

Torgar was hardly one to be outdone.

"Well, then, let me help you out. My asshole's pretty big too. Think they're hiding there?" Down went his trousers. "Here, take a look. See anything suspicious? Come stick your hand up and search—you look like you'd enjoy that sort of thing. Or maybe have Ingram come on down instead. He'd probably enjoy a poke."

Even from her distance, Madelyn could tell the guard leader's face was beet-red. Beside her, one of the servants blushed and looked away. Madelyn, however, wished she could throttle the big idiot. She wanted them to leave without incident, not be provoked into an unnecessary fight.

"You dare insult—" the guard started to say before Torgar interrupted him.

"Stop it, already. You want in? Well, you aren't getting in, not unless you come back with a shitload more men than what you got. We got walls, gates, and enough swords in here to cut you all down in seconds should you try breaking in. So either draw your blade and actually do something... or get the fuck out of here."

Without even waiting for an answer, Torgar put his back to the guard leader and returned to the house, buckling his pants as he did. Behind him, the guards stood looking strangely helpless. Madelyn held her breath, waiting for their response. Several of them were swearing, and none looked happy, but they marched back toward the castle in formation.

When Torgar stepped through the front doors, Madelyn was there, and she slapped the lug across the face. He smiled down at her with a wolfish grin.

"I wouldn't do that again, milady," he said.

"Are you out of your mind?" she asked him, hoping her harsh tone would hide her discomfort. Torgar shrugged as Laurie appeared, having watched from another room.

"There's no way Ingram gave them orders to fight their way in," said the mercenary, shooting a glance toward Laurie. "They came all show, no teeth. I figured I'd call them on it, and sure enough, they went running with their dicks tucked between their legs when I did."

"They'll be back," Laurie said. "And you insulted Ingram."

"He'll get over it. Now's your turn to talk your way out of this."

"And if I can't?"

Torgar nodded toward the window. "Then those boys out there will kill themselves a whole lot of city guard. You ain't even seen a scrap of how many we'll soon have. Sounds like Ingram tossed the mercenary guildleader into his prison. What I'm hearing, half the sellswords in the city are volunteering just to get some free food and a shot at payback."

Madelyn thought of open warfare filling her gardens and walkways with corpses, and blood running like rivers across the carpets of her mansion.

"Like Veldaren," she said. "Just like Veldaren. She did this. She brought them here, and now we'll suffer the same madness."

Laurie swallowed hard. "Do what needs to be done," he told Torgar. He looked to Madelyn. "I'm tired and shall take a rest."

She knew what that meant. They'd be sleeping in separate rooms that night, which was fine with her. Knowing that her best time to act was now, she went searching for Alyssa. She found her in the room with the two wounded troublemakers, sitting at Zusa's side.

Madelyn smiled sweetly at her. "How do your cousins fare?"

"Well enough," Alyssa said, standing. "May I help you?"

"You can," Madelyn said. "You can leave. Go back to Veldaren, where you belong. My husband doesn't need your help to handle the likes of Ingram and the Merchant Lords. And take these two wretches with you."

"Watch your tongue—"

"I will speak as I wish in my own household. You are guests, and I am being gracious calling you that. The city guard has left for now, but they'll come back. Go to Veldaren where you'll be beyond Ingram's reach. Don't treat me like a fool, Alyssa. I know no Gemcroft blood runs in either of their veins. I won't have you destroy my household just because of some crude attachment to your pet killers."

Alyssa did not back down, and more shocking, her hand fell to the hilt of a dagger attached to her belt.

"Do not presume to give me orders," she said. "I will not go running like a coward, nor refuse the protection your husband offered me. Now, if you please, Haern and Zusa need to rest."

Madelyn went to the door but could not resist one last parting shot. "You should be responsible for your own actions, your own errors. Too often the rest of the Trifect gets dragged down with you."

"You stupid woman," Alyssa said. "I'm the one who faced the thieves while you fled. It was my servants who died, my coin that paid for the mercenaries to stand against them. I earned our current peace with blood and gold while you stayed down here in Angelport, so eager in your safety to tell me everywhere I went wrong. Why do you think I'm here, Madelyn? It was your sole task to keep the Merchant Lords in line, and you and your husband have failed spectacularly. You once owned every boat sailing from Angelport, yet now hardly a ship bears your crest. The Merchant Lords have taken your boats, your trade, and now take aim at the last lucrative business you have left. I've come to help clean up your mess, and now you accuse *me* of being the cause of it?"

She reached into her pocket and flung a small bag at her. Madelyn caught it out of pure reflex, but only after it softly smacked against her chest. She was so stunned that she barely felt it.

"Try some Violet," Alyssa said. "It's stronger and more potent than even the best crimleaf your farmers can grow. Bite down on a leaf and breathe in deep, and when you do, imagine what will happen when the value of your crimleaf trade dwindles to nothing because of it. When I open my coffers to keep your family afloat, we'll see who drags who down."

Madelyn crushed the bag in shaking hands, and she heard the sound of crinkling leaves. "All three of you deserve nothing but the noose," she said. "One day, my husband will see that."

Alyssa slammed the door in her face.

At first Madelyn wanted to find Tori and hold her to her chest, to cry out all her anger and frustration, but she knew she could not. Not yet. Despite Laurie's subtle request for privacy, Madelyn went to their room. It was dark inside, heavy curtains blotting out the little light given off by the setting sun. Laurie lay half-naked across the bed, staring up at the ceiling. He didn't look at her when he spoke.

"I wish to be alone."

"I know."

Her dress fell to the floor. When she climbed into the bed, he tried to resist. She grabbed his wrists, pressed her mouth to his, and straddled him, ending the protest. She let the fire within her take over, riding out her fury as her husband moaned. When he climaxed, she lay atop him, her lips beside his ear.

"We're losing control," she whispered in the dark.

"I know."

"How did it happen? You were feared even among the Trifect. Your cruelty was legendary."

"Twelve long years happened. I'm sorry, Madelyn, I really am. The Merchant Lords were always a nuisance, a lowborn bunch pretending at wealth and power. But I gave them too much slack. I ignored their threat, kept my eyes on Veldaren instead of on my own home. Now their influence has spread, our fleet is a shadow of its former glory, and only our crimleaf trade keeps us afloat. I've failed us, all of us."

She nestled closer to him, resting a hand atop his chest. "It's not too late. Your cruelty was a tool, and we need it back. Everyone is against us: Ingram, the Merchant Lords, the elves, that murderous Wraith, even Alyssa. We can't trust them, not any of them. We were meant to rule. *You* were meant to rule. Can you not do so again?"

Laurie sighed, and she could tell he was staring at the ceiling, searching through his thoughts for the right words to say. That alone told her she wouldn't like what she would hear.

"Alyssa is one of the few left we can trust, Madelyn. And the elves are helping us, just as we are helping them. Did you not know?"

Madelyn felt her blood run cold. "We help the elves? How?"

"Alyssa paid for the buildings, but I secured places for the elves to stay within the city. We need their aid in stopping the Violet from spreading across Dezrel. If the merchants ever gained access to their forests and started growing it in crops..."

Madelyn felt a chill run through her as she thought of what Ingram would do if he ever discovered their involvement. Harboring fugitives was one thing, but to be aiding the elves? Ingram would never forgive it, never forget it. Elven arrows daily slaughtered innocent men, so much they approached war. What they did now could count as treason. She thought to challenge Laurie over this, but then bit her tongue. Her hand reached under her pillow to where she kept her dagger.

"You're not the man I married," she said.

"I suppose not, but neither are you the wife I once loved."

She plunged the dagger into his throat. He caught her wrists when it was an inch in, blood pooling about the tip. His neck tightened, and his eyes flared wide as he fought against her.

"Just stop," Madelyn said as she flung all her weight into the thrust. Tears ran down her face. "Please, stop, just stop, just let it go."

The tip sank farther in. He tried to scream, but all he could do was let out a quiet gurgle as he choked. He shifted his weight, but if there was any part of her stronger than her husband, it was her thighs, and she straddled him as she had only moments ago. His whole body began to shake violently. His eyes met hers, and she refused to look away despite the horror she saw. Despite the betrayal.

"I'm sorry," she whispered as his strength faded, and he could no longer stop the blade from sinking another inch. Her lips brushed his ear as blood smeared across her bare breasts. "But you aren't strong enough to save us. Tori needs better. I need better."

She stabbed again and again, turning and shredding flesh. *I do this for Taras*, she thought. *I do this for his child.* When her dagger revealed bone, she finally stopped. All at once, it seemed the room was painfully quiet. Only her breathing broke the silence, that and the soft patter of blood dripping from the drenched sheets to the floor. Madelyn felt something lurking heavy above her, like an animal ready to pounce, but she could not relent. She had to be strong, stronger than Laurie had ever been. Steeling herself, she took the dagger, knelt on the floor, and began to draw.

Taras, she thought, even as she scrawled the symbol left by his killer. *For you, Taras.*

It wasn't hard, the drawing. It'd been burned into her memory, haunted her eyes every time she looked to the little baby girl left in her care.

Compared to that, tearing Laurie's body to pieces was a simple but tiresome measure, especially with only a dagger to do the cutting. *It has to match*, she thought. *Has to be perfect.* Everything felt detached, her own actions that of a stranger. Was it really *her* twisting and pulling until an elbow joint snapped and the bloody flesh tore free? Was it really *her* jamming a dagger into her husband's eye sockets? Her tears running down her face, dripping into the innards spilling across the carpet, were the only thing that convinced her she was still human.

At last she stood in the center of the room, her naked body hopelessly stained red, her arms coated up to the elbow with gore. The hours had passed, each one threatening to crush her completely. The heavy weight felt closer, more dangerous. It clung to her shoulders, dragged at her arms, and threatened to tear away her eyelids so she'd see everything she'd done in that horrible room. That detached feeling was gone, though she wished for it to return.

Not done yet, she thought as panic clawed her throat. She slid underneath their bed, stabbed a hole into the feather mattress, and shoved the dagger inside. In the darkness, she could barely see but for the dim glow of a single lamp she'd lit. Removing it from its hook upon the wall, she set it on the ground so its light would spread underneath the bed. Dipping her hands in her washbasin to clean them, she retrieved a needle and some thread from their closet, crawled underneath, and began the painstaking process of sewing the mattress shut.

No one could know. No one could ever know.

With that done, she put everything away. Taking her husband's sword from the decorative crest above their dresser, she clutched the scabbard and breathed in deep. With three hits she smashed open a window, then put the sword back it in its place. At last, she was free. At last, she could invite the torment in, let the realization of what she'd done consume her like a brutal fire. Again and again she screamed, letting free every bit of her grief, fury, and loss.

In moments, the door burst open.

"He said he'd kill me if I made a noise," Madelyn sobbed, Laurie's horrific corpse held lovingly in her naked arms. "He said... he said..."

Her wail echoed throughout the mansion as guards poured in, once more baffled and furious at their inability to stop the Wraith from killing.

CHAPTER

11

The captain's quarters of the *Ravenshade* were even smaller than on the *Fireheart*, but they still had a bed, which was good enough for Darrel. Light streamed in as the whores opened the door to leave. Instead of shutting and leaving him in blessed silence, the door pushed wide, and in stepped Lord Ulrich Blackwater.

"Least you waited until I was finished this time," Darrel muttered.

"Two?" Ulrich asked, glancing behind him.

"Been a rough few days. Thought I deserved the indulgence."

Ulrich chuckled.

"What's so funny?" Darrel asked. "You think I can't handle two women?"

"I'm amused you know the word *indulgence*."

The captain grinned. "Ulrich, if there's ever a word I'm good friends with in this ugly world, it's that one."

"Fascinating. Put on some damn pants so we can talk. I'll be waiting on the deck."

He shut the door. Darrel scratched at his beard, waiting for his alcohol-soaked brain to remember just where he'd tossed his pants before the two women worked their magic on his dick. Finding them behind him on the bed, he pulled them on, tightened the strings, and grabbed a nearby shirt. He was still looping his arms through it as he stepped out onto the deck of his new ship. New to him, anyway, for the diminutive vessel had sailed the ocean for many years and only recently had been purchased as a replacement for the *Fireheart*.

"A real beauty, ain't she?" he said, seeing Ulrich looking over his ship.

"The best I could do at such short notice," the merchant said, unimpressed with his sarcasm. "You're lucky to even have a ship after what happened to my cargo."

"You know damn well that wasn't my fault. Three men keeping watch, and they died like they was still scabs. Every one of them knew how to kill, Ulrich, I assure you. Someone knew we had the Violet, and that someone didn't want us selling it. That Wraith fellow, maybe?"

"Maybe." Ulrich bit at his lip, and the captain noticed the way the man's hands were twitching.

"You need a drink?" he asked.

"I'm fine."

He pulled a tiny sliver of something green from his pocket, popped it on his tongue, and then chewed.

"So what is it you're here for?" Darrel asked, crossing his arms. He had no intention of watching his boss take little snippets of Violet, not when he couldn't have any himself. Every shred of it had gone down with the *Fireheart*, burning away a fortune and nearly killing him in his sleep to boot. He'd woken to the sound of warning cries and dove into the water just in time.

"Laurie Keenan died last night," Ulrich said, sniffing deeply. "Killed by the Wraith."

"No shit? Who's running the family fortune now?"

"His wife."

"Damn. What's that got to do with me?"

Ulrich appeared to visibly calm, and he gave Darrel a wide grin. "Things are coming to fruition, my dear captain, but we need to ensure everything goes our way. Madelyn's scooping up every mercenary in the city and throwing enough gold to break what little loyalty they had to us. We need a counter. I want you to start spreading orders to the rest of my ships, and my brother's too."

"What's that?"

"No one leaves Angelport. I don't care if the docks fill up, either. Beach along the coast if need be."

Darrel tried to do the math but knew that number was way beyond him. "You're talking a lot of waste and headaches," he said. "Any foodstuffs will spoil, and that's not touching the nonsense we'll encounter in every damn port we arrive late to, assuming we arrive at all. The other merchants all right with this?"

"They will be. We need as many fighting men as possible, all loyal to us. It's time this city learned who's really in charge. Any friends you know, bring them on board. Plenty of men may not consider themselves sellswords, but they'll still bleed and die for a bit of coin. I want them all."

"What if someone leaves anyway?" Darrel asked.

Ulrich gave him a pleasant smile. "Then all nearby ships are to board, tie up their crew, and burn them alive. No one leaves, Darrel. No one."

Darrel shrugged. "You're in charge, so I'll spread the word. What will you do in the meantime?"

"Why, give Madelyn Keenan my most heartfelt condolences for her loss, of course," Ulrich said, smacking the captain on the shoulder before heading down the plank to the dock with a bounce in his step.

They'd scoured the entire mansion top to bottom, but of course the guards found no sign of the Wraith. Madelyn had spent the night among her servants, red-eyed and unable to sleep. They all thought she was in shock, and they were partly right. But one thing weighed on her mind, and she could discuss it with no one: what to do with Alyssa Gemcroft come morning.

When at last light shone through the windows, she bathed, dressed, and then met with Torgar outside her door. He grunted at her rough appearance.

"You look like shit," he said.

"You look little better," she snapped back. It was true too. Despite his apparent lack of care, the mercenary had been a veritable demon while ordering around the house guards, and to her shock, he'd even gutted two who dared mouth off. Together they sported dark circles under their eyes, Madelyn from tears, him from lack of sleep.

"Sorry," Torgar mumbled, and she could tell he was finally realizing she was the head of the household now. "He can't be close, but we'll keep looking, keep searching. I'll find out how he got in, how he killed Laurie. That's a promise."

The certainty gave her a shiver, and she hid it with a half-hearted sob.

"Forgive me," she said. "I have much to do."

"Like what?"

Madelyn took a deep breath. "Why, I must inform our guests of Laurie's passing."

She started walking down the hallway, and Torgar joined her in step. He reached for her elbow to stop her but pulled back at the last moment.

"Sorry for the boldness, Madelyn, but you should be resting. Alyssa's already aware of what happened, I assure you. The whole damn city probably knows by now."

Her glare made him take a step back.

"Hold your tongue," she said. "I will do as I please. Do you understand me?"

Absently he nodded, and he looked to her as if seeing her for the first time. Scowling, she continued onward. She felt herself balancing on a knife's edge, and her outburst was a dangerous misstep. If she didn't play the grieving widow just right, people might start asking questions, might come to certain realizations that would end with her head on a pike or with her in chains before the other leaders of the Trifect. Given the respect Laurie commanded from their house guards, even they might turn on her if they knew the truth.

"Forgive me," Madelyn said, trying to soothe things over. "I'm still not comfortable with the thought of replacing Laurie, especially when it comes to dealing with other members of the Trifect."

"Of course," Torgar said, but he didn't sound too understanding. Forcing him out of her mind, she continued to Alyssa's room. She felt her anger rise as she pushed open the door. It was these three who had caused everything, who had forced her to do such... terrible things to her husband. Inside, she saw Alyssa already awake. She sat on the edge of her bed, with the other female servant of hers beside her. Blankets covered her up to her neck, and immediately Madelyn could tell she was with fever by the pale color of her skin.

"Madelyn," Alyssa said, standing at her entrance. "I heard and... please, I'm so sorry. Laurie was a great man."

Madelyn nodded, unsure of what to say to that. Had her husband been a great man? Perhaps once. But it wasn't a great man she'd stabbed and torn to pieces. That was a shell, a disgrace to the strength she'd married. As she paused, she noticed Haern leaning against a wall, his arm and shoulder bandaged. It was him, she thought. He was the criminal, the killer. More than anyone, he was to blame for the Wraith's ire against her family. Did his symbol in Taras's room not prove that?

"Lord Ingram will still be looking for you," she told him.

"Let him," said Haern.

The casual disrespect annoyed her. More than anything, she wanted to remove all three from the premises, but she had to think further ahead than that. She had to keep playing the role of grieving widow, and that meant respecting the dead.

"I only let you stay because it was my husband's last command," she said. "He sought to protect you, and so I shall honor that, no matter how much it might sicken me. Angelport is a dangerous place, but at least here you'll be safe."

"Safe?" said Alyssa.

Her face was a calm façade, but Madelyn knew her mind was whirring behind it, trying to understand. It wouldn't take her long. The Trifect could not be seen killing one another. It was a law all three houses had followed for centuries. But just because they couldn't be seen killing each other didn't mean more subtle methods might be employed. Subtle methods Madelyn hoped she might use, and soon.

"Yes, safe. All three of you should be safe here."

"After last night, forgive me for wondering," said Haern. "Besides, we must fetch a healer for Zusa."

Madelyn wanted to strangle him for such a comment, but she let it slide over her.

"I will send for someone," she said. "Now if you'll forgive me, I must be going."

"And I as well," said Alyssa. "I have plenty of coin, and I'm sure I can find someone who will not betray—"

"No," Madelyn said, her voice firm. Behind her, Torgar reached for his sword, as if he could read her mind. "No, you must stay. I will not have you endanger yourself out in the streets, not when Ingram is looking for any way to strike at us. All three of you must stay here. The Wraith will not get to you, I promise."

"Is that so?" Alyssa asked. "How kind of you."

"Torgar, assign a guard to watch over them," she said, her orders as much for Alyssa as the mercenary. "I'd hate for anything to happen."

"May I still wander the mansion?" Alyssa asked, but her words were dripping with false sympathy.

Madelyn smiled, letting the tiniest bit of her victory seep into her voice. "I don't think that'd be a good idea."

She shut the door, and Torgar followed her as she left.

"They're dangerous," he said, glancing back.

"Alyssa is but a child, and the other two are wounded."

"Wounded animals tend to be the most dangerous."

She whirled on him. "Then I expect your men to do their job," she said. "They don't leave. Gods know why I don't just cut off their heads and be done with all three."

Torgar stepped closer, and he lowered his voice. "So much for honoring your husband's final wishes," he said.

Dangerous ground, Madelyn realized, but she could not do it. Not when it came to that harlot, Alyssa.

"He's dead, and I'm in charge," she said softly. "And Alyssa's a disease rotting away at the Trifect's core. They don't leave that room until tonight, for any reason. Have I made myself clear?"

"Perfectly clear," said Torgar. He saluted her, his motions stiff and lacking any fluidity. "And may I ask just how long they will not be leaving that room?"

"The only way they leave that room are as corpses," she said. "And I expect you to make that happen come tonight."

A guard came from the front door, and he paused while waiting for acknowledgment.

"What?" asked Torgar, showing no reaction to Madelyn's orders.

"A man at the gate wishes to speak with you," he said.

"Go," said Madelyn. "And remember, I want a guard in there at all times."

"I'll handle it," Torgar said, suddenly grinning at her. It was so wolfish, so disgusting, she shivered. "Trust me, I got all this under control. What about the various stuffed shirts wishing to give their sympathy? I've got them corralled up at the front."

"Let them wait," she said. "I have no time for their false sorrow."

Glad to be away from the mercenary, Madelyn hurried to Taras's old room to once more join her servants. More than anything, she wanted to hold Tori in her arms, shut her eyes, and cry away the last memories of her husband, until nothing remained inside her but a faded shadow.

The entire estate looked to be on lockdown when Ulrich arrived at the front gate.

"Let me through," he said to one of the five guards who stood watch on the other side.

"No one enters."

"I am Ulrich Blackwater, and I am no commoner for you to turn away. Send for someone I may speak with if you insist I remain outside."

The guard sent someone off running, and a few minutes later they returned with a giant sellsword in tow.

"Ulrich, you bastard, what are you here for?" asked Torgar.

"I heard the grim news," Ulrich said. "I've come to offer my condolences."

Torgar turned and spat. "How long did I work for you?"

"Three years, if I remember. It was so long ago..."

"Aye, three years. How many times, in those three years I knew you, do you think I ever saw you feel sorry for anyone but yourself? You were more likely to cry over your spilled ale than a dead child lying at your feet."

Ulrich clenched his teeth, but he kept his face calm. "I'll forgive such rudeness if you let me in. It would be impolite of me to deny respect to such a man as Laurie."

Despite the rolling of his eyes, Torgar grumbled an order to the guards. They unlatched the gate and swung it open, slamming it shut behind Ulrich after he entered.

"Keep it short and sweet," said Torgar. "As you can see, we're not in the mood for guests."

"I've noticed," Ulrich said, glancing at the guards as Torgar escorted him toward the front door. Every section of the wall was guarded by mercenaries, many who had, until recently, been in his employ. The front door had a man on each side, standing with their swords drawn. Even when he looked to the windows, he swore he saw men with crossbows. No wonder

Lord Ingram had pulled the city guard away. The losses they'd suffer just trying to get past the gates...

"Fearing an invasion?" he asked, pretending not to know the reason for the security. He'd told Darrel that the Keenans were rounding up every mercenary they could find, but actually seeing it in person was another thing entirely. The place was crawling with them.

"Something like that. Between Lord Ingram and the Wraith, we're needing as much as we can get."

They went inside, and Ulrich found himself on the receiving end of several glares from petty nobles gathered in the front parlor. In return, he bowed low.

"Gentlemen," he said, giving them a mocking grin.

"You have no right to be here," said one, a middle-aged man with a graying beard. "Wretches like you are why the Wraith torments us so."

"Is that so?" Ulrich asked. "I was not aware you had spoken with the elusive butcher. Please, tell me, what did he have to say about me?"

"Shut up," Torgar said, and it seemed he spoke to both. "Madelyn's in Taras's old room. Follow me."

The sellsword led the way, his broad shoulders bumping into the finely dressed nobles who didn't move in time. Ulrich followed in his wake, and he winked at the bearded man, who looked ready to draw a sword if he had one. It only amused him further.

They walked down the hall, took a few turns, then stopped before an open door. Inside, he saw Madelyn sitting on a bed, dressed in a simple black outfit, laced tight. Leave it to her to find a way to make mourning look sexy, thought Ulrich. She held a baby in her arms—Taras's kid, if he remembered correctly. All around her, doting servants waited for the slightest request. Ulrich saw lines in her rouge from tears, as well as her pale complexion, and was surprised. He'd expected an icy woman like her to be taking things better.

"Milady," Ulrich said, offering a sweeping bow. "It pains me to see you in mourning yet again. Surely the gods are cruel to let such a fate befall you."

"Some say there is love in cruelty," Madelyn said, beckoning for him to enter. "Do you think so?"

"Cruel men can make love," Ulrich said. "I'm not so sure about the other way around."

Torgar gave a half-wave to Madelyn before stepping out. "Let me know when you're ready for him to leave," he said.

Ulrich stood before her, letting a silence stretch over them as he thought of what to say.

"How is your health?" he asked, though he could plainly see she looked ill.

"I will be better," she said. "Though you're not one known for compassion. Is there some business with my husband you'd like to discuss?"

Ulrich feigned insult. "Of course not. Laurie was a rival, not an enemy. I can still mourn his loss, can I not?"

She nodded, and Ulrich took no offense from the noncommittal response. She was right, of course. He was hardly known for his compassion, and his ego wasn't large enough to take offense from the truth. As for his business, well... he did have one issue to discuss, other than scouting out the mansion to see its defenses and confirm the mass hiring of mercenaries.

"We're to meet with Ingram and the elves in a few hours," he said, sitting beside her and gently patting her hand. Her skin felt clammy, cold. "I'll make sure they know the reason for your absence."

"Absence?" She yanked her hand away and rubbed it as if she'd been burned.

"Why, I merely thought..."

"No," Madelyn said, shaking her head. "Delay the meeting. How could anyone expect me to be there today?"

"Delay isn't an option," Ulrich said, making sure the slightest hint of condescension slipped into his voice. "The city is already full of unrest because of the elves' visit. If you must, have Alyssa speak for the Trifect."

"No!"

Ulrich was taken aback by the ferocity of her outburst. He chuckled, unsure of how else to react.

"Very well. Laurie made the Trifect's position clear, so I'm sure we'll do fine without anyone—"

"I will be there," Madelyn said. "I will not have my house absent. Nothing so important happens in Angelport without our approval."

Only the million things that pass underneath your nose every day, thought Ulrich.

"You are a brave woman," he said instead. He let the silence linger for a moment, then out of pure spite, brought the conversation back to Laurie's death. "What provokes this Wraith?" he asked. "What did Laurie ever do to earn his wrath?"

"He was weak," Madelyn said, rocking the sleeping babe in her arms. "But I won't be. Good day, Ulrich. I will see you at Ingram's mansion."

Ulrich stood, and he bowed again. Before leaving, he had one last thing to ask. "Forgive the intrusion, but by chance is the lovely Zusa Gemcroft here? We were in the midst of a fine conversation before we were interrupted."

Madelyn's face hardened into stone, and Ulrich marked the bizarre reaction.

"Zusa left with her husband for Veldaren," she said.

"A shame," Ulrich said, about his only honest reaction in

their entire conversation. "Might she return to Angelport soon, perhaps when things have settled?"

"I doubt it. Good-bye, Ulrich."

"May you endure," Ulrich said in return. He stepped out and found Torgar waiting not far down the hall, a wineskin in hand.

"Were you listening in on private conversation?" he asked.

"Course not," said Torgar. "Don't expect much interesting conversation between her crying and your ass-kissing."

Ulrich pulled the door shut behind him. "I was told you'd lead me to Zusa's room. She's leaving for Veldaren soon, and I wish to say my farewells."

The sellsword lifted an eyebrow. "That so?"

"It is."

Torgar shrugged. "Whatever."

He turned toward the back of the mansion, and Ulrich's heart began to race as he followed. Such a simple piece of intrigue, for sure. Did the newlyweds have a falling out with Madelyn? Were they injured? And what might happen if Torgar realized he'd been duped? Glancing about, he had a sudden, more dire thought. What would happen if Torgar decided to draw that giant sword of his and ram it through Ulrich's chest? Given their guards and wealth, the Keenan mansion might as well be a foreign nation. His brother might try for revenge, at least, but that'd be little comfort if he was deep in a grave...

Near the servants' quarters, they stopped before a door, and Torgar gestured for him to enter.

"It ain't locked," he said. "I broke it."

Another strange oddity. He pushed it open and stepped inside. The room was empty, the bedsheets ruffled and stained with blood.

Torgar stepped in, saw the same, and then drew his sword. "Fuck!"

It was then Ulrich saw the dead guard slumped in the corner to his right, his skin a pale white and his head at an awkward angle. Still clipped to his belt was an empty scabbard.

Suddenly Ulrich realized it wasn't just an oddity anymore.

"Time to go," Torgar said, grabbing his shoulder and pulling him out of the room. Normally Ulrich would have taken offense, but he knew a precarious situation when he saw one.

"Of course," he said. "I should prepare for the meeting, anyway."

"Yeah, yeah," Torgar said, clearly not listening. Instead of the front door, Ulrich found himself heading toward the back. At the first hallway crossing, Torgar spotted a guard and began shouting.

"Where are they?" he roared. The guard paled and took a step back, and even Ulrich felt intimidated.

"Who?" asked the befuddled guard.

"Who else? Alyssa and her pets! Gods, what I'd give for someone who knows what the fuck they're doing."

As Torgar ordered for them to sound an alert, Ulrich could only wonder the reason why Alyssa was being treated like an escaped prisoner. He knew the Trifect had its occasional infighting, but nothing like one taking the other hostage.

Torgar kicked open the back door and more shoved than led Ulrich through. The two guards, one on either side, lay bleeding on the ground. He couldn't tell if they were dead or unconscious, but it certainly seemed the former. Seeing this, Torgar looked ready to explode. More than ever, Ulrich felt ready to be gone.

"I can show myself out," he offered.

Torgar shot him a look, at first with eyes wide and feral.

Ulrich's throat tightened, and he felt no better when the sellsword suddenly grinned at him.

"Scared to get a little blood on your hands?" he asked him.

"Scared it'll be my own blood, yes."

The backyard was not as guarded as the front, for it lacked any passage or gate through the brick wall surrounding the estate. Near one wall lay three more bodies, their blood soaking into the grass and staining the nearby bricks.

"Not even an alarm," Torgar muttered. "Couldn't even raise a damn alarm."

He let out a cry, and from either side of the mansion mercenaries came running. Ulrich followed Torgar toward the bodies as he went to examine them, feeling unsure if he would be allowed to leave or not. So far the sellsword had made no outward threat, but still, he couldn't shake the feeling his life hung by a thread.

"Climbed over," Torgar said as the first arrived.

"Shit," said the first mercenary. "How'd this happen?"

"Love to know myself," said Torgar. "You three, form up squads, and get it done five minutes ago. Scour the area outside the mansion. I want those three found."

"What three?" asked one of the mercenaries.

"Alyssa!" Torgar roared. "Who else could I be talking about? Now go!"

As they burst into action, Torgar grabbed Ulrich by the shoulder and dragged him toward the front. Halfway there, out of sight of any possible witnesses, the sellsword pulled him close enough for Ulrich to smell the wine on his breath.

"You listen well, you little runt. Not a word of this gets out to anyone, understand? It does, I know who talked. I don't like people who talk about things that got nothing to do with them. They end up dead. Have I made myself clear?"

"You have," Ulrich said, trying to stand up tall despite how ridiculous it might look compared to the imposing sellsword. "Though you should remember, I don't take kindly to people who make threats."

"Threats? I'm not making threats, Blackwater. I'm stating a damn *fact*. Now get out of here. I've got work to do."

He shoved Ulrich toward the front gate and, no fool, Ulrich hurried away. The guards at the front looked him over, then let him pass. Outside the walls, Ulrich smoothed his clothing and glared at the mansion. Hardly a moment later, the first of several squads emerged, each heading in a different direction to search. Amused by their urgency, he wandered down one of the side streets that led to the back alley behind the Keenan estate. Leaning against the wall, he watched with a smirk as two different squads raced in and out of view, making a lot of noise but discovering little.

That smirk changed to a full-blown grin when, after the squads were gone, he saw a familiar blond-haired man suddenly step into view far down the street, turn, and beckon behind him. Trying not to look suspicious, Ulrich wandered their way as Haern vanished from view. Alyssa appeared next, and it seemed like Zusa leaned against her, needing help to stand. When the two women were outside his line of sight, he ran as fast as his legs could carry him.

Staying at least one block behind, he followed them as they made their way through the back alleys of Angelport. Once far enough from Madelyn's mansion, they traveled along the main roads, blending in with the sea of people. But Ulrich knew who they were despite the plain clothes they wore, no doubt as a disguise. He followed until they reached a place they seemed to deem safe, and stepped inside.

Ulrich could hardly contain his joy. He knew that building and, more important, knew who was being housed within.

"The elves?" he said, letting out an uncontrollable laugh. "Oh, my dear Alyssa, you couldn't have made it any easier for me if you tried."

He hurried back to his own mansion, eager to change and then speak with his brother. They had so much to discuss.

CHAPTER 12

Haern collapsed onto the floor beside the bed the elves had placed Zusa in, dropping the sword he'd taken from their guard back at the mansion. It clanked heavily against the wood. Gingerly touching his shoulder, he felt blood seeping from the reopened wound. It'd torn during his fight with the three near the outer wall. With secrecy so urgent, he'd forced on through the pain.

"Thank you for taking us in," Alyssa said to Ambassador Graeven, who smiled at her and gently patted her hand.

"Our doors are open, for this is your home too," he said.

"Things are not so simple," said an elegant elven woman in a green dress, coming to join them after hearing the commotion from their entrance. "Who are these two, and why have you brought them?"

Haern would have been more impressed with her beauty if

he hadn't been so dead tired. Based on her appearance, and how Alyssa bowed her head in a way she would never do to anyone below her station, Haern figured she was the princess, Laryssa. Alyssa had said little on their trek there, but the one thing she had reinforced was that no matter what Haern did, he was to treat Laryssa with the utmost respect.

Given how precarious their position appeared to be, Haern didn't risk giving Alyssa a chance to lie about his nature.

"I am the Watcher, who Lord Ingram sought to hang," he said. "Zusa rescued me, and injured herself in return. I was wrongfully imprisoned and will swear so until my death."

Laryssa looked none too pleased, and neither did the many elves who gathered around, discussing in rapid Elvish. Only the ambassador seemed unconcerned.

"Then why are they here?" she asked Alyssa. "Why not keep them with you, where you might bear the risk yourself?"

"Because with Laurie's death, Madelyn Keenan has turned against me. She imprisoned me in my room, under the pretext of safekeeping. In time, she would have executed me. I'm certain of it."

"Executed?" asked Graeven, sounding stunned. "Surely not? She is part of your Trifect."

"Madelyn seems to not care for history, respect, or alliances," Alyssa said. "If she has her way, the Trifect will crumble completely."

"This matters little to me, Lady Gemcroft," said Laryssa. "Our conflict with Angelport is far greater than any minor dispute between you and your associates. We cannot risk being found harboring fugitives. You must go."

"Surely they can stay until they have recovered," Graeven said, looking to Haern. "How bad are your wounds, Watcher?"

"Just Haern," he said. "And I'm fine. It's Zusa who worries me."

Behind him, Zusa lay very still upon the bed, the only sound that of her heavy breathing. With Alyssa's help she had managed to run, though Haern had offered to carry her the final stretch of the city streets. The faceless woman had proved her strength, and refused. Still, she seemed to be paying the price, breathing in thin, pained gasps.

"Wounded or not, this is not a risk we are in a position to take," said the elven princess. "The slightest misstep and we shall come to war. I do not trust this city's lord to react properly should he find out."

As she spoke, Graeven leaned closer to Zusa, a frown spreading across his face as he listened to her breathing.

"Her blood is poisoned by leaves of the nyecoa bush," Graeven said, pressing his fingers against her throat to feel her pulse. He pulled back her eyelids so he might see the yellow in her veins.

"Nyecoa?" asked Alyssa.

"A plant that grows from the roots of our trees. What you humans call the Violet."

"Poisoned?" asked Haern, feeling a distant touch of panic in his chest. "What do you mean poisoned? Will she get better?"

"Without our care?" Graeven glanced to Laryssa. "Unchecked, it will only grow worse. She will die in two days, maybe three."

The room grew silent but for the quiet muttering of a few male elves. Laryssa stood there, making eye contact with the ambassador. It was as if they could read each other without a word between them.

At last, the elven princess spoke. "We are grateful for your kindness, Alyssa, but we know it was done with your own aims in mind. If you stay, then we must go, and our final word with Angelport will be one of war should they continue to press our borders. The life of a single human servant is not worth the thousands who might die if Ingram discovers we helped you."

"Servant?" said Alyssa. "She is no servant. She is my friend, and you must help her!"

"Make your decision, Lady Gemcroft."

Haern watched her struggle, and he wished he had an answer. They'd come to the elves for aid, with Alyssa insisting the ambassador would offer it to her. Sadly, it appeared his sway was nothing compared to the princess's. Where else might they go? The few servants and mercenaries they'd brought with them to Angelport were back at Madelyn's estate, suffering who knew what fate. They were lost, alone.

"You would cast me out?" Alyssa asked, her voice cold. "Is that true?"

No hesitation. Laryssa nodded, and behind her, the various elven men spoke their agreement. There was no hiding the hurt in Alyssa's eyes.

"Will you tell others of my coming here?" she asked. "Or has my friendship been mistrusted so deeply you believe I have no other motivation than greed?"

"I will speak no lies," Laryssa said. "To stain my honor in such a way is disgraceful. We are people of our word, Alyssa. It would be best if you humans learned this."

They waited, all eyes on Alyssa. Haern wanted to be furious, but he was too exhausted, too distracted by the ache of his bandaged shoulder. He knelt by Zusa's bed, and he took her hand in his. It felt aflame with fever, and that heat ignited something deep inside him. Turning to the elves, he stood, and he felt the cold anger of the Watcher overcoming him.

"Cowards," he said. "You use caution to mask your fear. You speak the word *war* to hide your inability to act. We come seeking aid, yet you turn us away to further your own ends, then throw it back in our face to justify it? Your very presence in this city means people might die. Bite the hand that once offered you aid—it is your choice. But know the wild dogs of this city can smell blood, and you won't remain hidden for long, not from them. Not from me."

"Quiet, Haern," Alyssa said, glaring at him.

"Is that a threat?" asked Laryssa, standing perfectly still. Only her mouth moved. "Is it, Watcher?"

"Not unless Zusa dies from your cowardice."

"Enough!" Alyssa stepped between Haern and Laryssa. "I will not apologize for him," she said, and Haern was proud of how tall and regal she appeared before the elven princess. "For he speaks my mind. But I know the lives at stake, and I know what Zusa would choose. I will go, and I do so in hopes you will find a way to peace and save thousands of lives. But consider me friend and ally no more."

The ambassador stepped beside Laryssa and began speaking in Elvish, but several others behind him shouted him down. Laryssa shook her head, and the sadness in her eyes only fueled Haern's anger.

"Go," she said. "Be safe, Lady Gemcroft. It saddens my heart knowing this is the fate all agreements between our races must one day reach."

"Your choice," Alyssa said, shaking her head before turning to Haern. "Can you carry her?"

Haern scooped Zusa into his arms, shifting as much of her weight onto his good shoulder as he could. The pain was intense. *Well,* he thought, *at least all those years of training under my father's tutors will be good for something.* Locking the pain into a distant corner of his mind, he forced himself to not feel it. *Just an ache,* he thought. *Just a dull ache.*

"I can walk," Zusa murmured.

"Sure you can," Haern said, chuckling. "But you won't."

They left the house under the cold stares of the elves. Alyssa glanced back once when they exited, as if she expected someone to follow after them, but no one came. Suddenly thrust back onto the streets, Haern felt exposed, and it seemed every pair of eyes watched him as the people passed. It wasn't true, not entirely, but he was used to hiding in shadows and traveling by night. At least they wore simple clothing. As long as they could avoid guards, they might have a chance.

"Well," he said as Zusa wrapped her arms about his neck and shifted so he'd be more comfortable. "Where do we go?"

Alyssa looked down either direction of the street, then sighed. "I haven't the faintest clue, Haern. I wish I were home."

So did he. He'd give anything to have the rest of the Eschaton mercenaries there. Tarlak would have whipped up a few fireballs to convince the elves of their foolishness. Brug would have done a fine job ranting and raving, and of course Delysia would slide in right after, ready to speak a kind word to defuse...

He blinked.

"I have an idea," he said. "It's desperate, but it might serve for a few days until we figure something out."

"Lead us, then," she said. "I trust you."

"Let's hope I'm worthy of it."

When they'd first toured the city under the guise of newlyweds, he and Zusa had memorized the location of various places, generally the markets, the docks, and the homes of the

Merchant Lords. There was one building he'd noticed, not because of its grand size, but because of how diminutive it'd been. The only problem was that they'd need to pass through one of the three gates, which meant a cursory examination by the guards.

"When we're questioned, just speak the truth," he told her as they walked. "Our friend is sick, and we're seeking help."

"Are you certain?"

"Stop worrying," Zusa said, opening a sleepy eye. "You're braver than this."

Alyssa flushed, then quickened her step to keep pace with Haern.

They arrived at the heavy gates, two guards overlooking those passing by. Every now and then they'd turn someone away, usually if they were too poor to afford the bribe. They had let Haern through with hardly a glance when he'd been in his fine, borrowed clothing. Nobles could stand their ground without fear. The rest, though...

"Hold on up," said the heavier of the two guards as they tried to pass through. "What's wrong with her?"

"Sick with fever," Haern said, refusing to meet the guard's eye for long. He didn't want to seem memorable in any way.

"Fever?" said the other guard, wandering over. "We don't need any sort of plague getting near the docks. How bad?"

"She'll die soon," Alyssa said, stepping up.

"You his husband, miss?"

"Yes," Alyssa said without missing a beat. "Please, she's our friend."

She reached into her pocket and withdrew a handful of coins. Haern inwardly winced, and wasn't surprised when the guards narrowed their eyes. Every coin was gold, and freshly minted. Such wealth was beyond anyone dressed in the clothes they currently wore.

"Please," she said, offering three coins to each. "We are in a great hurry."

The second took the gold, but the heavier one scratched at his chin. Haern felt his eyes analyzing him, and he tensed, waiting for that moment of recognition. The guard leaned toward the other and whispered something.

"Don't be daft," said the other. "That ain't him."

"But how could you know?"

"'Course I know." The second guard stared Haern straight in the eye. "He saved my life. How could I forget that face?"

The heavier guard shrugged and pocketed his share of the coin. "Much appreciate the kindness," he said. "Hard work keeping these streets safe."

"I can imagine," Haern said.

The three continued on, then hooked a right.

"Next time, a handful of coppers will suffice," Haern said when they were out of earshot.

Alyssa blushed. "The least I have is a few silvers..."

Haern rolled his eyes. "Forget it. You could never pass as a commoner anyway. You don't have the slouch."

Alyssa started to protest but saw Zusa smiling amid her pain. She blushed and kept her mouth shut. They traveled down the street until Haern at last stopped them before their destination.

"A temple?" Alyssa asked.

"They may give us sanctuary," Haern said. "At the very least, they might be able to help Zusa. She's what is most important right now."

"Of course," Alyssa said, sounding ashamed. "I should have thought of this sooner."

They approached the entrance, a single door lacking any decorations. The outside was plain, a third the size of Ashhur's temple in Veldaren. The walls were wood instead of stone. Haern wondered if Karak's temple held far greater sway and attendance, or if the people of Angelport simply had no time for gods. Neither thought was comforting. A bronze knocker was nailed to the center of the door, and Alyssa rapped it twice. Within moments the door cracked open, and a young man of twelve or thirteen greeted them.

"May I help you?" he asked with practiced politeness.

"We seek succor," Haern said, tilting his head toward Zusa. "And our friend is in need of healing."

"One moment."

The door shut, and they heard a lock click from the other side. Haern began a new litany in his head, denouncing the pain he felt. Something warm trickled down his arm, and he knew his wound was bleeding through the bandage. Not much longer, he thought. He just had to hang on a little while longer. A minute later, the door swung wide, and the young man beckoned them in.

"I'm sorry for the wait. Please, follow me."

They entered immediately into the altar room, where benches of mismatched wood were lined before a single stepped dais.

Their host pointed to one of the benches. "Lay her down there."

"Sure thing, uh..."

"Oh." The young man seemed to snap out of his routine for a brief moment. "Logan. Sorry."

Haern noticed he'd kept something hidden from them in his arms, first at his chest when he led them in and now at his back. Setting Zusa down, he took a quick glance when their host wasn't looking. It looked like a weapon of some sort, a metal club perhaps.

"Are you the priest here?" Alyssa asked, looking around the simple room.

"Me?" Logan shook his head and grinned. "No, ma'am. Nole's in charge. I just help. He's out with a family, but he'll be back soon. Please stay in here, all right?"

"Sure thing," Haern said, squeezing Zusa's hand. "Might you bring us some blankets before you go?"

Logan flushed. "Of course."

He retreated into a single door behind the altar, returning moments later with several blankets in his arms.

"I didn't know how many you'd need," he said as Alyssa took them.

"Thank you," she said, laying two of them across Zusa, who had begun shivering.

Logan peered over her shoulder, then stepped back when he realized Haern was watching. "What's wrong with her?" he asked.

"She's sick," Haern said. "Is it not obvious?"

Logan nodded twice in rapid succession, then hurried into the back room after repeating that they stay there.

"Nervous little kid," Haern muttered.

"Be kind," Alyssa said, sitting on the bench by Zusa. Gently she stroked her friend's forehead.

The minutes passed in silence. Haern took a seat on a bench opposite the two women, and he held his stolen sword in both hands, gently poking the tip into the floor as a way to relieve his boredom. He hated this feeling of helplessness, hated the pain that refused to leave his shoulder, hated the blood that dripped down to his wrist before dropping to the floor. Most of all, he hated the raging desire for vengeance in his heart. It felt unwelcome in such a temple, no matter how small and plain it might be.

But he wouldn't deny it. Madelyn. Ingram. The elves. More than ever, he felt he understood the Wraith's desire to bring it all tumbling down. What was it he'd said? *You've walked into a house of cards.* Who was in the right? Could he even trust Alyssa?

The door opened behind them with a loud creak, and he turned toward it. In stepped a middle-aged man, his hair long but his face shaven. He wore the white robes of his order, which stood in stark contrast to his dark skin. Seeing them there, he smiled.

"I see we have guests," he said. "Welcome. I am Nole, priest and leader of this holy temple."

Haern stood so he could bow, while Alyssa remained seated next to Zusa, still holding the faceless woman's hand. From the back the door opened, and Logan hurried out.

"Have you made our guests feel comfortable?" Nole asked the young man.

"We've been treated well," Haern said, answering for him. "Though I feared Logan might strike us with a club at any moment."

Logan blushed and kicked his feet. "It's just, you know, robbers..."

"We've had many come claiming they seek forgiveness only to instead steal every last copper," Nole said. "I hate leaving him here alone, but someone must watch the temple when I am gone. And who might you three be?"

"My name is Haern. With me is Alyssa, and the sick lady is Zusa."

Nole frowned as he came closer to where Zusa lay.

Alyssa looked up at him expectantly. "Can you help her?" she asked. "I can pay well, I promise." She was already pulling out coins from her pocket when the priest waved her away.

"What has happened to her?" he asked, kneeling beside the bench.

"I'm not sure I can say. She caught fever a few days ago, and while she recovered at first, it's come back far worse."

Nole put his hands on Zusa's face, pressed his forehead against hers, and then closed his eyes. As he began to pray, Haern lay down on his own bench, unable to keep up his concentration. The pain in his shoulder came roaring back to life, and he gritted his teeth to endure. Meanwhile, white light flashed around the priest's hands, then vanished.

"I've seen this before," he said, standing. "Though never quite this extreme. Does she chew crimleaf?"

"No," Alyssa said. "Why?"

"Because that's what this reminds me of. Sometimes people try far too much at once, and it gets into them like a disease. Usually it only makes them sick for a day or two as it passes from their bodies, but this—"

"The Violet," Alyssa said. "It must be that."

"Violet?"

"Similar to crimleaf, only far stronger. I can't explain much more than that, Priest."

Nole shrugged. "I will do what I can. Logan, help me carry her into my room. She deserves a better bed than this hard bench."

Alyssa slid aside so they might take Zusa. She watched them go, worry evident in her eyes. Haern eyed her from upon his back, feeling incredibly tired.

"You love her, don't you?" he asked.

"Like a sister. Perhaps more."

"I wouldn't know what that's like. I had only one brother, and I didn't know him well."

She glanced his way. "What happened to him?"

Haern smiled even as the sadness and shame of it stung him. "I killed him at my father's request. I haven't thought about him in years."

Alyssa didn't seem to know what to say. She stared at the door behind which Zusa had vanished. Wringing her hands, she settled into the bench and pulled a blanket over her.

"I did the right thing, didn't I?" she asked. "Letting the elves stay?"

"You ask the wrong person," Haern said, closing his eyes. "I'm still in the dark. Why were you helping them? What do they have to do with you? And just what is this Violet?"

Alyssa sighed. "Laurie Keenan's wealth has faded, so his only real source of wealth comes from his domination of the crimleaf trade that grows in the fertile plains of the Ramere. But recently we heard rumors of this new leaf, which the Merchant Lords were calling the Violet. Everyone said the same thing, and after Zusa stole me some, I tried it myself to confirm it: the leaf is a hundred times more potent than crimleaf. The catch is that it only grows in the Quellan Forest. Something about the trees there, or the elves, I don't know. For two years, the merchants have tried growing it elsewhere without success. So now they've moved on to a new strategy."

"The elves," Haern said. "That's what is causing all this conflict?"

"Partly. Ingram's hatred of them is well known, and he's always been stirring up trouble. This time, though, he's gone too far, and he's clueless as to how badly the merchants have manipulated him to do so. He wants concessions of land, believing it'd be for his loggers and his boats. Since the elves have killed so many, he thinks this a fair compensation, as well as a way to cease the bloodshed. Once the land's handed over to Ingram, he'll dole it out to his various minor lords, and from then it's only a matter of time before they sell it to one of the Merchant Lords for an obscene sum."

"Except this time the elves won't back down," Haern said, thinking of the look on Laryssa's face. "Will they?"

Alyssa sighed again. "No, I don't think they will. There are some who wish to avoid war, and might consider parting with a few acres. But there are many elves who hope for otherwise. Lord Ingram's clueless to the change in attitude sweeping over the elves. He sees them as cowards, only cowards—"

"So you coming here, helping the elves…it was all just to protect Lord Keenan's investments?"

"Is that what you think of me?" she asked, and the cold fury in her voice made him open his eyes. "That my wealth, and that of the Trifect, is all that matters to me? I saw a war coming, Watcher, one Laurie failed to prevent on his own. I wanted to find a way to stop it. I know we have our sins, but the Merchant Lords are worse. They have no stake in anything, no land, no heritage. They have their boats, their gold, and their vices. Violet is dangerous, yet they'll flood all of Dezrel with it to fill their coffers. At least we've built an empire of mines, farms, villages. Ulrich, and those like him, will burn Neldar to the ground if they so desire. They'll sail their boats through a thousand floating corpses if it satisfies their greed."

Haern stared, unflinching, against her glare. "Why am I here?" he asked. "Why really?"

"Because Taras Keenan was a kind, worthy heir to his father's legacy, and that Wraith butchered him and left his newborn child sobbing amid the gore. I brought you here for vengeance."

"And I'm just a weapon at your disposal?"

"Of course," she said. "Is that not what you are? Dezrel's greatest killer?"

He settled back down on the bench, shifting so his bad shoulder would be comfortable. He thought of the awesome skill the Wraith had displayed in their fight. How easily he'd won.

"I'm not so sure anymore," he whispered.

CHAPTER

13

What in Karak's name is happening to my city? wondered Ingram as he took his seat in the expansive meeting hall of his mansion and waited for the rest to arrive. At his right sat Edgar, though to his left was bare, with Yorr late as always.

"Laurie's resistance to your men sets a dangerous precedent," said Edgar as he sampled from a bowl of fruits a servant set between him and Ingram.

"And he's dead now," said Ingram. "Good to know at least one of the gods has a sense of justice."

"There's still the matter of his wife, and if they're hiding the Watcher. If the masses start thinking you aren't in control..."

"Enough," Ingram said, waving his hand. "I have another round of hangings coming tonight, all to goad that bastard out. Never had such a wonderful excuse to clear my dungeons, either. All those bodies swinging will make sure the people know who runs this city."

Edgar leaned in closer, shaking his head. "But still, you should press Madelyn to turn them over, or at least allow an inspection of her mansion. It's shameful enough the Watcher escaped your dungeons, let alone with the Wraith openly mocking you."

"Enough!" Ingram roared. "Do you think I'm daft? Traitors house elves, mercenaries are accepting coin to fight against me, a vigilante openly defies my rule, and it seems every night some new lord or lady dies in their bed. Worst part is, I can't send my damn soldiers after any of them. Too many cowards, all of you. At least the elves have the courtesy to admit they're the ones killing our people who enter their cursed woods."

He grabbed a drink to calm himself. When he drained it, he held it out for a servant to refill. As he did, the first of their guests arrived, and it was not who he expected.

"Lady Madelyn," Ingram said, standing. "You surprise me."

Madelyn lowered her head in greeting. She wore dark mourning clothes, but her face was uncovered and even sported a hint of rouge. Her long ponytail was wrapped about her neck, as if it were a collection of necklaces. Escorting her was a large mercenary, enormously muscled and with a greatsword on his back.

"There will be time to grieve, but not now," she said, taking a seat. The mercenary remained standing behind her.

"I'd prefer all weapons be left outside," Edgar said, raising an eyebrow.

"Given recent events, I go nowhere unless Torgar is with me to keep me safe," said Madelyn.

Ingram let it drop, for he had far more pressing things to discuss. "I'm more surprised you would come given your... aggressive stance toward my investigation," he said, taking his seat.

"A regrettable event, I assure you. Indeed, that is one reason why I must speak with you. The Watcher did come seeking succor, but he is with us no longer. Alyssa Gemcroft is the one who brought him from Veldaren, and it was her mercenary who freed him from your prison."

"Is that so?" Ingram asked, feeling his heart race. A leader of the Trifect blatantly helping a wanted criminal? Could he have any better excuse to take those egotistical bastards down a peg?

"Then you must hand her over at once."

"I would, but she escaped my guards, and I do not know—"

"Milord, Laryssa and her escort," a servant announced at the door just before the elves entered. This time neither Edgar nor Ingram stood, for they both had tired of treating the elves with such dignity. Only Madelyn rose, and only just.

"Welcome," Ingram lied, his voice cold. "We are pleased to once again be in your company."

"As are we yours," Laryssa said, no doubt lying right back.

They took their seats, with the ambassador Graeven on her left and Sildur on her right. Ingram sort of liked Graeven. That elf seemed to see reason at times. Sildur, however, looked ready for war with every word he spoke, with only Laryssa keeping him in check. Behind them stood two bodyguards, ornate daggers in their belts. Ingram tried to shove the business with the Watcher out of his mind. After the meeting was done, he could question Madelyn more about Alyssa's involvement, as well as where they might have gone.

The elves had hardly settled in before Ulrich arrived representing the Merchant Lords, only this time he was accompanied by his brother, which was mildly surprising. The two bowed as a servant announced their presence, then took a seat opposite the elves at the long table. Ingram offered them greetings just as cold as he had the elves. The elves would one day go back to their forests and leave his city in peace. The same could not be said for the Blackwater brothers.

"Do you speak for your husband?" Laryssa asked, noticing Madelyn's presence.

"My husband is dead," she said. "I speak for myself."

"My apologies," Laryssa said. "I am sad to hear that."

"As are we," Ulrich said, butting in as Yorr finally arrived, taking a seat at Ingram's left. "Such a true shame, but I am glad to see you remain strong."

Ingram ignored the clear mockery in his words. They had everyone assembled but for Alyssa, and given what Madelyn had said, he doubted she would be making an appearance for the rest of the discussions.

"Thank you for coming, all of you," Ingram said, standing. The rest fell silent. "To begin, I'd like to share grim news I've received by messenger early this morning. Two days ago, a group of twenty-three loggers from the village of Redgrove were assaulted, their bodies filled with arrows and dumped outside the village grounds. Twenty-three. I hope all of you understand my rage at such an action. The life of every man, woman, and child in the Ramere is under my responsibility, and these murders your kind commit are an insult to my rule."

"We have made it clear to all villagers what risks they take setting foot in our lands," Sildur said, interrupting the ambassador, who had begun to apologize. "If what you say is true, then those humans have no one but themselves to blame."

"Yes, only themselves to blame for the arrows stuck in their sides, which I'm sure shot all on their own," Edgar said with a dramatic rolling of his eyes. "That lumber is the only means to their survival, after all, so without it they may as well take their own lives."

"You act as if we are butchers," Graeven said. "We are a

sovereign nation and may seal our borders if we so wish. You humans have done this before."

"Only in times of war," Yorr said, his words casting a dark pall across the table.

"We have not come here for that reason," Laryssa said, straightening in her seat. "We wish to avoid such a conflict; otherwise we would have remained in Quellassar. It is not our goal to cause strife or unrest within your city."

Before any could continue, Ulrich burst into laughter, so absurd and out of place that everyone stopped to stare.

"Not your goal to cause unrest?" Ulrich asked, a huge grin across his face. "My, my, that sounds amusing, especially with you protecting a wanted murderer."

Every elf froze as if they'd been struck. Ingram's jaw dropped, and it took a moment before he could compose himself.

"What do you mean?" he asked. "Explain yourself."

"Saw it with my own eyes," Ulrich said, leaning back in his chair, looking incredibly smug. "That Watcher you were going to hang? He and Alyssa fled to the elves, and to my eyes it sure looked like they were welcome guests."

Panic and anger swirled inside Ingram. If the accusation were true, they all deserved punishment, and he'd have no choice if he wished to save face. But that meant war, a war they could not hope to win without rapid, extensive aid from the king...

"Why would elves help Alyssa?" asked Edgar, since it seemed the elves would offer nothing on the matter unless prodded.

"Because she's the one who provided them a place to stay in the city," Madelyn said. "I know, for it was a secret of my husband's."

That appeared to be the final nail, and all eyes turned to Laryssa. She looked to be holding back her fury, her crystalline face starting to crack.

"Well?" Ingram asked. "Care to explain yourself?"

"What you say is true," the elven princess said. "But we gave her no aid, for we did not wish to risk your wrath. We turned her away. Where she is now, we do not know."

"Turned her away?" Madelyn asked. "She must have been furious."

Laryssa glanced her way, then nodded.

Ulrich clapped, as if thoroughly amused by the performance. "Excellent, excellent," he said. "I hope you don't begrudge us for doubting your word, though, especially with possible imprisonment at risk. That is why we have taken appropriate measures."

Ingram felt his heart skip a beat. Ulrich's brother Stern crossed his arms and leaned back as if telling a story before a fire.

"As of now," said Stern, speaking directly to Laryssa, "over a hundred men loyal to myself, and therefore loyal to Angelport, have surrounded the various homes and rooms Alyssa prepared for your stay. They have no orders to kill and will strike only in defense. All they want to do is search your residences for Alyssa and this Watcher. Surely your fellow elves won't object?"

Laryssa's lower lip quivered as she spoke. "I do not believe they will take kindly to such an intrusion."

"A shame," said Stern. "Any confrontation could be taken poorly, especially given Angelport's current... climate toward your kind. This matter of Alyssa and the Watcher does not concern your kind in any way. Surely elves will not interfere with the affairs of men as they search the premises for a fugitive sentenced to execution?"

Ingram gripped the table to steady himself, and it took all of his self-control to fight down his temper. He knew he was staring war in the face, and the damn Merchant Lords had provoked it beautifully. Worst of all, he couldn't contradict their actions; otherwise he would appear weak before the people and the merchants the strong ones willing to act. Everyone was conspiring against him. He just wanted a few acres of land for his villagers to cut down without fear of retaliation, as well as give the elves a little deserved humiliation. Was that really so terrible?

"I feel this discussion is at an end," Laryssa said, her entourage standing. "We shall return to our borrowed homes and check upon the safety of our kin."

"I would beware the streets," Ulrich said as they turned to leave. "I fear they aren't a safe place right now... for anyone."

Sildur tapped the hilt of his sword. "We do not walk in fear," he said. Without a bow or word of leaving, they exited the room to the sound of Ulrich's mocking laughter. When the door closed, Ingram turned to the Blackwater brothers and slammed his fists against the table.

"Have you lost your minds?" he roared.

"You have always been intolerant of their meddling," Stern said. "Yet now, when they harbor a murderer who threatened your life, you go soft? Have you forgotten how the Watcher snuck into your very room with death on his mind? The elves are protecting him—we all know that. That protection could be seen as a deliberate approval of his attempt, if not an act of war. Speaking of which..."

The two brothers stood, and they bowed low.

"We should see how things have progressed. I'm sure the searches went peacefully, of course. It's not like the elves want conflict."

"Of course not," Ulrich said with a wink as they left.

Ingram caught Madelyn whispering to her giant mercenary, Torgar, and then she, too, stood.

"There will be no compromise made until we know how this day ends," she said, curtsying. "And if what Ulrich says is true, I would like to be in the safety of my home before the streets turn dangerous."

With her gone, that left just Ingram and his two lords. He looked to them both, then shook his head. "What just happened?" he asked.

"To put it mildly," Edgar said, leaning back in his chair and chuckling, "we're fucked."

"There's still a chance this might blow over," Yorr cautioned.

"It won't," insisted Edgar.

Ingram shook his head. He'd had enough. "Both of you, send out riders. I want every soldier of yours you can muster brought into the city. Claim it's for quelling the riots."

"Are you sure there are riots?" asked Yorr.

In answer, Ingram led them from the room and to the front doors of his mansion. From the steps, they overlooked the city. Already smoke billowed from two different districts.

"Yes," he said. "I'm sure."

Laryssa hated the ugly layout of the city. There was nothing beautiful to it, nothing natural. They built their straight roads and their square box homes and stamped out every bit of life that might grow in the cracks. It was only if she climbed to the rooftops could she even see the stars, all because of their torches and lamps. More than ever she yearned for the forest, especially as her company descended the hill Lord Ingram's mansion was built upon. Below, the city seemed angry and vile. Every pair of eyes that looked upon them burned with hatred.

They were only five, all armed, including Laryssa. She

feared no ruffian or drunkard striking her. Humans were only frightening if in great numbers, and even then the people so far had only flung stones from hiding. Such cowardice. Laryssa preferred the company of wild dogs to the people of Angelport. At least they would bare their teeth and fight a creature that frightened them.

"Perhaps we should stay here in the mansion until things calm down," Graeven suggested, but Laryssa would have none of it.

"That man is a swine dressed in silk," she said. "I will not stay under his roof, nor will I fear his streets. We must see what fate has befallen our friends. We'd deserve nothing but Celestia's condemnation if they are in danger while we five hide in a human castle."

At first things seemed somewhat calm, the people of the city no more hostile than normal. If not for a hint of distant smoke blotting the sky, she might have thought the two Blackwater brothers lying. It was only when they reached the first gate that they saw the results of a riot. Loud screams and chanting came from down the street, and the gathered guards peered from underneath their helmets with frightened eyes. A group of lowborn humans were there with them, whether watching or waiting, she didn't know.

"You picked a bad time," one of the guards said to Laryssa as they pushed through the commoners. "I'd turn back, milady."

"What is going on?" Graeven asked.

"What's it look like? Something sparked a riot up north, and it's spreading like wildfire. Seen at least two squads head down that way, and they ain't come back. We've confined it at the gates, so far as I know. You go in there with them, though, you're likely to get hit."

"Let them try," Sildur said. He drew his sword, which only deepened the guard's frown.

"Naked steel ain't a good idea. You don't want this crowd smelling blood, sir. Trust me on that. Go back to Milord Ingram's mansion where you'll be safe."

"We cannot stand idly by while a mob rips apart our brethren," Laryssa said. "Let us through."

"And may Celestia watch over us all," Graeven said to himself as the soldiers parted, and they entered the strangely empty streets. It seemed those not intent on burning or breaking were in hiding. With Sildur leading the way, they traveled toward their home. A boy ran past them, blood dripping from his nose. They passed a two-story building, its windows billowing smoke. Broken doors marred several shops. A group of three ran toward them, saw their approach, and cut down an alley. All three held torches. Laryssa could only wonder at the twisted logic of humans. Furious at their situation, and at perceived damage done to their own kind many miles away, why did they then turn it on their own homes, their shops and walls? Still, it was better that than turning it on her own kind, as far as she was concerned.

"Perhaps we were wrong to seek a way to reason with men such as these," Graeven said, and coming from him, it was a harsh condemnation. The ambassador seemed to be one of the few Quellan elves not eager for war. As they walked past a slumped guard, his face beaten to a pulp, she felt certain even Graeven's hope for peace would reach its end.

The shouting grew louder, and then from another alley came a large gang. Only a few wielded weapons, the others lifting their fists or waving torches. Laryssa's hand fell to the ornate dagger belted to her waist as all around her the rest reached for their weapons.

"Murderers!" one shouted, and many others took up the chant. "Heathens! Go home! Go home!"

There were about fifteen of them, not enough to inspire any real bravery. When the five elves neared, the humans gave way, splitting so they were on either side. They cursed and hollered, turning their faces red, but she ignored their threats. They were mere products of ignorance and poverty. What could they say that would possibly mean anything to her? The rest of the elves lifted their weapons, easily keeping them at bay.

"We've still a ways to go," Graeven said as they made it past, the group lingering like a shadow.

"Then we should make haste," Laryssa said.

Come the next block, they encountered the true mob, and for the first time, Laryssa felt fear. At least a hundred of them gathered together, the air above them thick with the smoke of torches. They cheered and shouted as seven or eight tore down the door to a home. She couldn't begin to guess the reason why, though by what they cried, she worried one of her friends was hiding inside. Those near the edge first saw Laryssa and her escort, and word spread within seconds. The mob turned toward them, and they screamed for blood.

"Show no fear," Laryssa said.

"Don't stop moving, no matter what," Sildur ordered.

The mob surrounded them as they made their way to its very center. Once the elves were totally enclosed, lost in a cacophony of hate and screams, the first dared strike. He wielded no weapon, just a young man throwing a punch. Sildur ducked beneath, then with practiced precision cut off the man's fingers. As the blood spilled and the severed digits fell to the street, the rest howled with near-mindless fury.

"Cut through!" Laryssa cried in Elvish.

The surprise of their attack was the only thing that kept the elves alive. They lunged at the front group, tearing through them with ease, for they lacked weapons and armor. Her two bodyguards protected their rear, their long swords moving with dizzying speed. Laryssa ran, for as the bodies began to fall and shrieks of pain filled the air, most of the mob fled in fear. However, there were many who wanted blood, and they rushed on with mad abandon. Graeven cut a path through a group of five, slaughtering three of them, then turned back to Laryssa, ushering her on. Before she could follow, the gap closed, over thirty angry men rushing at her, thinking her helpless.

With her dagger, she could kill any lone human, but they were not alone. She stabbed anyway, killing the first to near, but the rest pressed on. Fists crashed against her face and chest. With no other recourse, she fled the other direction. It, too, was blocked. Amid a pile of corpses, Sildur battled back-to-back with one of her bodyguards. The numbers seemed endless, and as she watched, a man impaled himself on Sildur's blade. With his weapon immobilized, Sildur was helpless before the many others who leaped atop him.

Beside her she saw an alley, and she ran, wishing she could banish from her mind the sight of Sildur's face crunching inward as a heavy human smashed it with his heel. Three men moved to stop her, but she twirled, her dress a startling display of emeralds and blood. With them unable to match her speed, she cut the throat of the one closest, slipped past the other two, and fled as fast as her legs could carry her.

The sound of the mob faded behind her, and if any chased, they could not keep up. Not caring which direction she ran, Laryssa continued on. More than anything, she wanted out of the city, to go home as the people of Angelport desired. The city was a sickbed of hatred, wrath, and ignorance. If she had her way, she'd burn it to the ground, and if Celestia was willing, the humans would accomplish that for her before the day's end.

When the sound of chaos was in the distance, she slowed to catch her breath. Tears trickled down her cheeks, but she refused to let grief overcome her. Sildur, Graeven, her friends... all had lived for hundreds of years, and this was how it would end for them?

"Damn you, humans," Laryssa whispered, wiping a tear from her face. "Damn you to the Abyss your gods created."

Something hard struck the back of her head, and she let out a gasp as she fell. She caught herself, but then a hand grabbed her hair and rammed her forehead into the dirt. Her vision full of stars, she retched uncontrollably. Her limbs feeling numb, she tried to roll over, but a heavy weight pinned her to the ground. Something passed over her face, a cloth or bag of some sort. The air was hot in her lungs, and she could not see.

Fists rained down on her, and she tried to cry out against the abuse. Each time she did, her assailant struck harder. As if from a distant place, she struggled. She screamed.

"This is what happens when you turn on your friends," her attacker whispered in her ear. Fierce pain pierced her side, and she felt warmth pooling beneath her as she bled. Her attacker left, and despite his weight no longer atop her, she could not move. Her arms and legs refused to cooperate. Her breathing grew shallow as whatever was wrapped about her head suffocated her. Time passed, and she could only weep.

Someone touched her shoulder, and she screamed. But it was not her attacker returning as she'd feared. Off came the hood over her face, and squinting, she saw Graeven kneeling over her, his fine clothing covered with blood.

"Stay calm," he said, pressing his hands over the wound in her side. "Breathe slow. I won't let you die. Now stay with me."

She nodded as her whole body began to tremble. Her head lolled to one side, and there she saw it, drawn in her own blood. It meant nothing to her, but she would never forget it. Staring, mocking, the signature of her attacker: an open eye.

CHAPTER

14

Rain fell upon the city of Angelport, and from the roof of the temple, Haern watched. The water soaked through his clothes, and it dripped from his hair. The thick clouds gave the appearance of night, and the darkness was a comfort. As thunder rumbled, he wondered if the rain might wash away the violence of the past three days. He'd watched the riots spread, but he'd done nothing to stop them. It'd filled him with disgust, sure, but against those masses, what was he to do? Slaughter them all?

The casualties to the elves had been catastrophic, at least ten dead from what he'd heard. Most damning were the rumors of what had befallen the elven princess, Laryssa. For a little while, many had believed her dead. Only yesterday had the talk of the taverns claimed she'd survived. It didn't take much thought to know where it was all heading. The rioters justified their actions with the hundreds of deaths inflicted by elven arrows, but that wouldn't matter. Unless something changed, drastically, war would break out between humans and elves. Lightning flashed, and as its brilliance lit up the port, Haern wondered if perhaps the Wraith was right, that the world would be better if the rain swept them all into the ocean.

The loud ringing of a bell drew his attention south. The city guard had begun marching patrols with bronze bells to emphasize their presence and draw attention to their proclamations. Half the time, it was to alert the city to new hangings. Lord Ingram had been filling the gallows night and day, both to subdue the city and show the elves his disapproval of the attacks. Neither seemed to be working.

But as the patrol passed, he heard something that struck him as strange, so much that he snuck down to the streets and followed: gold bounty. They called for all interested to head to the square, and Haern diverted his path. At the gallows, a handful of men gathered, and by their dress Haern guessed them various mercenaries and a few curious peasants eager to share what they'd heard with their friends over drinks. A messenger stood on the wood platform, looking thoroughly miserable in the rain. He kept a sealed scroll underneath his cloak, protecting it best he could.

"Any word what this is about?" Haern asked, sliding up to one of the regular folk.

"They ain't said yet," the man answered, scratching at his neck. "But sounds like the reward's plenty, so it's got to be big, right?"

"So it'd seem."

They'd set up two torches burning on either side of the raised platform, and both flickered and died as a sudden gale blew through them. The messenger cursed, barely holding on to the scroll. Looking like he'd had enough, he opened it and began hollering at the top of his lungs.

"Having been given sufficient proof, Milord Ingram Murband declares Alyssa Gemcroft an enemy of both the elves and Angelport, having been responsible for the grievous attack on Laryssa Sinistel of Quellassar. A reward of twenty acres of Ingram's land, to be done with as he or she would please, will be given to whoever brings Alyssa to the city guard. No reward shall be given if she is dead. Another ten acres of land is offered for the man known as the Watcher, who made an attempt on our Lord Ingram's life, and carried out the attack upon Laryssa Sinistel. Reward will still be given if brought his corpse. So orders our lord of the city, may the gods protect his name."

Haern's jaw fell open as the news spread like lightning through the crowd. What madness was this? Fading away into the dark alleys, he ran back to the temple. Logan was waiting for him at the door, letting him in and handing him a dry cloak to wrap about his body.

"The rain letting up?" the young man asked.

"Doesn't look like it," Haern said, looking for and finding Alyssa sitting on a bench at the very front. Beside her lay Zusa, wrapped in blankets. She slept. Logan lingered nearby, polishing the altar and dais, as Alyssa nodded in greeting.

"Her convulsions have stopped," she said as he took a seat beside her. "I think the Violet's finally leaving her body."

Haern nodded, glad but unable to think much of the matter, not given what he'd just heard.

"Alyssa," he said. "Ingram just put a bounty worth twenty acres on your head."

Her jaw clenched, but she held her reaction well. "I'm not

surprised," she said. "I assumed Madelyn would try to turn him against me somehow."

Haern shook his head, and he fought to keep his fury down. "It's not that. It's Laryssa. He's claiming you're responsible for her attack."

"But why...no, she can't possibly think I'd retaliate, not even for what she did."

"It seems she does, and they claim I was the one to attack at your command. We have prices on both our heads."

She sat back, stunned, and grabbed Zusa's hand as if on instinct.

"What do we do?" she asked. Her voice had fallen to a whisper. "What can we do?"

Haern shook his head. "This whole city is rotten. Let us leave. Forget vengeance on the Wraith. Once we're back in Veldaren, you'll be safe from Madelyn's madness and Ingram's guards. Let this city meet its own fate."

"Even if that fate is war?"

"This city will have war no matter what we do! They run toward it with open arms. Do you think we can convince the elves to ignore the lynch mobs that tore their kin apart? Do you think we can convince the Merchant Lords to abandon their greed? Do you think we can make Ingram humble himself before the elves and take their side in these disputes?"

"We must do something!" Alyssa stood, as if sitting were too much for her anger. "I won't let the Ramere descend into chaos. Thousands will die, and call me greedy if you will, but I cannot lose the trade, the ships, the farmland...War in the south will cause irreparable harm to the Trifect, and already we limp on decaying legs. We helped create this mess, and we will fix it. Now think! Why would Laryssa or Ingram think you were to blame?"

"The eye," Zusa said, slowly sitting up. "And your yelling is bad for headaches."

Haern felt her words pierce his heart with ice. "The Wraith," he said. "It has to be. He wants this whole mess brought to a head, and now he's found a way."

Alyssa fussed over Zusa a moment, who pushed her away.

"He's attacked the elves before," Zusa said. "You must find him, Haern. Give him to the elves and let them take all the years they need to drag out a confession. If we clear Alyssa's name, we might stop all of this."

She made it sound so simple, but Haern knew it wasn't. Finding the Wraith would be close to impossible, and as for defeating him…

"And what about you?" he asked her, trying not to let his nerves get the best of him.

"The merchants have overstepped their bounds," Zusa said. "We must make them fear us, fear the fate awaiting them if they force Angelport into war."

She stood on unsteady feet. Alyssa pulled her back down to the bench, and the faceless woman could not resist.

"You're still weak," she said. "Rest another day. We're safe here."

"Can the city spare another day?"

Haern frowned, and he swung his arm in a circle. Nole had done well healing his shoulder, and he finally felt like he might fight at full strength. Perhaps the city could wait, as well the merchants, but the Wraith…

"I'll find him," he said. "Even if I have to tear Angelport apart until I do."

It was a hollow promise, for the city was an enormous place, but he had a feeling the Wraith would be looking for him. Looking to see if he'd join him. Part of him still wanted to. But if they were to have peace and clear his name, he'd have to take him down.

Haern reached into Alyssa's pocket, pulling out a handful of gold coins.

"Where are you going?" she asked as he headed for the door.

"To buy new swords."

Ambassador Graeven waited outside the city, in the same spot where Eravon had been killed. It only seemed appropriate. No tents this time, just a small fire to show his position. The rain had stopped, but thick clouds remained, convincing the elf it was a brief, but welcome, respite. Hour after hour came and went, and patient as ever, he let them pass until at last his guest joined him at the fire.

"Greetings, Scoutmaster," Graeven said, bowing. "Where is your magnificent horse?"

"I feared Sonowin would attract too much attention," the other elf said, and he bowed low to show his respect. His hair was brown and long, carefully cut and braided so it would not disrupt his vision. His clothes were a camouflaged mix of greens and browns. When he walked, he made not a sound, and it seemed even the grass hardly noticed his passing. He was Dieredon, scoutmaster of the Quellan elves and one of their greatest trackers. Hanging from his back was an enormous bow, with which his skill was legendary.

"I'm glad you've come," Graeven said. "The city has grown violent as of late, and I have need of your skills."

"So I have heard. Where is Laryssa now?"

"We've smuggled her out of the city for her own safety. Ceredon has ordered her to return to Quellassar, as is best. I will remain in charge of our negotiations, which brings me to why I need you."

They both sat opposite each other by the fire, on beds of grass Graeven had carefully dried out with a burning branch during the lengthy wait. He offered Dieredon a buttered piece of bread, but the other elf rejected it.

"I am not much for human food," he said.

"It's grown on me."

Dieredon looked to the city in the distance, his sharp eyes easily seeing a hundred details even Graeven could not.

"I am not alone in my arrival," he said. "Many more of our kind have come, and it takes little to guess their intentions. Already we infiltrate the city. By week's end, we'll have two hundred elves in disguise among their ranks, if not twice that. The response has been overwhelming."

"Which is why I summoned you," Graeven said, setting aside his food without taking a bite, despite what he'd said about human food. "My position is to speak for our kind, who are united in their desire for war. I have done my best, but since Laryssa's attack, I fear to utter even a word of peace lest I find myself reprimanded."

"Then why summon me?"

"Because you aren't like the rest of our kin. You have spent a century in the wild, amid orcs, wolves, and humans. If there is anyone who has seen the world for what it is, who I feel I can rely on in this matter, it is you."

Dieredon crossed his arms. "I am no friend of man, despite my efforts. But a war against Angelport is folly. We should be above revenge and pride, yet that is what drives so many of our kind into their city. If I can help prevent such madness, tell me and I will do what I can."

Graeven smiled. "Despite his bluster, I don't think Lord Ingram actually seeks war. He's a coward, and his fear and ignorance of us is truly impressive. He's done what he can to appease us, and placed a large bounty on those he believes responsible as a way of showing he was uninvolved. I, however, have little faith in his bounties or his soldiers. No, I trust you, Dieredon. If you hunt down the ones responsible for the attack on Laryssa and prove they acted on their own, we might have a chance. I'll still need to deal with the Merchant Lords, but I think Ingram has begun to fear their influence as much as ours. Perhaps a solution will present itself, but for now, we must worry about one thing at a time."

"Do we know who is responsible?" Dieredon asked. "I've heard rumors…"

"I feel certain Alyssa Gemcroft gave the order. I heard her fury when we cast her out, reneging on my earlier offer of safety." He handed Dieredon a small square piece of parchment, with a drawing of Alyssa he'd made with a thin stick of charcoal. "She is in hiding and must be found. But I do not believe she is physically capable of performing the act herself."

"Who was it, then?"

"I have looked into the matter, so trust my word in this. He is known as the Watcher, a killer from Veldaren who came south with Alyssa. The open eye is his symbol, which he drew using Laryssa's blood. Not only did he attack our princess, but he was also arrogant enough to ensure we knew why it was done."

"What does this… Watcher… look like?"

Graeven handed over a second square of parchment.

"It's crude, I know, but the best I could manage. He is skilled, far more than humans are usually capable of. Do not treat him lightly. I wonder how great a match he would be against you."

"How will I find him?" Dieredon asked, tucking both drawings into a pouch at his belt.

"If you find Alyssa, you will find him. He seems protective of her, perhaps because she has hired him, perhaps because they are lovers. It is little matter. With Alyssa found, he will come for her, if he is not with her already."

"I will do what I can, though I must travel in disguise, and that will slow things down."

"Make haste," Graeven said, standing. "Remember, everything I do, I do for Quellassar. We must not relinquish the slightest scrap of land to the humans. I understand that now. Once given a taste of power, they become addicted to it and will never stop clawing for more. But neither can we let a war begin that we are not prepared to win."

"It might not be within our power to stop."

Graeven's eyes twinkled, and he smiled in the absence of starlight.

"Within the land of humans, Dieredon, everything is possible. These events are ours to control. Bring me Alyssa and the Watcher, and I will do the rest."

Dieredon nodded, and he turned once more to the city. "I may have to kill to succeed," he said.

"Our cause is just. Celestia will understand and give you her blessing. The few you kill outnumber the thousands you save. Remember, if you see our brethren in disguise, keep your task to yourself. Their minds are set, and they will not appreciate any attempt toward peace."

"I understand. Go in peace, Ambassador, and may Celestia watch over you."

"And you as well."

Dieredon scattered the fire with his foot, then headed for the city. Graeven watched him go, for a moment doubting the wisdom of sending the scoutmaster after the Watcher. In the end, he shrugged and decided it was worth the risk.

CHAPTER

15

Dejected, Haern returned to the temple just before the break of dawn. He'd scoured the city, twice interrupting an attempted theft and once a rape, always careful to wound without killing. Still no sign of the Wraith, despite the possible attention. At least the rain had subsided, and no riots had broken out, which was a blessed relief.

As he walked to the door, it opened, and Logan startled for a moment finding him standing there so close.

"Heading out?" Haern asked.

"Errands," Logan said, hurrying away.

Inside, he found Alyssa still asleep on one of the benches, wrapped in a cocoon of blankets. Zusa sat beside her, and she nodded in greeting. Haern nodded back, and as he sat, Nole appeared from his room.

"Finally back?" the priest asked.

"I am," Haern said, keeping his voice low so he wouldn't

wake Alyssa. "Though I have little to show for a night's rest wasted."

"Come, use my bed, then," said Nole. "It is softer than the benches, and I have no need of it."

Haern didn't want to be a bother, given the kindness the priest had shown them over the past few days. Still, the benches were hardly comfortable, even with the padding of blankets. He removed his sword belt, pulled back his hood, and followed. The priest's room was small and bare, but it had a bed, and Haern sat on its side. The mattress was stuffed with feathers, and it felt divine after hours hunched over the side of buildings, watching and waiting.

"I'm sorry it isn't much," Nole said, tidying up his small desk and rolling up various scrolls. "You must be used to better, having come from Veldaren. Have you seen the temple there?"

Haern laid his swords down in a corner, then set his newly purchased cloak atop them. "A few times," he said, kicking off his boots. "It is a fine building."

"Fine?" Nole chuckled. "*Fine* does not do it justice. Great pillars, walls carved of marble from distant quarries. I hear they've begun coloring their windows so that the light swirls like a rainbow as it enters the temple."

The priest looked around his room, carved of plain wood, and he gestured out the door, to where simple benches rested atop uncarpeted floor.

"Sadly, I must make do with so very little."

"I take it Angelport is not so free gifting its coin?" Haern asked, lying down on the bed, his back popping multiple times as he did.

"I think the wealthy and the poor are all the same in every city, Haern, at least when it comes to their coin. No, the gods are not very important to the sailors and workers of Angelport.

I have a small congregation every sixth day, but their tokens are only enough to keep me and Logan fed and stave off the debtors for another year. Perhaps we do not impress them, perhaps I am an uninspiring servant of Ashhur, but at least Karak's presence here is just as weak."

"Well, at least there's that. Thank you for the bed."

"You're welcome. I will leave you be."

The priest blew out the small lamp and shut the door, closing him in darkness. Finding the room too hot, he removed his shirt and flung it into the same corner as his swords. He closed his eyes to rest, but then the door opened and Zusa slipped inside.

"Something wrong?" he asked.

"I wish to join you, if that is fine."

He furrowed his brow. "But it's morning."

"I could not sleep through the night, for I spent too many days asleep as is. But I am tired now. If I would bother you, I will return..."

"No, that's fine. The bed's large enough."

He shifted over, and she slid into the blankets. He turned, and he felt her press her back against his, and he was surprised by her closeness.

"We are a sad married couple," she whispered.

"We are, aren't we?" Haern said, laughing. "Seems there's not much need for the guise anymore. Probably best. I don't think either of us were very good at it."

She fell silent a moment, and he tried to focus on his breathing instead of the touch of her skin against his.

"You found nothing, didn't you?" she asked quietly.

"Nothing."

"I could tell. I fear we're but puppets in this farce."

He heard ruffling of blankets beside him, and then Zusa's

arms slid underneath his, and she pressed her face against his neck. He tensed despite himself. Her sudden closeness, the pressure of her breasts against his back, filled him with something almost akin to terror. What was it she wanted from him? And as Delysia's face flashed before his eyes in the darkness, he wondered if it would be right to give it.

"Not that," Zusa said, as if reading his thoughts. "My life is a lonely one, Watcher. The last time I slept with a man exiled me into wrappings. Please, let me enjoy your comfort knowing you need nothing in return."

Haern nodded, and felt embarrassed for the thought. Closing his eyes, he let his breathing slow. It was a strange but welcome feeling, her breath against his cheek, her arms loosely wrapped about him. She spoke of loneliness, and thinking of those long five years he'd spent living in the streets of Veldaren, he could sympathize with that ache. Solitude was an evil beast, and even after living in the Eschaton Tower among friends, he still felt its scars.

They were so alike, Haern realized, and with that thought he finally relaxed. His hands wrapped around hers, holding her tight against him, tilting his head so her short hair could be a pillow for her cheek. He slept, and it was peaceful, but not long.

"Haern?"

He stirred, the worried tone of Zusa's voice kicking in years of training. Fully alert, he sat up in bed, realizing that he was alone atop the mattress. Zusa knelt by the door, having cracked it open for just the tiniest sliver of light to pierce through.

"What's going on?" he asked.

"Dress, and prepare your swords," she said, shutting the door so they fell once more into darkness. She kept her voice low, as if afraid of being heard. "I fear we have been betrayed."

"Betrayed?"

Already he'd thrown on his shirt and cloak, locating them easily enough in the corner. He heard a ringing sound as Zusa drew her daggers.

"Yes, betrayed. I weep for this city, Haern. Even the faithful are faithless."

As he tightened his belt, he heard a heavily muffled noise. The second time, he guessed what it was, and he felt his throat tighten.

Voices were shouting from outside the temple.

"Alyssa?" he asked.

"Dead or sleeping, from what I can see. Move quickly."

The door cracked open again, then closed, and suddenly Haern felt a pair of lips ram against his mouth. It took him a full second to kiss back, so stunned was he.

"Don't die," Zusa whispered into his ear. "Perhaps, in time, I'll show you why Karak's priests made me one of the faceless."

Haern chuckled, then pulled his hood low. "Go," he said.

They burst through the door, weapons drawn. In seconds he took in the scene, and it was not what he expected. Alyssa lay very still on the front bench. Beside her sat Nole, looking very tired. Logan was nowhere to be found, the rest of the building completely empty. Zusa flung herself at the priest, grabbing the front of his robes and pulling him to the ground. Haern had a blade at his throat immediately.

"Check her," Haern said as outside someone bellowed for Alyssa and the Watcher to come forth. Zusa put her fingers against Alyssa's mouth as Nole slowly shook his head.

"She won't wake," the priest said. "Not for many hours. A simple leaf I crushed into her tea. I assure you, it will cause her no permanent harm."

"Why?" Haern asked, trying to remain calm as fury swept through him at the betrayal.

"You wouldn't understand," Nole said, remaining calm despite the weapon pressed against his neck. "I do this for Ashhur, and only for him."

Behind him, Zusa shook and slapped Alyssa, but the woman would not wake. Haern's knuckles turned white as he clutched the hilt of his saber. He thought of Robert Haern, his mentor, giving his life to protect a young Aaron Felhorn from the wrath of his father. To compare the two seemed foul, yet Nole was a priest, a holy man, while Robert had been just... Robert. And yet that old man had been so much stronger, so much braver.

"The temple's surrounded," Nole said softly, interrupting Haern's thoughts. "They won't enter out of respect, at least for now. Turn yourselves in. Spare us all the bloodshed. If you are innocent and your heart pure, you have nothing to fear, for even in death you will go to Ashhur's Golden Eternity."

"What reason do you truly sell us for?" Zusa asked, finally setting Alyssa back down on the bench. "Money? Respect? You are a disgrace."

"I do what must be done!"

Haern shook his head. "I've seen a man give his life to protect others, and it never had to be done," he said, pulling back his saber. "I'm the one who must kill. I'm the one who wraps his hands in death. That is my lot, my sin, and if Ashhur turns me away at his gates, then so be it. But I would never betray a man or woman I offered succor to, then claim it an act of faith. Damn you, Nole, are you so blind?"

He gave him no chance to answer, for he didn't want to hear it. He slammed the priest's head with the hilt of his saber, hard enough to knock him out, then let him drop to the floor. That done, he looked to Zusa, and he had no answers for her worried stare.

"We cannot take her," she said. "Not if we hope to escape."

"We can still try," he insisted.

"Dying will not help Alyssa."

"Then what, Zusa? What?"

Again the soldiers cried for them to come out, but this time it was all of them, not just the one. Their voices were like thunder shaking the walls. There had to be at least a hundred out there. They could not fight them off, especially trying to carry Alyssa's unconscious body. Nor would any stand at the doors succeed, not against that many. They had no options, no obvious choice. Either they died or they left Alyssa to her fate, and neither possibility was something Haern would willingly embrace. He could not leave her there, to suffer for a crime he knew she had not committed.

"What do we do?" he asked her again, feeling so helpless.

"We live," Zusa said softly. "We continue on, and in doing so, rescue her on our terms."

"You'd have us run. Have us wait." He shook his head. "You said we should do the same before, and because of it I watched children hang. I can't do it again. I'd rather fight and die knowing I was not a coward. How could you even suggest leaving her?"

Zusa's hand gently brushed Alyssa's face, but the softness of her movements there did not touch her voice, nor the fierce glare she gave Haern.

"Damn you, don't you see? Leaving her will be the hardest thing I have ever done, and I will still do so because I am no fool. I rescued you from your prison. I can rescue her. Now will you stay, or will you come with me?"

Haern looked to Alyssa, and more than ever he hated the city of Angelport.

"Lead on," he said, the words nearly catching in his throat.

"Don't stop moving," Zusa said, facing one of the slender

windows, the milky glass preventing them from seeing anything outside but a yellow haze of light. "Keep fighting, keep running, and if we separate, find me at the docks come nightfall."

Drawing her dagger across her palm, she clutched her cloak and let the fresh blood seep into it. Eyes closed, she whispered words that sounded strange to Haern's ears. Then the color spread throughout the cloak, and it shifted and swayed in an unnatural way. That done, she turned to the window and leaped, her body twisting sideways. Her fists smashed through, scattering glass and no doubt cutting her severely. Haern hesitated. The doors to the temple broke open. He almost stayed, almost assaulted the armored guards who came rushing up the aisle, but he had promised Zusa he would follow, and so he did. The glass cut into his clothes, and he felt a vicious sting on his left arm as he rolled along the ground, but none of it mattered. Pulling out of his roll, he caught sight of Zusa and followed.

The city guard had formed a circle around the building, but most were gathered near the front. At the side, the line was only two men deep, spread out enough that Haern knew they could punch through if they assaulted with enough ferocity. Zusa knew this as well, and she had already begun. Her daggers were brilliant flashes of steel, spinning and twirling in their bloody dance. Her cloak lashed out as if it had a mind of its own, and its edges were as sharp as knives. As Haern rushed to help her, he saw the cloak snap toward a guard, shift its angle, and then slice open his throat.

Haern kicked that same guard, and he fell. Landing atop the body, Haern heard Zusa cry out, "Left!" He followed without thinking, jointly assaulting a trio of soldiers who thrust at them with spears. Zusa shifted her body so she slid between them, and Haern parried away the sole spear aimed at his chest. Her feet hardly touching the ground, Zusa stabbed the one on her left, twisted the blade, then yanked it free in time to double-thrust into the other guard's chest. The chain mail there kept them from piercing, but the blow knocked out his wind, and Zusa's ensuing kick to his forehead took him down.

As for Haern, he ran right past his guard, lashing out with a saber as he did. The guard fell to one knee, holding a hand against the side of his neck to stem the blood flow. The two sprinted down the streets, leaving a pile of bleeding bodies behind them.

"Move!" Haern shouted, grabbing Zusa's wrist and pulling her to the ground as he glimpsed several guards behind him with crossbows taking aim. Bolts sailed over their heads, one catching the thigh of a woman haggling with a merchant. Her scream sent the early morning crowd into a frenzy. Once back on their feet, the two easily weaved through the chaos, while the city guard had to fight for every step.

They ducked into an alley once far enough away. Haern removed his hood, and he glanced at Zusa. Her clothes were stained with blood, but he had no clue how much was hers and how much that of the guards. The red of her cloak had faded, whatever magic infusing it now gone.

"You need new clothes," he said, nodding toward the blood.

"As do you," she said, pointing to the long scrape along his arm. It wasn't deep, but it'd certainly leave a scar.

"At least you're not wearing your wrappings," he said.

Neither laughed, for they were in no mood for humor. They drifted toward the more crowded marketplace, far away from where the guards still searched. Zusa remained hidden as Haern used the last of his money to purchase new clothes, plain grays and browns.

"A dress?" Zusa said when he returned.

"Best I could find," he said, handing it to her.

"I can't fight in a dress."

"I'm sure you'll manage."

The alley they hid within ended against a cracked stone wall, so Haern stood with his back to her as she changed, blocking sight of her best he could from the street ahead. When she finished, he turned around and gave a halfhearted chuckle at the comic sight of her short hair, exotic features, and slender form stuffed into a plain brown dress that hung loose around her shoulders.

"Perhaps we were better off with the bloody clothes," he said.

He changed into his own clothes, then tied their old outfits into a bundle he could throw over his shoulder. Zusa hid her daggers within the folds of her dress, while Haern stashed his sabers in the bundle.

"Very well," she said. "A simple couple we are once more. Where to now?"

Haern took her hand and led her out into the street. "We check on Alyssa."

They hurried toward Ingram's mansion, hoping to beat the guards there. At first Haern had thought they'd taken too long changing, but he found himself proven wrong. As they neared, a large group gathered along the sides of the road, following the escort of nearly fifty city guard carrying Alyssa to the dungeon.

"What's going on?" Zusa asked as they pushed to the front so they could see. "They're celebrating."

He could sense her anger rising, but he shook his head. "No," he said. "It's not what you think."

The men and women of the city cheered, many raising their arms or crying out at the top of their lungs. But they were not celebrating Alyssa's capture, nor the work of the city guard in doing so. Instead, they cried out against the elves and hailed her bravery.

"Unbelievable," Haern whispered into Zusa's ear. The small

mob gave way as Alyssa entered the gated compound, where the people of Angelport could not follow.

"Is that how much they hate the elves?" Zusa asked.

It seemed so, and suddenly unsure, the two watched as the guards took the city's heroine into the heavily protected dungeon as, all the while, people exalted her name.

CHAPTER 16

Madelyn sat in her room as her servants finished adjusting her clothes, tightening the laces of her corset, and applying various colored powders to her face and lips. Last was the ornate tying of her hair, four braids curling through one another so it formed a necklace around her neck that dipped into the curve of her breasts. She watched them work in the oval mirror hanging from one of the walls, the wood finely polished, the glass immaculate. No sign remained of the blood of her husband that had splashed across it days before. If only she could clean up the filth of Angelport as easily as she could slide a polishing cloth over that sheet of glass...

Her mood soured as Torgar stepped through the door and leaned against the frame with his arms crossed.

"Not sure this is a good idea," he said. "The streets still aren't the safest."

"If you and your men do your job, I have nothing to fear."

"We can't hold back a mob."

She glared at him, careful not to move her head and disrupt the work of the two servants still braiding her hair.

"There will be no mobs. Why would they bear any ill will toward me?"

The giant man shrugged, and he said nothing despite clearly disagreeing. One of the servants tugged too hard, and she snapped at the girl. "Watch what you're doing."

By the time they finished, she was glad to stand. She looked and felt like the regal ruler she truly was. Laurie might have tried to remain humble in his later years, but she had no such plans. She was beautiful, and she would let the city know it. Surely in time she could find a wealthy man to marry, one who would willingly accept a submissive role, given her status.

"Make sure you wake Tori for a feeding within the hour," she told Lily, who nodded as she cradled the baby.

"You ready?" Torgar asked.

"I am," she said, standing tall. The brute sneered at her but held his tongue.

With eight additional guards, they marched out to the streets, and she was surprised by how vacant they were. There was a hushed quality to the air, and she found herself nervous mere feet from her gates. Being beyond her home always made her nervous, but now she felt the nagging fear tugging with far greater strength.

"You all right, milady?" Torgar asked, still with that mocking tone.

"I'm fine," she said. "The city is a bit strange, that's all. I guess I should have expected as much after all the riots. Surely the commoners need to recover."

"They ain't recovering. They're holding their breath waiting for the next hit, and it ain't going to be from their own kind this time."

She shot him a glare as they walked south, toward Ingram's mansion.

"You think the elves will attack? Nonsense. I'm sure they've made vague threats, and those living near their forests should keep their doors locked tight, but here?"

Torgar pointed to the distance. "You see that man?"

She looked and caught a brief glimpse of someone ducking into an alley, his clothes a dull brown and his head covered by a similar-colored hood.

"Why, is he an elf?"

"No. But he could have been. Every man and woman you see hiding in the shadows might have ears a bit pointier than they're supposed to be. And don't forget, they have that tricky magic of theirs. I wonder how many poor and hungry travelers flooding into the city have masks over their faces and a bit of forest sap running in their veins..."

Madelyn tried to shrug off his words. He was just playing up stories, wild conspiracies lowborn like him loved to embrace. There was no proof to it. No truth.

"Hold your tongue," she said. "I don't wish to hear your exaggerations."

"He's just saying what we've been hearing," one of her other mercenaries chimed in, and she felt furious that the man thought it necessary to defend his captain.

"Then you've all been hearing nonsense, no more truthful than the blue jay that brings new babies and the trolls underneath children's beds."

"No trolls here in Angelport," Torgar said, shooting her a wink. "Just elves and wraiths under our beds."

She felt her blood freeze, but guilt over her husband's death made her bite her tongue. He laughed at her glare. When they arrived at Ingram's, she couldn't have been more relieved. The guards opened their gates at the top of the hill and welcomed her inside.

"This way," one said, and Madelyn ordered Torgar to stay at the gate.

"If you say so," he said, not seeming to care that she'd be alone but for Ingram's men. She might have been annoyed at his lack of concern for her safety, but she was too happy to get away from him to care. She followed the guard through the halls of the elaborate mansion, listening to him talk casually on the way.

"With things as they are, he's been very busy, so don't be insulted if he has to keep things short," said the guard.

"I understand."

"I heard about your husband. Frightening, really, knowing someone might break in like that. You'd like to think there's at least a few safe places left in the city."

"We've never been safe, not so long as our enemies live," she said as she stepped into Ingram's private study. "My husband learned this too late."

Ingram turned, and he smiled a tired smile. He sat in a small padded chair, a book in hand. Stretched out behind him was an entire wall filled with tightly wound scrolls and finely bound books, their lettering soft gold or shining silver. Putting aside his book, Ingram bowed, and she returned it with an elegant curtsy. She could tell he was impressed with her outfit, and she made sure to keep her lungs full during her curtsy to push her breasts out as far as she could. Laurie had once told her she had cleavage that could kill. Shame he never figured out her hands were just as deadly.

"Welcome, Lady Madelyn," he said, accepting her offered hand so he might kiss her fingers. "I am glad to see you have not completely lost your sense of womanhood amid your grief."

There was a bite to the comment, and so she smiled sweetly at him and asked, "Have you made any progress toward capturing the one who brought me such grief?"

Ingram's frown came and went like the flap of bird wings, but she saw it.

"This Wraith proves elusive," he said.

"I heard he mocked your guard when he helped the Watcher escape, all the while declaring the city his. Surely with such arrogance, you'll capture him soon. I would be much relieved to know my husband's killer has been found and given the punishment he deserves."

"Of course," Ingram said, then gestured to a nearby table where servants had rushed in a variety of drinks.

"White wine," she said, and a lurking servant brought her a glass.

"So what brings you here?" Ingram asked as she drank. She caught him glancing down the front of her corset, and she made sure to sip even slower. The thought of him touching her was repulsive, but given the immense amount of land he owned, and the power he wielded as the king's appointed ruler of the southern portion of Neldar known as the Ramere, there might be enough benefits for her to close her eyes and endure.

"I come because of Alyssa, of course."

Ingram sighed. "I take it you're here to demand her release, given how she's a member of your Trifect."

Madelyn had to hold in her smirk. She'd never been fond

of Maynard Gemcroft, and she was even less impressed by his rambunctious brat of a daughter. The idea of wielding her influence and wealth to demand Alyssa's release? Preposterous.

"Quite the opposite," Madelyn said, struggling to keep her smile pleasant. "No, Ingram, I've come to make sure you have the courage to punish her accordingly for her crimes. Even we of the Trifect are not above the King's Law."

Ingram raised an eyebrow. "Funny how your husband never shared the same opinion whenever Taras got into a scrap."

The mention of her son's name stabbed her heart like a dagger, and she discreetly tugged the top of her corset higher.

"I am not Laurie, and I would be thankful if you did not mention either of their names. The wounds are much too deep."

The lord bowed, and he quickly apologized. "At times I forget to tame my tongue. Please, forgive me. As for Alyssa, things are far from simple. I have little proof of any actual crime, other than fairly damning testimony from Laryssa. Of course, the word of an elf is worthless in any court, no matter how trustworthy they pretend to be. And then there's the nonsense with the commoners..."

Madelyn knew what he was talking about, and the very thought sickened her. Because the people believed Alyssa responsible for the attack on Laryssa, they hailed her as a hero, the first of their nobles and leaders to take decisive action against the elves slaughtering their kin at the forests' edges. The situation disgusted her to no end.

"So will you hand her over to their kind?" she asked.

Ingram went to his bar, waved away the servant, and poured himself a drink. He downed it in one long shot. "No," he said, slamming the cup down. "I can't."

"Why? I can assure you, no one in the Trifect will bear you ill will, not even Alyssa's successor..."

To her surprise, Ingram broke out into laughter. "You? You think I'm worried about you? Look out the window, Madelyn, and see the remains of the fires those mobs set the past few nights. Nearly burned half my city to the ground and killed seventeen of my guard. And now they've branded Alyssa a hero. But even that I could handle. Given time, I could claim politics, or bargaining chips, or whatever I need to say to remind them I know best, not them. But the Merchant Lords are spinning this as well, Madelyn. Every damn one of them is grandstanding about how I'm a terrible leader for this city, and it should be *them* in charge. They say they'd never, ever think of surrendering Alyssa for trial and execution. So if I hand Alyssa over to those elves, I'll have mobs surrounding my estate, ready to burn me alive."

He downed a second glass.

"Gods damn it, how did this happen? You know what I had to do yesterday? I had to beg and grovel like a damn peasant to convince Graeven, that ambassador of theirs, that I meant no ill will. And he claims he's one of the few who *doesn't* want war. Hah!"

Madelyn did her best to smile. The opening she'd hoped for was right before her, and she slid closer and poured him a third glass.

"So it's the merchants stirring up trouble?"

Ingram shrugged. "It seems everyone is, but they've been particularly unhelpful. If I make any move against them now, Angelport suffers. We live and die by their boats, you know that, and gods help me if the elves actually put us under siege. I can't imagine how badly the merchants would fuck us over if we had to rely on them for food and supplies—pardon my language."

When he didn't drink, she took the glass from him and downed it herself. It burned, and her eyes watered, but she forced herself to show no sign. She wanted him to know she could be just as tough as any man, especially when it came to what she was about to propose.

"The merchants have been a thorn in my side for as long as they've been one in yours," she said. "My husband failed to deal with them properly, but I won't. Give me the word, and I will take my army of mercenaries and storm their homes, their docks, their warehouses. Let me crush them beneath my heel like the insects they are. They're the lowest of the lowborn, sons of whores and sailors. They think their money gives them power, but I'll show them what true station and coin can bring. They've played at being lords for far too long. Let me show them what fate awaits those who dare give orders to their betters."

She put her hand on his, and she could sense the rapid increase of his breathing.

"There would be chaos for months," he said, "trying to get all the boat captains in line, trade agreements remade..."

"The city is already in chaos, and besides, if you're going to create something new, you must spill a little blood and endure a little pain. That's a lesson we women learn early."

She could tell he was weakening. Just a little more, and she'd have the bloodbath she craved. Alyssa had dared call her husband a failure, and worse, she'd been right. Madelyn would not have that same failure hanging over her head for the rest of her life. No, she'd excise it in a single night of slaughter, the one thing she knew Torgar could do better than anything else.

"I have over five hundred men at my disposal," she said, lowering her voice. "If I fail, you can denounce me in public, threaten me for a bit, and in return I'll hand over a few of my mercenaries for you to hang. If I succeed, though . . ."

She thought of what Torgar had said, and she knew Ingram had to be hearing the same rumors. Perhaps she could use that.

"If I succeed, you'll save this city from the hundreds of elves that have already infiltrated your walls."

He twitched as if she'd cut him with her fingernails.

"How do you know?" he asked.

"Only rumors," she said. "But sometimes stories turn out to be true. Give me permission. End this now. With the Merchant Lords crushed, the pressure on you to receive lands from the elves will relent. We can have peace."

Ingram walked to the window, and he stared at his city. She calmly waited, her hands crossed behind her back.

"Do it," he said. "But know you alone will bear the consequences. You'll receive no help from me."

"Thank you," she said, curtsying. He waved her away, and the servant at the door came to escort her back to Torgar.

"How'd it go?" he asked her.

"Prepare all but a handful of the house guards," she told him as she hurried toward the street. "Ingram's given me the freedom to deal with the Merchant Lords as I wish. I hope you haven't drunk away what little skill you used to have."

Torgar flashed her a grin. "A bunch of fat merchants waiting for a butcher? Madelyn, if you think I can't handle them, you sorely insult me."

Ulrich lay naked from the waist up, eyes closed so he might better enjoy the sensations. In his left hand he held what little

Violet he had left, made all the more frustrating since he'd had to steal it from his brother. The elves had abandoned all pretense of civility. Every day brought new reports of casualties. So far the human camps hadn't struck back, but it'd only be a matter of time before they brought out the torches. Ulrich wondered if Violet would grow in the ashes of the forest. If so, perhaps they could change their tactics...

He took out his last leaf, hardly the size of his thumb. He crushed it between his fingers and, on a whim, pressed it to the bottom of his nose. It was the aroma that did it, he knew, when the leaf was crushed between a man's teeth. With so little of the Violet, he didn't expect much, but as he inhaled through his nostrils, it hit him with twice the strength such a small amount should have. He snorted out of instinct, and suddenly his whole body was alive with sensations. He rode it like a wave, time lacking any meaning. As he felt it ebb, a realization hit him so strong he rolled off the bed.

Breathing it in through the nose increased the Violet's power tremendously. They didn't need even a fifth of what they'd thought necessary to flood Dezrel with the plant.

"Stern!" he cried out, thoroughly excited to tell him. For some reason he'd seen his brother standing in the corner, waiting, but it was a trick of the meager light playing shadows across his coat. Laughing, Ulrich dressed himself. As he was fighting with his twitching fingers to button his shirt, he heard shouts from down below. At first he thought it was the rest of the merchants, thrilled about his discovery, but then again, he hadn't told them yet. *Think*, he told himself, *think. What was that noise?*

The clang of steel pierced his haze. Fighting? Screaming? But why?

He opened his door and stepped out. From his balcony he

looked down and saw armored men rushing in through his front door, fifty of them at least. The few guards he had were fighting valiantly, but they were badly outnumbered.

"Shit," Ulrich said, and he spoke it so calmly it surprised him.

He dashed back into his room, slammed the door shut, and pushed in the lock. Hitting his head against the door, he tried to think, to understand what was going on. Nothing was coming to him. The king? The Trifect? Who would dare strike against him? He felt his hands reaching for the pouch with the Violet, but it was empty. Screaming, he flung it against the door. His troops, his loyal men that he'd had Darrel buy, were still scattered throughout the city, awaiting his orders. Gods damn it, he needed them *here*, to protect him!

But no, he was alone, helpless, and listening to the screams of his dying guards and servants. He had minutes until they stormed into his room. Or seconds. The Violet was still draining away, and without its presence, it felt so fucking hard to think.

"Deep breath, Ulrich, deep breath."

He closed his eyes, forced himself to ignore the pounding of his heart, forced himself to think. His mansion was overrun. Already he heard heavy footsteps thumping up the stairs. He had to escape, to live long enough to bring together his fighting men, but how?

Opening his eyes, he spun about, putting his back to the door so he could face the heavy curtains across his bedroom window.

"Why not?" he said, rushing toward it as behind him a fist struck against the wood. The lock held, but it rattled, the strength of the bolt far from impressive. Heart in his throat, Ulrich yanked down the curtain and pressed his nose against the glass. He was on the second floor, and beneath the window was a large enough ledge to stand on. Grabbing his sword off the wall, he broke the window with the hilt, then stepped outside. Blood ran down his arm as his elbow caught on a jagged edge. He didn't even feel it.

From the rooftop, he could better see what was going on. The gate to his mansion had been smashed open, and he saw the trampled bodies of his guards beside the wreckage. A squad of men guarded the exit, while the rest poured into the mansion, with only a few circling about. Ulrich felt panic creeping through his chest, and he tried to ignore it. He thought for certain they'd have noticed him, but so far no one had. Running toward the back, and away from the gathered group, he looked for another way out.

Behind him he heard shouts, and a quick glance showed the first of many mercenaries climbing onto the rooftop, having broken through the door to his room. Swearing, Ulrich hurried to the edge of the rooftop, but there was no way down other than a painful fall. Worse, even if he made it down, he'd have to climb over the iron gate surrounding his property. He might make the climb...or he might die with a blade shoved in his back as he desperately scrambled up it.

Ulrich drew his sword, flung the scabbard to the ground, and held his weapon with both hands.

"Come on!" he shouted, wiping sweat from his eyes with his forearm. "I can still kill plenty of you before I die!"

Four mercenaries were up there with him, and they paused. For a moment Ulrich thought his threat had disturbed them, but then he saw their eyes were not looking at him, but beyond.

Torn between curiosity and certain death, he clenched his jaw and refused to turn.

"Scared?" he asked them, and shockingly enough, it seemed they were.

And then the Wraith vaulted over his head, landing on the slanted roof with ease. His sword flashed in his hand, killing the nearest. The mercenaries rushed him, but the Wraith danced between their strikes, his cloak twirling to hide his presence. Another mercenary fell. The final two tried to run, but the moment their guard went down, the Wraith lunged, shredding into them with his sword and kicking their bodies off the roof.

Done, the Wraith turned to Ulrich, who lifted his sword in defense.

"Stay away," he said.

"No."

"I said stay back!"

The Wraith laughed. All but his smile was hidden by the deep shadow of his hood, a shadow that seemed oblivious to the actual position of the sun. No matter which way he turned, there was only that smile, that maniacal grin.

"If you want to live, then put down that sword and follow me."

An arrow sailed over their heads, and both dropped to their knees. Ulrich chewed on his lower lip. He was in no position to think clearly, not with Violet and battle lust pounding through his veins, but it didn't appear he had any choice. Despite the bounty on his head, despite his killing of William Amour, it seemed the Wraith was willing to be an ally. But why?

"Lead on," he said. "If you can keep me safe, I'll reward you beyond your wildest dreams."

"You don't have the power to give me what I seek. But I will accept your help in smaller things. Now hurry!"

A few more arrows flew over, wild guesses to their actual positions. Running with his back bent, the Wraith led Ulrich to the southern side of his mansion, which faced the docks. From there, he saw smoke rising to the evening sky.

"What's going on?" Ulrich asked him. "The whole city gone to the Abyss?"

"You are not the only one in danger," said the Wraith. "It seems Madelyn is trying to eradicate all the Merchant Lords from Angelport. I doubt she'll be successful, stupid woman. How dare she believe she could do such a thing without my noticing?"

By the shouts inside the mansion, the mercenaries clearly realized Ulrich had fled to the roof. He felt trapped, but with the frighteningly skilled fighter protecting him, he dared believe they had a chance. The Wraith peered over the edge, then rolled onto his back, his sword lying across his chest.

"Jump down," he said, glancing over. "Roll when you land, and make sure you brace with your arms, not your legs. Better you're unable to hold a sword than unable to walk."

Ulrich nodded, and then the Wraith rolled off the roof to the ground below. A trio of mercenaries were passing underneath, and Ulrich watched as they fell in an explosion of gore. With them dead, the Wraith beckoned him to follow. Given no choice, Ulrich hung from the edge by his hands, then let go. He hit hard, and his right knee popped. Before he could cry out in pain, the Wraith was there, yanking him to his feet.

"Run, you fool!"

The Wraith pulled him along, and every bit of his strength

was necessary. The slightest weight on his right knee flooded it with pain, and by the time they reached the fence, Ulrich was more stumbling than running. Looking up at the rows of spikes he'd had installed along the top of the fence, he wondered how he was to cross.

"Here," the Wraith said, offering his hands for Ulrich to step upon. "Step with your good leg, then jump. Do not think, now do it!"

Over ten armed men turned the corner from the front, and they let out an alarm upon spotting the two by the fence. One let fly an arrow, and it clacked into the bars mere feet away. That was enough to get Ulrich moving. He planted his left foot on the Wraith's hands and was stunned by how it felt like he stepped onto stone. As he moved to jump, he felt himself lifted, and suddenly he was sailing headfirst over the fence. He landed flat on his back, the impact blasting the air from his lungs. Tears ran down his face as he tried to stand. His right knee was in total agony, and when he took a step with it, it buckled under his weight.

Before the mercenaries could arrive, the Wraith jumped over the fence, not needing a running start. Ulrich could hardly believe the sight. The man glared down at him, and for once his smile was gone.

"I told you to brace with your arms."

"I know."

The Wraith pulled him back up, and he let a bit of his weight rest on his shoulders.

"Move fast, and in rhythm. We must get you to your brother, where the battle still rages."

Step by step they ran toward the docks, Ulrich feeling like troublesome baggage. As they came closer, he saw a great pillar of smoke, and his throat tightened.

"That's my brother's home," he said.

"Stay calm. He fled sooner than most and has gathered his men. He is why the others might live."

"Why isn't the city guard doing something to stop it?"

The Wraith laughed. "Because Ingram has signed off on it, you dim-witted animal. They've rolled the dice together, hoping to wipe out your group forever. A desperate maneuver, one that shows how truly afraid of you they are."

Ulrich picked up the pace, limping along as fast as his leg could go. Rage burned in his chest at the thought of Madelyn striking against them. Perhaps she did so to protect Alyssa? The Trifect always stuck together, their combined wealth and might nearly unassailable. Perhaps Ingram had promised Alyssa's freedom for Madelyn's attack...

Stern's home was far smaller than Ulrich's, though his brother had an equal amount of wealth, if not more. He didn't flaunt it as openly, but that didn't mean his home lacked defensive measures. He, too, had a large wall around it, made of thick stone and topped with steel spears. The building itself was in flames. Sailors and lowborn men fought against the mercenaries, nearly outnumbering them two to one. Strangely, it was Madelyn's men trapped within the wall between the mob and the fire, not his brother's.

"Stern came around back and ambushed them," the Wraith said. "Very good."

Something pierced Ulrich's back, and he screamed as he collapsed. The Wraith immediately let him drop so he could face the new threat. Ulrich rolled to one side, and he caught a glimpse of a quarrel sticking out from beneath his shoulder blade. Far down the street, several mercenaries gathered, one of them reloading a crossbow. Whether they had chased from Ulrich's place, or come to help from elsewhere, he didn't know, nor did it matter. The Wraith weaved side to side as he ran toward them, avoiding a second bolt that wasn't even close.

Warm blood pooled below him as Ulrich watched the mercenaries try in vain to match the Wraith's wicked skill. Their swords were slow by comparison, each defense always seeming to be the wrong one. The Wraith feinted, took off the head of one man, parried a desperate lunge, and then whirled. Gore splashed across the ground as two more fell, huge gashes in their throats. Ulrich's heart skipped as the crossbowman fired again, and this time it seemed his aim was true.

It didn't take him down, and the bolt lodged in the Wraith's side only seemed to increase his fury. The remaining two died in a furious display, his sword severing limbs and tearing flesh with its frighteningly keen edge. The last of them dealt with, he fell to one knee, grabbed the shaft, and tore it free. He made no cry of pain. When he dropped the bloody projectile to the ground and turned, he was smiling.

Never before had Ulrich doubted the man's mortality until seeing that smile.

"Can you stand?" the Wraith asked as he approached. "We must hurry if we are to turn the battle in your favor."

His upper back throbbed with pain, and his right knee felt almost as bad. Gingerly he stood, bracing his weight on his left leg. The Wraith leaned down to help him, and Ulrich realized he was staring into the shadowed hood from mere inches away. Even so close, the darkness remained. It had to be magical, Ulrich realized. Clearly he saw his chin, his curling lips, but the rest was there, a faint outline that even the darkness could not completely conceal. As Ulrich reached for support, he brushed the side of the hood, just enough so he might see. He'd meant it to be subtle, accidental, but his surprise was too great for his drug-addled mind to handle. His mouth dropped.

"You! But—"

A sword rammed through his throat, and his whole body went rigid, his arms and legs wracked with spasms. Ulrich's vision darkened, then exploded with light. If not for the horrendous pain, he would have found it amusing how similar it was to a heavy dose of Violet. As it carried him, he heard the Wraith's voice float away.

"You damn fool, you could have lived. You were useful..."

CHAPTER

17

Haern crouched on the rooftop as he watched Ulrich Blackwater's mansion burn in the night like an enormous pyre.

"What madness is this?" he wondered aloud. "Have you not had your fill of betrayal, Madelyn?"

He wore his assassin's colors, his gray cloaks, and his hood pulled low. In the shadows of the fire, he felt himself become the Watcher once more. At least the cursed city hadn't stolen that from him, no matter the doubts it had brought him.

Zusa landed beside him, her long cloak trailing after her in the air.

"The other Blackwater's home is damaged but not destroyed," she said. "I see two other houses damaged by fire, but both still stand. Men patrol them, and they are not Madelyn's."

"They failed, then," Haern said, pressing his knuckles to his lips as he thought. "Now the question is, how will the Merchant Lords respond?"

"They are not known for their forgiveness. No doubt Madelyn hides in her mansion, surrounded by what's left of her mercenaries. With her high walls, she can survive anything they throw at her...assuming Lord Ingram does not intervene."

"That man has lost all control of the city. Anarchy will follow if things continue as they have."

Zusa shrugged. "Then we will thrive in the anarchy. I think it's time we made those in power fear our presence."

Haern looked to the dying fire. "Who will you go after?"

She grinned, and the eagerness in it was both frightening and exhilarating. Her face remained uncovered, for there seemed little point in disguising her identity.

"Ingram has given you an ultimatum, but he knows nothing of me. Alyssa has stayed in his dungeons long enough. Either he frees her, or I slit his throat."

"He said if he dies, his guards are to execute every prisoner. That includes Alyssa."

"Ingram is a coward," she said, drawing her daggers. "And cowards will always give up every promise to protect their lives. You should have learned this by now, Watcher."

Zusa turned and ran, leaping from rooftop to rooftop toward the distant mansion on the hill. Haern watched her go, wishing he could share her reckless abandon. But he had his own man to find, a Wraith that had framed him for a vicious attempted murder. Deep down, he felt confident Zusa could free Alyssa without his aid. But even if she escaped, they needed some sort of proof to their innocence; otherwise they'd be hiding forever. And to prove his innocence meant finding the Wraith. Haern's instincts told him the Wraith would be lingering about the fires, watching. No man could declare Angelport his, then ignore the bloodshed that had filled the streets during the day.

Haern dropped to the ground and began circling the

compound. Every nerve in his body remained on alert, and his eyes scanned the deepest shadows. Twice he looped around the burning mansion, then moved on to the next place Madelyn's men had assaulted. From his initial scouting of Angelport, he'd learned it belonged to Arren Goldsail. The attacks had gone worse there for the merchants. By the time Haern had learned of the attack, it'd been halfway over. He and Zusa had watched to the very end, unwilling to help either side. Arren had been dragged out from his mansion, strung up by his feet from the branches of a nearby tree, and then had his stomach slit open. They'd wrapped his intestines around his neck before he finally died.

After watching that, Haern knew it was only a matter of time before the merchants retaliated, even if Zusa was right about the Keenan mansion being able to repel an attack. Given Haern's distaste for both of them, he had no qualms with them killing each other, but innocent lives would be quickly dragged in. Haern would not mourn the loss of someone like Arren Goldsail, but his servants, his guards, they'd all died as well. Did they deserve the same fate as their master?

Of course not, Haern knew. But there was nothing he could do to stop such a blood feud. *Focus on the task at hand*, he told himself. As he looked upon the ruins of the Goldsail mansion, lost in thought, he felt a tingle in the back of his mind. Peering over his shoulder, he spotted a hunched shadow, nearly invisible in the darkness. Someone was following him.

"Let's play," Haern whispered, suddenly bolting to his right. Figuring it was the Wraith, he moved at full speed, his legs pumping. He weaved through the quiet street, then cut into an alley. A glance behind showed no pursuer, but he knew that wasn't true. That left but one place. Digging in his heels, he changed directions, running straight at a wall. Leaping into it, his knees pressed into his chest, he somersaulted into the air. As he'd guessed, his pursuer came crashing down from the rooftops, blades slashing. He hit nothing, unprepared for Haern's maneuver. As Haern landed, he drew his swords, his eyes narrowing.

Whoever this attacker was, it wasn't the Wraith.

"Why do you follow me?" Haern asked, his whole body crouched low and ready to spring, his sabers angled outward.

The attacker turned, and he removed his hood. Pointed ears poked out from beneath his brown hair, which was long and tied away from his face. He wielded two ornate knives, each one gleaming with silver. His cold eyes stared, and Haern felt his every feature being analyzed.

"Are you the Watcher of Veldaren?" this strange elf asked.

"If I am, will you attack again?"

The elf glared, clearly not amused. "I have little patience for human sarcasm."

"And I for unwarranted attacks. Be gone. I have no wish to hurt you."

The elf chuckled, a small smile pulling at the edges of his mouth. "You won't."

He moved to attack, and Haern went to block, only too late realizing it was a feint. The elf slashed again, one knee bent so his whole body could attack at a bizarre angle. Haern blocked the first, and as the knife slid off with a loud scraping of steel, he used his other hand to parry the second attack. But the elf stood just before contact, and he tilted the knife so it avoided the parry. Pure instinct saved Haern's life. As the knife went for his throat, he went limp, falling so it only cut the air above his head. When he hit the ground, he rolled, then kicked away, avoiding a double thrust that would have impaled him.

Upon landing, he crouched again, eyeing the elf with newfound respect. No, he wasn't the Wraith, though he was just as good. Any hope of surviving relied on Haern overwhelming the man on the offensive, praying the elf made a mistake before he did. The elf remained back for a moment, as if he, too, were reassessing the skill of his opponent.

Haern assaulted, pushing his skills to their limit. He let his countless hours of training throughout his childhood take over, let his sabers act as if they were their own sentient beings. The elf countered the first three hits, and each time Haern twisted side to side, narrowly avoiding the killing thrusts. His sabers a blur, he slashed with one and thrust with the other, doing so even as a knife passed within an inch of his cheek. The elf battered away the thrust, but he was not fast enough to avoid the other. The saber pierced his shoulder, but he twisted so that the wound remained shallow.

As the elf retreated a step, Haern kept back. He peered from underneath his hood, and he fought to keep his breathing under control. Keeping pace required tremendous exertion, and he knew the fight was far from over. The nameless elf didn't seem winded, and if not for the tiny trickle of blood running down his chest, he might have looked like he hadn't fought at all.

"Most amazing, for a human," the elf said.

"Who are you?" Haern asked, frustrated at how he sounded out of breath.

"You deserve as much. My name is Dieredon, and I've been sent to kill you."

Before Haern could protest, the elf attacked. He fought his initial instinct to retreat, and instead met the charge head-on. Their weapons danced, and they shifted their feet and twisted their bodies so neither could find advantage. Dieredon gave him no opening except false openings, traps he refused to fall for. Haern felt sweat drip across his forehead, his vision narrowing so that he saw only his opponent and the dark street around them. Still, he sensed the fight slipping away. Dieredon pressed the attack, his knives scoring a dozen shallow cuts. Haern bled but would not go down.

At last the elf made a mistake. Haern narrowly ducked a swipe, then vaulted away. As his body curled through the air, his foot connected with Dieredon's chin, snapping his head back. His vision dazed, he retreated, his knives slashing in a bewildering defense. But Haern had no intention of attacking.

He ran. A quick look behind showed him at least fifty yards ahead, and that would be enough. After the past few nights he'd searched for the Wraith, he felt confident he knew the city better than any outsider elf. He weaved and ducked through the alleys, sometimes looping back, sometimes taking to the rooftops. At last he felt himself safe as he neared the docks, dropped behind a stack of three barrels, and collapsed against the wall of a tavern. He gasped in air as his chest ached and the many thin wounds bled and stung.

"First the Wraith, now you," he said, remembering Dieredon's amazing speed with his knives. "Why, Ashhur, does the whole world hate me?"

Ashhur gave him no answer. Two opponents, each more skilled than any foe he'd fought before, and both seeking him out without explanation. Frustrated, Haern returned to the small room he and Zusa had rented. He was in no shape to fight the Wraith, and he didn't want to imagine what would happen if he was spotted by Dieredon again. After bandaging his wounds, he lay on the shoddy straw bed, closed his eyes, and hoped Zusa fared far better.

"I want watch set up in three shifts," Torgar said as Madelyn clutched Tori to her chest and watched her mercenaries take up positions throughout her yard and along the wall. Several of the men were wounded, and all looked tired, but they did not complain. Even Torgar sported a fresh cut across his already ugly face, but he didn't seem bothered by it.

"They can't make it through, can they?" she asked as the minor captains spread out, organizing shifts.

Torgar shrugged and gestured for Madelyn to go back inside. "No reason they should, not with how many bodies we have watching the gate. Trust me on that."

"Like I trusted you to handle the Merchant Lords?"

Torgar made a noise akin to a growl, and he put a massive hand on her shoulder. "Go inside," he said. "Now."

She might have argued, but she held Tori in her arms and feared something might happen to the baby. She slipped inside as told, and to her surprise, Torgar followed. The door slammed shut behind him with a heavy crack.

"Take her," Torgar said to Lily, who stood waiting beside the door.

The servant looked nervous, as if unsure she should follow the mercenary's orders. Madelyn handed little Tori over, and she whispered soothing words as she stroked her head. Her eyes met Lily's briefly.

"Get my guard," Madelyn whispered before turning to face Torgar.

"We need to talk," said the mercenary. "Either here or somewhere private. I don't give a damn which."

"About what, may I ask? What is so important you believe you can give *me* orders?"

Torgar grinned, and his tone was full of mockery. "The Wraith, and how he killed Laurie."

She swallowed, forcing herself to make no outward reaction. "My husband's old study, then," she said. "Lead the way."

"Oh no, ladies first," he said. "I insist."

Madelyn walked to the study, every muscle in her body stiff. She kept telling herself there was no way he could know, no way he could prove it, but that grin of his... Once inside, she put her back to a wall and crossed her arms over her chest. Torgar walked in casually, his hand resting on the handle of his giant sword. He kicked the door shut behind him, and her heart jumped at the loud bang.

"I don't know what you're thinking, but I can assure you—"

"Be quiet," Torgar said.

She did, and that alone worried her. The mercenary paced before her, tapping his lips as if in thought. His eyes never left her.

"You said you wished to talk," she said, regaining her composure. "We're here now, so talk."

"I've been thinking about that night," Torgar said. He stopped pacing and leaned his back against the door, as if reminding her she had nowhere to go. "The Wraith's good, and stealthy—I have no doubt about that. I've fought him, seen what he can do. But to make it into your room unnoticed, without killing a single guard? That seems a bit much, don't you think?"

"I don't know how he got in, Torgar. I woke with Laurie dead and a hand over my mouth. Perhaps the window?"

"That glass breaking is what alerted us, Madelyn. If he got in, then he got in through the door. He left through the window... at least, looks like it, don't it? I looked at the window, though, and it don't seem right. Don't seem the shape it should be. Course, I'm not the smartest, but then I saw something I really didn't like."

He stepped closer, and when she tried to slide away, he shoved an arm in her way. Towering over her, he leaned in, grinning. It was false, though, for anyone could see the fury that burned in his eyes.

"I saw blood in your washbasin."

"There was blood everywhere," she said, her lower lip quivering. It took all her willpower to meet his gaze.

"Aye, but not that far. Sure, a few drops could have landed in there...or maybe someone cleaned up afterward. But that don't make much sense, does it? Made me wonder, though. Wonder how he got in. How he got away. How no one saw him. All we had was your word, and, milady, that don't mean shit to me."

"I'll hang you for this," she said softly.

"That so? I don't think so. Not knowing what I know."

He reached into a pocket of his vest. When she saw the dagger in his hand, her legs went weak. The hilt was golden, the sharp blade still stained with dried blood.

"You recognize this, don't you?" he asked.

"Should I?" she said, trying to feign innocence.

"I tore your damn room apart, Madelyn, and I found this sewn up in your mattress. Look at it. Look at it! It don't take much guessing to know whose blood is dried on the edge."

"What do you want?" she asked. Under such conditions, she normally would have flaunted her body, used her sex to subdue his anger and put herself under his protection. But something about Torgar always made her uncomfortable, and deep down she knew any advance she made would be met by a blow from the back of his hand.

Torgar jammed the dagger into the wall. Her breath caught in her throat. He leaned closer, and she knew he could smell victory.

"Laurie's dead, so you're the one with the coin purse. Let's try to be fair about this, shall we? I've taken on far more responsibilities around here, what with fighting off the merchants and the city guard. Oh, and let's not forget my fun with that elven slut. So let's have my pay go through the roof, you hear me?"

"I can arrange that," she said, her voice hoarse.

"Not just that. I don't want you trying anything stupid, like killing me to protect your little secrets. So this is the other catch. I know you won't ever let me join the family, so if you want me to keep my lips shut, you need to make me Tori's godfather."

The door burst open, and a dozen guards rushed in. They said nothing, only looked around as if confused.

"Are you all right, milady?" asked one.

"She's fine," Torgar said, flashing a smile. He turned back to her. "What's it going to be? Or should I have a talk with the Conningtons, or whoever will be running Alyssa's house once she's dead?"

"I'll do it," she said, thinking of a hundred ways she could delay making such an arrangement legal. "And I'll trust you to hold your word."

Torgar laughed, and he walked through the group of guards looking completely unworried by their presence.

"I'd say you're not the one who needs to worry about getting stabbed in the back," he called over his shoulder.

Madelyn felt her blood run cold, and she nearly gave the order for her guards to execute him on the spot. The look on the guards' faces stopped her. Some were inquisitive, but most seemed angry, or in doubt. How many of them knew, or at least questioned Laurie's death? Oh dear gods, what if Torgar had told them already? His presence might have been the only thing keeping them in line.

She caught several of them staring at the dagger embedded in the wall, and that was the last straw.

"I'm fine," she said. "Go on, back to your posts."

They filtered out, and when they were gone, she yanked the dagger free. The study had a fireplace, and she hurled the dagger into the center of the coals, not caring whether it would burn or not. She just didn't want to see it anymore.

"Damn you, all of you," she said, thinking of Torgar, her late husband, the merchants. Every sick member of Angelport who seemed to relish destruction and bloodshed. The fire popped, and she saw the tip of the dagger sticking out from the center. As the blood blackened, she wondered how to kill Torgar without blame or suspicion. There had to be a way, and she would find it. For once, the Keenan fortune was fully under her control. No one would take that from her.

No one, not even the brutish guard who knew her darkest secret.

CHAPTER

18

Zusa remained patient as she crept toward Ingram's compound, knowing the slightest mistake could be her last. Between the mobs, the elves, and the merchants, every guard would be on high alert, and that wasn't even counting the added protection because of the Wraith, or Haern's earlier midnight visit. Still, she was one of the faceless, if not the last. Nothing would stop her from getting in. Her patience was infinite, the shadows her friends.

Of course, getting *out* was another matter. She couldn't help but think of her and Haern's disastrous escape. If not for the Wraith, they'd be two corpses, or even worse, still suffering through torture in the deepest parts of Ingram's dungeon.

When she reached the gate, she pressed her back to a wall, blending into the long shadows made by the starlight. Even with her impressive skills, she wondered just how much patience it'd take when she saw how many armed men patrolled the wall. Torches had been set up every fifty feet, no doubt hoping to eliminate any chance of stealth by someone like Haern or herself. Every window was lit with lamps, and the patrolling men also carried torches. She doubted there was anywhere else in Angelport closer to having daylight at night than Lord Ingram's mansion.

As she was pondering a route in, something caught her eye. It was a shadow that didn't seem quite right, stretching out far longer than the wall that created it. And then it moved. Curious, Zusa watched as a single shadowy form approached the mansion wall. As it arrived, her eyes widened. Six more figures followed, sprinting across the street with both incredible speed and unnerving silence.

Elves, thought Zusa. *They had to be*. The question was... should she consider them friend or foe?

Either way, she had to follow and keep them in sight. She wouldn't let them endanger Alyssa, no matter their goal. As she ran, the seven scaled the wall with ease, then descended upon a patrol walking past. Zusa sprinted across the street, pressing her body flat against the stone wall. She listened for cries of alarm or sounds of combat, but there were none. The elves had slaughtered a full patrol with hardly a noise. Her respect for them went up tenfold. From her own watch, she knew it'd be about a minute before the next one appeared. The elves would have to move fast to accomplish what they desired in such a small window of opportunity. Zusa leaped, grabbed the top ledge of the wall, and vaulted over.

She landed amid the bodies, all five of the patrol. They lay crumpled about, their throats slashed with fine precision. She looked to the mansion farther up the hill, yet saw no one. She frowned. It didn't matter their speed; she should have seen movement. Unless...

Zusa sprinted along the wall, a lump growing in her throat. Sure enough, as she rounded the side, she found another patrol, dead from sliced throats and stabs through the back and into lungs. Deadly killers, all seven, and they weren't heading for Ingram in his mansion. They were making their way to the dungeon.

They wanted Alyssa.

"You won't have her," she whispered. She thought of raising an alarm, but no patrols were near, and the mansion was too far away to break a window with a stone to alert the guard. Besides, shouting and hollering would alert the elves to her own approach, and she would arrive far sooner than any guard. Drawing her daggers, she steeled herself to fight such incredible opponents. *It'll be like fighting Haern*, she told herself. She'd sparred with him plenty on the trip to Angelport. That was the speed to expect, the level of skill to anticipate.

And there were seven of them.

At the entrance to the dungeon, she found two guards slumped beside the door, long darts sticking out from underneath their helmets. The huge door was open, and from within she heard the sound of shouting and combat. With the dungeon buried under the earth, the noise was well contained, and unless someone made it out, no one would raise the alarm. Gripping her daggers tighter, she knew it might be far too late by the time someone did.

Her rescue nearly ended before it began. As she passed through the entryway, every nerve in her body fired off warning. Reacting on instinct, she plummeted to one knee, ducked, and flung her daggers up in a desperate defense. From above the entrance fell an elf, and his sword connected with the daggers with a loud clang. Zusa rolled, knowing he would try to finish her before she regained her footing. Sure enough, she heard the sound of blades scraping against the stone floor, failed slashes mere inches behind her.

Reaching a wall, she spun, putting her back to it. The elf lunged, his thrust aimed for her chest. She batted the thrust aside with both daggers. Before she could react further, he continued in with his charge, despite his sword clanging against the wall beside her. His foot connected with her abdomen, and when she swung, he twirled to one side, his fist striking her across the face. Nose bleeding, her stomach cramping, Zusa lifted her daggers and tried to smile.

"Come on," she said. "You can do better."

The elf's face was painted in a smoothly blended mix of blacks and grays, making his brown eyes shine in the contrast. He grinned, his white teeth vibrant compared to the black of his lips.

"A skilled human," the elf said. "Still, nothing compared to us."

He looped his sword through an intricate display designed to confuse her, but she did not watch the blade, only the movements of his arms and the positioning of his legs. When he tensed, ready to lunge, she fell backward through the shadows of the wall, reappearing on the other side of the entryway. As his sword hit the wall hard enough to create sparks, she leaped at him. Her knees rammed his back, her daggers puncturing his soft leather armor.

"If you insist," she hissed into his ear as she twisted the blades.

Zusa let him go, and as the body collapsed, she fought a wave of dizziness. Traveling through shadows would not be something she could rely on, not with how drained it left her afterward. She wiped her wrist beneath her nose, and it came back sticky with blood. *Broken*, she thought. *Wonderful.* Her abdomen still ached, and deep within the dungeon, the sounds of conflict lessened.

One elf down. Six more to go.

Seeing their skill, and having heard the contempt in the elf's voice, she was convinced the rest would expect no attack from the entrance. Surprise was her best weapon, perhaps her only real chance against them. She ran through the dungeon, and at the very first intersection, she saw dead guards leading every direction.

Shit.

There were three main wings to the dungeon, and Alyssa might be down any of them. She was certain the elves had broken up to investigate all three, which left her with no time to think, only react.

She ran straight ahead, hoping they'd placed Alyssa in the same cell they'd placed Haern. All around her, the prisoners made a ruckus, most seeming amused by the slaughter of the guards they'd witnessed.

"You're dead, girl!" one cried as she passed, and her heart jumped into her throat, for before her were two elves hurrying along, each one checking the cells on their side for Alyssa. The cry didn't grab their attention, and with all her fury she crashed into the pair, her daggers slashing like the claws of a wild beast. She focused on just one, knowing if she got greedy and failed to kill both at once, it'd leave her outnumbered, and therefore dead. Blood spilled across her hands, and she kicked the corpse away so she could fight.

The remaining elf was a woman, her hair pulled behind her and tightly braided. Blood ran from her forehead, the lone cut Zusa had managed to score after killing the other. The elf wielded a long, curved blade in one hand and a dagger in the other, the two weaving through the air in perfect tandem. Zusa refused to back down, nor be intimidated by their speed. Compared to Haern, the elf was actually slower, and unlike Haern, her blades did not both have a longer reach.

Zusa fell into a rhythm, blocking and parrying for a good ten seconds. She saw the other woman grow confused, as if baffled Zusa could even stand toe-to-toe with her. Zusa chose that moment to strike, slipping between a dual-thrust that she'd parried wide to either side of her. But the elf fell back, and her swords sliced back in, so Zusa did the only attack that would still hit: a snap-kick to her face. The blow momentarily stole her balance, and Zusa dropped to one knee and swept out the elf's feet from underneath her.

Instead of landing hard, perhaps knocking the wind out of her lungs, the elf woman was already rolling. Zusa's daggers missed flesh, hitting only stone. Swearing, she chased after. The elf pulled out of the roll, landed softly on her feet, and met her charge. Four blades danced, parrying and blocking in a blur creatable only by the best. But Zusa would be better. She had to be. In her heart, she thought of Alyssa and what the elves might do. The fury gave her strength, and when she stole the offensive, she hammered away at the elf's blades as if they were mere playthings in her way. The elf tried to flee, but Zusa would not let her. Sensing her hesitation, she feinted, then took out her knee with a solid blow from her heel. As the elf fell, Zusa crosscut, tearing open her throat.

Elven blood poured across the cold stone.

"Alyssa?" Zusa called out as she staggered toward the end of the hall. She came upon the same dark cell Haern had been in, and in the thin sliver of light, she saw it empty. Her heart sank. She had guessed wrong. Running back toward the entrance, she prayed that somehow she would make it in time. She didn't care if Karak heard or if Ashhur answered. It didn't matter. Alyssa mattered. The cell doors flashed by, the jeers and catcalls only distant groans of insects to her.

Back at the initial intersection, she saw them, four elves hurrying in tandem. Slung across one of their shoulders, bound and gagged, was Alyssa. Their backs were to her, but they must have noticed the other elves' absence and were on alert. One turned to face her, his painted face glaring as he readied his long blade. The other three shouted something in Elvish and ran toward the exit.

"Did you kill Celias and Treyarch?" he asked in the human tongue as she readied her daggers.

"Don't forget whoever was at the door," she said, flashing him a smile that felt born of mania and desperation.

His face hardened in the dim torchlight. "I'll make sure your death is painful."

He lashed out, an upward swipe that passed an inch away from her face, cutting strands of her hair. This elf was faster, and she felt slower, her battle lust fading. Zusa retreated, but the elf matched her step for step. Her daggers batted left to right, blocking his smoothly connected strikes. His sword was a blur, and she had to fight to keep herself focused. *No time for this*, she thought, but already defeat clawed at her mind. The elves would escape, and Alyssa with them. She'd failed.

The elf backed her into a corner, and she felt the heat of a torch burning beside her head.

"You ended lives that walked this land for hundreds of

years," he said. "No greater sin poisons this world than that of your kind."

His sword danced, and she was a poor partner. Without room, her dodges were limited, and his speed incredible. Any time she countered, he'd leap back, slap the weapon aside, and then lunge, relying on his greater reach. With every passing moment, her exhaustion ebbed away at her reflexes. He scored cut after cut, and at least once she saw him purposefully twist the blade to the side so it did not embed into her flesh.

The elf was mocking her, covering her body with a dozen gashes. The insult was too much. She weakly slumped back against the wall, tears in her eyes.

"Just end it," said Zusa.

The elf frowned, obviously disappointed. He closed in, the tip of his blade aiming for her throat. No comment this time, no biting words. The muscles in his body were tense, and death was in his eyes.

When he thrust, Zusa parried it to the left, letting out a cry as the tip slashed across her cheek. Her other hand reached out, and he moved to dodge, but she wasn't stabbing with it. She was throwing. The dagger hurled true, piercing his side. It wasn't fatal, but the delay was enough. She yanked the torch from the wall and swung. He blocked, but the fire was in his eyes. She swung again and again, always toward his face. At last she let it drop, and she could see his pupils dilating. In that brief moment as the torch fell, when his vision would be all spots and shapes, she closed the distance between them, wrapping her free arm around him as if in an embrace. Her other rammed the blade of her dagger through his ribs and into his heart.

She let him drop, then spat on his corpse.

"Never talk to me of sin," she said.

Zusa looked to the exit, to where the starlight shone on an empty walkway. Guards would be there soon, but they would not catch the elves, nor would they catch her. She ran.

Haern woke to the sound of his door opening. He looked up, the sleepiness in his head vanishing at the sight of Zusa standing there, her wrappings cut and torn, seemingly every inch soaked with blood.

"Zusa?" he asked, stumbling out of bed.

She took a limping step closer, then collapsed into his arms. "They took her," she said.

"Took her? Who? Alyssa? Who took her?"

Her fingers clawed against his chest, and her whole body shook. At first he thought it was weakness, maybe from blood loss, but when she looked into his eyes, he realized it was rage struggling to break free.

"The elves took Alyssa," she said. "They'll kill her. I know it. They'll kill her, but I'll make them pay. All of them, this whole damn city, will pay in blood."

He held her close, and she pressed her bruised forehead against his chin.

"I don't care if this city burns," she said, her voice suddenly softening. "I just want her back. Please, that's all I want. Without her..."

Haern wrapped his arms tighter about her, and she felt so small then, so close to breaking.

"We'll find her," he said. "All's not lost yet. We'll find her, save her. I promise."

She pulled away.

"Don't make promises you cannot keep," she said, beginning to undress. "Now help me bandage these cuts, and quickly. If we're to act, we have little time to spare. There's only one place the elves would take her."

"Where's that?" he asked.

She gave him a look as if he were a simpleton. "To their forest," she said. "They'll take her to Quellassar, and once there, not even the greatest army of man could save her from their blades."

CHAPTER

19

Alyssa awoke in the middle of the act of vomiting, her stomach heaving while her abdomen tightly cramped. Vertigo came next, the ground seemingly above her. Closing her eyes, she realized she was slung over someone's shoulder. Soft whispers in a language she assumed was Elvish came from either side of her. Daring to open her eyes once more, she saw they were running. With strange glee she noticed she'd vomited on her elven captor's boots.

When she tried to look up, she felt pressure on both her neck and her wrists. They were tied together, she realized, with an intricate knot. Testing, she tried pulling her wrists apart, only to choke off her next breath. Struggling would be useless. Trying to relax, she looked up as much as she could without strangling herself, in the vain hope she'd recognize her surroundings. But there were no nearby buildings, no distinguishable landmarks. Instead she saw hills, and grass, and the occasional cluster of trees.

Her heart sank. The elves had captured her from her prison, knocked her unconscious, and then smuggled her out of Angelport. Whatever safety she might have known in her cell, it was gone.

"Where are you taking me?" she asked.

The elf tensed, and the sickening motion of his running halted. The ground pitched before her, and then she hit, having been unceremoniously dumped to the grass. She rolled over, forced to sit on her hands since they were tied low and behind her back. Three camouflaged elves gathered about her, two men and one woman. Their faces were painted in various shades of blacks and grays, their clothing dark and loose. They'd pulled off their hoods, though, and there was no mistaking the point of their ears.

"You have no right to ask questions," said the one who had carried her. He was the tallest of the three, with long golden hair stretching to his waist.

"Why not?" she asked, knowing she had to get them talking if she were to have any hope.

"Does the butcher tell the pig where it's going on the way to the slaughter?" asked the female.

"I am no pig."

"I know others who might disagree."

The third elf snapped at them in Elvish, and the two fell silent. He was shorter than the female, with emerald eyes that were mesmerizing to behold. Alyssa tensed as he knelt before her and grabbed her chin with his fingers, tilting her head so she would look directly into his face.

"You are to be granted an audience no human deserves," he said. "We will let you kneel in the presence of our princess and hear her pronounce judgment against you for your crimes. You sent your pet after her, but we are no fools. We know the evil that lurks in mankind's heart. Others may be naïve enough to seek peace, but we are not. You will die, Alyssa. Your corpse will be burned, so perhaps your ashes will foster life in our forest to atone for your betrayal."

He leaned closer, as if he were about to kiss her.

"That is, if we do not send your head back to the lords of Angelport so they know Celestia's children will no longer suffer their foolishness and greed."

Alyssa swallowed, and every bit of contempt her position had fostered over her lifetime surfaced to protect her with a strong mask. "If your princess would be so foolish as to execute me, then prepare to be the last of Celestia's children. War will follow, and make no mistake, your race will not survive."

He gently cupped her cheek in his palm and smiled. "Strong words," he said. "Strong, hollow words. Stand up."

Slowly she obeyed, grimacing at the aches in her lower back and legs. Stealing a glance behind her, she saw the fading lights of Angelport at least a mile in the distance. She tried not to let her disappointment show at being so far away. Still, no matter the distance, Zusa and Haern would find out about the break from the prison and come looking for her. The question was, would she still be alive by then?

The elf with emerald eyes slashed the rope that bound her ankles tightly together, but left the others.

"Run away if you wish," he told her. "I would gladly accept a reason to kill you."

Instead Alyssa stood as straight as her bonds allowed, refusing to let them defeat her in any way.

"Lead on," she said. "I do not fear your princess, nor any fate she decrees."

The tall elf laughed, and the female grabbed the severed rope at her feet. She looped it about Alyssa's neck and then held the end. "Come, dog," she said. "Stand proud if you wish. You will still arrive on a leash."

They led her farther from Angelport, toward a copse of trees that appeared to be growing around a pond. Every noise made Alyssa tense. Every shadow she hoped was Zusa peering out from the darkness. The rustle of leaves and grass in the wind was the Watcher's approach. Yet on and on they walked, and no one came. As they neared the copse, Alyssa realized the pond was nothing but an illusion, and with each step it faded away, revealing a large tent built behind a roaring bonfire.

Several elves stood around it, but one in particular caught her eye. It was Laryssa, sitting beside the fire in an elegant dress. In the yellow light, Alyssa could see the bruises fading from her face, as well as a bulge in the side of her slender dress, no doubt from her bandages. Her skin had faded, looking pale and sickly. Alyssa's heart ached seeing such damage. To see a beautiful woman of noble birth beaten and marred in such a way felt vile and against all proper order of things. She could understand their anger as they led her toward the fire, but that did not change her mood. Her life depended on maintaining her composure and convincing them of her innocence.

"Greetings, Lady Laryssa Sinistel," she called out as the light of the fire reached her skin. "I heard you'd returned to Quellassar. Consider me both surprised and pleased to be a guest in your presence, as you were once a guest in mine."

By the way Laryssa's face twitched, she could tell the comment stung. Alyssa knew much of mankind's traditions in court and nobility were based on the elves' own culture, and to appear inferior in any way insulted their sensibilities.

"Remove her bonds," Laryssa ordered. "She poses no threat and must still give her testimony before I pass judgment."

Alyssa stared at her as the elves cut her free. Absently she rubbed her throat, which felt raw from contact with the rope. Glancing at herself, she saw her dirty, torn dress, the same she'd worn since being taken from the temple days ago. No doubt she looked the pauper amid the finely dressed elves. Even those who had captured her, in their leather armor, appeared more prepared for a pleasant evening than she did.

Laryssa asked one of the elves something in her native tongue, and when given the answer, she frowned. Alyssa could only guess the reason.

"Do you know of a woman with dark skin?" Laryssa asked. "Her hair is black, cut short, her body wrapped in strange clothing. One of your servants, perhaps?"

Alyssa wondered why they asked but knew she couldn't risk lying. The elvenkind were known for their excellent skill at detecting lies, and beyond that, she had no idea what magic might be cast about the camp. Every lie she spoke might let out a great plume of smoke for all she knew.

"The woman you describe sounds like a companion of mine named Zusa," she said. "Why do you ask?"

Again Laryssa spoke with the three who had brought her. Her frown deepened.

"Because she appears to have killed four of my warriors. Your crimes against me only grow, Alyssa."

"No doubt she thought she was protecting me," Alyssa said. "Indeed, what else might she have thought when elves come at night, break into a human prison, and drag me across the land for a secret trial? I have sworn no allegiance to you, Laryssa. Only to the king's justice do I bow, and only he may administer it. You have no authority here, not in our lands, and not with one of the king's citizens."

This caused a stir among the elves, and more puzzling, she saw that it was not just anger at her words. A spark of hope burned in her chest. Could it be there were elves, even in this dark court, who actually agreed? Rarely were humans unified in thought when it came to anything. Surely it made sense elves were the same, even if to a lesser extent. More than anything, she wished she had learned their language. Her old advisor had suggested it many times, but she'd shrugged him off, not seeing the point. Listening to the fluid words all about her, she now saw otherwise. Too late, of course. That tended to be how those things went.

"We have tried finding justice in your courts," Laryssa said, ending the argument. "Just as we have tried for peace. Ingram hanged men he claims killed Sildur, but I know he only guesses, only hopes we accept such a petty token. Angelport is sick with betrayal, rife with anger, and ruled by cowards and greedy men. No, out here, in the wild, we will pass our judgment and have our justice. You may not accept any court other than your king's, but your crimes have gone beyond the human realm and into ours. As for your war..."

Laryssa stood, leaning heavily on her chair. Despite the shaking of her arm, she let it go and stood to her full height without aid. Looking down at Alyssa, she shook her head.

"We do not fear the blades and fires of man. We are Celestia's children. My father walked the land when your gods first breathed life into the dust, creating such imperfect servants. We saw you come from dust and will still be here when you return to it, having learned nothing, accomplished nothing. Only destruction. It is all you humans know."

All about her, the elves cheered, and whatever hope Alyssa had dwindled and died. She was not on trial, not anymore. There in the starlight, she stood representing the crimes of all her race. Her innocence didn't matter. Her words of defense would not change anything. The elves wanted blood for Laryssa's wounds and for the others killed by the mobs. Random lowborn peasants hanging from ropes would not satisfy them. They wanted the highborn, the nobles. Someone whose death would matter. Someone like Alyssa.

She prayed her execution would be swift, and without pain.

"Look at me," Laryssa said, stirring Alyssa from her thoughts. "I heard the words whispered to me as I lay dying, a bag over my head. I saw the eye drawn in my own blood beside me in the dirt. You sent the Watcher after me, your little pet from Veldaren. 'This is what happens when you turn on your friends,' he told me. What further proof do I need? Was your anger truly so great, all because we would not risk our lives for you?"

Alyssa stood tall, refusing to be humbled, regardless of her attire or the filth of the dungeon caked to her skin.

"When the mob attacked you, I was in hiding at a temple of Ashhur. I did not send the Watcher after you. Even now, you are manipulated by the fools you so openly deride. Do you think you would have lived if I had sent the Watcher? Do you think he'd be so foolish as to leave his mark? You believe the lies you hear because you desire vengeance, and I fit every falsehood you put upon my kind. You want to believe us betrayers, murderers, a race without hope, without redemption. Even those who helped you might turn on you—that's what you want to believe. You need it, all so you can justify the bloodshed you wish to create."

She turned and spat, knowing full well how great an insult it was to do so in front of their princess.

"I will have no part of it and will accept no blame. I never betrayed you. It was you who betrayed me. I never struck against you. It was you who came after me, killing all in your way. I have tried to prevent warfare, yet you have courted it with every word you speak and every arrow you fire. Execute me if you wish, but I die innocent, and the war you so desperately seek will destroy the last hope of peace between our kind. Go on, Laryssa. Kill me. Let me see the hatred, ignorance, and bloodlust in your eyes so I may know elf and man are alike in every . . . single . . . way."

The camp went silent. She could sense the mood about her, and it had turned decisively cold. A sarcastic smile tugged at her lips, and she truly could not care. For so long she had helped the elves, trying to find a compromise that would benefit the Trifect while minimizing the loss of life. If they wanted to kill her for it, then so be it. Her heart ached for Nathaniel, and she wished to hold him in her arms and say good-bye, but the world was a cruel place. She'd learned that long ago, sitting in her own father's dungeon, shivering in the cold.

"On your knees," Laryssa said. When Alyssa refused, two elves approached, grabbed her shoulders, and forced her to obey. One of them tugged her hair so she would lower her head respectfully.

"Alyssa Gemcroft, I find you guilty of your accused crimes. You have struck against my kind, inspired mobs to riot, and nearly took my own life. You deserve a lengthy execution, but because of your rank, and your past cooperation, I will give you a painless death."

The elf with the emerald eyes drew his sword, the blade sliding smoothly out of the oiled scabbard. Pulling back on her hair, he lifted her up so she might face Laryssa. The keen edge of his sword pressed against her throat, and all around her, the elves held their collective breath.

"Do you have any last words for me to pass on?" the elven princess asked. "A final good-bye to your son, perhaps?"

Alyssa winced at the pain from her pulled hair.

"No good-byes," she said, catching sight of movement just beyond the ring of elves. "Not yet."

Zusa leaped from behind one of the trees, and before the other elves could react, her dagger pressed against Laryssa's throat. All around, elves drew weaponry and reached for bows, but Laryssa cried for them to halt.

"That's a smart girl," Zusa whispered into the elf's ear. "Now let Alyssa go before I start cutting."

"No," Laryssa said. Alyssa felt the sword against her throat turn, angling sharper into her flesh. Blood trickled down the blade. "Once she is safely away, you will kill me."

"I will kill you if she stays. This is not a negotiation."

Alyssa could feel the tension, so thick it made breathing feel difficult. Zusa's stealth had been perfect, her plan simple enough, but it seemed Laryssa had no intention of playing along.

"I am not alone," Zusa cried to the others. She pulled the princess closer, one arm holding her head, the other positioning the dagger. "One false move, Laryssa dies, and you will face the Watcher."

"You will suffer for this," Laryssa said. "I am no hostage to be taken. Release me, or Alyssa dies."

Zusa looked to the elf who held Alyssa, addressing only him. "If Alyssa dies, I lose my employer. If Laryssa dies, you lose your princess. I wonder who will suffer more when we return to our homes?"

"Do not listen to her," Laryssa insisted. "We have given in to their fear for too long!"

Alyssa could sense the uncertainty of her captor. He pulled harder on her hair, but the sword no longer cut into her skin. Zusa's eyes swept the camp. They were badly outnumbered, and while holding Laryssa kept them from attacking, so far it had not bought her and Alyssa an escape. The threat of fighting Haern seemed to have carried little weight as well.

A far cry made Alyssa jump, and pain streaked across her throat, the blade giving her a shallow cut. She wished to turn and look but could not. Instead, she heard a body drop, and then Haern speak.

"He was to release an arrow," said the Watcher. "A bad decision."

Haern on one side, Zusa on the other, with Alyssa caught in the center. Both sides were eager to fight, but neither was willing to risk the death of their hostage. She tried to think of a solution, but could not. Part of her just wanted them to flee, to live. She saw no way for them to escape alive. But she didn't need to.

"Laryssa!"

She recognized that voice. Storming into the camp came the ambassador, his face livid. He shouted something in Elvish, turning and berating many of them at once. Laryssa said something in argument, but Graeven didn't even let her finish. He turned to Alyssa and bowed.

"Forgive us this horrible travesty," he said. "I can assure you, these elves do not represent Quellassar in any way."

"I find that hard to believe," Zusa said.

"If you wish to live, you must. They will not harm you, but first you must let Laryssa go."

Alyssa looked to Zusa, who shrugged. The emerald-eyed elf started to object, but Graeven shouted him down in their language. Again he bowed low.

"Please, Alyssa. You must trust me. There is no other way out of here alive."

Alyssa swallowed and, praying she was making the right decision, she ordered Zusa to let the princess go. Laryssa hurried away and collapsed into the arms of another elf. Blood seeped from the bandages in her side, the red staining her dress. Meanwhile, the elf holding Alyssa tensed, but Graeven lowered his voice and spoke with undeniable authority. The blade left her throat, and she felt the pressure on her head disappear as he released her hair. She accepted Graeven's offered hand.

"Come with me, all of you," he said, glancing at Zusa and Haern. "Don't worry... we won't be followed."

The last comment seemed more directed to Laryssa, who openly glared at the ambassador. Zusa slid in beside her, grabbing her hand as they rushed along the green countryside.

"I am glad to see you well," she said.

Alyssa allowed herself to smile. "Me too."

Haern moved to the other side of her, constantly turning his head so he might watch the elven camp.

"Too easy," he said, as if in doubt of their escape.

"You're right," Graeven said, leading them on a path toward the main road running south into Angelport. "You are only safe in my presence. The rest will hunt you, rest assured of that."

"How is it you may overrule the demands of a princess?" asked Alyssa.

"Because she was ordered to return to Quellassar and leave all dealings with humans to my discretion. If Laryssa disobeyed and caused a war, then she might have faced potential banishment if there was enough uproar about it."

"Would there be?"

Graeven spun, fast enough all three tensed. "Make no mistake," said the elf. "Doing this puts my reputation at great risk. I requested your release under terrible pressure, and my objections are well known to the rest of our nobility. There are many who believe your death will avert a war, and they question where my loyalties lie. You are safe in my presence, but the moment I am gone, they will take their justice knowing there is little I can do to punish them."

He turned and continued on.

"Ingram has refused handing you over because he knows the recent riots will be nothing compared to the fury he would face should word reach the commoners. Many of my colleagues in Quellassar have taken a similar hard line and will march upon Angelport if that's what it takes to bring their desired justice. Whether you deserve it or not, you've become a focal point, a symbol of human aggression against elvenkind. More will die until Ingram regains control of his city, and my own people acknowledge the truth staring them in the face."

"And what truth is that?" asked Haern.

The ambassador turned and gave him a look Alyssa could not decipher.

"That we are fading," he said. "Our rule over Dezrel has long ended. Our numbers dwindle, and every day the power of man tightens around our borders. Already one of your kings chased the Dezren elves across the nations and burned their beloved city to the ground." Graeven shook his head. "One day, those same torches will come for us. I must do all that I can to prevent that, or at the least delay it. I will not see those I love perish in such a way. I will not let the tragedy at Dezerea happen again."

They reached the road, and Alyssa joined Haern in looking behind them.

"You won't see them," Graeven said. "But they are following, I assure you. We have little time."

"There must be something I can do," Alyssa said. "Some way to prevent all this."

"There is." Graeven looked to Angelport. "You disappear. My people will look, of course, and they'll believe Ingram has you in hiding. Still, that gives me more to work with than if my kind knew for certain you were in his custody. Ingram will do a fine job accusing us of lying in return, since we broke into his dungeon. That alone will be a fine mess to explain. But so long as you remain a mystery, I believe I can keep things from worsening."

"We need to return to Veldaren," Haern said, his hands resting on the hilts of his sabers. "Only there will you be safe, Alyssa."

"No," Graeven insisted. "You will never make it. They'll watch the roads and track you with ease. A dozen arrows would pierce your body long before reaching Veldaren. Come with me to Angelport. I know a place you may hide, and the city walls will delay them long enough for you to disappear. And, if we're blessed, we might even discover whoever it was who *did* attack Laryssa."

Alyssa chewed her lip, and she looked at the other two. Haern shrugged, and Zusa put a hand on her shoulder.

"Do what you think is right," she said.

Thinking of that tense moment in the camp, and how the ambassador had defused it, she nodded. "Lead on," she told Graeven. "And let us pray to whatever gods might listen that we find a way to save us from war."

Graeven smiled, and he bowed low. "Of course, milady," he said. "Follow me."

CHAPTER 20

At the Port and Loan, Warrick Sun met with the last surviving members of the Merchant Lords, taking count of casualties and losses. Their meeting table was overloaded with strong alcohol as they toasted and drank. No one cared it was hardly an hour past sunrise. It was not a time for sobriety.

"I am fortunate enough to have my wealth forever on the water," said Warrick, leaning back and resting his hands in his lap. "Madelyn's mercenaries burned my home, but that is no sore loss. A shame about my paintings, though. Those commissions were not cheap."

"I'm sure Arren wished he had gotten away so lightly," Stern said, downing another shot. "You see what they did to his body? Gave him a damn necklace made of his own guts. Fuckers. Glad I gave as good as I got when it comes to killing."

"That is because you have a demon's luck," said Durgo

Flynn. "I lost five ships to their fire, and many good crewmen. But I did not have the Wraith fighting to protect my home."

A stir spread through them, merely at the mention of the Wraith's name.

"Demon's luck?" asked Stern. "I stumbled upon my brother's corpse in a bloody alley, a week after attending the funeral of my only daughter, and you'd accuse me of a demon's luck?"

Beside him, Flint Amour shifted uncomfortably.

"We ran when we saw the mercenaries coming," he said. "Not much we could do. They killed my brothers as well, all of them."

"Yes, I'm sure," Stern said, rolling his eyes. "Mighty convenient, that."

Flint flushed and focused on drinking instead of responding.

"There is that strange business, the Wraith's aid," Warrick said, scratching at his nose with his wrinkled hands. "He has struck at us before, yet now he protects us, despite our ineffective bounty on his head? What game does he play?"

"Well, if it is a game, I'd like to join." Stern hurled his cup against a wall, just above the head of a servant. "We lost hundreds of thousands of gold coins' worth of supplies, homes, plus two of our lords, yet Ingram does nothing. Madelyn's sitting safe behind her walls, and our lord won't do a damn thing to bring justice."

"Justice in Angelport has always been brought about by our hand," Warrick said, doing his best to be patient. Stern was usually more levelheaded, but the loss of his daughter, and now Ulrich, had left him raw and unpredictable. "And we still have many fighting men at our disposal. If we had known of Madelyn's attack in advance, we would have crushed them at our gates. Alas, she was one step ahead, but we cannot let that happen again. We must remove her as a threat, but how?"

"She's got too many mercenaries left for us to assault her mansion," Stern said. "And any attack we make risks bringing the city guard down on our heads. Gods know Ingram would love the excuse."

"Our riots have left him frightened," Warrick said. "They served their purpose. One false step, and we will have him supplanted as ruler, the city delivered to us by the hands of its own people. He will not interfere."

Durgo stood, striking the table with an enormous fist. His surprising outburst, contrary to his soft-spoken nature, left Warrick more annoyed than anything.

"We must act like cowards no longer," Durgo said, glaring at all of them. "Damn Ingram, damn Madelyn, damn the whole city. It is time we stopped fearing their reactions, their plans, and do as we please. Madelyn needs to die, regardless of what Ingram thinks. I say we gather who we have, then attack. We'll hang her body at the docks and let every lord and noble see what happens when they oppose us."

Slow, mocking applause met his speech, and they all turned to see a hooded figure enter the dark room, a grand smile on his face.

"Well spoken," said the Wraith. "Brave, but stupid, just as I've come to expect from you Merchant Lords."

Stern bolted to his feet, his hand falling to the hilt of his sword. Durgo armed himself as well, though Flint stood perfectly still. Warrick felt only tired amusement at the attempted grand entrance.

"You," said Flint, sounding terrified. "How did you get past the guards?"

The Wraith hopped atop the round table, crouching down as he grinned at Flint. "I killed them, of course."

"We want no trouble here," Stern said, tensing.

The Wraith shifted his way. "Strange, given that amusing bounty you placed on my head. Are you still upset about my killing William? His replacement, while young, seems far more competent. I thought you'd be happy for the improvement."

Warrick knew he'd be furious at such a statement made against his own father, but Flint just sat there looking sick. So much for the bravado, he thought. At least William wouldn't have pissed his pants staring face-to-face with a murderer. The others had been happy to see William go, but they had never truly seen William's strength, his ability to make deals without his pride getting in the way.

"Why are you here?" Warrick asked. "I'm too old for games, and not foolish enough to believe we stand a chance should you wish us dead. Now speak, or draw your blade."

Wraith bowed, and Warrick held in his smile. The man wasn't there to kill, after all. If it came to deals, then who in Angelport was better at making them than him?

"Luckily for you I am not much for wasting time, either. Your plans for revenge are amusing, I must admit, but they are irrelevant. Madelyn Keenan is not your worry. Lord Ingram is."

"He's got armored men," Stern said. "Well trained, with many of them killers and thugs long before adopting his standard. Even with our forces combined, we cannot yet challenge him, especially without a valid reason to do so. King Edwin will be furious at us deposing one of his appointed lords."

The Wraith's grin grew. "You simple men with your simple ideas. I don't want you to overthrow Ingram. I want you to save him."

Stern's brow furrowed, and Warrick tilted his head to one side and tapped his lips.

"How so?" he asked.

The Wraith hopped down from the table and walked over to one wall, which was decorated with a painting of the docks, the waters full of majestic boats and tanned men hard at work.

"Tonight, a large group of elves will launch an attack against the city," he said as he looked the painting over. "Don't worry about your walls...they're already inside. They'll kill everyone in Ingram's mansion, in his dungeons, and they'll come hunting for you as well. This is their last desperate attempt, a hope to win a war before it even starts."

Warrick leaned back in his chair, his hands pressed against his chin as the gears in his head began turning.

"Why come to us?" Stern asked, glancing at the others as if to gauge their opinions. "And why would we help Ingram?"

"My affairs are my own," the Wraith said. "And I come to you because the elves must not win. Prepare your forces. Prepare for battle! Let them find an ambush waiting for them, instead of fat merchants and helpless servants. Otherwise..."

He pulled something from his pocket, rubbed his fingers together, and then touched the painting. Fire spread across the canvas, consuming the docks and turning the boats to ash. The Wraith turned back to them, his grin looking demonic in the red light.

"Fight them. Kill them. Or watch every last remnant of your wealth burn."

"Thank you for this warning," Warrick said, slowly standing. "You have given us much to think about, and discuss."

The Wraith bowed low. "I aim to help," he said. Shooting one last grin at Flint, he headed for the door. Just before leaving, he turned back. "Oh, and should you cooperate, I have a fine gift for you, one I'm sure you'll appreciate. I'll give you an hour to discuss, then return for your answer."

With that, he exited the room, having never once drawn his

sword. Immediately the tension lessened, and Stern plopped back into his seat. The others looked about, as if unsure what to say.

"Well?" Stern asked, throwing up his hands. "Do we trust him?"

"He's killed too many," Durgo said, shaking his head. "Lies are not beyond him."

"No," Warrick said. "I think he's telling the truth."

Stern nodded, and despite his apparent frustration, he seemed to agree.

"The elves know of our insistence on receiving portions of their lands. When they're done with Ingram, they'll come for us. Should we prepare and do what the Wraith says?"

Warrick's wrinkled face stretched into a smile. All around him, he saw the others take notice of the sparkle in his eyes, the sheer amusement at manipulating one who thought himself above all manipulation.

"As he says?" Warrick shook his head. "Oh no, not quite."

Darrel sat in the back of the tavern, his beard soaked with spilled ale. He was in no mood for cheer or talk, and his glare made that clear to several women who drifted over. Any other day, he might have taken one or three back to his ship...

"Damn it," he muttered, spilling his mug when he reached for it. As the liquid splashed across the floor, he realized a man had joined him at the table.

"What in Karak's name do you want?" Darrel asked.

"A sober man to talk to," said Stern, frowning at him. "Though it appears I hope for too much."

"Fuck off."

He waved for one of the wenches to bring him more, but Stern's look sent them back to the bar, leaving Darrel dry and unhappy.

"We have matters to discuss," Stern said. "And I'd prefer you keep your attention on me, not your mug."

"Far as I know, you don't give me orders," Darrel said. "That was your brother. How's the fellow doing, anyway? Oh, that's right. He's dead. Bastard. Did he leave the ship in my name? 'Course not. I got no gold and no crew, all because he wanted us here to fight instead of doing our damn jobs and sailing out with cargo."

"Much of Ulrich's belongings are now mine," Stern said, leaning back in his chair. "That means I can give you back the *Ravenshade*, if I felt it a wise decision."

Through Darrel's alcohol-clouded mind, a realization forced its way through. He straightened up and decided that just maybe he should be a bit nicer to Stern.

"Been on boats since I was nine," he said, trying to wipe ale from his beard, a hopeless task. "I know my crew, my boat, and every trick the seas can throw at me. You won't find yourself a better captain."

Stern's smile was full of condescension, but Darrel tried not to show he noticed.

"Have no worries—the *Ravenshade* is yours," Stern said. "But first, there's something you must do for me. My brother trusted you, and you never betrayed him. I'm hoping I might be able to trust you as well."

"These lips stay sealed," Darrel said. "I don't even mutter secrets to my whores. I'll forgive plenty, but oathbreakers deserve to be strung up by their toes and beaten with rods. You want something done, I'll get it done."

Stern scratched at his neck and looked him over. "Perhaps," he said, motioning over a serving wench.

Darrel grinned as two large mugs were set before them, both frothing at the top. "So what is it you need?" he asked as he took one into his hands. "Special cargo? Message delivered? A body to vanish?"

Stern smiled. "I have someone I need you to kill."

Ingram paced the halls of his mansion, muttering to himself. "Where is that damn elf?" he wondered aloud.

"He may not come at all," said Yorr, lounging in a chair with a bowl of cherries on the table beside him. After each one, he'd spit a pit out and place it atop the fine polished oak.

"He should! He's their ambassador, and his elves broke into my prison and slaughtered my guards. Graeven should be right here, on his knees, ready to kiss my ass from sunrise to sunset."

Edgar leaned against the wall opposite Yorr, his arms crossed over his chest. "If he doesn't, perhaps it means the elves have chosen war."

Ingram looked once more to the door, his patience wearing all the more thin. "They wouldn't," he said. "Not yet."

Edgar shrugged but said no more. Yorr continued eating, and Ingram finally gave in and poured himself a stiff drink. Halfway through downing it, he saw the door creep open and a servant stepped inside.

"Ambassador Graeven of the elves desires an audience."

"About time. Bring him in."

Moments later the door flung open, and in stepped the ambassador. He looked surprisingly harried, at least for an elf. His robes were wrinkled, and strands of his hair hung out of place over his face. He bowed low, his easy smile seeming to belie his appearance.

"Greetings, milords," he said. "I wish I could come to you under better circumstances."

"I imagine so," Ingram said as Yorr stood and pushed away

his bowl. "I have no time for bullshit, so please, what reason can you offer for elves climbing my gates, killing my soldiers, and kidnapping my prisoners?"

Graeven sighed, and he crossed his hands behind his back. "A small faction of elves are not happy with the way our delegations have gone, and I cannot blame them. They took it upon themselves to bring Alyssa to trial."

"You admit it?" Yorr said, sounding stunned.

"I admit nothing. I only speak the truth. Their actions do not represent all elves, nor the prevailing opinions of Quellassar. I assure you, I am as appalled as you are."

"I'm sure," Edgar said, running a hand through his curly hair. "Do you know who these elves are? Will you give them to us for punishment?"

Graeven shifted uncomfortably. "They have been sent back to the Quellan Forest and will be dealt with accordingly."

Edgar laughed, and Ingram shared in his contempt.

"Of course," Ingram said. "You'll send murderers of my guards to Quellassar for your own justice, all while demanding Alyssa be handed over instead of undergoing a trial here. We humans tend to be imperfect, but at least we haven't mastered hypocrisy as well as elvenkind."

Graeven shifted closer, his frustration obvious on his face. "I understand, I really do, but I am doing the best I can under the circumstances. Given the mob's brutal killing of Laryssa's escort, antihuman sentiment is rather high."

"You've killed plenty more with your arrows," Yorr said. "Every day we get families traveling here in hopes of finding a better life, with work that doesn't involve your patrols butchering every farmer and woodcutter that sets foot in your forest."

"Killings that would stop if you would only reach an agreement with us and stop pressuring for large allocations of land!"

Ingram put his back to the elf to calm down, and he refilled his glass. "Then what about Alyssa?" he asked. "Will you be returning her to my protection?"

"I would if I could."

Ingram turned, not at all surprised. "Why can't you?" he asked, his voice dripping with contempt.

"I cannot say, other than that she is safely within Angelport's walls. I am doing this for her own protection."

"Like shit you are," Yorr interrupted. "You're using her somehow, aren't you?"

The door cracked open, the sound slicing through the tension.

"Uh, milord," said the servant, looking nervous. "I... please, if you would bring your attention to the docks. I feel it best you take a look."

Ingram raised an eyebrow, but the other two lords only shrugged. He walked over to the curtains across one of the windows and pulled them open with a heavy string. Sunlight flooded in, and from their high perch, they overlooked the docks below. Ingram's mouth dropped open at what he saw.

"What in blazes is going on?" he wondered aloud.

Nearly every last boat in Angelport, regardless of its size, had left port. The sea was full of them, but instead of sailing northeast to the lost coast or west for Ker, they remained close, as if keeping some sort of strange vigil. The few boats remaining at port had been set aflame, and the smoke blotted the sky.

The rest joined him at the window, Graeven included. He peered out, wearing a deep frown.

"Whose boats were burned?" he asked.

"It's too far to know," Edgar said. "What game is this, Ingram?"

"I don't know," Ingram said. He shot a glare at the elf. "What about you? Care to illuminate us with your fabled elven wisdom?"

Graeven shook his head. "I... this is unexpected, to say the least. I can think of only two things. Either they expect an attack or plan on making one themselves."

Ingram ground his teeth, the sight of all those boats in the distance filling him with fury.

"Get out," he told the ambassador. "Go back to your elves. Let them know I will declare war in the name of King Edwin Vaelor against the Quellan Kingdom should even a single elf make another aggressive act against my city. I don't care what reason you give me or how many apologies you make. You've tried our patience, and were you any other kingdom of man, we'd have already sent troops marching to your borders. This is your last chance for peace. Do not waste it. As for the Merchant Lords..." He nodded toward the ships. "We obviously have much to discuss. Consider their claims against your lands dismissed. I want no concessions, no repayments. Just stop the killings. We still need to work something out over our loggers, but that can come another time. I don't want war. I mean that, I really do. So for once, listen to me, and do what I ask."

Graeven looked stunned for a moment, then smiled and bowed. "Thank you," he said. "I'll do my best."

When he was gone, Ingram slammed a fist against the window and refused to look at the docks. "What do we do now?" he asked.

"I'm still not quite happy with what I just heard," Edgar said, frowning. "Do you know how many of my villagers those elves have killed? Yet we're going to make peace without even an apology?"

"Enough! We worry about my city first. Warrick and his merchants look like they're about to launch a damn revolt. I couldn't care less about a few backwater villagers. Now again, what do we do?"

"We flee."

Ingram and Edgar gave Yorr looks of complete shock.

"Could you repeat that?" Edgar asked.

"I said we flee." Yorr gestured to the grand window. "They have their men gathered, their boats ready. If Angelport is a fruit, they're the worm that's eaten its way to the core. We must get out of their reach. They have no real armies, no proper training. If given a month to prepare, I could summon several thousand armed men ready to fight, and I know you can do the same, Edgar. It doesn't matter what the merchants do. When we return, we'll crush them to pieces, take their boats, and end their threat once and for all."

"Are you mad?" asked Ingram. "You want me to run like a coward?"

"A rebellion of peasants and merchants is no light thing," Yorr insisted. "Send word to Veldaren and to all the lords in the north. An uprising of commoners against our rule is a threat to us all and must be stamped out with due urgency."

Edgar took a step closer, his whole body tense. "You want us to flee," he said. "Abandoning the crown jewel of the sea and, with our tails tucked between our legs, go begging for aid from the king?"

Yorr shrugged. "If you want to put it so indelicately, yes."

Another step.

"And how much did the merchants pay you to say that?"

Yorr raised an eyebrow, and his confusion only worsened when Edgar drew his sword. Before another word could pass his lips, the sword thrust through his throat. His body convulsed, and blood splashed across them both, dripping down to stain the floor. A twist, and Edgar pulled the blade free, wiping the edge clean with a cloth from his pocket.

Ingram watched it all with his mouth hanging open. "Have you lost your damn mind?" he asked, shocked.

"That man was practically begging for us to commit treason," Edgar said, sheathing his sword. "King Edwin has given you the Ramere to rule, and Angelport as its seat. To abandon now and let those merchants take over? I don't care if they rule for a day, or a month, or a year while we prepare. That humiliation will end us, all of us, and it cannot happen. We stay, and we fight. The words Yorr spoke, they were what the Merchant Lords paid him to speak. I'd risk my life on it."

Ingram glanced at the corpse, then nodded. "You're right. How many men do you have with you?"

"About a hundred trained soldiers."

"Bring them here." Ingram hurried toward the door, and he began calling out for the captain of his guard. "When they land their boats, we'll be ready. I want every person at our disposal here, at the mansion. I don't care how many ruffians they've given a sword. They'll break against our walls."

"And the rest of the city?"

Ingram shrugged. "It can burn for all I care. When they've tried, and failed, to take over, we'll come storming out. We'll seize their boats and hang every last Merchant Lord from their ankles. While we're at it, we might even have a few rough words with Madelyn, given her own failure in dealing with them. These families, these merchants and lords of coin and trade, they've all pretended at power for too long. With your help, we'll take it all back."

"Of course," said Lord Edgar, bowing low. "I'll begin immediately."

CHAPTER

21

Haern sat restless in the single-room home Graeven had brought them to, nestled into a quiet section of Angelport against one of the inner walls. Inside it were plain, barren walls and a dirt floor that always seemed to be wet no matter the time of day.

"I did not think you would provide us a place to stay," the elf had told Alyssa as they sneaked inside during the cover of night. "I had a human on friendly terms with us procure it for our use. When you agreed to house us, I felt it best to keep this place in case something went wrong."

"Something did," had been Alyssa's only response.

The windows were covered with curtains, leaving the interior dark despite the midday sun. They'd had little to eat, just a small loaf of bread Haern had purchased at the market. None of them seemed to have any real appetite.

"It's painful to sit and wait," Zusa said from her position sprawled out across the only bed. Alyssa sat at the foot of it, looking very tired. She wore a fine dress of elven make, a shimmering silver to replace her dirty, worn clothing from the dungeon.

"What else is there to do?" she asked. "Ingram would imprison me, the merchants would kill me, and the elves would send me off for trial and execution. We'll wait and see what Graeven can figure out."

"I don't like relying on others for your survival," Haern said, peering out the window to the dull street. The curtain felt scratchy between his fingers, as irritating as his own mood. "We should get you out of Angelport, tonight."

"Graeven said they'd track us."

Haern shrugged. "I'm scared of no elf, and I doubt Zusa is either. We're about the best bodyguards you can have. With just the three of us, we should make it back unnoticed."

Alyssa lay down on the bed, Zusa sliding over to make room. With her hand across her eyes, Alyssa sighed.

"I know. You're right. I need to be back in Veldaren, where I can deal with Madelyn appropriately. I miss my little boy too. Let's at least wait for Graeven. I will not disappear to leave him worried, nor repay all his kindness with such insult."

Haern shrugged. "If you insist." He stood and reached for the door.

"Where are you going?" Zusa asked.

"Out."

He kept his sabers hidden within his cloak, his head low and his hood removed so he appeared like every other poor, tired worker of the city. At first, Haern didn't know where he wandered; he just let his instincts guide him. At one point, he'd promised the Wraith he'd investigate the city to learn its secrets, but there was nothing particularly striking or secretive about it. Everyone wanted power. Everyone wanted everyone else crushed underneath their heel. Even Alyssa wasn't completely innocent, though her intentions seemed more noble than the norm in this wretched city.

To his surprise, when he stirred from his thoughts, he found himself staring up at the meager temple to Ashhur. His anger came and went, and despite himself, he entered. Logan was at the door, and he started to greet him until he saw Haern's face. His skin paled, and he dropped the cloth he'd been using to clean the floor.

Haern held a finger to his lips. "Not a word," he said. "Go to Nole's room, lock the door, and do not leave for an hour. Understood?"

The young man swallowed, and he nodded rapidly.

"Good."

Logan scurried toward the back of the temple, with Haern following. Beyond the benches, at the altar, Nole knelt, his head bowed in prayer. Normally interrupting such a private act would have bothered him, but Haern had no patience for the man's piety, not this time. As Logan went rushing past, Haern hopped onto the bench beside Nole and leaned his weight on his heels. At the noise, the priest opened his eyes and looked up. His reaction was hardly any better than Logan's.

"You," he said, startling bad enough he fell to his rear. "Please, no, don't kill me."

Haern felt as if ice flowed in his blood, but at the same time, he felt so tired, so drained, that he could not muster the anger he thought the man deserved.

"Tell me," he asked instead. "Do you sleep well at night?"

Nole was breathing heavily through his nose, and he glanced around as if unsure whether the question was a trick.

"No," he admitted. "Not since . . . you know."

"You betrayed us?"

Nole swallowed. "Yes."

Haern stared at him, as if trying to see through the robes, the fear, and his own anger, to the man underneath it all.

"Why?" he asked. "We trusted you."

"Logan told me of the bounty," Nole said, sighing. "I thought if I sold those acres, I could rebuild this temple into something magnificent. Something people would feel proud to enter. And there you were, supposed criminals. All I had to do was turn you in."

"You'd rebuild your temple with blood money?"

"Don't you understand? Look around. This place is empty, broken. Every day I pray to Ashhur, yet all I feel is isolation. The weight of a whole city lies upon me, and for once, just once, it seemed like I saw a way through. I did it for the souls of thousands, Haern! What does one little whispered word to a guard matter when compared to eternity for so many?"

Haern's fists clenched. "You'd break your trust and profane Ashhur's ideals, all to serve him?"

"Are you any better? I've learned of you, heard the stories spoken since you came down to join us in Angelport. You keep the thieves in line in Veldaren. You kill to prevent killing. Whose blood is on my hands? Whose lives did I end? Yet I see it in your eyes—you are ready to draw that blade and cut my throat."

Haern did feel that urge, but instead he shook his head. "This city deserves better than you."

Nole chuckled. "In that, we are in agreement."

As Haern headed for the door, he stopped and turned back to the priest. "Did Ingram give you your acres of land?"

Nole shook his head as he slowly rose to his feet. "No, he did not. What of you? Have you brought Veldaren any peace? Or does death and killing still plague its nights?"

Haern wished he had a better answer, but instead thought of the dead child he'd given to the gravekeeper. "No. Innocents still die."

Nole gestured about him, to the empty hall of worship. "We're not men meant to sleep well through the night," he said. "For whatever it is worth, I wish I could take it back and that you'd forgive my moment of pride. Even if I could haul in the rarest marble and hang the finest silks from the ceiling, it'd still be just me, preaching to a small few in my weakness. I'm the failure here, and not the finest of constructions will hide that."

"Then why continue, if you have failed so poorly?"

"Because maybe I'll at least save one life," Nole said. "That makes this all matter, right? Besides... there's no one else who will."

Haern put his hand on the door, and the weight of the temple's silence was heavy on his shoulders.

"At least in that, I understand," he said, and then he left, feeling no better than when he'd arrived. Turning toward the south, he froze, for billowing smoke met his eyes. He felt his throat turn dry, and he clenched his fists as he stared at the boats pulling out from the docks, all but those that burned.

"What madness is this?" he wondered before sprinting through the street. Under normal circumstances, men and women should have been rushing toward the water to aid in putting out the fires, but circumstances were far from normal. Between the riots, the hangings, and the attacks on the Merchant Lords' mansions, it'd left the people in fear, kept them in their homes while Haern rushed as fast as his legs could carry him.

The wood planks of the docks thudded beneath his feet as he neared the last boat still yet to catch fire. Several men stood beside it, hurling torches and splashing oil from thick buckets.

Haern drew his swords as he saw the symbol carved into the side of the bulkhead, recognized it as belonging to the Keenan family. *So the Merchant Lords are finally retaliating*, he thought as he descended upon the men.

Only one cried out in alarm, the rest too busy with the burning. Haern stabbed him through the gut, twisted the blade, and then yanked it free. As the body fell, he leaped upon the remaining three, cutting and slashing before they could realize they were even under attack. Two fell quickly, but the third he left untouched. The man, bare-chested and deeply tanned, pulled out a heavy knife and did his best to slash at Haern. Clumsy thrusts, Haern barely even noticed them. Instead he pitched one way, then another, using the confusion to slash across the man's wrist, disarming him.

Two kicks to the face left him dazed, and a slash to the ankle took him down. Haern fell atop him, sabers pressed against his throat.

"Where are they going?" he asked, his face inches from the other man's.

"Not telling you shit," the man said.

Haern pressed harder, drawing a drop of blood. "You die like the others if you don't. What are your friends planning? Do they hope to return later, like some conquering army?"

The man laughed despite his obvious pain. "Army? You got it all wrong, you freak. We're not the ones coming to fight tonight. We're just getting out of the way."

Haern stood, removing his weight from the man, though he kept the tips of his blades pressed against the man's neck. He felt dread building in the pit of his stomach, but he asked the question anyway.

"If not your masters," he asked, "then who? Whose army comes in the night?"

The man spat blood to the plank beside him, glared upward, and then gave him his answer.

When Graeven returned, Alyssa's heart immediately dropped at the sight of him. The elf looked flustered, and in a great hurry.

"What's wrong?" she asked, sitting up on the bed so her back rested against the wall.

"It is nothing," Graeven said, but it was an obvious lie.

"Then what 'nothing' bothers you?" asked Zusa, who had begun doing various training stretches to keep herself from going stir-crazy in the small room. Meanwhile, the elf was rifling through one of the few shelves, removing a few personal objects Alyssa didn't recognize.

"The merchants have...done something interesting, and I must try to deal with it accordingly. They launched all their boats from the harbor, burning what few belonged to the Keenans."

"What does it mean?" Alyssa asked.

"I don't know, and I need to find out. Please, stay here tonight. I have a feeling it will not be safe for anyone."

He glanced around. "Where's the Watcher?"

Zusa shrugged. "Out."

Graeven went to Alyssa, and he grabbed her hands. His were soft, and she could feel the sweat on them.

"Please," he insisted. "Promise me you will stay. Your safety is now my responsibility, and I do not want to bear the shame of something happening to you, especially with all I have gone through."

Alyssa tried to decide how to respond, especially given her precarious situation.

"I will," she said. "Only because you have been so kind. Good luck, Graeven."

The elf smiled. "I won't need your luck, Alyssa."

He bowed and then left. Zusa came up behind her and wrapped her arms around her as they stared out the window.

"It isn't safe," the faceless woman whispered.

"Here, or leaving?"

"Both."

Alyssa sighed. "I know. But what else can I do? No wonder Laurie had such trouble keeping things in line here in Angelport. I have done no better. I never should have made my coming here a secret. I should have marched down with a thousand men and killed anyone who moved against us. It seems everyone here has their guards, their mercenaries, and their fighting men. What do I have?"

Behind her, Zusa laughed. "You have me and the Watcher. Are we so terrible?"

Alyssa put her hand on Zusa's. "No, but I'd rather lose a thousand fighting men instead of you."

The door opened, and Haern stepped inside, his face locked in a scowl. There was blood on his boots.

"Something wrong?" Alyssa asked, stepping away from Zusa.

"The docks," he said. "Every boat's fled, except a few belonging to Madelyn Keenan that were burned."

"We know," Zusa said. "Graeven told us."

"Did he tell you *why*?"

Alyssa shook her head. "I can only assume they're planning—"

"They're planning nothing," Haern interrupted. He drew a saber, showing them the blood on it. "I ambushed some men left behind to start the fires. The Merchant Lords have no attack planned. Instead, they're making sure they're safe on the water when the bloodshed starts tonight."

Alyssa knew what that meant, but she had to ask, had to hear it out loud. "Safe from who?"

Haern's scowl deepened. "The elves. Tonight, they'll make their move."

The room they hid in suddenly seemed so small, the area of the city far less safe than it once was. Alyssa wrapped her arms about her, and she thought of the chaos that would follow.

"Surely they lied to you," she said. "If the elves kill Ingram, it'll be war the moment King Edwin hears of his death."

"He wasn't lying," Haern said. "And it might be war already. Something this brazen? What can we do?"

Zusa gestured to her daggers, lying sheathed upon the floor. "We can stop them."

Haern looked to her, then nodded.

"I don't know what hope we have," Alyssa told them. "And I don't know what you think of me, or my reasons for coming here, but believe me when I say we must save the hundreds of thousands who might die because of their actions this night. Do what you can, the two of you. Save us from ourselves."

They readied their weapons, donned their cloaks, hid their faces, and then vanished into the streets of Angelport, where the sun was beginning to set.

CHAPTER

22

Gregory stood at the wall surrounding the mansion, his hand on his sword hilt. It remained in the scabbard, but he liked the assurance of knowing it was there, felt comforted by its cold metal touch. At some point that night, he'd get to use it.

"Think those merchant bastards will be foolish enough to attack?" asked the man next to him, a large but gruff guard named Turk. Refusing the standard-issue sword, he kept a large ax on his back, which he claimed was a family heirloom.

"I hope not," Gregory said. "Don't make much sense otherwise, though. They sailed off and burned those ships. They got to know we won't go easy on them when they land, no matter what they say."

Turk scratched at his beard. "Maybe. But we're ready. Why would they attack when we're ready?"

Gregory shrugged. Everyone had been assigned a squadmate

to fight with and protect each other's back. Turk was Gregory's. He'd been happy about the situation, given how solid a fighter Turk was. But he wasn't much for thinking or stimulating conversation.

"Maybe because they think they'll win no matter what?"

Turk laughed. "Well, they're stupid, then. Look how many we got."

Indeed, thought Gregory. He glanced about the exterior of the mansion. The outer city walls were left with just a skeleton crew, and nearly every guard who had ever lifted a sword had been called in to protect Ingram and his home. A thousand men in various amounts of armor crowded the grounds, with at least a hundred patrolling the outer walls. The fine grass had been trampled into mud, the gardens crushed beneath mailed feet. Many windows were boarded up or otherwise occupied by archers. Around the corner, at the gate where the fighting would be most vital, waited Lord Edgar's men, armed and trained, numbering over a hundred.

From Gregory's position, the wall blocked their sight of the harbor. Still, they'd hastily constructed ladders over the course of the day, and one of them had been given to the pair. Climbing up the three steps, Gregory peered over the wall to the distant harbor.

"Still not moving," he said. The boats were large shadows on the moonlit water. As he watched, he heard cries of alarm west, and he glanced in that direction. Far off, near the main entrance to the city, a building had somehow caught fire.

"What's going on?" Turk asked from below.

"There's a fire."

"Well, that's bad. We going to put it out?"

Gregory shrugged, but he doubted it. Within a minute, orders came hollering out from the mansion, and various captains repeated them. No one was to leave. It'd be up to the peasants to put it out themselves. Gregory was hardly surprised. From what little he knew of Ingram, the man would be content to let the city burn, so long as he survived. Of course, there was the question of who had started the fire...

Smoke blotted out the stars as another fire began, this one closer to the center of the city.

"Shit," Gregory muttered.

"What now?" asked Turk.

Gregory stepped down so the man could look for himself. Seeing the fire, Turk swore long and loud.

"You live near there?" Gregory asked.

"No. Worried that's the Nag's Head they burned down. Spiteful little fuckers. That's my favorite pub. The folks rioting again?"

As smoke drifted higher, this time from a third location, Gregory began to wonder, as did many of the men circling the mansion.

"The boats still out there?" he asked.

Turk looked that way, then nodded. "Sure are."

"Then what in blazes is going—"

He stopped as cries of alarm sounded from the opposite end of the compound. His hand instinctively reached for his sword, and he tensed, looking for enemies.

"What's going on?" asked Turk, twisting on the ladder.

"Quiet," Gregory said, trying to figure it out. More shouts, plus a shriek of pain. They were under attack.

"How'd they get back?" Turk wondered. "The boats are still out there."

He suddenly jerked backward, losing his footing on the steps. Down he fell, landing hard on his back. Gregory was at his side in a heartbeat, wincing at the thick arrow shaft embedded in the guard's chest.

"Bloody cunts," Turk said, glaring down at the arrow. "They shot me."

Outside the wall, chaos erupted. The men on patrol screamed in pain, and the sound of steel on steel rang loud. The men gathered at the gates drew their blades, and cries of warning came from all directions.

"We need to get you inside," Gregory said, reaching to remove Turk's armor so he could better see the wound.

"To the Abyss with that," Turk said, slapping his hand away. "I ain't dying to no *elf*."

Elf? Gregory stepped back, and when Turk snapped the arrow shaft in half, he realized its peculiar make and how much longer it was than their own. Almost in denial, he hurried up the rungs and peered over the wall.

Over thirty bodies lay scattered across the ground, nearly all of them city guard. Twenty more guards remained standing, but they were surrounded and with their backs to the wall. Fighting them was a squad of fifteen elves, their faces and hands painted in camouflage, their long, curved blades slashing through armor as if it were cloth. One in the back noticed him watching, and he pulled a bow off his back. Gregory ducked, and as the arrow flew over his head, he could hardly believe the sheer speed of it.

Suddenly their walls and numbers seemed so insignificant.

"Can you stand?" he asked, offering his hand to Turk. The man took it, and he grunted loudly as he got to his feet.

"Hurts," was all he said when Gregory inquired.

Shouted orders came in, demanding they form up. Gregory understood the necessity. Weight of numbers was their only advantage against such an enemy. From that brief glimpse, he knew they would not win skill versus skill. Turk was unable to run, so they hurried toward the front gate as all around them the city guard did the same.

Halfway there, he heard the clatter of metal. Glancing back, he saw a rope hurled over the wall, a heavy grappling hook attached to the end. In seconds elves were vaulting over the fortification with ease.

"Move!" Gregory shouted, pushing Turk along. They joined a formation of about fifty, all men who had fled the walls. Gregory drew his sword, and Turk readied his ax. A captain cried out for them to hold, to stand firm, and Gregory did his best as ten elves raced toward them. They were in no lines, no formations, just a brazen, lightning-fast attack in hopes of catching them unprepared. Bracing himself, Gregory swore not to run. Not to panic. High above, bolts rained down upon the battleground from crossbowmen at the windows. As if the elves could read their thoughts, they weaved side to side, avoiding nearly every one.

"Stand tall!" shouted their captain. "Fight like men, you bastards, and cut them all down!"

The numbers were in their favor, and against any other opponent, the fight would have ended in moments. The elves, though, twisted and pushed through their formation in a blur of steel and blood. As one neared, Gregory held back and let Turk slash with his ax. The elf ducked below, and as he twisted to stab Turk in the side, Gregory lunged. His blade hit flesh, and he let out a whoop. The elf turned on instinct, tearing open the hole in his side further. Roaring, Turk swung his ax, and the injured elf could not dodge in time. The heavy blade tore through his shoulder, splitting him like a log.

"Back!" Gregory cried. Turk heard and obeyed, flinging himself toward the side of the mansion. An elf's blade missed, and the attacker pivoted to charge again. Turk got his ax in the way to block the first hit, but the second slipped beneath and into his side. Praying it wouldn't be fatal, Gregory flanked the elf, thrusting for his spine. Instead, the elf weaved back and forth, blocking and parrying both ax and sword with stunning speed. Gregory tried to match it, but he found himself unable to position his blade correctly. What was supposed to be a killing thrust turned into a weak chop, and the elf suddenly lunged at him, smacking the attack away with ease. Defenseless, Gregory tensed, his left arm pulling up as meager protection.

The elf jerked sideways, then fell, a crossbow bolt lodged in his neck. From one of the windows above, he heard a crossbowman cheer. Turk drove his ax into the dying elf's chest, just to be sure.

The elves pulled back, their sudden retreat leaving the remaining thirty guards off balance and unsure. Of the initial ten elves, six remained. In similar smooth motions, they pulled the bows off their backs, drew arrows, and fired. Gregory turned sideways to minimize himself as a target, but they were not aiming his way. They were aiming at the windows. Two volleys later, the guards finally had the sense to rush forward, before the elves could turn that deadly accuracy on them. Gregory tried to be on the front line, but Turk took a few steps before staggering. Refusing to leave him behind, he stopped, one eye on the fight, the other on his squadmate.

"Goddamn arrow," Turk muttered before coughing up blood. He fell to one knee and would not stand, despite Gregory's help.

Glancing back at the fight, he watched the elves cut down the initial wave. Without their firm lines, the guards had even less chance of victory. Gregory felt his heart sink as he watched discipline waver, then break. Those who turned to flee found swords stabbing into their backs. Even worse, coming around from the back of the mansion were at least twenty elves, linking up with the six and shredding through the remaining human forces.

"Get into the house," Turk said, shoving Gregory away. "You got a chance there."

"I'm not—"

"Now!"

Turk backhanded him, and that was enough to finally make Gregory let him go. Looking once more to the broken lines, he knew he alone could do nothing to help. Saluting Turk, he ran toward the front gate. Behind him, Turk managed to stand, and he lifted his ax defiantly as the elves came rushing by. Gregory refused to watch the ensuing execution, and he hoped the giant man might find plenty of fun in whatever world awaited him after.

Bodies littered the ground as he hurried, and he felt strangely alone on the battlefield. Reaching the door, he found the majority of the city guard gathered together, at least two hundred. They had spread from the gate, for the elves had avoided it entirely. The gate itself, though, was open, and the sight horrified Gregory to no end. Lord Edgar's men, the trained soldiers meant to anchor their defense, were nowhere to be seen.

"Where's Edgar?" he cried as he joined their ranks.

"Fled, the little bitch," said their captain. "How many?"

Gregory nodded behind him. "Twenty-five, maybe thirty."

"Shit."

Elves appeared from both sides, Gregory's twenty-five, and another forty from the other direction. Outnumbered by the human forces four to one, they should have been easy prey, but instead the city guard tightened their lines and prepared for a slaughter.

"Be brave," several shouted, but when the elves readied their bows, Gregory knew they were in a dire situation. Break ranks and charge or suffer the arrows. Either way meant death. This time the guards held their ground, and the few with shields did their best to protect the rest. Arrows flew in, deadly accurate. Volley after volley hit, until the elves were out of ammunition. Their opponent's ranks softened, they drew their swords, cried out in their native tongue, and charged.

Gregory had never considered himself a man afraid of death, and as the elves came rushing in, he tried to remain true to that. He stood on the front line, and he braced himself to swing, trying to guess the timing instead of reading his opponent, since he'd seen how near impossible that was with the elves' speed. When he swung, he struck air, but not because his timing was off. Instead, the area before him erupted in a chaos of gray and red cloaks. The elven charge faltered, for a pair of enemies had landed amid them in an explosion of blood and gore. Not willing to risk losing such a huge advantage, Gregory rushed forward, barely aware he was screaming at the top of his lungs.

The rest of the guards followed, and they slammed into the elves with wild abandon. Many of their attacks were parried or blocked, but they were a wave, and even as one fell, two more surged forward with blades already swinging. Gregory managed to cut down one too focused on dodging a man to his right. A second turned on him, kept him at bay with a shallow thrust, then tried to flee. One of the unexpected allies, a woman with a red cloak and strange, tightly wrapped clothing, dove upon the elf's back, her daggers shredding flesh.

Gregory had no idea who she might be, but as the other slipped through their lines to aid the opposite side, he saw the man's garb and knew him.

"The Watcher?" Gregory murmured aloud. Without thinking, he followed. The woman remained and seemed to have that side under control. The other, however...

The Watcher dove into where combat was at its thickest, seemingly unafraid of the flailing weapons and press of the elves. His sabers twisted and danced, cutting down elves who were yet unaware of his arrival. He tore through the city guard, like a phantom come to their aid. When he finally reached the elven lines, he let out a cry. Gregory followed, knowing the cloaked man was their only hope of survival, and he was far from alone in thinking so. The rest of the guard rushed ahead, and though the elves cut them down, the Watcher formed their spearhead, and because of it, they did not break. They did not falter. Gregory kept to the Watcher's back, hoping to help where he could, but usually just finishing off opponents the man left bleeding on the ground.

Without any signal he could hear, Gregory saw the elves initiate a full retreat. He let out a whoop and held his weapon aloft. With their speed, he couldn't hope to chase, and it seemed the Watcher had no desire to either. He turned, and from what little of his face Gregory could see, he was smiling. Of the initial two hundred men, a third remained, but they'd held.

Gregory looked to the mansion, wondering how the people within fared. At a window, he caught a glint of light, then camouflage. His smile vanished. Without thinking, he dove forward. The arrow struck him in the chest, and he let out a gasp. As he hit the ground, the rest of the guard took up shouts, their heavy footsteps rushing into the house, where elves had no doubt entered through the windows and back entrances. Gregory felt a reflex to cough, but the pain was too incredible, and he forced it down.

The Watcher leaned over him, and he mouthed a question Gregory suddenly couldn't hear. Gregory tried to speak, to tell him that it was his life the Watcher had saved from the Wraith all those nights ago, but the words were silent on his tongue, his muscle spasms beyond his control. His vision darkened. Not long after, he left to join Turk.

As the fires spread, Madelyn watched from the window of her room, sleeping Tori clutched to her chest. When the door opened and she saw it was Torgar, she had to bite her tongue.

"Our walls are secure," he said, leaning against the door frame. "It seems we are not their target."

"Nor should we be. Laurie helped them, after all. We do share a mutual enemy in the Merchant Lords."

Torgar grunted. Madelyn refused to look at him, instead staring out the window. She rocked Tori a few times, trying hard not to show unease at the huge mercenary's presence. When he didn't leave immediately, she turned and glared.

"Do you have something you wish to say?" she asked.

"I do, not that you'll listen. The merchants pulled out all their ships, and no doubt got their fighting men with them. You know what'll happen, don't you? The elves will kill Ingram, and with him dead, those boats will sail back in. Just like that, we'll have a new ruler over Angelport. How long do you think we'll survive once that happens?"

Her anger grew along with her panic. How dare he try to frighten her so?

"They won't dare," she insisted. "The king would be furious at them for—"

"The king will be told the elves did the killing," Torgar interrupted. "And anyone who might say otherwise, anyone like you and me, will find themselves missing a head."

"No," she said. "Ingram has many men at his disposal. They won't kill him—I know it. The elves will lose, and then they'll pay for their foolishness, as will the merchants for such cowardly behavior."

Torgar shook his head, and his voice hardened as his patience ended. "Even if through some miracle Ingram survives this night, he'll still want to know why we didn't help. Why we stood here and hid while the lord of our city fought for his life. Either way, you risk the noose. We *must* go out there. Let me take half our men. If the battle's close, we might be enough to turn the tide. The fate of Angelport will be decided tonight, and we cannot remain here and do nothing!"

"We can, and we will!" Madelyn snapped. "I am lady of the household, and you will do as I say. I control the Keenan fortune, not you. All you have is...guesses. You know nothing. You're a stupid mercenary, more drunk than sober!"

Instead of getting angry at her outburst, Torgar only grinned. "You seem to forget a few things," he said. "Speaking of which...have you named me godfather to Tori yet?"

She instinctively clutched the babe tighter. "I've had my advisors begin preparations," she said.

"No," Torgar said, shaking his head. "No more stalling. I want it done now. Tonight."

"Tonight?" she asked, looking at him as if he were out of his mind.

"Yes," he said, his grin slipping. "Tonight. Unless you want me to start telling stories to my men."

Madelyn felt acutely aware of how alone they were, with not even Lily there to provide witness. Swallowing, she gave him a nod. "If you insist," she said.

She left the room, Torgar following closely behind her. Downstairs she found one of her advisors watching from a window, and she ordered him to bring her a quill and some parchment. As he was leaving, she caught his shoulder.

"I'll want several of my guards as well," she said. "To provide witnesses."

The advisor gave her a worried look, then nodded. He no doubt knew that the word of those guards would be worthless in any royal court. For her to ask meant she was in trouble. They went to the front parlor, where she found Lily.

"Please take her," she said quietly as Torgar lingered behind them at the door. "Take her somewhere safe."

The advisor returned, carrying both the supplies she requested as well as a group of six guards. They gathered behind him, their hands on their weapons.

"Good, you're here," Torgar said, grinning at them. "Let's get this distraction over with, shall we? Just in case someone decides to climb our walls."

Madelyn felt better with the guards there, and she took the quill and dipped it in the inkwell.

"What do you wish me to write?" she asked.

"The obvious. State I'm the godfather."

She sat on the floor, a hardwood table before her. The light of the torches was dim, and she squinted as she wrote the letters. Normally she'd make an advisor do the work, but she knew Torgar would only accept something written in her own hand.

When finished, she signed it and offered it to the mercenary. He took it, then glanced at the guards.

"Jenson," he said, offering the parchment. "You can read. Tell me what that says."

The guard accepted the paper, tilted it so he might see better, then frowned. "Just says you're charged to protect Tori," he said.

Torgar clucked his tongue and shook his head, taking the parchment back. "Not good enough," he said. "Try again. With loose language like that, someone else might swoop in claiming to be the real godfather. Someone like, say, Stern Blackwater. You wouldn't want one of them Merchant Lords raising Tori, would you?"

Better them than you, thought Madelyn, but she bit her tongue.

"Forgive me," she said instead. "I'm not used to writing such documents."

Torgar chuckled. "Sure thing, milady. Still . . . try again."

This time she wrote the document correctly, deciding she could cancel it at any time. Once the business with the elves and the merchants was over, the troublesome mercenary had to be the next priority. The risk was too great. Signing him godfather and protector of her granddaughter above all others, she gave it directly to Jenson, who read it aloud. Every word the man spoke was like a nail against her spine, but she consoled herself by thinking it was only temporary. It was only a stall until she could regain the upper hand.

"Excellent," Torgar said, nodding as Jenson reached the end of the document. "That'll do."

He lashed out, his fist striking her across the chin. She spun, her head hitting the table on her way to the ground. Spots filled her vision, and coughing, she spat blood from a bleeding lip.

"Guards!" she cried, her voice weak. Looking up through tear-filled eyes, she saw them standing there. Doing nothing. Torgar strode over, no more grins, no more amused expressions. His eyes were cold. She went to cry out again, but he kicked her in the teeth.

"Did you see that?" Torgar said to his guards, and only then did she realize how badly she'd erred. "How about you?"

She tried to stand, but he struck her again, blasting the air from her lungs and robbing her sob of any power.

"It's that damn Wraith again! How'd he get in here?"

Another kick rolled her onto her back. Tears streamed across her face as Torgar leaned down and grabbed her by the hair. "Almost impossible to keep him from killing, ain't it?" he asked.

Behind him, a couple of the guards laughed. Madelyn felt ready to vomit.

"Please," she whispered. "Please, don't do this."

"You have no right to beg," Torgar said, glaring. "Laurie was a good man, a powerful man, and he deserved a lot better fate than what you gave him. Getting his throat cut by his own wife? Fuck. You're lucky I don't let every guard in this mansion have a turn with you for that."

"Please don't hurt Tori," she pleaded, trying not to imagine such a fate. "Please, whatever you do, don't…don't…"

Torgar leaned closer, and when his grin returned, her dread only grew.

"Taras was like my own kid," he said. "I helped raise him better than you ever did. Tori's as much my grandchild as yours. I'll never hurt a hair on her head, so you can die knowing that. I'll teach her, protect her. After all, I'm her godfather…which means until she comes of age, this mansion, and all its fortunes, are mine."

The reality hit her like one of his fists. She tried to cry out, to deny it, but Torgar drew a dagger from his belt and stabbed her in the breast. As she felt blood drip across her blouse, she saw the dagger and realized it was her own. Ash from the fireplace still covered the handle. Her mouth opened and closed silently, and then she collapsed.

Her last thoughts were of Tori, and who she might become with a man like Torgar as her father.

CHAPTER

23

As Lord Edgar's men marched through the barren city streets, forming a protective barrier of shield and blade, Ingram glanced back at his mansion and felt a tug of sorrow.

"It had to be done," said Edgar beside him. "Sailors and ruffians are one thing, but an army of elves?"

Ingram scowled. He understood, all right, but that didn't mean he liked it. The second the attack began, Edgar had hurried into the mansion and found Ingram watching from one of the front windows. His idea had been simple, though on the cowardly side. They'd flung a helmet on Ingram's head, a coat of mail over his chest, and given him a shield. As the elves were scaling the walls, they pushed open the gates, Ingram hidden in the center of the hundred armed men. The city guard had sworn up a storm, but they could not stop them.

"They might keep looking if they discover I'm not there,"

Ingram said, forcing himself to look away from the mansion. He kept expecting it to go up in flames at any moment.

"They can look for only so long before they must flee. Daylight will not be their friend."

The streets were quiet, any man with half a mind smart enough to know that tonight was a night to remain indoors. As fast as they could march, they made for the front gates. Ingram thought Edgar meant to leave the city entirely, and go against his entire treason rant earlier, but then they veered aside, to a path that ended at one of the walls.

"In there," Edgar said, gesturing to a plain-looking home. It had a single window, the glass broken and the back of it boarded up. "You should be safe."

Ingram took a step, something feeling amiss. "Where is this?" he asked.

"A safe house I've kept ever since the Wraith started killing. Hurry. We can't stay in the open for long, else we'll be noticed."

Ingram tested the door and found it unlocked. Pushing it open, he entered the small room. A round table was in the center, a lit candle atop it in a glass base. The fireplace burned bright, casting long shadows across the far wall. At the back, a set of stairs led to the second floor. In one of the two chairs sat a man Ingram did not recognize. He reached for a weapon but realized he carried none, only a shield. He didn't remember forfeiting his dagger. Had it been when they put on his mail?

The door shut behind him, and the sound sent shivers up his spine.

"Who is this?" Ingram asked. "What's going on?"

The man in the chair stood. He was dark-skinned, bearded, with a long scar running from his lip to his chin. He sipped hard liquor from a bottle, while in his left hand he held a long blade.

"Glad to see you're a man of your word," he said, setting the bottle down atop the table.

Ingram pulled the shield off his back, and for a moment he stood there, shaking. The stranger laughed as behind him the door reopened.

"Make it quick, Darrel," said Edgar, his voice suddenly different. It was darker, angrier. "We have much still to do."

The door shut, leaving Ingram alone with the brute.

"Traitor," he muttered, eliciting a laugh from Darrel.

"To you, maybe," said the man, tossing the weapon hand to hand, his grin so big he looked like a child given a cherished present. "But we've been paying him plenty, and for years. I'm thinking he might be the most loyal man in the city."

Ingram lifted the shield, his face nothing but a mask of fear. Darrel slapped at it with his sword, which Ingram barely blocked in time. The big man shook his head, as if disappointed.

"This is going to be way too easy."

When he pulled his sword back to stab, Ingram gave him no reason to think otherwise. But when he thrust again, Ingram launched himself forward. The sword hit the center of the shield and veered outward. Distance closed, Ingram rammed his knee into Darrel's crotch, then followed it with an uppercut with his free hand. The man staggered backward on unsteady legs.

"You little shit!" Darrel cried, grabbing his sword with both hands and swinging. Ingram moved his shield to block, but he guessed too high. The sword clipped the bottom before continuing on, striking his mail shirt. The weapon could not cut through, but the blow knocked the air from his lungs and sent him sprawling into the table. Dropping the shield, Ingram fell to the ground, the killing blow missing and instead embedding a solid inch into the wood. Beneath the table, Ingram kicked out Darrel's knee, and as he fell, he took another shot at the man's crotch, this time with his heel.

The effect was better the second time around. Darrel fell to both knees, and he had to grab the table to remain upright. Despite his trouble breathing, with several of his ribs cracked or broken, Ingram flung himself at the man, wrapping his arms around his neck. The two hit the ground and rolled. In the scuffle, Ingram found himself flung off, with Darrel lying on his chest before the fireplace.

"Stay down!" Ingram said, kicking him in the ribs. Darrel dropped, but he pushed up again. Knowing he stood little chance in a prolonged fight, Ingram crawled closer, then wrapped his arms around Darrel's neck again. Darrel's enormous fists closed about his arms, and they struggled, but Ingram had the better positioning. Inch by inch he lowered Darrel's face, then at the last moment, he twisted and flung him forward. Darrel's face smashed into the burning coals, eliciting a howl that chilled Ingram to the core. It took all his strength to hold the man there for a moment longer. When he released, he scrambled for what lay beside him on the floor: the spilled bottle Darrel had been drinking from when they first entered.

As Darrel rolled himself out of the fire, Ingram took the bottle by the neck, turned, and swung it with both hands. It smashed against Darrel's nose, crunching it inward before the bottle broke against his skull. Alcohol splashed across his face and beard, igniting a few coals that had remained lodged against him. His beard caught fire first, followed by the rest. As the man howled and flailed, Ingram staggered toward the steps. There was no way Edgar would leave the front entrance unguarded, not until he saw a body. But perhaps up top, he might escape…

He climbed the stairs to the second floor. The room was even smaller, the roof slanted in sharp angles. Within was a dresser, a bed, and an open, dirt-covered window. On the bed, as if he'd been waiting for him the whole while, sat the Wraith.

"You lasted this long," the Wraith said. "I will give you credit for that."

His sword lashed out, cleanly slicing through Ingram's throat. He collapsed, clutching his neck as blood gushed through his fingers. Gasping for air, he saw the Wraith lean over, a sad smile on his face.

"I would have saved you from their treachery, Ingram. Truly, I would have. But then you weakened and dared to offer peace. So disappointing."

As he died, Ingram watched the Wraith leap out the window and into the bloody night.

Upon seeing his own kind besieging Ingram's mansion, Dieredon felt torn between loyalty and fury. Surely such a brazen attack had not been condoned by Graeven, nor Neyvar Sinistel. He'd heard of the attempt at the jail, and best he could tell, it'd been initiated by Laryssa. His gut told him Laryssa had done the same tonight. The attack might as well be a declaration of war, something she had no authority to do.

But at the same time, as the humans battled and fired their crossbows, he watched many elves, some he'd known for hundreds of years, fall and bleed out on the grass. The sight was enough to make his stomach sick. He knelt from the rooftop of a nearby home, just barely able to peer over the stone wall.

"This is your doing," Dieredon said, shaking his head. "I won't help you start a war, Laryssa."

He wanted to go but could not. He watched the ebb and flow of the fight, which at first was drastically in the elves' favor, despite their fewer numbers. The humans gathered at the front, for what appeared to be their last hurrah before dying in a blur of elven steel.

But then *they* arrived.

Dieredon had never seen the woman before, but the man spinning and slashing with those sabers could be no one else. His movements were too fluid, his skill far beyond what any normal human could hope to attain. Suddenly things became far clearer in Dieredon's mind. He might not support Laryssa in her attempts at a pointless war, but to see the one who'd nearly killed elven royalty now slaughtering elven troops...

Leaping off the rooftop, he hit the ground and rolled, his long, ornate knives flashing into his hands. He wished he had his bow, but he'd left the enormous thing in hiding outside Angelport, knowing he couldn't carry it around without drawing immediate attention. Still, his knives would be sufficient, despite the Watcher's surprising skill. Not many opponents fought Dieredon and lived for a second encounter.

Despite his speed, Dieredon kept his approach low and hidden, wanting no one, not even the other elves, to know of his presence. Should word get back to Quellassar that he had witnessed the battle and not helped, there'd be many eager to deem him a coward and a traitor. He had no intention of delving into that type of political nonsense. As he was halfway there, smoke billowed out the windows of the mansion, and elves fled from all directions. One side or the other had set it aflame, though Dieredon couldn't begin to guess which. He dove into the cover of shadows as they fled, and he waited.

The Watcher vaulted over the wall in chase, and Dieredon followed him in return. Far down an alley, his target having eluded him, the Watcher slowed. Dieredon did not. Only sheer honor kept him from stabbing the man in the back. Someone who fought with such skill deserved to die in fair combat.

"Watcher!" Dieredon called, mere seconds before he launched himself into an attack. The human spun, his cloaks whipping about. His eyes widened at the sight of him, and Dieredon felt the tiniest amusement at the worry he saw. Even against the Watcher, Dieredon still carried a frightening reputation.

Their blades clashed, and this time Dieredon was prepared for his speed. He settled into an attack routine, keeping on the offense. At last the Watcher tried for a riposte, and Dieredon slid into the opening. His foot shot out, connecting against the human's chin.

"Blow for blow," Dieredon said, grinning despite the horror of the night. Armies of humans might soon march upon their forests, but at least for now he could fight an opponent of equal skill and know the human deserved death.

The Watcher didn't seem as amused. He fled toward a nearby building. Grabbing the side of a low-hanging roof, he vaulted atop it. As Dieredon was about to follow, his finely honed instincts cried out in warning. Instead he dropped back down and spun, his knives already out to parry.

The red-cloaked woman slammed into him, her daggers ringing as Dieredon parried slash after slash. Her speed was nearly equal to the Watcher's, but it was her fluidity that struck him, and as he launched an offensive to ensure she couldn't pin his back to the building, he felt as if he were fighting another elf. Her skill with the daggers, however, was not anywhere as finely honed. He parried a thrust to the side, stabbing with his right hand. She twisted and should have avoided his thrust, but it was just a feint. Instead he closed the distance between them, batting both her daggers outward when she tried to bring them in. Her defenses broken, Dieredon pulled back for a killing thrust.

The Watcher's heels slammed into his shoulder before he could. Sabers slashed the air where he'd been as Dieredon rolled with the blow, then leaped twice to give himself some space. Both the Watcher and the woman faced him, their weapons clutched tightly in their hands. Dieredon tensed, realizing that, skilled as he was, combined they posed too dangerous a fight.

"I have no quarrel with you," he said to the woman.

"Nor I with you," she said, her body slanting lower. "But you're not killing Haern."

She attacked, and the Watcher followed. Her daggers danced like snakes, and Dieredon could only defend against them with just his left hand, for the Watcher assaulted the other side. The elf felt his skills tested as never before, twisting and shifting as his two knives blocked and parried with nearly every movement he made. The woman increased her ferocity, but Dieredon faked a counter, then launched himself at the Watcher. The two intertwined, a chaotic clash of blades, kicks, and punches. Blood flew.

Dieredon rolled away, his chest stinging from a shallow cut. The Watcher fared no better, two fresh wounds bleeding from his left arm. The woman came at him, refusing to give him rest. He blocked her daggers, shoved them aside, and then caught her with his hilts on the way back. As her body twisted with the blow, he kicked out, delivering a satisfying hit to her midsection. She let out a cry as she staggered away. Dieredon took the time to gain some distance between them and catch his breath. The Watcher looked ready for another attack, his legs braced for a leap.

"Why do you hunt me?" the man asked, shifting the angle of his sabers every few moments to ensure Dieredon did not anticipate his next move. "I have never struck at elves before tonight."

"You stabbed Laryssa and left her dead. There will be no courts for you, no lies, only justice."

"Justice?"

Dieredon took advantage of the man's confusion, breaking into a dead run. When the woman tried to intervene, he slide-kicked, forcing her to leap away to avoid his low slash. He rolled once, then kicked out of it with his knives leading. The Watcher was ready, unafraid to meet his charge. Knife and saber collided, the alley ringing with the sound of their contact. Dieredon's arms weaved at the very limits of their speed, and the Watcher met him blow for blow. Each scored another pair of cuts, shallow wounds that would do little else other than bleed.

Again came the damn woman, forcing Dieredon to split his attention. This time the Watcher did not fall for a feint needed to buy him separation. The elf knew he must flee, but the two pressed, eventually linking up side to side as they stabbed and thrust. Dieredon's knives were a twisting blur, viciously slamming away every attempted hit. At last they overextended, and instead of countering, Dieredon tried to run. He underestimated their speed. The woman kicked out a leg, and as he rolled, another foot connected with his sides. He continued until striking a wall, hitting his head hard. As he felt his balance tremble, he stumbled to one knee, still attempting to block the killing blow, but it did not come. Not yet.

"Justice," said the Watcher, sounding very much out of breath. "I never attacked Laryssa, you fool. How is killing me justice?"

"Your mark," Dieredon said, slowly standing. His stomach was doing flips, but he tried to keep a calm façade. "You drew it in her own blood."

"My mark? How do you know that, Dieredon? Who told you?"

The Watcher's apparent confusion left Dieredon puzzled. He'd thought the symbol common knowledge, a well-known calling. What was this man trying to get at before killing him?

"Our ambassador," Dieredon said, refusing to lie. "He said the open eye is yours."

The Watcher glanced once at the woman, and she mouthed the name *Alyssa*. He stood up straight, falling out of his combat stance.

"Listen to me, elf, and listen closely. I have not used that symbol for nearly two years, and when I did, it was hundreds of miles from here, in Veldaren, a city of humans. Here in Angelport, only one man has used that symbol, the man calling himself Wraith. Tell me, Dieredon, how does your ambassador know that eye was first mine? *How does he know?*"

Suddenly it was Dieredon's turn to be confused. Neither the woman, nor the Watcher, looked ready to kill him despite their conflict. Trying to force his mind to work through the pain, he shook his head. No, what they were insinuating...it couldn't be right.

"I didn't come here to cause a war," the Watcher insisted. "I didn't attack Laryssa. You must trust me."

"And why would I dare trust a human?"

The Watcher looked to the distance, and he clearly had something pressing on his mind. "Because I can prove my innocence," he said. He pointed at him with the tip of his saber. "What will it be?"

Dieredon looked to them both, stood to his full height, and then answered.

CHAPTER 24

Haern rushed through the quiet streets as fast as his tired legs could carry him. Not far behind hurried Zusa, limping slightly after the brutal kick she'd suffered. They weaved through back alleys, doing everything they could to maintain a straight path. What time they had was limited, and it might already be too late.

When they arrived at the safe house given to them, Haern paused to gather his breath. Heart in his throat, he pushed open the door and stepped inside. The Wraith leaned against the far wall, his arms crossed. The unhidden lower part of his face was wrapped in a smile. Alyssa was nowhere to be seen.

"About time," said the Wraith. "I expected you here far sooner."

"Why?" Haern asked as Zusa slipped in beside him. "How could you betray us so?"

The Wraith pulled off his hood. When he spoke, his voice

changed, more forceful and deep. "That is such a vague question," said Graeven, pulling his sword off his back. "You'll need to do better."

"Where is Alyssa?" Zusa asked, taking a step forward.

Graeven turned and directed his smile to her. "Such care, such love. You've been an unexpected nuisance, Zusa, but not enough to truly cause any worry. If you want to find Alyssa, she's hanging from a post at the docks. It shouldn't be long before the merchants have her. I doubt her fate will be kind once those ships land... nor will it be very long."

Zusa drew her daggers, and they shook in her hands.

"I thought you wanted peace," Haern said, freeing his own blades. "I thought you never wanted war."

"Ignore the words I've spoken as a politician, Watcher, and think on what I told you in Ingram's prison. This city is wretched, a blight on Dezrel. It's full of hate, murder, and it will only grow worse when Violet floods its streets. I've done what's needed to set things right. Every step I've taken, even as our ambassador, has brought us closer to war. We'll burn Angelport to the ground, all of it. There's still time for you to join me. We do not have to be enemies."

"I need to get to the docks," Zusa whispered, and Haern nodded.

"Go," he told her. "And may Ashhur help us all."

With her gone, Graeven paced before him, watching, mocking. "You won't win on your own," he said.

"I know."

Dieredon stepped in through the open door, knives in hand. Seeing him, Graeven sadly shook his head.

"You've always been incapable of performing the simplest tasks."

"Why did you bring me here?" Dieredon asked. "Why strike

at our royalty? Would you slaughter Ceredon's own daughter to achieve your ends?"

"I never touched her!" Graeven said, anger flaring in his eyes for the first time. "I twisted her tragedy to help my cause, and it sickened my stomach doing even that. As for why... you've lived among the humans. You've seen their destructive behavior, their riots, their sins. Surely you understand what I have done, what still needs to be done. Those who would work for peace, even those with our own blood, must suffer for their delusions."

Dieredon settled into a combat stance, and it was answer enough. Graeven sighed.

"You can't defeat me," he said, pulling his hood back over his face. Shadows enclosed all but his eyes and mouth, and his voice immediately changed. "I've always been the better, but my station has never given me a chance to prove it. Besides, it would have been an insult for me to challenge someone so lowborn as yourself. I'd hoped the Watcher would kill you. Nothing would have given me greater pleasure than to spread word of how your legacy ended at the hands of a *human*."

Dieredon launched himself at Graeven, and Haern remained behind to wait for an opening. The room was cramped, and it'd be difficult for them to fight side by side. Graeven's sword connected with the knives, hard enough to send sparks floating to the ground. The two exchanged hits, and Haern felt a chill crawl up his spine at the sight. He knew Dieredon's skill, having so recently received a painful lesson in the elf's abilities. Yet as the two elves battled, Haern knew who was the better. Graeven had told no lie. He was the superior fighter. His sword weaved and feinted like a true extension of his body. With every stab and slash Dieredon made, he found himself out of position. Not by a lot, and he always recovered or pulled his slashes back to block a fatal blow, but all it'd take was one mistake and he'd be bleeding out on the floor.

Which meant he had to help. When Dieredon fell back, Haern stepped in, his surprise attack as ineffective as he'd expected. Graeven parried it away, forced his sabers up to block what turned out to be a feint, and then brought his attention back to Dieredon. The two exchanged another set of blows, adding a slight gash across Dieredon's arm, before Graeven had to return to the defensive, parrying and blocking their four weapons with his one with amazing skill.

Still, against two powerful opponents in the cramped space, his maneuvers were limited, and Graeven knew it. Just as they were about to corner him, the elf lunged at Haern, startling him with his sudden, vicious speed. Haern failed to parry the sword in time, only shifting its aim so that instead of piercing his heart it slashed across the bones in his shoulder. It stung like the Abyss, and Haern fell away in fear of an onslaught. Instead, Graeven bolted for the door, Dieredon at his heels. Haern clutched his shoulder, forced the pain back into the recesses of his mind, and then ran, all the while knowing he could never match either of their speed. But he had to try.

No matter what, the Wraith had to die tonight.

The salty air stung as it blew against the cuts on Alyssa's arms. That pain was the first thing she noticed as consciousness returned to her. The second was the realization that she hung from the air by her wrists, putting painful pressure on her shoulders and back. Last was of how Graeven had betrayed her far worse than anyone in her life had before. He'd come in the middle of the night, while she'd sat awake atop her bed, unable to sleep.

"What's happening out there?" she'd asked him. In response, he'd smiled, offered her his hand, and then struck her across the face upon accepting it. Two more blows came, and then darkness followed.

Her eyes fluttered open, and she saw the heavy shadows of boats, lit by a few carefully protected lanterns. Fear clawed at her heart as she realized those shadows were growing ever close. The Merchant Lords were coming home to port.

"Help," she cried weakly, hardly a whisper. She struggled against the rope, twisting her body about so she might glance deeper into the city. "Help!"

The second scream was better, but it still seemed weak. Worse than the pervading silence about her was the unnatural quiet that enveloped the city. No one was about. No one would come to save her. Tears rolled down her cheeks. This was it. This was how she'd die. She couldn't begin to understand why the elf had betrayed her, though as the boats neared, she wondered if the merchants had offered him a bounty. Perhaps the elves figured her dying was good enough, regardless of whether it was at their hands or the merchants. Maybe Graeven wasn't as ardent in his belief of her innocence. In the end, it didn't matter.

The only thing that mattered was the cold, triumphant smile on Warrick Sun's face as he stepped down the plank and onto the dock. Armed sailors and mercenaries accompanied him. More boats arrived, and amid the din, Warrick approached. She hung from a heavy post, the rope expertly tied about her wrists so that her squirming only tightened it. The old man cupped her face in his gnarled hand so she would look him in the eye. She made no attempt to hide her revulsion at his touch.

"Aaah, Alyssa," said Warrick. "We have some business arrangements to discuss. I hope you don't mind."

She refused to respond. Men came from the other boats, some of whom she recognized.

"Goddamn," said Stern, shaking his head in disbelief. "I can't believe the Wraith actually kept his word. A fine gift, indeed."

"Cut her down," Warrick told one of his men.

A ruffian pulled out his dagger and began sawing at the thick ropes. When it finally snapped, he caught her, not out of any inclination to protect her from the fall, but just to have a grab at her breasts. He set her on the ground, then backed away. Alyssa pulled her hands free from the rest of the bonds. Trying to be brave, she stood before Warrick with her back straight, her arms at her sides, and addressed him with a firm tone.

"What is the meaning of this?" she asked. "What is it you think you'll gain?"

"We stand to gain much," Warrick said. "Tonight is the night we celebrate our ascension to lords and rulers of both Angelport and the rest of the Ramere. Not just that, though. We'll celebrate the complete and total dissolution of the Trifect."

Alyssa swallowed down her fear. "Killing me accomplishes nothing," she said. "My son still lives, and make no mistake, he will hunt you down and slaughter you all once he comes of age."

Stern backhanded her, looking almost bored as he did it. She spat at him, feeling her cheek already starting to swell.

"Try not to be so shortsighted," he told her.

"What about you?" Alyssa asked. "It's your granddaughter who will eventually suffer for all this, yet you call me shortsighted?"

"She'll inherit sooner than you think," Stern said. "And free of you, Tori's fate will be far better. We'll be her allies now, not you, not the Conningtons. Here in Angelport she'll flourish, free of your influence, free of the games you play in Veldaren."

"What makes you think—"

Warrick cleared his throat to interrupt her, then reached into his coat. From it he pulled out a heavy, unsealed scroll. He offered it to her, and she reluctantly took it. As the rest watched, she unrolled it and read. Written in a careful hand that had to be Warrick's own, the wording was simple, the scroll addressed to King Edwin. In it, she declared that the Trifect no longer existed, negating all trading agreements made with the other members and swearing to make no similar allegiances for a span of twenty years.

"This will mean nothing, not forced at knifepoint," she said. "The others of the Trifect will know, and their wrath will be terrible."

"Terrible?" Warrick asked, and his smile was ugly and full of missing teeth. "Is that so? Come now, who could refute this if key nobles bore witness?"

"What witnesses could possibly matter?"

"The head of the Keenan wealth."

Alyssa's sense of betrayal grew. First Madelyn had tried to kill her, and now she'd shatter the Trifect to pieces, despite the hundreds of years it had existed? Why? What madness had taken over her? She stood there, rubbing her sore wrists, and looked to the streets. Sure enough, she saw a large group of mercenaries coming their way. If only Laurie were alive, she thought. He never would have let something so terrible happen. She expected Madelyn to be amid the group, but she saw only Torgar leading the way.

"Where is Madelyn?" she asked, confused, as Torgar came up to them and bowed.

"Such a shame, that," Torgar said, grinning. "The Wraith killed her, just like he killed her husband. Looks like little Tori's in charge, but I'm her godfather, so I'll be watching over things until she comes of age."

Alyssa's mouth dropped open. The entire Keenan wealth... in the hands of this drunken oaf? What was Madelyn thinking? Dumbfounded, she watched as Warrick took the scroll from her hands and gave it to Torgar, along with a small quill. Torgar signed his X at the bottom, then handed both back.

"We have no need of your help," Torgar said to Alyssa. "You can stay up in Veldaren and rot, same with all the Conningtons. There's far better friends for us down here. Ain't that right, Stern?"

Stern crossed his arms, and despite Torgar's grin, he seemed none too happy with the brute. "I expect Tori to be well cared for," he said. "And we will have much to discuss, you and I."

"Sure thing," said Torgar. "We have all the time in the world."

Alyssa watched it all as a numbness crawled through her mind. It felt as if ice water ran through her veins. With Alyssa's forced agreement, and Torgar's own eager signing, that meant two of the three members of the Trifect were accepting total dissolution. Even if the Connington family could appoint a leader to the household in time to challenge it, there'd be little anyone could do. Everything they'd built up over centuries would collapse. It'd be over, all of it, and the merchants would be there waiting to pick up the pieces.

"We have all the witnesses we need," Warrick said, turning back to Alyssa. "Now will you sign, or must we become more... persuasive?"

They'd torture her, she knew. How long until she broke? Because she would. In time, with enough pain, anyone would. But even knowing that, she could not bring herself to relent. Not to scum like them.

"I won't," she said. "I don't care what it is you've done. I won't sign. My son will inherit a fortune, not the pauper's kingdom you'd leave him with. Consider me rejecting your proposal."

"Stubborn as always," Stern said, gesturing for one of his larger men to come over. "But you'll see wisdom in this agreement. Bind her again, and take her to the water."

When they grabbed her arms and pulled them behind her back, she refused to give them the satisfaction of a struggle. They tied her wrists tight, wrapped the rope about her waist, and then dragged her to the edge of the dock. A heavy blow sent her to her knees, and a foot blasted the air from her lungs. As she lay on the sea-worn wood, she felt the rope wrapping about her ankles.

"Have a good swim," the ruffian said, then tossed her off the pier. She gasped in air before the freezing water enveloped her, shockingly cold. The pressure around her waist tightened, and she felt disorientated as something pulled her upward, but only halfway. Her legs emerged, but her upper half remained below water, and as the air burned in her chest, she clenched her teeth and squirmed. Her skin started to numb, and flashes of color swam across her eyelids. At last she could hold it in no more, and gasped in water. Her insides roiled, and as she gagged and spurted they lifted her up and out.

"So," said Warrick, kneeling at the edge of the dock as Alyssa coughed up icy water. "What do you think of our counterproposal?"

She spoke, but her lips were trembling, her lungs too busy gasping in air to make much noise. Warrick leaned closer.

"What was that?"

"Bastard."

"I thought so."

They dropped her again, and this time she wasn't able to prepare. The cold was almost welcome, a numbing sensation overwhelming her raw nerves throughout her body. All but her lungs. They felt aflame, and she had to resist the desire to open her mouth and let the water pour in, lest it be the last breath she ever took.

She endured, and when they pulled her out, she managed another desperate gasp before they dunked her back in. Still, that one was the worst of all. Her headed pounded from the blood rushing into it, her legs trembled and shook in the exposed air, and her nostrils ached from the water pouring into them and then pooling in the back of her throat. All thoughts of resisting fled from her mind. They'd continue to dunk her, spend all night if they needed, until she cracked. Here she was, her lungs about to burst, and it was just the third time. How would she survive another ten minutes? Twenty? An hour?

For Nathaniel, she thought. *I'll do it for my son.* Even if it meant dying a cold, ignoble death, she'd make sure his fortune survived.

In and out of the water, every breath a sweet gift that was never enough. At last she could hardly think, could hardly feel, and it was then they pulled her onto the docks and left her lying there, soaked and shivering. Warrick knelt over her, and when he put his hand on her cheek, she felt nothing.

"I ask for only what is right, my dear Alyssa," he said to her, and in her waterlogged ears, it almost sounded like he was trying to feign paternal affection. "The Trifect has dominated for too many years, and it's time for the rest of Neldar to trade, barter, and live without your iron control over their lives. You've ruled by your heritage, lasted on a wealth prepared for you decades before your birth. But the old guard must crumble and die. You may mock us for calling ourselves lords, but despite our lack of lands, our lack of noble birth, we carry far more influence than anyone else here in the Ramere. It is our agility, our determination, our ruthlessness that you cannot hope to match. We thrive because we are your betters, not because we were born into such a position. We are the future, Alyssa, not you. Now will you sign?"

Alyssa lay with her cheek pressed against the wood, and with red eyes watched a shadow crawl across a rooftop in the not-so-far distance.

"I won't," she said, her voice cracking. "And you won't make me."

"Is that so?" asked Warrick. "What makes you so certain?"

"Because you'll be dead."

And then Zusa landed amid them, her daggers unleashing a bloody spray from the bodies around her. Alyssa watched, unable to move. The faceless woman was a true spectacle, dipping and weaving through a crowd of nearly fifty men. In all her time, Alyssa had never seen her fight in such a way, not even when battling the dark paladin Ethric or protecting her from the various thieves who made attempts on her life. She made no blocks or parries, instead relying on pure speed to carry her through. She dodged and twisted, and her daggers sliced through throats and plunged into eye sockets and chests.

"Stop her!" Stern cried out beside her. Alyssa tilted her head, trying to follow. The men had managed to regroup after the surprise attack, and they lashed at her with their weapons. Zusa's progress slowed, many of her attacks missing or being blocked. Still the bodies gathered, and Alyssa dared to hope.

Panicking, Stern grabbed her by the hair and put a dagger to her throat.

"Won't stop her..." Alyssa muttered, and it seemed Stern realized that as well.

The battle shifted, and Alyssa saw that Zusa was bleeding, her wrappings torn, with many hanging by threads. Still she battled, now on the defensive. They left her nowhere to run, but then she vaulted over them, sailing into the sky as if the world could not contain her. She landed so close to Alyssa that she wanted to reach out, to merely touch her to confirm she was real. But then Torgar was there, and his giant fist caught Zusa across the side of the head. Zusa staggered, and he followed it up with a roundhouse across the face. As the faceless woman collapsed, Torgar took his blade and prepared to stab.

"No!" Alyssa screamed.

Torgar paused and looked her way. He kicked away Zusa's daggers, then rested his foot atop her throat. Warrick grabbed Alyssa by the neck and hefted her to her feet with surprising strength for his age.

"You value her life, then, if not your own?" he asked. "Then sign, right now, or I will make you watch as that brute cuts strips of her flesh off one by one. I'll make you *wear* them, Alyssa, just as that lady over there garbs herself with cloth."

Zusa's eyes were unfocused and gazing up at the sky. Alyssa felt tears running down her face. Torgar grinned at her, and he put the tip of his sword against Zusa's palm and pressed. Zusa screamed, and Alyssa did as well.

"I will!" she cried. "Please, don't...don't kill her. I'll sign whatever you wish."

Warrick's smile spread ear to ear. "That's a smart girl. Get her a quill."

They untied her wrists, and one of the ruffians had to hold her so she could stand. Her hands shook violently, so much that Stern brought over a torch and held it below her wrists. Alyssa stared at Zusa the whole while, at the pain on her face as blood spilled from her palm. Torgar twisted the edge, seemingly for no other reason than malicious glee. Zusa did not cry out, and as feeling returned to Alyssa's fingers, she refused to cry out as well despite the throbbing agony it awoke.

When at last she could hold the quill steady, they presented her the scroll. Before she could sign it, one of the men called out, and the rest looked to the north. A large squad of soldiers marched their way, and Alyssa dared to hope. She recognized that banner. Lord Edgar, one of the most powerful lords sworn to Lord Ingram. They'd come armed for battle, and she had no doubt as to their foe. Ingram had finally sent his men to slaughter the Merchant Lords like the pests they were. He'd finally come to prove that he ruled Angelport, not them. She wanted to call to them, to cheer, but she was so tired, and Torgar's blade remained pressed against Zusa's flesh, his heel against her slender neck.

Warrick, however, appeared unworried, and that gave her pause. When the troops neared, the rest gave way, letting Lord Edgar walk without conflict up to Warrick Sun, draw his sword…and then kneel. As his knee touched the dock, the last hope in Alyssa's heart died.

"The city's yours," Edgar said, rising. "Ingram is dead."

"You've done well," Warrick said. "Your rewards have already been great, and they will grow greater still. The people have rallied to our side, and in this chaos, we will be the ones seen bringing about order. In time, even the king will accept my appointing as lord and protector of Angelport. I promise you, Edgar, your rewards then will be far greater than Ingram ever doled out."

"You can start with giving me Yorr's lands," Edgar said. "He might have recently perished due to my sword getting shoved down his throat."

"Of course," Warrick said, and he looked disgustingly amused. "Of course."

Edgar looked at Alyssa, and then he bowed low. "Forgive me if I am…intruding," he said, grinning.

"No intrusion," said Stern. "Alyssa was just about to sign an agreement, and you'd make another fine witness should she try to renege on it before the king."

"But of course. Go on, then, Alyssa. Sign. We're all here."

Alyssa felt trapped, helpless. She took the quill, the scroll, and read through it once more. Every line meant the dissolution of years of trade. It meant the halt of all minimum prices on the bulk of their goods. It meant the end of the safety and strength of the Trifect. They'd be on their own, competing against one another, as well as struggling to recover as all the while the Merchant Lords swarmed north in attempts to steal away every last coin.

But not signing it meant the loss of her life, and Zusa's. She'd never get to see her son again. Whatever strength she'd had, it meant nothing now. She took the quill, signed her name, and then let it drop to the dock.

"There," she said. "It is done. Now let me and Zusa go."

"Not quite," said Warrick, who nodded at Torgar. The man chuckled, pulled back his sword, and slashed Zusa across the stomach. Alyssa's vision exploded with red. She screamed. She flung herself at Torgar, but he let go of the blade and grabbed her by the throat.

"You want to hurt me, bitch?" he asked, punching her in the gut. As she leaned over and gagged, she heard Warrick speaking to Lord Edgar.

"Send her to the elves," said the old man. "We'll need to pacify them so we can solidify our control over the Ramere. I can't imagine a better gift."

"No," Alyssa said, trying to deny the unfairness of it all.

"You hear that?" Torgar said, pulling her closer so he could growl into her ear. "You're going to lose your head for attacking that cute little elven slut. And you know what's best? That was me. My sword. You'll die for my crimes, you stupid cunt, while I rule over Laurie's fortune. I can't imagine a better, more proper fate for a stuffed-up highborn like you."

With that, he let her head drop back to the wet wooden planks.

"Torgar, enough!" Stern yelled when he reached for her again.

Through blurred vision, Alyssa saw the two glaring and did not understand. Turning her eyes down, she saw Zusa lying close, facing her. Her body was trembling, one wrapped hand holding back the bleeding, the other reaching toward her. Alyssa reached back, and their fingers touched.

"I'm so sorry," Alyssa whispered.

"You three," said Stern, gesturing to men about him. "Take her."

Several men grabbed her, lifting her to her feet. They were dragging her away, to the castle, to its dungeon. When they were almost out of sight, she managed to steal a look back. Zusa lay on the dock in a pool of her own blood, all but forgotten.

CHAPTER 25

The Wraith fled down the streets, and Dieredon gave chase. More than ever he wished he'd brought his bow with him instead of stashing it. Against someone like Graeven, taking him down at a distance seemed the wisest, and safest, course of action. Instead he had to close in, and when Graeven climbed to the rooftops, he had to follow. They leaped across them, heading away from the docks. The homes crowded together, their roofs forming a slanted, uneven road for them to race upon. As Graeven reached a street, he tensed as if to leap over, but then spun. Dieredon twirled his knives in hand. By most he was considered the finest fighter of elvenkind. He showed no fear, no hesitation, regardless of the opponent. He would show none now.

They clashed together, this time with far more room to duel than in the home. Despite the unevenness of the footing, Dieredon felt better with the open space. Wielding two weapons to Graeven's one should have granted him an advantage, but

Graeven kept on the offensive, striking with so much strength that Dieredon could not block with just one hand, nor parry with his thin, light knives. His only hope was in a counter, but every time he ducked underneath a blow and moved to attack, Graeven had already pulled back or shifted his blade for a thrust.

Dieredon still kept on, refusing to back down. But he was bleeding and had suffered wounds fighting Haern and Zusa. As the fight progressed, each second an agonizing whirlwind of parry and thrust, slash and dodge, he feared what he'd always known: Graeven was his equal, if not his superior.

The sword swung low, and when Dieredon blocked it with both his blades, he tried stepping in to close the distance between them. Graeven continued pressing, forcing the blades to remain low, and then his head shot out, ramming Dieredon's nose with his forehead. As stars exploded in his vision, he tried leaping away, but Graeven caught him with his fist. Using his elbow to knock Dieredon's thrust aside, he rammed his forearm into his throat. Blind and gagging, Dieredon made one last desperate stab, which amounted to nothing. Graeven somersaulted away, his foot catching Dieredon's chin. The blow jammed his teeth shut, and he felt a piece of his tongue tear. Blood spilled warm across his mouth.

Dieredon fell to one knee, spitting out a tiny chunk of flesh. His breath came in ragged, and he glared at Graeven as the other elf slowly stalked closer.

"You shame us all," he said.

"I do what must be done. I do what we should have done *centuries* ago. We can no longer overlook the threat humans present to us, nor the evil they carry in their hearts. Look what they did to our Dezren brethren. They sent mobs carrying fire and blade, and despite all our skill, all our magic, we still had to flee. I was there, Dieredon. I watched the smoke spread for hundreds of miles. I watched our children taken down by thousands of arrows. And now the people of Angelport press our borders, and many of us would kneel and present them our necks, all the better for our executioners. I won't let it happen, damn them all. *I won't let it!*"

Dieredon flung his knives in the way as Graeven's blade descended. His arms jarred at the contact, and he felt the muscles in his neck and chest tighten as he fought against its downward progress. Graeven knelt with all his weight into it, his feet positioned so that even if Dieredon tried to kick them out, he'd still be able to dodge in time. Closer and closer came the tip, its edge shifting so it aimed straight for his left eye. And then it thrust, accompanied by a shriek of metal as it slid across his knives.

It stabbed the rooftop instead, shoved upward by Dieredon at the last moment. He kicked for Graeven's knee, but instead hit only air. The two were both badly positioned, flailing for footing, but it was Graeven who recovered first. The sword slashed across Dieredon's chest twice, and as he stumbled back, Graeven stepped in behind him and cut the back of his leg. The pain was incredible. Crumpling to one knee, he tried to defend, but Graeven smacked the weapons aside as if they were playthings. Another cut, this one on his arm.

Dieredon fell to his back, Graeven hovering over him, smiling out from the shadows of his hood.

"I told you I was the better," he said. "It's a shame no one else will ever know."

Dieredon flung his knives, which Graeven parried aside. He slapped him across the face with the flat of his blade, as if rebuking a student.

"Maybe," Dieredon said, laying his head atop the roof. "But you forgot someone."

With a flutter of cloaks, the Watcher arrived, looking like Graeven's reflection in the fading starlight.

Haern landed atop the roof, his sabers drawn and his pulse pounding. Dieredon had clearly been defeated, but he looked alive, so at least there was that. Bracing his legs, he prepared for an attack should Graeven make the slightest threatening motion toward Dieredon.

"Step away," he commanded.

Graeven only laughed. "Why?" he asked. "Do you care for him? Have you ever seen him before? He is our dog, our hunting beast. You shouldn't mourn his loss."

"I said step away."

Graeven angled his sword so the tip pressed against Dieredon's throat. "Of the two of us, I don't think you're the one in a position to make demands, Watcher."

Haern took a single step, watching Dieredon as much as he was Graeven. Another step, and the tip pressed tighter against flesh.

"This won't end how you want it," said Haern.

"I beg to differ."

Dieredon met his gaze, and in the slightest of nods, he saw the order to attack. Haern lunged, and before Graeven could execute him, Dieredon batted aside the sword with his arms, accepting the vicious cut it dealt him. With him rolling away, Graeven could not follow, for in came Haern on the attack. His sabers connected with Graeven's long blade, and the ringing noise it created was like a death knell in Haern's mind. His primal instincts took over. His sabers slashed low and high, Graeven batting aside the low while ducking underneath the other. Spinning, his sword slashed for Haern's knees, but he spun himself, avoiding the cut as well as flinging his cloak into Graeven's face.

Graeven took the offensive once he could see, using every advantage of his longer reach. Haern parried several strikes with both his sabers, trying to adjust to the elf's vicious speed, then attempted to go on the offensive. His sabers lashed out, but he still hadn't judged correctly. Graeven batted both aside, stepped close, and then rammed his elbow into Haern's throat. As he gagged, Graeven struck again, this time with the hilt of his sword atop his head. Haern collapsed to his knees, and he expected a flash of pain as the elven steel claimed his life, but it did not.

Instead, Graeven paced before him, just outside the reach of his sabers.

"Why do we fight?" he asked. "I swear, human, your blindness is sometimes baffling."

"You're a heartless murderer," Haern said, staggering to his feet. "Why would I let you live?"

Graeven chuckled at that. "I'll live regardless of what you do. Don't you see how alike you and I are? Look around. Can't you see what I've accomplished?"

Fires burned across the city, guards patrolled the area surrounding Ingram's mansion, and Alyssa hung at the docks waiting for Zusa to rescue her. Yes, Haern thought, he could see it just fine.

"Nothing," he said. "You and I are nothing alike."

"Try opening your eyes, then, and perhaps you'll see differently."

Haern stepped to the side, feinted a thrust, and then came rushing in, his sabers slashing with all his strength.

"What could you know of me?" he cried as his sabers whirled and cut, flooding the rooftop with the sound of steel on steel as Graeven blocked each one with a deft twist of his blade. Growing desperate, Haern tried a complicated series of short thrusts he'd learned from one of his many trainers. The idea was to overwhelm his opponents with attacks so that when one finally slipped through, Haern could step in and put all his force behind it. But Graeven was no normal opponent, and he retreated step by step to each thrust, parrying only when Haern tried to press in. When Haern at last could not keep it up, he tried to pull back, and that's when Graeven struck.

Haern flung his sabers up in defense as the elf charged in, but he left himself vulnerable to one side, and in slipped Graeven's foot, tripping him. He hit the ground with a thud, the blow knocking the wind out of him. Again he expected a killing blow, but Graeven retreated, twirling his sword as if he were bored.

"I know so much about you, Haern," he said. "I know the role you played against the guilds and the Trifect. When rumors of that pathetic little war's end reached my ears—all blamed on the actions of one man—I scoffed. But the truce lasted, so in disguise I came to Veldaren. Piece by piece, story by story, I learned what you did. I listened to the way the scum of the city spoke your name. You were a beacon of hope to me in this dying world. My race is outnumbered, and every day it dwindles while the race of man spreads like an unstoppable plague. But your cities, your true places of power, were your weakness. If I could bring them toppling down, we might survive. And there you were, one man, with an entire city in your grip.

"And then there was Angelport, reaching to our forests with its bloody fingers. Within every faction, even my own, I slaughtered those who desired peace, who would rather make deals and concessions than face the true ugliness and conflict that must be fought if we are to endure another century. When I first used your bloody eye, I did so as an homage, not a calling. Imagine my delight when you actually arrived. I thought you could help me, that you would see the need for this. Angelport is worse than Veldaren ever was. There is no salvation in it, no desire for peace, no hope for something better. There is greed, and hatred, and nothing else."

Haern took to his feet, and Graeven attacked him with such viciousness he had to retreat. The long blade sliced through the air, always a half second behind.

"You tamed the vile darkness in Veldaren," the elf said as he chased. "You killed hundreds to force a final confrontation and subdue the guilty. Help me do the same here. Everything I've done has been to force the war needed to bring everything into focus, to give clarity to the nations. My kind will burn this city to the ground, a glorious purification that all Dezrel, both elf and man, so desperately needs."

"I am not you!" Haern cried, attempting a counter that was quickly blocked. "I will not murder the innocent!"

"You murder innocents with your actions, you damn fool. You've left children to starve, wives without protection, guilds so weak others tore them to pieces. Celestia help me, how are you so naïve?"

Haern tried to shut him out, to ignore the words that echoed his own thoughts, awakening guilt he'd carried for years but done his best to deny. Graeven could see his torment, and he fought closer, forcing an opening in his sabers so he might slash a shallow cut across Haern's chest. As Haern stumbled back, blood dripping down his shirt, Graeven shook the droplets from his sword.

"We are alike, Watcher. I am your mirror, your shadow, the natural progression to what you began. Do not throw your life away without reason. Look what we have done by ourselves, through manipulation and sheer brute strength. Imagine what we could do together! We can thrust the darkness of mankind into the light. We can find the vile corners in which the sickness hides and burn it all to the ground. Help me. Fight beside me. We have the same goals, the same methods. Do you not see?"

"Our methods might be the same," Haern said, mustering the last of his strength. "But I never wanted to destroy Veldaren, only save it. I won't be the monster you want me to be."

Graeven shook his head. "Then to Veldaren I will go next. I'll finish what you started. I'll hunt down everyone you knew, everyone you loved. No one betrays me, Watcher. Whatever legacy you had, I'll destroy it and replace it with my own."

Haern felt time slowing as he settled once more into a stance. He thought of the Wraith running loose in Veldaren, slaughtering priests, thieves, mercenaries, all to bring about chaos and riots. He thought of every step of his life made worthless, the brittle peace breaking into a slaughter worse than it had ever been before. He thought of Tarlak and Brug trying to fight it, only to be overwhelmed. Most of all, he thought of Delysia, dying at the hands of the Wraith.

"No," he said, shifting his weight onto his back leg. "You won't."

Help me, Ashhur, he prayed as Graeven twirled his sword. *Not for me, but for them.*

The elf leaped, and Haern met the charge. They crashed together in the air, a brutal collision of kicks and slashes. The sword cut a wound across his thigh, the pain terrible. His heel caught Graeven's jaw, and a saber slashed across his knuckles. They landed with their backs to each other. Graeven swung behind him, twisting his body while keeping his feet planted. Haern arched backward, the edge slicing the air above his chest. Returning to a stand, he thrust both his blades, but the elf looped his arm around, smacking them away.

Now face-to-face, they dueled once more, Haern driven on by a fury approaching madness. He kept on the attack, spinning and thrusting with such precision he couldn't help think his father would be proud. All his inhibitions, all his doubt, faded away as his sabers sang out a song of violence. He'd once thought himself a monster, but now he faced a true monster, a being sworn to death and destruction, to whom life was only to be taken, not preserved. Whatever limits he knew, he pushed beyond them, despite the pain of his cuts, the ache of his muscles, and the blood that poured across his cloaks.

But Graeven would not fall, and at last Haern knew his energy was almost at an end. He had but one final trick, the cloak dance he'd relied on for years. Graeven had defeated it before, but Haern trusted it, knew how he might react when facing him a second time. Pulling back, he weaved himself into a spin, his cloaks separating and flailing in a bizarre pattern to hide his weapons and the positioning of his hands and feet. As Haern's vision was momentarily blocked, up came the expected smoke. Graeven had been shifting left just before vanishing, and denying every instinct, every piece of information he'd seen otherwise from the elf's stance, eyes, and momentum, Haern turned and thrust his sabers blindly to the right.

Graeven's sword slashed across his arm, spilling blood but failing to achieve the lethal hit he desired. His eyes grew wide, and his momentum carried him all the way into Haern's arms, as if in an embrace. His mouth opened, his lips trembling. With a twist of his wrists, Haern pulled his sabers free from deep in Graeven's belly. The elf fell on his back in a clang of metal and rustle of cloth. Haern stood over him, watching, his sabers dripping blood.

"Killing me stops nothing," Graeven said, coughing. Blood spilled across his lips. "Your war, your hatred, it's a disease that will destroy you, a flame that will consume you. Even without me, you humans will destroy one another."

"I know."

"Then why this, Watcher? Why stop me?"

Haern knelt over Graeven, and he made sure the elf could see the fire in his eyes. "Because I must. I will *fight* it, until my dying breath. I will fight our failures, our weakness, our destruction. Whether I succeed or not, I will never sit by and watch our world burn. There is good in us, even if you cannot see it. Somehow I'll find a way to save it."

Graeven rolled onto his stomach, and he crawled toward where Dieredon knelt on one knee, having watched the entire encounter.

"They will consume us," the elf said, his voice growing weak. "Just as they consume themselves. But must we die with them?"

Dieredon shook his head. "Never your place, Graeven. Die now, and may Celestia grant you the mercy I cannot give."

Haern put his saber against the elf's back, its tip aimed for the heart. "Farewell," he said, thrusting.

Graeven gasped, his hands twitched, and then he lay still.

Dieredon slowly rose to his feet, careful to put as little weight on his wounded leg as possible. Meanwhile, Haern took a saber to his own cloak and cut off his hood. Tossing the cloth aside, he removed Graeven's hood and held it in his hands. Flecks of blood stained it, but they were well hidden by the dark material. Taking a deep breath, he pulled it over his head. Shadows immediately covered his face, and when he spoke, his voice changed, a subtle magic weaving over his words.

"It's finished," he said.

Dieredon frowned at him. "You would honor him in his death?" he asked, gesturing to the hood.

Haern shook his head. "No honor, and not for him," he said. "Remembrance, so I might never forget."

"And what is that?"

He glanced at Graeven's corpse. "We're men, not gods, regardless of how many lives we take. Can you run?"

Dieredon shook his head. "Go on without me. Find your friends at the docks. I'll not be far behind."

"I'll be waiting."

No running, no leaping from rooftops. Haern carefully climbed down from the roof, put his feet on solid ground, and limped toward the docks.

CHAPTER

26

Dawn was fast approaching, but that only meant the night was at its darkest as Haern slowly approached the docks. Even from afar, he saw a sight that made his heart ache. Clenching his teeth, he tried to hope for the best.

"No," he whispered. "Please, Ashhur...no, it can't end like this. It can't be this way."

Yet Zusa's body lay so very still.

Holding his cloaks tighter, for he suddenly felt terribly cold, he kept walking. Alyssa was nowhere in sight. Even the many docked boats appeared empty. Haern could imagine where they'd gone, to Ingram's most likely. Let them fight over the city, he thought. Far as he was concerned, they could have it.

At Zusa's body, he knelt and put his hand against her neck. He held his breath and closed his eyes, not wanting to see the bloody wound across her stomach, not wanting to think about who had done it.

There was a pulse.

"Thank you," he whispered.

Tearing at his cloak, he stuffed the cleanest parts he could find against the wound to stem the soft blood flow. After that he tied it, careful when he lifted her. She grunted at the movement, and he saw her open her eyes. With tender care, he removed the wrappings from her face so he could see her better. A moment later her eyes came into focus, and she looked his way. Despite her obvious pain, a hint of a smile crossed her lips.

"Knew... you would," she said, her voice hoarse.

"Shush," he told her, focusing on bandaging the wound. "Lie still until I can look at this better. Can't believe you're even alive."

He heard the sound of soft footsteps on the wood, and he glanced back to see Dieredon approaching. He'd wrapped his wounded leg and somewhere had found a long stick of wood to use as a crutch.

"Where is Lady Gemcroft?" the elf asked, glancing about the empty dock.

"They took her," Zusa said, having to swallow repeatedly so her voice would not crack.

"Who?" Haern asked.

"Merchants... they're giving her to the elves."

Dieredon shook his head and muttered a few words in Elvish. "I can save her, if I act quickly. Can you escape the city on your own?"

"We'll need to heal her first," said Haern. "Give me an hour or so, and I think I can get us out."

The elf nodded. "I cannot be seen in here come daylight," he said. "I don't think the guards would take too kindly to my presence."

Haern chuckled. "Where shall we find you, then?"

"I'll find you," Dieredon said. "That's what I'm best at. Just stay on the roads, and good luck, Watcher."

He hurried away, moving at a remarkable pace for having to use a crutch. Haern watched him go, then turned back to Zusa. Her dark skin was growing pale, and he knew time was short.

"Should be used to this by now," he muttered as he took her into his arms.

"Still don't...like it," she said, and despite the chaos of the night, he laughed.

Step by step, he told himself as he took her down the quiet street. *Step by step.*

At the entrance to the temple, he tried the door and found it locked. Beating on it with his fists, he waited, leaning beside the door to help support both his weight and Zusa's. When he was met with only silence, he tried again, then a third time, refusing to be turned away. At last the door cracked open, first only a little, then wide as Nole realized who was there.

"We had nowhere else to go," Haern told him. "She needs healing, and quickly. Will you help us?"

Nole chewed on his lower lip. "You would trust me?" he asked.

"As I said...I have little choice."

The priest nodded. "Bring her in."

Haern carried her into the empty temple.

"I sent Logan home when the fires started," said the priest as he gestured to the nearest bench. "Thought it best he be with his family should something happen. This city grows worse with every day. What happened to Zusa?"

"She was cut by a blade," Haern said, stepping away so he

could lean against a wall. His breathing had grown short, and carrying Zusa had sapped what little strength he had left.

Nole looked over the wound, a deep frown across his face. "I'm not sure I can heal this," he said.

"You better damn well try."

"You don't understand. My faith the past few years has been... weak. I fear this is beyond me. Ashhur may not hear my prayers."

Haern took a step toward him, then suddenly lunged and grabbed the priest by the front of his robe, yanking him close so they could speak face-to-face.

"I don't care," he said. "You hear me? I don't care what you did, that you betrayed me or how badly you've failed before. You kneel there and you heal her. Don't give Ashhur a choice to hear you, understand?"

Nole nodded, and he looked visibly relieved when Haern let him go. Turning back to Zusa, the priest knelt, his hands on her wounds. He bowed his head and began to pray. Too scared to watch, Haern closed his eyes and waited. And hoped.

At last the prayers ceased. Still hesitant to look, he waited, head low, until he felt a hand touch his face. Opening his eyes, he saw Zusa standing there, her bloody bandages still on the bench, her revealed skin scarred but healed. Nole sat beside her, bewildered and in tears.

"Thank you," she said to both of them, gently resting her head against Haern's chest as her arms wrapped about him. "Just... thank you."

"We have little time," he said. "Are you ready to go?"

She nodded. Haern put his hand on Nole's shoulder, squeezed it, and then left him kneeling there on the floor as they slowly limped out of the temple and toward the city's walls.

* * *

Lord Edgar and newly named Lord Warrick were in the mansion discussing their future plans for the city when the servant knocked at the door.

"Yes?" Warrick asked.

The servant came in and bowed low, looking incredibly nervous. He'd been one of many originally staffed by Ingram, and it seemed every single one, from top to bottom, thought they were a heartbeat away from being executed should they show a lack of skill at their position.

"Milord, we've received word from the messenger you sent to the elves."

"Already?" asked Edgar. "But it's hardly been an hour."

"I know," said the servant, licking his lips. "Your messenger said an elf was waiting outside the city, as if expecting him. The elf said he'll accept your, uh, gift."

Edgar shrugged. "Not entirely surprising. Shall I fetch her?"

"No," Warrick said. "I must be the one to do this. It only feels just. You..."

"Jarl," said the servant.

"Good, Jarl. Go tell this elf that we will be bringing Alyssa to him, if he will kindly wait for us."

The servant bowed low, then hurried away. Warrick promised Edgar he'd return soon, then ventured out into the mansion grounds. They'd cleaned away most of the bodies, but the blood still remained. The grass would grow strong next spring, he thought, feeling a bit of grim amusement. The understaffed servants hurried about, trying to put everything back in order as if the battle had never happened. They'd never succeed, of course. Warrick was in charge now. Things would never be as they were, and the city would be all the better for it.

At the entrance to the dungeon, the city guards bowed low, both men looking uncomfortable. Warrick knew Ingram was hardly loved among the city folk, but compared to him, Warrick was an unknown, a frightening entity suddenly come to power. He'd overlook their stuttered words and shifting eyes for a little while. At some point, though, he'd have to either win them over or terrify them into submission.

"Go fetch me Alyssa," he told them. "Make sure she remains unharmed."

The first guard bowed low and then hurried inside. As Warrick waited, he called over another of his guards and requested an escort. He would not travel through the city without the support of shields and blades, not with fires and riots fresh in his memory. Granted, he'd caused most of them, but that was irrelevant.

When the guard returned with Alyssa, Warrick bowed as low as his old spine allowed. "I hope your stay has been pleasant," he said.

Alyssa's face and dress were covered with dirt, and she sported fresh bruises from the previous night's entertainment at the docks. At his words, she smiled so sweetly, as if he'd brought her down from Veldaren for tea.

"A most exquisite locale," she said. "I hope you get a chance to sample its pleasures."

Warrick chuckled. "One day, perhaps, but I fear I'll be dead before I spend any time in those cells."

"We can only hope."

"Save some of your charm for the elves. You'll need it to keep your head."

He nodded to his guards, and with Alyssa still in chains, they left the compound and headed for the gates of the city. As they walked, Warrick took in the sights with a fresh set of eyes.

No longer were the various stores just his partners in trade or the taverns places his underlings could fritter away their coin. They were his now, his protection, his servants. They would pay taxes to him, kneel at his feet, and show respect far beyond what he'd known as a lowborn man sailing the seas in search of wealth. Even the people seemed different, for they were *his* people now.

Of course, the other Merchant Lords would have their say in things, and each would obtain parcels of land in the surrounding areas. The Ramere was theirs now, after all.

At the gates, the soldiers saluted and gave way.

"Where is the elf?" Warrick asked as they paused a moment underneath the stone arch of the gateway.

"If your eyes are sharp, you can see him from here," said the guard, pointing to a far hill.

Warrick shook his head, able to see only a blur, but he knew his eyes were not the same eyes of his youth, when he'd sat in the crow's nest, calling out banners of distant ships. He could see hills easily enough, though, and he and his escort headed out. The minutes passed, the only sound the clatter of his guards' armor and the clinking of Alyssa's chains. As they neared, Warrick saw the elf but failed to recognize him.

"Hail, elf of Quellassar," he called out.

"Hail, Lord of Angelport," the elf returned.

Warrick smiled. At least he was polite enough. They closed the distance, and he took a better look at him. The elf had long brown hair, carefully braided so it would not interfere with his vision. His eyes sparkled as he bowed low, refusing to move from his spot atop the hill.

"I must apologize for all our misunderstandings," Warrick said, offering a half-bow. "But I am Lord of Angelport now and must try to make amends. I believe your people have been demanding Lady Alyssa for trial, and I have come offering her as a gift to start a new friendship between us."

The elf nodded, his face somber. "I accept and will bring her to Quellassar where she may have a trial. Release her from her chains."

Warrick raised an eyebrow. "Would it not be better to keep her bound until she reaches your forests?"

"Do not insult me. I am not alone, and she cannot escape from us, not in the wilds."

"Of course," Warrick said, bowing again. He looked to his guards. "Release her."

They unclamped the chains from her wrists and ankles. Alyssa absently rubbed the raw flesh as she took a hesitant step toward the elf. Warrick felt glad to be rid of her. After everything, he had little doubt to her fate. Once the elves took her head, the Trifect would crumble, nearly every strong leader among them broken. After that, he and his comrades would spread north to pick up the pieces.

"Farewell," the elf said, and he bowed deeply. He did not leave, though, only stood there with Alyssa at his side, as if waiting for Warrick. Warrick wondered if it was a custom he was unaware of and resolved to learn more about the elves since his dealings with them would be of the utmost importance over the next few years. With Alyssa gone, he felt a great weight off his shoulders, and when he reentered Angelport, it was with a smile on his face.

Alyssa waited beside the elf until Warrick and his escort were far out of sight before stepping away from him and crossing her arms over her chest.

"I have refused elven justice once already," she said. "Who

am I to go to now? Will Laryssa hang me in secret, or do we head to Quellassar for a sham of a trial?"

The elf turned to her, and she noticed he did so with a poorly concealed limp.

"Not exactly," he said, and a smile crossed his face as he put his fingers to his lips and whistled.

At the bottom of the hill, hidden from sight of Angelport, was a heavy gathering of brush, and from its center Haern and Zusa stood up from their hiding place. Relief flooded through her, the sight of Zusa alive and well sending her to tears. She ran down the hill at a breakneck pace, and when she reached Zusa, she flung herself against her.

"Careful," Zusa said, pulling back. "My wounds are still tender."

Alyssa laughed, then brought her attention to Haern, who she hugged and kissed his cheek.

"Thank you, both of you," she said.

The elf joined them, and Haern bowed his head respectfully.

"We cannot thank you enough, Dieredon," he said.

"I should be thanking you," said the elf. "Ceredon will not enjoy hearing it, but he must learn of Laryssa's misconduct, as well as Graeven's manipulation of these events. I feel tensions between our races will never vanish, but at least this might pull us back from war for a time."

Dieredon retrieved a cane he'd placed by the brush, saluted them all, and then started walking toward Quellassar. Alyssa watched him go for a moment, then called out his name.

"I never attacked Laryssa," she told him when he glanced back. "But I know who did. It was Torgar, a mercenary who now rules the Keenan household. He confessed as much to me, when he still thought I would die."

Dieredon froze, and the look in his eyes was chilling. Without a word, he continued on. Feeling a little better, Alyssa began heading north with Zusa, toward home. To her surprise, Haern did not follow, instead climbing the hill toward Angelport.

"Where are you going?" she asked him.

He glanced back, and his gaze was disturbingly hollow. "How can we leave like this?" he asked. "Walking home beaten, bloodied, having failed so terribly?"

Alyssa thought of setting foot in Angelport, and her revulsion was overwhelming. "No," she said. "Leave them be. There's nothing left for us there, not anymore."

"I disagree."

Haern ran back toward the city's walls, and Alyssa felt her heart ache at the sight.

"What is he hoping to accomplish?" she asked.

"We'll give him a night," Zusa said, watching him go. "Dierdon gave me enough coin to buy food and passage back to Veldaren, so we do not need to hurry. Let him find what he needs. He'll return to us, though, I know it."

Alyssa clutched Zusa's hand, and they embraced once more.

"Never do that to me again," she said.

"I'll try."

They walked north, gaining enough distance from Angelport to feel comfortable, then set up camp off the road to wait out the night and give the Watcher his chance to come back.

CHAPTER

27

Despite the severe lack of the many comforts still to be relocated from his old home, Warrick stayed the night at Ingram's mansion. *His* mansion, he tried to remind himself as he changed into a thick bed robe. It'd take several weeks before he stopped thinking of it as Ingram's, but he had to try. He was an old man, and change was not something he was well accustomed to.

The bed was absurdly large, with curtains across the bedposts. At least it'd be warm in winter, thought Warrick as he washed his face and hands in a basin of cool water. As he dried his hands on a wool cloth, he heard a soft creak, faint enough he might have imagined it. When he looked back, he knew it was no trick of his ears. A man knelt by the window, swords drawn. He recognized that shadowed face, though he lacked his characteristic smile.

"What is it you come for, Wraith?" Warrick asked, trying not to sound afraid.

"The Wraith is dead," said the intruder, shaking his head.

Warrick frowned, and he took a step closer. He knew if the man was skilled enough to make it past his guards, ascend the walls, and sneak in through his window, there was little chance he could escape now. He might as well see if he could learn something first.

"If not him," Warrick said, thinking aloud, "then... are you Veldaren's Watcher?"

"I am," said the man. His voice was a cold whisper, the harsh edge to it enough to convince Warrick what his plans were. His throat suddenly dry, Warrick tried to remain calm. He was an old man, and not afraid of death. It was just losing everything he'd accomplished, all on the night of his greatest triumph, that struck him most. Only a cruel world would allow something like that.

"Why are you here, Watcher?" he asked. "Have you come to kill me?"

"The thought has crossed my mind."

"And why is that? I have never met you before and have committed no crime against you. Surely we can talk reason... unless you've been paid, and even then I might offer you a more advantageous sum."

The Watcher chuckled, as if amused, but there was no amusement in the whites of his eyes that shone out from the hood.

"You sold Alyssa out for death. Why should you live?"

Warrick sighed. "Is that really it? Elves came into this city as if our walls meant nothing. Do you think Angelport can endure a second night like that? Of course I gave her over. If they want to hang her, I won't shed a tear, but I don't care if they send her back to Veldaren with only a paddling. The Trifect is a dying beast, with or without Alyssa's help."

The Watcher shook his head. "You are a plague upon Dezrel,

locusts who will consume and not build. I cannot let you remain rulers of the Ramere."

"Wait," Warrick said, his anger overriding his panic. "Who has told you that? Who has judged us so? You've come a long way to here, Watcher. Who whispered that judgment against us in your ear? Alyssa? Laurie, before he died? The Trifect dares claim we only reap, not sow? Who are they to speak of such things, when they have held kings in their pockets and broken down anyone who might oppose them? They are hardly innocent, Watcher, no more so than we. Ingram was a fool and a coward. He would have led Angelport to war against the elves one day, regardless of our interference. His guards were corrupt, his justice shortsighted and brutal. How many men did he hang in *your* name, Watcher? Yet you come bearing swords against *me*?"

"What of the Violet? I've seen what it can do. It's a danger, and you've nearly caused a war in your desire to claim it."

Warrick sat down atop his bed, observing how each step he took made the Watcher tense.

"I will admit, it would have been a wonderful weapon to wield against the Trifect," he said, deciding there was no reason to attempt lying to the strange man. "With it, we might have thoroughly destroyed the last significant remains of the Keenan's trading empire, for even a few months of disruption would have carried permanent damage. But the Violet cannot grow beyond the elves' forest, and you were in Angelport last night. You saw what just a few of those elves did, slaughtering hundreds, and that was with Ingram's soldiers prepared for the attack. Trust me when I say our hope for obtaining significant trade for the Violet has faded."

"That doesn't mean you won't risk war again if you feel you have a chance to obtain the leaf again."

Warrick shook his head. "So stubborn in your thinking. I

want peace now, perhaps even more than Ingram ever wanted it. We're merchants, not knights and kings. So long as I can keep the coin flowing, I will remain happy. Angelport is ours. The lands and titles always denied to us will finally flow. We will compete with the Trifect, and we will slowly destroy it, only now on even terms. War? I am too old for a war. The threat was what we needed, a looming crisis to make people panic and give up what they might not otherwise. But now I have a city to run, and all the lands of the Ramere soon to be sworn into my care, assuming our glorious king isn't as dumb as his reputation claims. What do I now care for a simple weed? Why would I desire a war that would burn all my hard-won rewards to the ground?"

The Watcher had nothing to say to that, and Warrick laughed at the utter stupidity of it all.

"You came here knowing little, Watcher, only what you have heard. People lie. People exaggerate. They view the world through tainted glass, yet see themselves in a gilded mirror. Did you think you could come into this city like some dark reaper and bring us justice? You cannot fix all of Dezrel, and I dare-say it isn't your damn place to do so, either. You were a fool if you thought otherwise. Now kill me, if you still think yourself justified in doing so. Watch Angelport descend into anarchy as the remaining Merchant Lords squabble among themselves for rule, and Lord Edgar tries to retake it for himself when he realizes he won't receive his promised rewards. Watch as the minor nobles at the edges of the Ramere form alliances out of fear, then come here to conquer. Take your blind justice and watch thousands suffer for it. Either that, or leave me to run my damn city."

The Watcher stood, not quite as tall as when he'd entered. His sabers slid into their scabbards.

"You truly believe you can rule this city, lead it to peace?" he asked.

"Far better than that paranoid fool Ingram, yes."

"Then I leave for Veldaren. Know I will keep my eyes south, and my ears will always be listening. Should you, or any other lord of the Ramere begin pressing the elven borders for the Violet—"

"Your threats are unnecessary," Warrick said.

"Not quite," said the Watcher. He lifted a rolled scroll, with Warrick's own seal pushed into the fresh wax. A scroll that should still have been in his dresser. Slowly, strip by strip, the man tore it into dozens of pieces. "Consider the treaty you tortured out of Lady Gemcroft to have never existed, Warrick. Alyssa goes not to the elves, either, but home. If you cherish your life, you won't dare try such a scheme again."

"Very well," said Warrick. "Amusing as it might have been, that scroll isn't necessary. As I said, the Trifect is a wounded animal, even with Alyssa's survival. It won't need our help to die. Go on home. No one will miss you here."

The cloaked man leaped out the window, onto the rooftop, and into the night. Warrick let out a sigh of relief, then vowed to have the damn window boarded up first thing in the morning.

Haern saw the fire as he traveled north, yet almost did not go to it. He didn't think it could be them, not with how close it was to the city. If they'd walked a steady pace north, they should have been several miles beyond. Still, he went, and sure enough saw Alyssa and Zusa lying side by side, with only each other and the fire to keep warm amid the cold night. Haern took a seat beside it, tossing on a few branches to bring it roaring back to life. On the other side, Zusa stirred, and she sat up alert, as if she had not even been sleeping.

"Oh," Zusa said, seeing him there.

Haern pulled the hood off his head and tossed it to the dirt beside him.

"Why did you wait for me?" he asked after a moment of uncomfortable silence.

To that, Zusa laughed. "Go to sleep, Watcher," she said. "And try not to ask foolish questions."

The casual dismissal put his mind at ease, and spreading out his cloaks as a blanket, he slept beside the roaring fire.

EPILOGUE

I really have no choice in this?" Torgar asked the eldest of his newly appointed advisors, a spindly man named Yates or Bates or something like that. Already he felt his mind fraying with the bewildering amounts of names and people and places he was suddenly expected to remember. They stood in the den of the Keenan mansion, him before the fire, the advisor beside a large stack of books he'd been writing in most of the day.

"Given the precarious position our house is in," the man said, shifting from foot to foot as if he had no choice but to fidget, "I feel it best you meet with him quickly. If you could make peace with the merchants now, it'd mean a great deal for—"

"So your answer is yes?" Torgar asked, glaring at him. "Fine. Get out. I know where I'm going, and I sure as shit don't need a chaperone."

Once the old man was gone, Torgar went to his room, retrieved his sword. He glanced at his armor, rolled his eyes. He felt exhausted enough as is. Going through the tiresome process of putting it on didn't feel worth it. So he slung his sword across his back and made a quick stop in Tori's room.

"She still eating well?" he asked Lily, who held the baby in her arms.

"Crying more than eating," Lily said, pulling up at her dress to hide her exposed breast. "I think she's growing a tooth."

Torgar ran a hand through the scattered fuzz that was Tori's hair, and when she looked up at him, he laughed.

"Stupid kid," he said. "Just eat, will you?"

He left Lily to handle the babe as she resumed crying, heading out the main doors and to the gate beyond. Slamming the gate behind him was immensely satisfying, for it made him think he might be free of his responsibilities, if only for a brief while. Keeping things sane seemed far harder than it had for Laurie, or even Madelyn. So many people wanting things, making offers, calling up debts. No matter how much wealth Torgar's new advisors insisted they had, it never seemed enough.

"Damn shame Madelyn killed you," Torgar murmured, imagining a ghostly Laurie walking beside him. "Should be you doing this, not me."

Down the dark street he walked. The sky was heavily clouded, and the sun soon to set. Still, it put his mind at ease, quiet streets amid open air. Even a bit of rain wouldn't put a damper on his mood, so long as a bolt of lightning didn't also come to say hello. Once he neared the docks, he started paying more attention to where he went, until at last he found the Port and Loan building, unguarded, its door unlocked.

Stepping inside, Torgar passed through the slender entryway and into the large oval room beyond. It was dimly lit with a few candles set atop the table, and sitting alone in one of the chairs was Stern Blackwater. The man rose to his feet at Torgar's entrance, though he stayed where he was and did not offer his hand in greeting.

"It has taken far too long for you to agree to such a meeting," Stern said.

"Grumble all you want," Torgar said, pulling his sword and sheath off his back and setting it atop the table. The metal rattled on the dark wood. "But I have things to do, as you can imagine."

"I can," Stern said. "But I am Tori's grandfather. Keeping me from her is disrespectful, and against what you told me earlier."

Torgar pulled out a chair at the table and plopped down into it. Something about sitting at the table exclusively reserved for the Merchant Lords amused him, and he propped up his dirty boots on the table as well. His heels kicked the handle of his sword, spun it a few degrees.

"Well, I'm here now," Torgar said. "What is so terribly important that we must speak in the dark of night?"

From outside, the first echo of distant thunder breached the walls, followed by the howl of the warm southern winds.

"I don't know how you conned Madelyn," Stern said, "but we both know you're in over your head."

"Never stopped me before."

"But it needs to stop now. Hand Tori over to me. Give up your status as her protector and let me be the one to safeguard her wealth. I'll do a far better job than you."

Torgar let out a snort. "I thought you might try something like this," he said. "But you see, I have a big sword, and you're an annoying soft-handed merchant. You can't intimidate me, and you won't convince me otherwise. Everything of Laurie's and Madelyn's is mine, and even if I need to hire a dozen advisors to tell me what scroll to put my X on, I'll do it. Tori ain't yours, her money ain't yours, and if you try something like this again, I'll make sure you won't speak a word to her until her sixteenth birthday. Have I made myself clear?"

Stern glanced at the sword on the table, at Torgar's wide grin. "Perfectly clear," he said. "Now is my time to make myself clear. That document you have is nothing, a scrap of paper with a dead woman's signature. Such a thing may carry more weight here in Angelport than elsewhere, but I've learned a thing or two from our guests from Veldaren..."

A deeper rumble sounded from outside, the heavy storm rolling in from the ocean. The door to the room swung inward, and in stepped an elf, his face painted in camouflage, his clothes a mixture of greens and browns. In his hand he held an enormous bow. An arrow was pressed against the string, but not yet pulled taut.

"Greetings, Torgar," said the elf as the building shook from thunder.

"What do you want?" Torgar asked, trying to sound more annoyed than afraid.

"You should know. I spoke with Alyssa, and she had a very interesting story to tell me, about a boast Stern confirmed overhearing."

Torgar's sword was still on the table, the handle beside the heel of his boot. He had no chance of reaching it in time.

"Ah, fuck me," he said as the arrow flew.

Haern sat atop the hill, staring at the lights of Veldaren in the distance. The Wraith's old hood lay in his lap, and beside him on the grass were his sabers. He held his chin in his hand, his elbow resting on his knee. He more heard than saw Delysia's approach. With a soft rustle of her robes, which shone silver in the starlight, she sat beside him. Her arm slid about him, and he felt her head rest against his shoulder.

"Are you all right?" she asked. "You've been morose ever since returning, and I don't think you've gone out at night once to patrol."

Haern started to say something defensive but fought it down. Instead he leaned against her, and he closed his eyes as he forced himself to relax.

"Back at Angelport...I met a man who I might have become. A man who thought the city was his, who felt he could control every faction by a twist of his blade. Deep down, he truly believed he was justified in doing what he did. He was protecting those he loved, his friends and family back in Quellassar. And so he killed and reveled in his hatred for the men he viewed guilty. And now I come here, where I've killed to establish control, where I've murdered and punished all to protect my own friends, my own family..."

He waved a hand toward the lights of Veldaren.

"I started thinking of Veldaren as *my* city. But those thoughts don't belong to me. They belong to someone like the Wraith. Someone like my father. Have I truly become anything better? By my hands, even innocent people die. And it's all because of my own anger, my own hatred toward the thief guilds."

"Do you really think that?" Delysia asked.

Haern shook his head. "I don't know."

He felt her lips press against his cheek, and it seemed time slowed.

"You never really hated the guilds, Haern. I know you better than that. You never fought against them. You never fought to destroy the Trifect. You wanted to save Veldaren from the world you escaped from. You wanted people to live without fear. It was never for you. So long as you remember that, I trust you. Go do what must be done, and we'll be here when you need us."

Haern wrapped his arms about her, kissed her lips, and then held her tight as he felt his body shiver. His guilt drained away, and he clutched her as a man might hold a piece of driftwood in a storm.

"Always be there for me," he whispered. "If you're there, if you're able to forgive me, I can continue to go on. I'll know I'm still me, still something worthwhile to save..."

She kissed him again, then handed him his hood. He put it on, and as the shadows enveloped his face, he grabbed his sabers and hooked them to his belt. Waving good-bye, he ran to Veldaren, to the many secret ways over the walls and into the dens of thieves and nobles. There was comfort in those shadows, a freedom as he leaped from the wall to the roof of the nearest house. He'd stalk the night and let his determination fuel the fear he bestowed upon those who turned their blades against the innocent. The slaughters of the past, the riots, the betrayals...they'd not happen, not here, not again. Not while he watched.

Warrick was right. He couldn't save all of Dezrel. But Veldaren was his home, the place of his father, the city of his friends.

Along the rooftops ran the Watcher, cloaks trailing, sabers in hand.

A NOTE FROM THE AUTHOR

This might amuse some of you. When I first created the story line to this book a long while back, the ending was . . . well, significantly different. Instead of Dieredon intercepting Alyssa on the way to the elves and then releasing her, she was kept in Warrick's prison. The elves were to demand her execution still, despite everything, and Warrick would do it as a way of ensuring peace as well as getting rid of her. That execution was going to be successful. I meant to have Haern and Zusa watching, and then despite Haern's attempts to stop her, Zusa lunging onto the platform to free her, only to die as dozens of arrows shot her down. Haern was to slink away back to Veldaren, alone, thoroughly defeated.

I don't know why I was so determined to have this book end so . . . drearily. At the time, Shadowdance was only to be a trilogy, and I think I fell for this belief that for the book to feel nice and final, it had to be dark and brutal and depressing. Because that's how you end a proper trilogy, right? Heck, the original name of the book was *A Dance of Death*, a title I hated less than a month after publishing. In addition to all this, having Zusa and Alyssa die helped explain why they weren't in my later Half-Orc novels. All dead, nice and easy explanation. However, I told a good friend of mine, Rob Duperre, the overall plotline. His reaction, paraphrased?

"That'd be awesome! But you know you can't."

"What? Why not?"

"Is that really how you want Alyssa's story to end? Seems kind of pointless, really, and depressing."

And it was. I looked back and realized I had her come to power over the death of her father, had her son kidnapped and brutalized, had her suitor try to kill her, and then when she comes to Angelport, she ends up getting executed in a ploy to prevent a war, and her best friend, Zusa, dies at her feet. So perhaps that did happen in an alternate timeline of Dezrel, but for me, I couldn't do it. Didn't feel right, didn't feel appropriate. They both deserved better, and more important, I didn't want to sacrifice the ability to tell more stories with either of them. I've made that mistake before, and I didn't want to make it again.

Of course, some of you may be sitting here thinking, "That'd have been epic!" Maybe you're right. And if you disagree, well, then it's all Rob's stupid idea.

Anyway, even despite taking the ending down a notch in terms of depression and suckiness, my original version (the pre-Orbit edition, if you will) still had a downer of an ending. Angelport had defeated Haern, leaving him feeling beaten and confused. And coming back to the book with fresh eyes, I really couldn't tell why I did even that. More of my determination to have some sort of foreboding heaviness, I guess. Haern recounted a summary of the events at the end, and reading it, I wondered what book he'd been involved in, because it wasn't the one I wrote. So the ending I have now rewritten rather heavily. It's not sunshine and rainbows, but it's not the crushing loss I first tried to make it out to be. Haern still faced a mirror of himself, saw what he could become. But he also defeated it.

And Delysia's still there, ready to help him pick up the pieces.

Speaking of Delysia...when I first ended the story here, I had plenty of people pissed off at me, wondering what happened with Zusa and Delysia, how their relationship with Haern worked, etc. Well, when I started what is now Shadowdance number four, I swore to elaborate on that relationship. I also dropped the ball in the original version of *that*, but hey, that's what this whole process with Orbit has been for me, this one shot to get everything down, get it right, get the editorial oversight I truly need. Because I'm lazy, and willing to let crap go if I think I can get away with it. Thankfully, Devi (editor lady) doesn't let me get away with anything. Except maybe these notes from the author. I have full power here, bwahahahaha.

That's right. Stereotypical evil laugh.

Anyway, I used to feel this book was the best of the initial three, but over time I realized *Dance of Blades* was the one best put together and most consistent in terms of tone and plot. However, now that I've gotten to tear into *Dance of Mirrors*, get all these threads nailed down, the ending reworked, the various players far better clarified...I think this might be my favorite of them again. Graeven in particular was a blast to write, especially once he was revealed as the Wraith and could make his appeals to both Haern and Dieredon. With only a few tweaks, I could have made him a hero, and really, that was the whole dang point.

Oh, and lastly: if you're wondering where the heck Thren

Felhorn went, I promise he's right back to prominence in book four. I haven't forgotten him. In fact, he's going to be around more than ever, and if there's anything I love, it's that crazy ruthless bastard...

Quick thanks to those who deserve it: Devi, who I think I've finally convinced I am capable of learning; Rob, for all the advice; Michael, for dealing with all the headaches involving contracts and deadlines so I don't have to; and Sam, for raising our two beautiful daughters and dealing with *that* headache while I'm off in the library writing.

And of course you, dear reader. I hope I've given you characters that you enjoy, that you might remember, that remind you why you read fantasy fiction in the first place. If I can pull that off, then hopefully you'll get to read many, many more rambling notes like this from me in the future.

David Dalglish
April 18, 2013

extras

meet the author

Mike Scott Photography

DAVID DALGLISH currently lives in rural Missouri with his wife, Samantha, and daughters Morgan and Katherine. He graduated from Missouri Southern State University in 2006 with a degree in mathematics and currently spends his free time wishing he was far, far better at Call of Duty.

introducing

If you enjoyed
A DANCE OF MIRRORS,
look out for

A DANCE OF SHADOWS

Shadowdance: Book 4

by David Dalglish

1

Haern returned home to the Eschaton Tower exhausted. He'd scoured the area surrounding the murder as best he could and tracked down several runners of the Spider Guild. The few he found had heard nothing, seen nothing, and even when threatened they showed no sign of lying. Leaving Veldaren for the tower beyond the city walls, he'd felt nothing but frustration and bafflement. He kept repeating the phrase in his head.

Tongue of gold, eyes of silver…

As he opened the door, the smell of cooked eggs welcomed him home. Delysia was the only one awake, and she sat beside the fireplace with a plate on her lap. The orange light shone across her red hair, making it seem all the more vibrant. Seeing him, she smiled. The smile faded from her youthful face when she noticed his sour mood.

“Something wrong?” she asked.

“I’ll talk about it later,” he promised, heading for the stairs.

“Don’t you want something to eat?”

He shook his head. He just wanted sleep. Hopefully when he woke up, he’d have new ideas as to why someone had killed a member of the Spider Guild in such a ritualistic—not to mention expensive—manner. Besides, the thought of eating twisted his stomach. He’d seen a lot of horrible things, but for some reason he couldn’t get the image out of his head of the corpse’s vacant eye sockets replaced with coins.

Eyes of silver...

Haern climbed the stairs until he reached the fifth floor and his room. Hurrying inside, he sat down on his bed, removed his sword belt, and drew out his sabers. Carefully, he cleaned them with a cloth, refusing to go to bed with dirty swords no matter how tired he was. That was lazy and sloppy, and laziness and sloppiness had a way of sneaking out of one habit and into another. His many tutors had hammered that into his head while growing up, all so he could be a worthy heir to his father’s empire of thieves and murderers. He chuckled, then put away his swords. *Not quite according to plan*, he thought, imagining Thren scowling. *Not quite at all.*

Run, run, little spider...

His bed felt like the most wonderful thing in the world, and with a heavy cloth draped over his window, he closed his eyes amid blessed darkness. Sleep came quickly, despite his troubled mind. It did not, however, last very long.

“Hey, Haern.”

He opened an eye and saw his mercenary leader sitting beside him on the bed. His red beard and hair were unkempt from a night’s sleep. He wore his wizard’s robes, strangely dyed a yellow color for reasons he was sure he'd never hear. Trying not to smack the man, Haern rolled over.

"Go away, Tarlak."

"Good morning to you, too, Haern."

Haern sighed. The wizard had something to say, and he wasn't going to leave until he said it. Rolling back, Haern shot him a tired glare.

"What?"

"Some fancy new noble is returning to the city today," Tarlak said, rubbing his fingernails against his robe and staring at them as if he were only mildly interested. "Lord Victor Kane. Perhaps you've heard of him?"

The name was only vaguely familiar, which meant he'd been gone from Veldaren for a very long time. If he remembered correctly, he was just another one of those lords who lived outside the city and liked to occasionally make a scene proclaiming how horrible Veldaren was and how much better it'd be if their ideas were listened to. All hot air, no substance.

"Why should I care?" Haern asked, leaning against his pillow and closing his eyes.

"Because he'll be meeting the king soon, perhaps within the hour. Normally this wouldn't be a big deal, but it sounds like he's bringing a veritable army with him."

"As if King Vaelor would let them pass through the gates."

"That's the thing," Tarlak said. "It sounds like he will. He sent a message to the king. I won't bore you with all the details. Much of it was the standard pompous nonsense these lords are fond of. But one comment in particular was interesting enough my informant thought it worth waking me up early."

Haern put his forearm across his eyes.

"And what was that?"

"I believe it was something to the extent of: '*Right now, thieves police thieves, yet when I am done, there will be no thieves at all.*'" Tarlak stood from the bed, then walked over to the door. "Sounds like someone plans on taking your job."

He left. The room once more returned to quiet darkness.

Haern sat up, tossing the blankets aside.

"Damn it all..."

2

Her servant women fussed over her, fitting clothes, applying rouge, and brushing her hair until Alyssa Gemcroft finally sent them away, unable to take any more. They filed out, leaving her alone in her extravagant bedroom. Well, not quite alone...

"Come down, Zusa," she said. "Tell me what is wrong."

From a far corner of the room, hidden in a dark space unlit by light from the windows, a woman fell to the ground. Despite the many years it had been since leaving Karak's cult of faceless women, Zusa still wore the tight wrappings across her body, strips of cloth colored various shades of black and purple. Her head, at least, she kept exposed: dark skin, dark hair cut short at the neck, and beautiful green eyes. A long gray cloak hung from her shoulders, the thin material curling about her body with the slightest tugs of Zusa's fingers.

"There is nothing wrong," Zusa said, crossing her arms over her chest and leaning against the wall.

"I'm used to you keeping an eye on me, but you only hide on the ceiling when you're nervous." She smiled at her friend. "You know I trust your instincts, so tell me."

Zusa gestured to the dress.

"You doll yourself up worse than a whore. Powder everywhere, rouge, perfume on your neck...and I must say, I pity your breasts."

Alyssa looked down at herself. She'd let her servants prepare her for her meeting, but had they gotten carried away? Her dress was a sultry red, tightly fitted, with a ring of rubies sewn along the neck. A gold chain held a large emerald tucked into the curve of her breasts, which, true to Zusa's words, her corset had rammed almost unnaturally high.

"This is what is expected of me," Alyssa said, sighing. She wanted to sit down but feared wrinkling her dress or, even worse, straining the ties of the corset. The realization made her blush, and she could tell Zusa knew her defense was a flimsy one.

"Since when did Lady Gemcroft do the expected?" Zusa asked, the last of her nerves fading away with a smile. "But you are beautiful, even if overdone. I only wonder why. Lord Stephen is but a child, young even compared to you. Your smile alone should impress him."

Alyssa paced, keeping her movements slow and controlled lest she muss her appearance.

"It's been a year since his appointment, and I have yet to meet him. I fear he'll think I have snubbed him or deemed him unworthy of his position. I wish only to make a good impression."

Zusa sat down on the bed, shifting the daggers tied to her waist so they did not poke into the soft mattress.

"He will think it anyway," she said. "Though I fear his impression will be that you are making advances on him."

Alyssa opened her mouth, closed it, and then looked to her dress. She sighed.

"Help me, will you?" she asked.

Ten minutes later she was in a far more comfortable dress, and they'd wiped clean her face. Alyssa left her hair the same, having always enjoyed the sight of thin braids interlocked and weaved throughout her long red locks. Able to breathe and move far more freely, she hugged Zusa, then attached a simple lace of silver about her neck.

"We have kept Stephen waiting long enough," she said. "Let's go."

A litter waited outside her mansion, and she and Zusa climbed inside. As they traveled through the streets of Veldaren, Alyssa felt butterflies in her stomach and did her best to belittle them. It was stupid to be nervous. Of the three families of the Trifect, she'd been in power the longest and had clearly solidified her position as ruler of the Gemcroft fortune. Stephen Connington was but a bastard of his father, Leon. Still, he was the only one with a clear biological relation. It'd taken several years before he'd been granted control of the estate from the caretakers. In the end, they'd had no choice. Leon had killed most of his family members and steadfastly refused to have named heirs, lest they drown him in his bath.

She winced at the memory of Leon. He'd been unpleasant at times, if not repulsive. The fat had rolled off him, yet his tiny eyes had always been of a young, starving man eager to take, and take, regardless the vice. She'd heard stories of what his gentle touchers—his private group of elite torturers—could do to a man to make him break. A shudder ran through her. She prayed that Stephen had inherited very little of his father beyond his name.

As for the last family of the Trifect, the Keenans, they'd yet to recover from the fiasco in Angelport two years before, when both Madelyn and Laurie had been murdered along with their temporary successor, Torgar. Their grandchild, Tori, was the biological heir, but it would be many years before she could take over rule. That had left Stern Blackwater in charge of the Keenan fortune down in Angelport. There were benefits to this, a ceasing of significant conflict with the Merchant Lords of the south that had done their best to destroy them. Still, even Stern's rule was conflicted, and he rarely made any appearances beyond the walls of Angelport. If he thought the Trifect was no longer in his granddaughter's interest, he'd cast them off in a heartbeat.

That meant Alyssa was the pillar of strength of the Trifect, the one holding it all together. She had to be strong, confident. Zusa had been right. Terrible as it was, the last thing she wanted to do was flaunt her feminine qualities when she needed Stephen to take her seriously.

"I should have brought Nathaniel with me," Alyssa said as the litter bounced across the rough street.

"Your son is better served with an honorable man like Lord Gandrem than dealing with worms like the Conningtons," Zusa said.

Alyssa frowned and glanced out the curtained window to the passing homes.

"Perhaps," she said. "But it won't be long before he must put away foolish fantasies of knights and armies. I won't have all I've built squandered and broken like it has for the Keenans. In time, he must learn to deal with the worms as well as the dragons."